PELICAN BOOKS

JAPAN VERSUS EUROPE

Endymion Wilkinson was born in Sussex in 1941 and educated at Gordonstoun School and King's College, Cambridge, where he read History and Oriental Studies. On going down in 1964, he continued research on East Asia in Peking (1964–6), Princeton (1966–8), and Tokyo (1968–9), gaining a Princeton Ph.D. in 1970. After four years as lecturer in the history of the Far East at the University of London, he left the academic world in 1974 to become an EEC diplomat, serving as head of the economic and trade department of the EEC delegation in Tokyo for six years. Then in 1979 he returned to EEC headquarters in Brussels where he was in charge of the China desk until 1982. Dr Wilkinson is fluent in Japanese and Chinese and is currently stationed in Bangkok as Deputy Head of the EEC delegation to Southeast Asia.

His other publications include several books on China – *The History of Imperial China: A Research Guide* (1973) and *Studies in Chinese Price History* (1980), as well as two translations from the Chinese, *The People's Comic Book* (1973) and *Landlord and Labour in Late Imperial China* (1978).

Japan versus Europe was a bestseller in Japan (where it was published under the title *Misunderstanding*) and has also been published in German and Italian. In 1981 Dr Wilkinson presented a four-hour series based on the book on Japanese television.

Japan
versus Europe
A History of Misunderstanding

ENDYMION WILKINSON

PENGUIN BOOKS

Penguin Books Ltd, Harmondsworth, Middlesex, England
Penguin Books, 40 West 23rd Street, New York, New York 10022, U.S.A.
Penguin Books Australia Ltd, Ringwood, Victoria, Australia
Penguin Books Canada Ltd, 2801 John Street, Markham, Ontario, Canada L3R 1B4
Penguin Books (N.Z.) Ltd, 182–190 Wairau Road, Auckland 10, New Zealand

First published in Japan by Chuokoron-Sha Inc. 1980
English language edition published under the title
Misunderstanding: Europe vs. Japan 1981
First published in Great Britain in a revised edition
under the title *Japan versus Europe* by Penguin Books 1983

Made and printed in Great Britain by
Cox & Wyman Ltd, Reading
Set in Linotron Times by
Rowland Phototypesetting Ltd
Bury St Edmunds, Suffolk

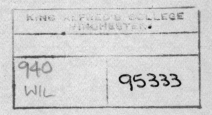

For S.W., F.W., and G.B.

Contents

III   Open Markets and Double-Bolted Doors

IV   What is to be Done?

List of Maps and Tables

Maps

Tables

Preface

Until 1974 I lived the gentle life of a university lecturer, teaching at the University of London and spending occasional summers as a research fellow at Harvard. It must be one of the few professions left where you are paid to pursue the hobby of your choice. In my case Japanese and Chinese history, and economics. The responsibilities were small, which no doubt explains why the pay was low. But in compensation I enjoyed the peculiar sense of buoyancy, so trying to those who are not academics, which comes from playing with ideas, without having to put them into practice, or even to test them very vigorously. Instead I and my colleagues tested the students, who could usually be relied upon to know less than ourselves.

This happy state of affairs would probably have prolonged itself indefinitely; long vacations alternating with mercifully short terms. Meanwhile, my learned publications slowly but neatly accumulated in a small pile, like sand in an hour glass.

But all that was to change abruptly, and the change took place in Japan.

I went to Tokyo in autumn 1973 on academic study leave to finish a book on Chinese agriculture. When I arrived I found that my income only allowed me to rent a small apartment in a noisy student quarter. It was next to a railway line. There were cramming schools nearby from which came the droning of students memorizing the answers to university entrance exams. None of this would in itself have mattered very much. What was difficult to accept was that I had lived in Japan for a year in 1968 as a graduate student working on a doctorate in very similar circumstances, although in a quieter part of town. Something seemed to be wrong if my living conditions were no better than they had been five years before. And then came the oil shock of October 1973 and a winter of rapid inflation. I began to live like a church-mouse, even worse than I had done as a student.

That was the final straw.

Already in England, and for similar reasons, I had begun to wonder whether to continue my career as an academic. Now these experiences in Tokyo served to crystallize my thoughts and I decided in the bleak winter of 1973 to change my profession.

After several false starts, my chance came in the spring of 1974 when back in Europe I was invited to join the EC Commission, and as my first task, to do the spadework to set up the Commission's permanent diplomatic delegation to Japan. Instead of staying six months in Tokyo as I had originally intended, I settled down for a long stay, which in the event lasted for six years.

One way to write a book about another country is to record the impressions of the first few weeks while they are still fresh, and then leave rapidly, before conflicting impressions blur the original picture. This approach usually reveals more about the author than the country through which he passes.

Another way is to work in a foreign country for a number of years, until one day the awful moment arrives when you suddenly realize that your time is nearly up and you will have to leave. This is what happened to me. When I heard that I had to return to Europe, I asked myself what I had managed to learn during my stay in Japan. The only way to find out was to start writing. The result is this book, which reflects my experiences, informed by reading, during the various times I have lived and worked in Japan – first from 1968 to 1969, then from 1973 to 1979 and on numerous visits since.

Many people taught me all sorts of things about Japan. Impossible to list them all by name. But I would like to thank my old friend Hiroshi Hayakawa. It was he who gave me the practical encouragement to sit down and start writing.

My former colleagues in the EC Delegation in Tokyo, in addition to the daily round of office work, helped me in innumerable ways. In particular, my thanks to Hajime Takahashi for his effective and loyal support and good judgement, Natsuo Taku and Takuro Tsukatani for their perceptive comments on early drafts, Kyoko Tanaka for her ungrudging efforts not only to check my statistics but frequently to produce better ones.

While translating the book into Japanese, Takao Tokuoka gave me a great deal of advice and encouragement. I am very grateful to Roy Denman, Leslie Fielding and Michael Hardy, who commented on early drafts of the text. Ron Dore gave excellent guidance with detailed observations on the entire manuscript.

As anyone who has ever tried to write a book in their spare time before breakfast or late at night, on Sundays or on occasional vacations, will know, it cannot be done without the understanding of an able secretary. My thanks therefore to Marion Chapman, Kiyoko Furusawa, Patricia Quinn and Hiroko Deguchi, Yoshiko Masuko and Annette Graf.

It should be made crystal clear that this book is in no sense the expression of an official view. It represents nothing more than the individual opinions of its author.

The first Japanese language edition went to the publisher in the spring of 1980. Since then I have completely revised the book and brought it up to date for the Penguin edition.

London and Brussels
October 1982

Introduction

Main Themes

There will be more strains and stresses on the relations between Europe and Japan for the remainder of the 1980s than ever before. It is going to be a chilly time. Even if the world remains at peace there is no guarantee that the prices of oil and other raw materials will not continue to go up and down by fits and starts. Growth rates in the industrialized countries are going to be much lower than in the 1950s and 1960s but inflation and unemployment, especially in Europe, will be high. World trade will not be growing very fast and the newly industrializing countries will increase their shares of export markets. Under these conditions, the competition between industrialized countries for markets, resources and investments will intensify. Europe and Japan will be two of the main contenders.

Slower economic growth and higher levels of unemployment in Europe than in Japan will make it more difficult for Europeans to keep up by adapting and modernizing their industries. Besides, the Japanese have already established a better track record for industrial adaptation and technological innovation. It is likely therefore that the 1980s will continue to see a widening gap between industrial efficiency in most of Europe and in Japan.

Trade frictions, if not trade war, caused mainly by rapid and concentrated Japanese export drives on the European market, which were common enough in the 1970s, have now become endemic.

At times such as these, it pays to step back and take a long cool look at the illusions which Europeans and Japanese hold about each other, and to question the assumptions upon which our relations are based. Only by tracking down past images can we begin to understand present-day actions and the full range of metaphor available today as, hopefully, we rid ourselves of old prejudices and take a fresh look at each other.

In the first half of the book I have tried to put economic and trade frictions between Japan and Europe into perspective, by placing them in their broader cultural context and by tracing the development of European and Japanese attitudes towards each other. I have not attempted to write a history of Europe–Japan relations, interesting though such a history would be. Instead, I have traced the accumulation of mutual prejudices and popular images which are the essential background to the trade frictions discussed in Part III.

The story has its harsh as well as its light moments.

The scene is set by the weakening of direct political relations between Europe and Japan in the twentieth century, brought about by the decline of Europe's role in the world and by its withdrawal from Asia in particular. Europe has become more inward-looking, concentrating ever larger amounts of its trade and investments in markets closer to home. One expression of this trend, which has also acted as a stimulus, is the shift towards regional integration in the European Community. Japan on the other hand during the post-war years quietly assumed a greater role on the world stage whose main expression has been economic rather than political.

These changes have not always been accompanied by corresponding changes of attitude.

The Europeans have found it exceedingly hard, and at best belatedly, to adjust their over-blown self-image to a diminishing role on the world stage. They often still behave as if Europe was the world's leading centre of culture. The Japanese on the other hand have found it equally hard to adjust their understated self-image to accord with their rising importance on the international scene. They still often behave as if theirs was an aspiring nation, 'on the make', nervously grabbing at every rung on the international status ladder. While awaiting the outcome of these two essentially internal adjustments of self-perceptions, Europe and Japan find it particularly hard to talk to each other, for neither is sure where it or the other quite stands. So both tend to fall back on modes inherited from the past – the Europeans arrogant and talkative, the Japanese falsely humble and silent. In line with this posturing, each also sees the other in terms which owe more to past perceptions than to present realities.

In Part I, 'The Upside-Down Land: Japan as Seen by the Europeans', I examine the European image of Japan and find it composed of an arsenal of stereotypes founded on the shifting sands of indifference, ignorance, prejudice and fear, rather than based on any effort to seriously understand Japan. Stereotypes which are at best gross caricatures and at worst simply beside the point. I have deliberately quoted at length from all sorts of sources so that the reader may enjoy the authenticity of the originals.

Part II, 'The Cultural Museum: Europe as Seen by the Japanese', completes the picture by tracing Japanese attitudes towards the West and the formation of images of Europe. Because they have seen themselves as learners, the Japanese have been able to form more timely and accurate images of Europe than the Europeans, who saw themselves as teachers, formed of Japan. On the other hand, the Japanese have not yet been able to project a very clear or attractive image of themselves.

In Part III, I turn to the most lively form of dialogue between Japan and Europe in recent years, namely economic and trade frictions. That it should take this form is surely indication enough of the poverty of the current dialogue. Trade frictions have become frequent because of greater Japanese competitiveness in certain key industries such as steel, ships, cars or electronics and a corresponding decline in Europe. They have been exacerbated by stagflation and unemployment at home and by the end of the era of cheap raw materials and energy supplies abroad.

The trade frictions have festered like maggots in a rotting apple because there has been no broad interchange and understanding between Europe and Japan, but instead, prejudice and outmoded images.

It is, I believe, in neither European nor Japanese interests that this state of affairs should be allowed to continue. In Part IV therefore I suggest various measures both to avoid trade frictions and to improve communications between Europe and Japan. It is pointless to attempt the one without the other, for without a change in the way in which Europeans and Japanese perceive and understand each other, there can be no improvement of the trade relations and vice versa. If we fail to take these measures, then the dialogue between Europe and Japan will be limited to trade frictions and ill-informed mutual accusations which can only reinforce negative images and therefore make hostile and negative responses even more likely the next time round.

The book is written for all those, whether Japanese or European, who have made efforts to understand each other's point of view.

I hope that as a result of reading it some European readers may conclude that it is time to form more accurate images of themselves and of Japan. I hope too some Japanese readers may be reinforced in their view that the time has now come to concentrate on projecting an unambiguous image of their country and their role in the world, rather than simply reacting to what others think of Japan.

In the last resort, I shall be happy enough if the reader, be he Japanese or European, can share with me now and again, as he glances through these pages, that sudden acute excitement which comes from an unexpected moment of self-recognition.

Out-of-Date Images

What disturbs and alarms man are not things, but his opinions and fancies about things.

EPICTETUS

When I first launched my boat into EC – Japan waters in 1974, I began reading up on the subject. The more I read, the more I found the same things about Japan and the Japanese appearing over and over again. Even the examples used were often the same. Observations of Japanologists of the nineteenth century would suddenly pop up in late-twentieth-century works. Intrigued, I pressed my inquiries further back to the earliest European writers on Japan in the sixteenth and seventeenth centuries. The same thing: their comments appeared to have been echoed, not entirely or even clearly, but echoed nevertheless, in the nineteenth and twentieth centuries. I decided then that I would jot down the most often repeated stereotypes and see if any pattern emerged.

Several years passed; my reading was spasmodic but broad. Also, during the years while I was stationed in Tokyo, I had the opportunity to listen to the comments about Japan made by numerous visitors of every kind: tourists, businessmen, officials, journalists, politicians and university professors.

My net was trawled through many waters – the astonishing thing was that at the end of the day my catch was usually composed of the same fish. I concluded that in the collective European mind there has formed a limited stock of images both positive and negative about Japan and the Japanese from which, depending on the mood of the day, the relevant image can be recalled any number of times.

So I have devoted considerable attention to images which were formed in the past, because even though they may seem to belong to a remote age, they have not been discarded. On the contrary, they are still part of the basic vocabulary, the inherited scripts, as it were, by whose logic a European's view of Japan is deeply and often unconsciously influenced.

Here and there I found characteristics attributed to the Japanese which bore a striking resemblance to what the Europeans have thought about other 'Oriental' peoples. This is of course not surprising: Japan, for example, has consistently been confused with China for at least five centuries. I have attempted to note this deeper layer in the European stock of images about Japan whenever I have been able to identify it for what it is.

During my stay in Japan, I also had numerous occasions to learn at first hand about Japanese popular images of Europe and Europeans. But even after my identity as a European had been established I was constantly reminded that I fell into the larger category of *gaijin* – 'outside person', a word used for Westerners (but not, for example, for Chinese foreigners). Over the years I can count on the fingers of one hand the Japanese I met who reacted to me as just another human being. More usually, in the politest possible way, one was continually put in one's place, reminded that one was an outsider by incredulous questions and naive comments such as 'What do you think of Japan?', 'Is Tokyo easy to live in?', 'When are you leaving Japan?' or 'Oh, how skilfully you use chopsticks!', 'How fluently you speak Japanese!' As if it was amazing that a foreigner other than a Japanese could be expected to use chopsticks or speak even a few words of Japanese after six years in the country. Such comments are no doubt made with the best possible intentions. Foreign tourists are certainly flattered. It is also true that such remarks are heard less from the post-war generations which do not necessarily see 'foreign' and 'Japanese' as exclusive categories, and pride themselves on being 'international'.

In the end I became used to being regarded as something of a curiosity. After all, I had been warned: all the textbooks both Japanese and foreign had drummed home the point that the Japanese had been isolated and regarded themselves as utterly unique. It was therefore only natural for them to draw a very sharp line between themselves and 'foreigners'. And no doubt they found it as hard to distinguish one Westerner from another, as most Westerners have difficulty in telling the difference between a Chinese, a Japanese and a Korean.

Indeed, in 1968, when I first went to Japan, it was so commonly assumed that all 'foreigners' were American, that I was often asked as a first question, 'What State are you from?' Later when I went back in the mid 1970s, the American influence had sufficiently waned for one to be greeted by the more broadminded question, 'Excuse me, but what country are you from?' On learning that I was from England, my questioners invariably reacted with the same flattering stereotype which somehow assumed that I was a representative of my country: 'Oh, the English are gentlemen, aren't they?' Next, I would be questioned in one form or another about the English 'love of tradition', 'the class society in England' and, less flatteringly, the 'English disease', meaning the social roots of economic decline.

On inquiring amongst European friends from France, Germany, Italy, Switzerland and Sweden I found that they had encountered the same kind of polite stereotypes about their countries. Friends from smaller, lesser known European countries such as Belgium were met with puzzlement. Polls of Japanese attitudes towards foreign countries reveal exactly the same 'tourist poster' handful of characteristics associated with each major foreign country.

Of course there is nothing particularly remarkable about this and I hastened to deepen my efforts to understand Japanese images of Europe by reading, observation and discussion. I have described what I found in Part II. In general, just as with European images of Japan, it seems that in the collective Japanese mind there has formed a limited stock of images both positive and negative about Europe and the Europeans from which, depending on the mood of the day, the relevant image can be recalled any number of times.

The key difference is that Japanese images of Europe have tended to be more positive and closer to reality than European images of Japan. The reasons are clear; at the formative period of modern Japan, Europeans were regarded with a mixture of fear and respect, two excellent reasons for wanting to learn from somebody else. The Europeans on the other hand have regarded the Japanese with indifference, sometimes with scorn and sometimes with fear, but seldom with respect. I state this as a matter of fact and also as a matter of regret. One of my aims in writing this book has been to try and analyse clearly and dispassionately the nature of European and Japanese attitudes towards each other and to suggest how mutual understanding can be improved.

Had I been writing about European *knowledge* of Japan or Japanese *knowledge* of Europe, I would have concentrated on the works of Japanologists and experts on Europe and on the findings of specialists in international relations, the social sciences and comparative literature. Such was not my aim. Nations conduct their foreign affairs on the basis not of what is but of what they perceive it to be. People are disturbed and alarmed not by things but by their 'opinions and fancies' about things.

Despite greater opportunities for travel and direct contacts, and despite television and instant communications, the grip of inherited prejudices appears to be as strong today as in the past.

Even with the rapidity of modern communications it still appears to take at least one generation to absorb and encapsulate in a memorable stereotype perceptions of another country. *Idées reçues* are not formed overnight in the minds of individuals, still less so in the collective unconscious of a country.

By the time the stereotype has become embedded in the literature and the elementary textbooks, and passed down to the following generation, the reality which originally inspired it is likely to have changed. To take a trivial example, decades after Paris had ceased to be a centre of European painting, would-be Japanese artists were making their way to Montmartre. In a similar fashion European visitors to Japan frequently express surprise on arriving in Tokyo. This is either because they expected it to be exotic, in which case their image of it was a hundred years out of date, or because they expected it to be unbearably polluted, in which case the image was only fifteen years behind the times.

In the following pages many examples are given of such out-of-date images hampering understanding – and not all of them are as trivial by any means.

If the reader is in any doubt as to the gap between the reality of a country and the perception and formation of an image of it by the people of another country, let him consider the articulation of foreign policy. The political leaders of a country are usually at least in their late fifties and sixties, if not in their seventies and eighties. Their images of other countries were formed in their childhood and youth. Such images must already have been a generation behind reality because of the time it takes to encapsulate perceptions of another country and pass them on to the next generation. Granted that politicians are capable, like everybody else, of adjusting what they learnt as children in the light of later experience, nevertheless after middle age it becomes increasingly difficult to make such adjustments. The result is that foreign policy decisions, even of the most revolutionary governments, are extremely conservative and can often only be understood as initiatives and responses to the political leaders' experience and perceptions of international realities in their youth – perceptions which were probably even then already out of date! While generals are preparing to fight the previous war, if not the previous war but one, statesmen are manoeuvring to avoid it.

So I wanted to understand the inherited scripts, the range of metaphor available to decision-makers in Europe and Japan as they considered each other's countries – a level of basic attitudes, even prejudices, sometimes held unconsciously and derived not from the reading of academic monographs, but learnt from parents, at school, and later enforced by early formative experiences. As illustrations of these popular images I frequently quote from such diverse sources as opinion polls, light operas, textbooks, fiction and the mass media. I have used, for example, bestseller lists as a handy and reliable index to the attitudes of an age or generation. Scholars are as prejudiced as anyone else. Occasionally too their ideas can have a shaping influence on the popular mind. When that has happened I have quoted them.

A second reason which led me to focus on popular images is that today they play a more direct role in international relations than in the past. It can matter very much what particular illusion about a foreign country is uppermost in this or that segment of society or pressure group. Politicians are aware of this and although demagoguery is certainly not always the outcome, decision-makers ignore popular prejudices at their peril. It also goes without saying that the policy-maker himself may hold popular images or be influenced by them.

I have used the word 'image' loosely to cover two broad ranges of meaning. In the first sense, the emphasis is on the emotional attitudes, whether positive or negative, the prejudices or illusions, which colour or even determine the pictures that we form of reality. In the second sense, an image is merely a picture of reality which may or may not have congealed into a stereotype and which may be either true or false.

When there is no necessity felt to learn about another country, then knowledge of it will be slight and the images which are held of it will tend to be subjective, emotional and extreme. In general this has been true of European images of Japan. Conversely in Japan, where there was once a strongly felt necessity to learn about Europe, images were formed which were less emotive and closer to reality.

In talking of 'the European image' or 'the Japanese image', I am guilty of a gross over-simplification whose only excuse is that these are a convenient shorthand. For a start not all European countries have held the same images of Japan.

Secondly, consider the images which two individuals hold of each other; they may be simple or complex, they may change as the years go by, or more frequently they congeal into stereotypes, but their formation and content are relatively easy to grasp when compared with the images which are held in one country of another. In the case of a country, many people are involved, there are numerous channels of communication and numerous images. Almost invariably different age groups will hold different images of the outside world, as will also different social and work groups. Thus a tourist will usually have a more rosy view of a country than a businessman working there. And a successful businessman will form a more positive view than a less successful one, and so on and so forth. Each individual forms his own personal mix of experiences and impressions of another country.

This is not to deny however that there are certain images, often passed from one generation to the next, which seep into every level of a country's imagination and form, as it were, a sediment of commonly held prejudice. During the colonial period, racial prejudice was of this kind and images which emerge at a time of war are also of a similar nature.

The relationship between image and reality is a subtle one, often complicated by the fact that images, whether true or false, tend to take on a life of their own, now vigorous and demanding attention, now fading away, only to reappear when least expected. And always suddenly or slowly influencing reality. Parts I and II trace the evolution of European and Japanese images of each other.

As he glances through these pages, the reader will frequently come across images of his country held by foreigners which will probably strike him as absurd or funny, perhaps even insulting and certainly very far from the realities which he himself knows so well. When this happens I would ask him not to form too hasty a judgement of the stupidity of foreigners. Firstly, because even the most exaggerated caricatures usually contain a kernel of truth. Secondly, if there is a communications gap, it is not always the result of the recipient of a signal not receiving it correctly. Sometimes the original transmitter of the signal may not be sending it clearly.

So I would ask the reader to bear in mind a simple question, who is responsible for what other people think of you? You yourself, or the people who form an image of you?

PART I

The Upside-Down Land:
Japan as Seen by the Europeans

1

First Impressions

Chipangu is an island towards the East in the high seas, 1,500 miles distant from the Continent; and a very great island it is. The people are white, civilized and well-favoured.

MARCO POLO, 1307

A recent survey of European images of Japan found that a majority associated the atomic bomb with the country. But they had got it wrong. One third thought that Japan possessed the bomb and no less than a half thought that she either possessed it or intended to get it. They had apparently forgotten the fact that Japan is the only country to have *been* atom-bombed.[1] Such complete reversals of the truth are common, particularly when one culture has failed to build up a tradition of basic knowledge of another. And this is precisely the situation in Europe where Japan has been (until quite recently) peripheral to the European mind.

Other countries in East Asia, notably China, have at one time or another played an essential part in the formation of the modern European consciousness of the world. Not so Japan. In the eighteenth century, for example, the discovery that China had a recorded past more ancient than the biblical chronology led to the fundamental revision of the European concept of history and to the birth of cultural relativism. The pages of Voltaire, Montesquieu, Leibniz and Gibbon are filled with references to China – but contain virtually nothing on Japan. While the *philosophes* were reshaping the European mind using China as one of their tools, Japan was closed to the outside world, voluntarily shut in upon herself.

In the nineteenth century the Europeans continued their exploration of many of the countries of East Asia in search of new markets. In the process of trading, and in some cases conquering, settling and administering these countries, there developed a practical necessity to learn about them. In this way, interest groups gradually formed within Europe who either had direct experience to draw on or who were informed by those who had worked in and studied the area. Japan was never colonized by the Europeans and there was therefore no such necessity to learn about her.

There is another important reason why Europeans tended to ignore Japan; towards the end of the nineteenth and in the early twentieth century they were convinced that after India, China presented them with a boundless market for their manufactured goods. Japan was felt to be far less promising in this respect because she was already beginning to build up a domestic industry of her own capable of competing with Europe. Major commercial efforts, therefore, were directed towards China rather than Japan. It was the Europeans after all who 'opened' China, and the Americans who 'opened' Japan.

These are some of the reasons why Europeans have tended to ignore Japan and concentrated on China.

In the late nineteenth century when they did finally 'discover' Japan, it was at a period when Europe was far more powerful than Japan and Europeans felt themselves superior to 'Asiatics'. These prejudices have been slow to change. So, Europeans, feeling no urgent need to learn about Japan, clung to romantic images of an Oriental fantasy land.

Small wonder that they constantly underestimated Japan. When she began forcing herself into the European consciousness by the defeat of China in 1895, or the victories over Russia in 1904 and 1905, Europeans were completely taken by surprise: they had thought her fragile as a fan. They now found her hard as an ironclad. Reeling from the shock they quickly decided that they had been cheated, that they had been given a false impression. Negative images were evoked and the ones most readily available were the immemorial images of the Orient. So Japan was seen as a 'Yellow Peril', an image which owed more to past fears of Attila or Genghis Khan or Tamerlane, rather than to any comprehension of the policies of the Meiji oligarchs.

Later, the same pattern was to be repeated and for the same reasons. European attitudes of superiority persisted with the same inability to learn about or to form accurate images of Japan. Europeans were completely taken by surprise by the Japanese attack on Pearl Harbor and by the fall of their colonies in Southeast Asia in 1941 and 1942, and again by Japan's rapid economic recovery after the war and successful export drive to the European market starting from the late 1960s.

Each time Europe was caught by surprise the shock was blamed on the Japanese for being unpredictable; each time that negative reaction was tinged with vague fears of the Orient.

It is to the Orient then that we must turn to begin our inquiry into the formation of European images of Japan.

Since time immemorial 'the Orient' has been an object of wonder and fear in the West; its image both powerful and contradictory. It was seen as the source of light and hence wisdom, but at the same time as filled with cruelty and torture. East is opposite of West, so by an unconscious reflex the East was often made the embodiment of values diametrically opposed to those in the West. If the Greeks were democratic and civilized, the Persians were despotic and barbarous; if the Occident was dynamic, then the Orient was stagnant. If the West was materialistic, the East was spiritual.

It was also common to regard 'Oriental' peoples as inferior, a racist reflex to justify privilege and aggression. For example, the literature is filled with examples of descriptions of 'the Orientals' as sub-humans, or animals or ants. In the twentieth century when industrialism came to Asia, this habit continued and 'Orientals' were often referred to as machines or robots, totally divested of human attributes.

The phrase, 'the Orient', was applied indiscriminately to many countries, being gradually extended to cover Persia, Arabia, India, China, Mongolia and, last of all, Japan. As contacts were made with each new country, past images were simply transferred to them. China, for example, was squeezed into a strait-jacket of images which had begun to grow with Greek perceptions of ancient Persia, and Japan is still often palmed off with these cast-off clothes of the European imagination.

It would be natural to suppose that as Europeans came into direct contact with all the countries of the Orient, gradually pushing the frontiers of their knowledge further east, and the jumbo jet tourism and instant communications of our own day had made once distant countries almost as close as our immediate neighbours, the catch-all phrases 'the Orient' and 'the East' and all the stereotypes associated with them would have faded into disuse. But it has not happened that way. We may live in a world of annihilated distance but it still remains a world of inherited misperceptions. Certainly there is a great deal of specialized knowledge available about individual Oriental countries, but the old myths live on as potent as ever, possibly because the geographic extent of 'the Orient' has grown so huge and the meaning of the word has become so blurred.[2]

In many ways the images of Japan in the West have been the most extreme embodiment of the myths of the Orient. Japan is in the furthest East, indeed in the earliest European literature it was actually thought to be the Antipodes. Europeans never tired of writing that in Japan everything was antipodal, topsy-turvy and back to front. An absurd, Alice-in-Wonderland world, not worth taking seriously. Thus the fundamental image of Japan in the West was of a country of extreme and paradoxical contrasts. The *locus classicus* of this view was expressed by an Italian Jesuit missionary, Alessandro Valignano, in 1583:

They also have rites and ceremonies so different from those of all the other nations that it seems they deliberately try to be unlike any other people. The things which they do in this respect are beyond imagining and it may truly be said that Japan is a world the reverse of Europe; everything is so different and opposite that they are like us in practically nothing. So great is the difference in their food, clothing, honours, ceremonies, language, management of the household, in their way of negotiating, sitting, building, curing the wounded and sick, teaching and bringing up children, and in everything else, that it can be neither desired nor understood.[3]

Another Jesuit, the Spaniard, Luis Frois, spelled out in detail in 1585 just what those contrasts were:

Most people in Europe grow tall and have good figures; the Japanese are mostly smaller than we are in body and stature.

The women in Europe do not go out of the house without their husbands' permission; Japanese women are free to go wherever they please without the husband knowing about it.

With us it is not very common that women can write; the noble ladies of Japan consider it a humiliation not to be able to write.

In Europe the men are tailors, and in Japan the women.

Our children first learn to read and then to write; Japanese children first begin to write and thereafter to read.

We believe in future glory or punishment and in the immortality of the soul; the Zen bonzes deny all that and avow that there is nothing more than birth and death.

Our churches are high and narrow; the Japanese temples are broad and low.

We bury our dead; the Japanese cremate most of theirs.

People in Europe love baked and boiled fish; the Japanese much prefer it raw.

We wash our hands at the beginning and at the end of the meal; the Japanese, who do not touch their food with their hands, do not find it necessary to wash them.

We mount a horse with the left foot first; the Japanese with the right.

Our paper is only of four or five types; the Japanese have more than fifty varieties.

We consider precious stones and decorations of gold and silver as being valuable; the Japanese value old kettles, old and broken porcelain, earthenware vessels, etc.[4]

Almost exactly three centuries later the first British Minister in Tokyo, Sir Rutherford Alcock, could go no further than adopt the same theme, so little had Europeans learnt of Japan in the interim, larding it with numerous examples:

Japan is essentially a country of paradoxes and anomalies, where all, even familiar things, put on new faces, and are curiously reversed. Except that they do not walk on their heads instead of their feet, there are few things in which they do not seem, by some occult law, to have been impelled in a perfectly opposite direction and a reversed order. They write from top to bottom, from right to left, in perpendicular instead of horizontal lines, and their books begin where ours end, thus furnishing good examples of the curious perfection this rule of contraries has attained. Their locks, though imitated from Europe, are all made to lock by turning the key from left to right. The course of all sublunary things appears reversed. Their day is for the most part our night, and this principle of antagonism crops up in the most unexpected and *bizarre* way in all their moral being, customs, and habits . . . Their old men fly kites while the children look on; the carpenter uses his plane by drawing it *to* him, and their tailors stitch *from* them; . . . and, finally, the utter confusion of sexes in the public bathhouses, making that correct which we in the West deem so shocking and improper, I leave as I find it – a problem to solve.[5]

Twenty-five years later, the Boston astronomer Percival Lowell observed that 'the boyish belief that on the other side of our globe all things are of necessity upside down is startlingly brought back to the man when he first sets foot at Yokohama . . . Intellectually, at least, their attitude sets gravity at defiance. For to the mind's eye their world is one huge, comical antithesis of our own.'[6] Lowell at least had the excuse that he was writing of a country virtually unknown in the West. But eighty years later, in 1979, a Tokyo-based foreign correspondent could still write:

An outside observer may find more than a touch of the unreal in the reality that is Japan. What at first appears to be straightforward at a second glance quickly takes on aspects of the absurd.[7]

The author of one of the earliest guide-books on Japan (which although a hundred years out of date is still in print and on sale in every major hotel and foreign bookstore in Japan), Professor Chamberlain, even included a special section on 'Topsy-turvydom'. It is largely based on Alcock, but he adds a number of further examples: 'On leaving an inn, you fee not the waiter, but the proprietor . . . They carry babies, not in their arms, but on their backs . . . Politeness prompts them to remove, not their head-gear, but their footgear . . . Strangest of all, after a bath the Japanese dry themselves with a damp towel!'[8]

The famous nineteenth-century Japanophile Lafcadio Hearn, most of whose books are still in print, wrote in 1904, after having lived fourteen years in the country:

Further acquaintance with this fantastic world will in nowise diminish the sense of strangeness evoked by the first vision of it. You will soon observe that even the physical actions of the people are unfamiliar – that their work is done in ways the opposite of Western ways. Tools are of surprising shapes, and are handled after surprising methods: the black-smith squats at his anvil . . . ; the carpenter pulls, instead of pushing, his extraordinary plane and saw. Always the left is the right side, and the right side the wrong; and keys must be turned, to open or close a lock, in what we are accustomed to think the wrong direction.[9]

These early experts on Japan never tired of repeating each other, driving home the same point, even using the same ex-amples. Constant repetition gave their views a wide currency. Besides, the second half of the nineteenth century was the first period in which Europeans of all sorts came into sustained contact with Japan. As with people, so with cultures, first impressions are all important. So frequently were things Japanese presented as antipodally contrary to those in Europe at this impressionistic period of Europe–Japan relations, that that is how they became firmly embedded in the European mind. It is now almost axioma-tic that a writer or journalist, or any other European pundit on Japan, will begin his remarks by reassuring his audience that Japan is indeed an 'upside-down land' where all is diametrically the opposite of what he is used to back home in Europe.

'Most people who go to Japan from Europe or America,' pontificated the London *Economist* in 1977, 'recognize at once that Japanese society is strikingly different from what they are accustomed to in the West. The explanation of this difference seems to be that Japanese society is organized "vertically", while Western society is organized "horizontally".' Or listen to an academic authority lecturing in 1979: 'the key to Japan . . . lies in realizing that the Japanese sense of identity is quite different from ours. We emphasize the abstract-intellectual. They emphasize the situational-emotional.'[10] The jargon is contemporary-scientific, but the basic thought dates back to the nineteenth century and beyond that to the very first European contacts with Japan in the sixteenth century.

There is nothing unusual in catching the reader's interest by saying that everything in the distant land about to be described is

quite different from what he has experienced before. The technique has been used by story tellers the world over since time
immemorial. But it is nothing more than a device – the trouble is
that if taken too literally, it fastens the attention on the quaint and
the arbitrary, for the point of departure is not the land being
described, but those features of it most different from what the
writer and his audience are most used to at home. The approach,
in other words, is purely subjective; even if some of the examples
chosen as contrasts are correct, they may not be significant in
terms of the objective realities of the country being described. In
surveying an uncharted land, both the lowlands and the highlands
have to be taken equally into account, and only then can the
similarities and differences with one's own country be traced.

   So insistently has the exotic, upside-down image of Japan been
repeated in Europe, that today, when a European visitor arrives
in Tokyo or Osaka, try as he will to conceal it, there is often a
sense of disappointment: here is no land of Oriental exotica; on
the contrary the urban sprawl is all too familiar. In search of the
fantasy land which past generations have led him to expect, such a
visitor will hurry off to Kyoto and there find with relief that in its
Buddhist temples and zen gardens he has at last been able to find
something 'Oriental'. His Japanese hosts usually understand
Western expectations so they will arrange trips to shrines, and in
the evenings, dinners with bilingual geishas. Thanks to these
ministrations, the visitor will be able to leave with his expectations
intact. On his return, with all the enthusiasm of someone who has
made a new discovery, he will tell you that Japan is a country of
extreme contrasts: between the silence of the zen rock garden and
the bustle of Tokyo's streets; between the bowing, smiling geisha
and the sharp-elbowed business commuter; between the neat
rice-paddies and the chaotic urban alleys and so on and so forth.

   Japan was not alone in being painted as a country of antipodal
contrasts – at the opposite extreme to Europe and filled with
extreme contrasts within herself. The same happened to most of
the other countries in the Orient as well. Nor was the picture
limited to quaint details of everyday life. At one time or another
the Orient was felt to contain all that Europe most lacked as well

In 1639, the last of the missionaries were expelled from Japan and the leaders of the country chose a policy of isolation for the next two centuries.

The only continuous European contact was the tiny Dutch trading station in Nagasaki. The Dutch merchants however were more interested in account books than writing accounts of Japan. The discoveries of the Jesuits and the occasional visits of Japanese delegations to Europe in the sixteenth century were all but forgotten.

The legacy of these early sporadic contacts was an important one. Educated Europeans, if they thought about Japan at all, were convinced that it was a rich appanage to China. This view, although based in part on the objective reality of the day, has beclouded the European perception of East Asia and Japan's role in it right up to our own times. Indeed, an opinion poll conducted in 1977 in five European countries found that a majority of high school children still believed Japan to be a part of China.[13]

This China bias was early recognized by the small number in the Dutch settlement who actually took an interest in the country to which they were posted. Such men were usually doctors, like Isaac Titsingh (1745–1812), who underlined the desirability of writing on 'a people almost unknown, though fully deserving the attention since a number of years so profusely lavished on the Chinese'.[14] But scholarly doctors such as Kaempfer (1651–1716), Thunberg or Von Siebold (1796–1866), although important in the history of European studies of Japan, were quite marginal in Europe itself and their voices went largely unheard.

The various editions of the *Encyclopaedia Britannica* can serve as a very rough measure of the extent of interest in and knowledge of Japan from the late eighteenth to mid nineteenth century. The first edition (1771) simply contained an abbreviated geographical entry stating, 'Japan, or Islands of Japan are situated between 130° and 144° of E. long. and between 30° and 40° N. lat.' In contrast, the same edition had no less than eight double column pages on China.

In the second edition of the *Britannica* (1780), the entry on Japan was lengthened and repeated substantially unchanged up to the sixth edition of 1823. The description is taken largely from Kaempfer's *History of Japan* (1726–8), which remarkable work was based on the author's two-year residence in Deshima at the end of the seventeenth century as physician to the Dutch trading station. The country is described as surrounded by 'such shallow and boisterous seas' that it seems as though 'Providence had designed it to be a kind of little world by itself.' It is a land of earthquakes, with a much revered conical volcano (Mt Fuji). Its people 'embrace, in the most public manner, a voluntary death, either by drowning, hanging or flinging themselves down from a precipice, or by poison, dagger, or any other quick riddance'. The Japanese have a sharply contrasted character: on the one hand they are modest, patient, courteous, hard-working and clean as well as artistic and ingenuous, while on the other hand they are proud, ambitious, cruel and uncharitable as well as passionate and revengeful.

The article did not quote from an earlier work of Kaempfer's written in 1692, in which he had argued that the Japanese did not need the Dutch trade, which was mainly in luxuries, and that it was 'conducive for the good of the Japanese Empire, to keep it shut up, as it now is, and not to suffer its inhabitants, to have any commerce with foreign nations, either at home or abroad'.[15] Later this point of view was frequently held by European romantics, who wished to preserve exotic societies in the state in which they found them, untrammelled by the contact with industrialism. But Kaempfer was only stating the plain truth – there just was not very much in his day which the Europeans possessed that the Japanese did not already have. His conclusion, though, cannot have satisfied the growing rumours of Japan's great wealth or those jealous of the Dutch monopoly of her trade with Europe.

The nineteenth-century search for new markets for Europe's new manufactures is reflected in the seventh edition of the *Britannica* (1842) which drew on a report made during Sir Stamford Raffles's exploratory expedition to Japan in 1812. The article stated that Raffles, while governor of Java, 'was deeply impressed with the importance of opening a commercial intercourse with the Japanese . . . The Japanese islands, containing, according to his estimate, about 25 millions of inhabitants, who require woollens, hardwares, iron manufactures, and glass, besides many other articles, might, he justly conceived, afford a very extensive market for British goods.'

The Raffles report also suggests that the Dutch had deliberately misrepresented the Japanese as being bigoted and intolerant in order to discourage others from trying to get a share of the market. On the contrary, they were

a nervous, vigorous, people, assimilated by their bodily and mental powers much nearer to Europeans than to Asiatics. The traits of a vigorous intellect are displayed in a greater progress they have made in the sciences and in the arts, which are carried to the much higher degree of perfection among them than among the Chinese, with whom they are frequently confounded but to whom they consider it as a great disgrace to be compared; and the only occasion in which the writer of the report saw a Japanese surprised into passion, and, relinquishing his habitual polite-ness, lay his hand upon his sword, was on an unguarded comparison being made between the two nations.

The report continued that the Japanese were

eager of novelty, and warm in their attachments, open to strangers, and, bating the restrictions of their political institutions, a people who seemed inclined to throw themselves into the hands of any nation of superior intelligence. They have at the same time a great contempt and disregard of everything below their own standard of morals and habits, as instanced in the case of the Chinese.[16]

It was also recorded in the seventh edition that 'many of the women live with Europeans and others, receiving the wages of prostitution'. In this blunt observation, presumably of conditions in Nagasaki, we get a foreshadowing of the later image of Japan as a land of geisha, a paradise for men.

Although the *Britannica* had gradually extended its articles on Japan, the coverage on China was still much more detailed and balanced. It was not until the end of the nineteenth century that entries on Japan began to reflect more than the summary of missionary reports, tales of shipwrecked sojourners and occasion-al residents or visitors to the Dutch trading station. Indeed the actual knowledge of Japan in the West just before Commodore Perry sailed into Edo Bay must still have been practically nil. 'As far as general impressions go,' wrote a contemporary, 'the ordinary floating feeling – we cannot call it knowledge – about Japan, is, that it seems to realize a good deal of the notions conveyed by Swift's Flying Island. We get to think of it as of some Atlantis of the East, a mystery or marvel seldom or very partially revealed to the sons of men.'[17]

If the general knowledge of Japan in mid-nineteenth-century Europe was practically nil, nevertheless the reader will recognize in the long-forgotten encyclopaedia articles which appeared between 1780 and 1842, many of the stereotypes which were later to become inseparable from the European image of Japan: an isolated, impenetrable world; earthquakes, volcanoes, Mt Fuji, suicides, a clean, hardworking, nervous people anxious to learn, characterized by extreme virtues and extreme vices; a tantalizing market for manufactured goods.

In the second half of the nineteenth century this cluster of images was enlarged to include two further vital elements. These were the image of Japan as a land of exquisite artistic refinement and the land of the charming geisha girl.

3

Japan as an Aesthetic Vogue

In the mid nineteenth century, Japan's period of isolation finally came to an end, as under strong foreign pressure she rapidly began to open to the West. One result was a flow of Japanese woodblock prints, decorative art and fabrics to Europe, and sumptuous Japanese displays at International Exhibitions in London, Paris, Vienna and the United States.

Very soon a craze for Japanese prints and objets d'art swept across Europe. This sudden boom for *Japonaiserie* (the word was coined by Baudelaire in 1861) is surely not hard to understand. For decades rumours had been circulating in Europe about the riches and marvels of Japan, a distant 'double-bolted land' in Herman Melville's phrase, whose products and civilization had for so long been totally inaccessible to the West. Now for the first time she began to reveal herself in bold prints and exquisitely refined handicrafts to a Europe whose painting was suffering in the iron grip of academic realism, and whose handicrafts were stifled by the mass-produced kitsch turned out by its new industries.

The Japanese prints were not totally strange. In the eighteenth century Japanese painters and woodblock artists had absorbed some of the techniques of European perspective from the Dutch. There was therefore not the total shock of finding something entirely alien, but rather the pleasing sense of discovering something long forgotten but vaguely familiar, not too strange to be incomprehensible, yet sufficiently different to intrigue.

For a while painters such as Degas, Manet, Lautrec, Van Gogh, Monet and Bonnard experimented with Japanese techniques of line and form in two-dimensional patterns. In the evening they would gather in their favourite cabaret, the Divan Japonais, where the waitresses wore kimonos and the walls were hung with fans. Their interest in Japanese prints incidentally has been amply repaid in Japan, where the French impressionists remain to this day by far the most popular Western school of painting.

The echoes of the new discovery of Japan were also felt in European ceramics and literature and even as far afield as in film, where a pioneer such as Eisenstein later acknowledged the inspiration he had drawn from Kabuki.[18]

The aesthetic infatuation with Japan was at its strongest in the last quarter of the nineteenth century and it was duly satirized, for example, by the younger Dumas, in his comedy *Francillon* (1887):

Henri: Annette, may I ask you the recipe of the salad we had this evening? It would appear that it was your own mixture.
Annette: The Japanese salad?
Henri: It's Japanese?
Annette: That's what I call it.
Henri: Why?
Annette: So it has a name: everything is Japanese nowadays.[19]

In London Gilbert and Sullivan's *Mikado* made the same point to packed houses from its opening night in 1885:

If you want to know who we are,
We are gentlemen of Japan.
On many a vase and jar –
On many a screen and fan,
We figure in lively paint:
Our attitude's queer and quaint –
You're wrong if you think it ain't.[20]

Typically, such infatuations are over almost as quickly as they begin because the novelty value of the newly discovered culture soon wears off. After the honeymoon of mutual discovery comes the humdrum round of day to day existence together, and occasional conflict. Indeed, the fashion in the salons and studios of Europe soon switched from the exotic to the primitive, and by the turn of the century it was African art which had become all the rage. Nevertheless the period of *Japonisme* is unusual in that it remains to this day one of the only periods when Europe has rushed to learn from Japan.

Europe's acquaintance with Japan since the 1850s was not only limited to the welcome imports of prints and objets d'art and occasional exhibitions. Increasingly travellers and merchants were making their way there, especially after the opening of the Suez Canal in the 1870s. To these early visitors, Japan seemed like an exotic Eden, untouched by the West, yet highly civilized. One such traveller, the Comte de Beauvoir, who visited Japan on a world trip in the 1870s, was entranced by the sight of men and women bathing together: 'In Japan one lives in full daylight; modesty, or rather immodesty, is not known; it is the innocence of the early paradise, and the costumes of our first parents have nothing which shocks the sentiments of these people who still live in a golden age.'[21]

The Victorian poet Sir Edwin Arnold, during a stay in Japan in 1891, told an audience in Tokyo that Japan

appears to me as close an approach to Lotus-land as I shall ever find . By many a pool of water-lilies in temple grounds and in fairy-like gardens, amid the beautiful rural scenery of Kama-kura or Nikko; under long avenues of cryptomeria; in weird and dreamy Shinto shrines; on the white matting of the teahouses; in the bright bazaars; by your sleeping lakes, and under your stately mountains, I have felt further removed than ever before from the flurry and vulgarity of our European life . . . Yet what I find here more marvellous to me than Fuji-san, lovelier than the embroidered and gilded silks, precious beyond all the daintily carved ivories, more delicate than the cloisonné enamels is . . . that almost divine sweetness of disposition which, I frankly believe, places Japan in these respects higher than any other nation . . . Retain, I beseech you, gentlemen, this national characteristic, which you did not import, and can never, alas, export.[22]

Sir Edwin was of course referring to Japanese women as the highest expression of Japan's aesthetic sensibility. Nor should this be in the least surprising – underlying the aesthetic attraction for Japanese art there was always a strong current of eroticism. Zola decorated the stair of his Paris house with Japanese erotic prints (*shunga*) which he referred to as 'furious fornications'. It is doubtful whether he would have put up French pornography in the same place. The point is that the word 'pornography' in one's own language has a below-the-stairs, furtive feel, while *shunga* carries an exotic, far-away thrill. Japan was a land of pure otherness where the ordinary rules did not apply. At least part of the interest of travel in distant places has always been escape from restrictions at home coupled with the expectations of romance and the excitement of chance encounters abroad.

For Europeans the Orient as a dream setting for enchanted, if not forbidden, pleasures is at least as old as the garden of Eden. Tales of sweet temptation and wild voluptuousness in the sumptuous courts and harems of the East have always beguiled us, because, by the law of opposites, if the West was Christian and moral, the East was by definition heathen and immoral, a perfect setting for tales of passionate and guiltless romance.

In recent centuries the rich tradition of Oriental exoticism took a new form as colonial conquest and rule provided the opportunity in the form of readily available girls, and encouraged Europeans to think of the West as active and masculine and the East as passive and feminine.

One outcome was the novel of exotic romance, of 'paresse et caresse'; the love of a white man and an Oriental woman. Considering that Japan had always been regarded as being in the furthest reaches of the Orient, and that the Japanese appeared to find no contradiction between erotic and religious love, it is perhaps small wonder that one of the first settings of the new novel of exotic romance was Japan.

The new genre was the creation of a young French 'man of action', the naval officer and writer, Julian Viaud (1850–1923), better known by his pen-name, Pierre Loti, who based his novel *Madam Chrysanthemum* on a brief visit to Nagasaki in 1885.

Nagasaki had long been the port through which Japanese trade with Europe was centred. Girls were easily available to foreigners, as the Italian adventurer Francesco Carletti pointed out already in the early 1600s:

As soon as ever these Portuguese arrive and disembark, the pimps who control this traffic in women call on them in the houses in which they are

quartered for the time of their stay, and enquire whether they would like
to purchase, or acquire in any other method they please, a girl, for the
period of their sojourn, or to keep her for so many months, or for a night,
or for a day, or for an hour, a contract being first made with these brokers
or an agreement entered into with the girls' relations, and the money paid
down . . . And many of these Portuguese, upon whose testimony I am
relying, fall in with this custom, as the fancy takes them, driving the best
bargain they can for a few pence. And so it often happens that they will get
hold of a pretty little girl of fourteen or fifteen years of age, for three or
four *scudi* . . . with no other responsibility beyond that of sending her
back home when done with . . . To sum up, the country is more plentifully
supplied than any other with these sort of means of gratifying the passion
for sexual indulgence, just as it abounds in every other sort of vice, in
which it surpasses every other place in the world.[23]

Since Carletti's day, the few Europeans who stayed at the
Dutch trading station in Nagasaki were forbidden to bring their
women with them: girls were provided. Occasionally too news
must have filtered back to Europe of adventurers who had stayed
on in Japan to marry and settle down with a Japanese wife (the
example of the sixteenth-century English pilot, Will Adams,
whose story has recently been made into the bestseller *Shōgun*,
comes to mind). Thus by the time Pierre Loti's ship put into
Nagasaki harbour for repairs in the summer of 1885, the port's
reputation, at least amongst European sailors, was well established. It was Loti's contribution to turn the humdrum realities of
prostitution in an Oriental harbour town into a romantic tale
which has coloured the European image of Japan ever since.

Loti's reputation had already been made as the author of
romances set in far-away lands such as Tahiti, Turkey and
Montenegro. The formula was usually the same. A young naval
officer (Loti himself) for one reason or another has to spend a few
weeks or a few months on shore. To while away the time and to
'penetrate the soul' of the strange culture, he has what might be
called an 'aventure de plage'. The girl is usually a teenager and so
infatuated with him that when he leaves, she pines away if not
actually dying of sorrow.

Loti's books were reprinted hundreds of times and were translated into all the European languages. His readers' imaginations

were no doubt titillated by the dream of romance unfettered by strict nineteenth-century European moral conventions and responsibilities. The setting, too, was an escape from the ugliness of early industrial Europe to countries and places inaccessible in an age when travel was still an adventure. Finally, Loti's style was undemanding. His speciality was the impressionistic sketch of local detail enmeshed in the sentimental moods of the hero – himself. The mistresses in his novel are curiously stereotyped, treated like pets and discarded as easily on leaving. He has been credited with creating the 'colonial novel' and the 'novel of desertion'. More accurate terms would be the 'novel of escape' or the 'novel of sexploitation'.[24]

His most famous book set in Japan, *Madam Chrysanthemum* (1887), followed the usual formula, but with a difference. In an introductory note to the first edition he explained that the three principal characters were 'MYSELF, JAPAN and the EFFECT which this country has on me'. Unlike in his other books, however, Loti made no secret of his dislike for the *mousmé* (prostitute) Chrysanthemum, with whom he and his inseparable companion Yves lived in that summer of 1885 in Nagasaki. Paradoxically in view of the book's later reputation, he also paints the Japanese with many a diminutive as a quaint, ridiculous people, living in a country which is only occasionally exotic. Summing it up, he wrote: 'I find it [Japan] little, aged, with worn-out blood and worn-out sap; I feel more fully its antediluvian antiquity, its centuries of mummification, which will soon degenerate into hopeless and grotesque buffoonery, as it comes into contact with Western novelties.'[25]

The Japanese are mercilessly caricatured as an inferior yellow people – they are small, fragile, and feminine. They are decadent, dangerous and contradictory; full of trickery, superb imitators like comic, aged monkeys.

Loti himself was a tiny, effeminate man, cold-blooded, snobbish, vain and terrified of old age. It is likely that in writing of the Japanese he projected onto them all those qualities he disliked most in himself. In doing so he made the image of Japan more 'real' for his readers at home, who could now associate the country with many of the familiar negative images of the Orient.

His bored, patronizing tone must also have been congenial to the colonial prejudices of the day. Above all, perhaps unwittingly, he added to the image of Japan as an aesthetic paradise the attraction of the *petite* eroticism of the *mousmé*.

The fundamental reason for the enormous success of *Madam Chrysanthemum* was that it articulated for the first time in a popular form the European fascination with Japanese women.

An English writer of the time fumbled towards the reason for this attraction: 'The Japanese woman is the crown of the charm of Japan. In the noble lady and in her frailest and most unfortunate sister alike there is an indefinable something which is fascinating at first sight and grows only more pleasing on acquaintance . . . the key to the character of the Japanese women lies in the word obedience.'[26]

A few of Loti's more discerning readers in the West took a dislike to *Madam Chrysanthemum*, including Henry James, who wrote soon after its appearance:

The author's taste is for the primitive and the beautiful, the large and free, and the Japanese strike him as ugly and complicated, tiny and conventional. His attitude is more profane than our own prejudice can like it to be; he quite declines to take them seriously . . . I may be altogether mistaken, but we treat ourselves to the conviction that he fails of justice to the wonderful little people who have renewed, for Europe and America, the whole idea of Taste.[27]

Yet, even while criticizing Loti's attitude towards the Japanese, Henry James shares his condescending tone in referring to them as 'wonderful little people'. In doing so he was merely repeating a fundamental conviction of the day, that of the smallness of everything to do with Japan, a view which Loti developed to its furthest extremes.

Loti was occasionally criticized by his contemporaries, and today most would find his attitude either distasteful or laughable, but in the late nineteenth century Loti's Japan became Europe's Japan. His novels were instant bestsellers; *Madam Chrysanthemum* went through twenty-five impressions in French alone in the first five years after its publication. His influence on his contemporaries was immense – just as Gaugin left for Tahiti after reading Loti's *Rarahu*, *Madam Chrysanthemum* was one of the two books which decided Lafcadio Hearn to go to Japan. Van Gogh painted an imaginary portrait of Chrysanthemum, and in 1900 the book was turned into a smash-hit play which so impressed Puccini when he saw it in London that he used it for the basis of his opera *Madam Butterfly* (1904), thereby giving the tale an even wider appeal.[28]

'To tell the truth,' wrote André Chéradam in 1906, 'before the war [that is to say, the Russo-Japanese war of 1904–5], apart from a limited number of specialists and scholars who kept themselves informed by their travels and serious works (seldom read), for us, the rest of the French, what we knew of Japan was that above all it was the country of Madam Chrysanthemum.'[29] If this was true of the French it was also true for other Europeans, including the Russians, whose failure to take seriously Japan's intentions for war in 1903–4 may have been in part due to the prevailing image of Japan as a land of *mousmés* (the word itself had by then entered the French language), full of tricks to be sure, but fragile as a butterfly and certainly unwarlike. As late as 1904, we know that the Russian Minister in Washington was still referring scornfully to the Japanese as 'little yellow monkeys'. The phrase is Loti's.

Even after the shock of Japan's victory over Russia, Loti's image of Japan exerted a powerful influence – the book continued to sell well and his imitators were legion. To take but one example from England, a popular novelist and authority on faking photographs, Clive Holland, published a slim volume entitled *My Japanese Wife* in 1895. The book went through sixteen editions in the next twenty years and also appeared with slight alterations under a number of different titles such as *Mousmé*. Holland shamelessly copied Loti, the only difference being that the author-hero, less ruthless than Loti or more hypocritical perhaps, says that he intends to bring his *mousmé*, Hyacinth, whom he has met in a tea shop in Nagasaki, back to England. As in Loti, Japan is described as 'tiny, toylike and ridiculous'.[30]

French variations on the Chrysanthemum theme such as *Poupée Japonaise*, *Petite Mousmé* or *The Honourable Picnic* abounded; there even developed a colonial sub-genre, set in Indo-China, with titles such as *Poupée Parfumée* or *Thisen, La*

Petite Amie Exotique. The theme was also treated in a first novel by a young British colonial policeman named George Orwell in *Burmese Days*, and inevitably it was taken up by Somerset Maugham in his Malayan short stories.[31]

No doubt the organized movement for women's equality in Europe only made the dream of escape to a submissive lover in an exotic land ever more attractive. Be this as it may, the genre long outlasted the feminist movement, as well as the European colonial presence in Asia, and after a temporary hiatus brought about by the Pacific War, made a triumphant return with a spate of bestsellers all set in Japan: *Sayonara*, *Tea House of the August Moon*, *You Only Live Twice* or *Shōgun* all contained large doses of the original Loti formula. At a slightly more 'highbrow' level, take Resnais's *Hiroshima Mon Amour* (1959), an influential film, sometimes even picked as one of the ten best films of the century. The plot is little more than the Chrysanthemum theme in modern clothing. The main difference is that the European having a passing affair in Japan is a woman, not a man (a reflection of the enhanced status of European women or the abject state of Japan after the war?). The heroine, Emanuelle Riva, picks up a Japanese lover in Hiroshima, Okada Eiji, who in the best traditions of Loti's Oriental love-objects, merely acts as a foil to Riva's moods. It is his role to be passionate when she requires it, and for the rest, to listen in sympathetic silence as she dominates the entire film with a monologue about her childhood affair with a German soldier. The film could have been set anywhere, but the authors chose to exploit the contemporary horror of atomic war by making Hiroshima the backdrop, and by interspersing the love scenes with shots of A-bomb victims (cribbed from Sekigawa's *Hiroshima*, 1953).

Only a particularly unpleasant form of French provincialism could have rehashed such a stale image of Japan – a land of extreme contrasts, a sensuous, horrific Oriental country, and as such, an 'exciting' setting for the French heroine's self-discovery.

It is with a sense of relief that one turns to a more light-hearted but also immensely successful film which makes Japan its setting, *You Only Live Twice*, based on Ian Fleming's bestselling book of the same title (1964). It contains an amusing pastiche of the

Chrysanthemum theme, right from the opening lines, 'the geisha called Trembling Leaf, on her knees beside James Bond, leant forward from the waist and kissed him chastely on the right cheek', to the closing scene, when Bond, on leaving Japan, the exotic Oriental setting of the film, also incidentally deserts the girl who has cared for him and fallen in love with him: 'his life on Kuno, his love of Kissy Suzuki, were . . . of as little account as sparrows' tears'.[32]

The exotic-aesthetic image of Japan in Europe was created by artists, connoisseurs and romantics, many of whom followed Paul Valéry's excellent advice, that 'in order that the word Orient produces its complete and entire effect on someone's spirit, above all it is essential *never to have been* in the country which it so uncertainly indicates'.[33] Those few of their number who actually did visit the country and willingly stayed on to become 'Japanified', or '*tatamisé*', as the French put it, were appalled by the first signs of Japanese industrialization. After all, this was precisely what they were escaping from at home: brick buildings and iron railings, gas lamps and tramways, crinolines and buttonboots hardly fitted the stereotype of an exotic Oriental land. So alongside the romantic image of Japan as an aesthetic paradise peopled by obedient *mousmés*, there also developed a contradictory image, an image mainly of Japanese men, as ridiculous, unaesthetic, untrustworthy imitators of the West. 'As a moral being, the Japanese woman does not seem to belong to the same race as the Japanese man!' wrote a contemporary.[34]

This negative image of the men was also no doubt in part derived from the frustrations of the local Western business community: for those forced to live in Lotus-land, it was Lotus-land no longer. They were confined to the Treaty Ports and limited in their contacts. An American traveller, Mrs Bacon, explained as follows:

The employment of the merchant being formally the lowest of the respectable callings, one does not find even yet in Japan many great stores or a very high standard of business morality . . . Hence English and American merchants, who only see Japan from the business side, continually speak of the Japanese as dishonest, tricky and altogether unreliable, and greatly prefer to deal with the Chinese, who have much of the business virtue that is characteristic of the English as a nation.[35]

Kipling quoted an English trader he met in a hotel in Kyoto in 1889 as saying, 'The Jap has no business savvy. God knows I hate the Chinaman . . . but you can do business with him. The Jap's a little huckster who can't see beyond his nose.' Later in his travels he met a businessman on the train to Yokohama who told him, 'Can't say that I altogether like the Jap way o' doing business . . . Give me a Chinaman to deal with . . . You'll find that opinion in most of the treaty ports.'[36]

One example of the sort of business practice which angered the foreigners will suffice:

If truth must be told, greed leads the Japanese into the most shameless impositions. Half the goods sold as foreign eatables and drinkables are compounded of vile and unwholesome trash, manufactured in Tokyo and elsewhere, put up in bottles and jars with the names and labels of such highly respectable makers as Bass, Martell, Guinness, and Crosse and Blackwell, upon them . . . But to secure themselves in their trade of forgery, these unconscionable villains have establishments at Tokyo, not only for the manufacture of the compounds, but of the labels which give them currency, and some of these are such adroit forgeries as to be completely successful, while others would effectually deceive a purchaser were it not for certain inscrutable vagaries in spelling . . .[37]

However much foreigners disliked Japanese business practices, they did not regard the Japanese as serious commercial rivals. The dominant Treaty Port view is summed up in a comment in the leading English-language newspaper of the day:

Wealthy we do not at all think [Japan] will ever become: the advantages conferred by nature, with the exception of climate, and the love of indolence and pleasure of the people themselves, forbid it. The Japanese are a happy race, and being content with little, are not likely to achieve much.

Japan Herald, 9 April 1881

Another aspect of the new Japan which Europeans invariably found out of keeping with their images of an unspoiled Oriental paradise was the early craze for Western styles. Clothing styles especially caught the eye. The following quotation is taken from the circular of a Tokyo tailor opening his shop in 1871:

> What strange sights we see these days! We see many a man wearing a Prussian cap and French shoes, with a coat of the British navy and the trousers of the American army – a mosaic of different Western countries plaited on a Japanese basis.[38]

An American traveller indicates how incongruous such sights appeared:

> It is usually the case, too, that a young Japanese who puts on foreign garments thinks it necessary to adopt other foreign customs, and, not having a very clear idea as to what they are, makes a ridiculous spectacle of himself with the best of intentions. He puts his hat on the back of his head, sticks a cigar in the corner of his mouth, takes a cane in his hand, and thinks that he is the perfect model of an American or English gentleman, when in fact he is a poor imitation of a loafer.[39]

At the other end of the social scale, Japanese in high society wearing European clothes appeared equally bizarre. In 1883 the government had opened a ballroom, the Rokumeikan, for the purpose of entertaining foreigners with cards, billiards, Western music and lavish balls. It was intended to give a cosmopolitan atmosphere to the new capital and thus help convince the Western powers that Japan was 'civilized'. Three years after it was opened, Loti was invited to a society ball at the Rokumeikan, which was, he wrote, 'built in the European style, all fresh, all white, all new and looks, my God, like a casino in one of our watering places and you could truly believe yourself to be anywhere but in Yeddo . . .' At the dance there were 'innumerable Japanese gentlemen; these ministers, admirals, officers and officials are a little too over-bedecked in gold braid, all dressed up for the ball . . . And how strangely they wear their swallowtails. No doubt their backs were not made to wear this sort of thing; impossible to say for what reason but I find all of them always in some indescribable way very similar to monkeys . . .' And, as for the women, 'they dance quite correctly, my Japanese in French costumes. But one feels that it is something *learnt*; they dance like automatons, without the least personal initiative . . .' Or, as a German observer of the same scene put it somewhat more wittily: 'most of them showed by the expression of their faces that they were making a sacrifice on the altar of civilization'.

Loti contrasts the Chinese at the ball with their Japanese hosts:

At ten o'clock, entrance of the Embassy of the Celestial Empire: a dozen superb personages, with mocking eyes, standing a head above this crowd of tiny Japanese. Chinese of the fair race of the North, they have in their bearing, under their dazzling silks, a noble grace. And also they show good taste and dignity in keeping to their national costume, the long magnificently brocaded and embroidered robe.[40]

Of course to a Japanese observer, it would have probably been the Chinese who appeared ridiculous, and the Japanese in their Western clothes would have seemed to be in the height of fashion. This is in fact the theme of Akutagawa Ryūnosuke's short story, 'The Ball', which is discussed in Part II.

The sight of Japanese adopting Western ways led Europeans to ridicule them as 'pitifully grotesque'. As Hearn put it, 'I fear the future demoralization of Japan is to be effected by Japanese in frock-coats and loud neck-ties.'[41] Many prophesied the end of 'Old' Japan and echoed Hearn's lament, 'the opening of the country was very wrong – a crime. Fairyland is already dead.'[42]

Kipling on a visit in 1889, three years after Loti was invited to the ball at the Rokumeikan, foresaw that 'the cultured Japanese of the English pattern will corrupt and defile the tastes of his neighbours till . . . Japan altogether ceases to exist as a separate nation and becomes a button-hole manufacturing appanage of America'.[43]

In another characteristically bitter-sweet comment he wrote:

Japan is a great people. Her masons play with stone, her carpenters with wood, her smiths with iron, and her artists with life, death, and all the eye can take in. Mercifully she has been denied the last touch of firmness in her character which would enable her to play with the whole round world. We possess that – We, the nation of the glass flower-shade, the pink worsted mat, the red and green China puppy dog, and the poisonous Brussels carpet. It is our compensation.[44]

The compensation has long been denied the British, and the rest of the Europeans too. Japan has shifted from the traditional to the modern – from the tatami to the carpet. In her rush to catch up with the industrialized West she has also displayed a sufficient 'touch of firmness in her character', if not to play with the whole round world, then at least to shake it at times.

The more Japan industrialized, however, the more Europeans clung to the old topsy-turvy image of Japan as a quaint fairyland whose only traces could now be found in a supposedly exotic past. After all, it was far more reassuring to live with this illusion than have to acknowledge the arrival of a new power and competitor on the international scene. Europeans were therefore poorly prepared for the rapid changes which Japan was already undergoing in the late nineteenth century. When they finally woke up to those changes it was with a profound sense of shock and disappointment; the *mousmé* was charming so long as she was obedient; she rapidly became intolerable when she took on a life of her own.

4

Japan as a Military and Colonial Power

The essentially frivolous image of Japan formed by Europeans in the second half of the nineteenth century was abruptly challenged by the Japanese victory over China in 1895.

A French commentator, De Villenoisy, pointed out that for the British Foreign Office, which had thought China would win the war, 'it was painful to see rising on the furthest borders of Asia a real European state of yellow people without having guessed that its birth was about to take place'. Not without some Gallic satisfaction he noted that the war was 'one of the most important events of modern times' because the emergence of an Asian sea power would inevitably lead to the decline of British influence. He also predicted an eventual rejuvenation of China and 'the awakening of the yellow peoples who would be in competition with Europe'.[45] A view shared by some of his contemporaries:

'Consider what a Japan-governed China would be,' a British writer exhorted the readers of the *St James's Gazette* in October 1894,

think what the Chinese are; think of their powers of silent endurance under suffering and cruelty; think of their frugality; think of their patient perseverance; their slow, dogged persistence, their recklessness of life. Fancy this people ruled by a nation of born organisers, who, half-allied to them, would understand their temperament and their habits. The Oriental, with his power of retaining health under conditions under which no European could live, with his savage daring when aroused, with his inborn cunning, lacks only the superior knowledge of civilization to be the equal of the European in warfare as well as in industry.[46]

These warnings, however, did not help to prepare public opinion in Europe for the Japanese victories over Russia in 1904 and 1905, which in the words of a contemporary, 'dumbfounded the chancelleries and surprised the people'.[47]

Europeans, it appeared, were simply not in the habit of taking Japan seriously. As *The Times* editorialized in February 1904, just after the sinking of three Russian ships and the Japanese declaration of war:

> The story of the last ten days must have fallen upon the Western world with the rapidity of a tropical thunderstorm . . . That is the trouble at the root of the present situation – the past inability of the West to take Japan seriously . . . All this is due to the superficial study of Japan which has characterized Western contact with it. We as a nation alone appear to have formed a shrewder estimate [the Anglo-Japanese alliance had been signed in 1902] . . . But for the rest, they still were pleased to look upon the Japanese through the eyes of the aesthetic penman, and thought of the nation as a people of pretty dolls dressed in flowered silks and dwelling in paper houses of the capacity of matchboxes . . .[48]

European reaction was swift and extreme, particularly in France, which had not only been chiefly responsible for the 'aesthetic penman's' image of Japan, but was also allied to Russia; it was pointed out that Japan's war with Russia was a revival of the struggle between East and West which had started with the Persian Wars of ancient Greece.

Fears of a new yellow peril had been circulating in the West for some time. One of the earliest writers on the subject was Bakunin, who travelled across Siberia to the Pacific in the late 1860s, and foresaw an alliance of China and Japan newly armed with Western skills, threatening the West by the end of that century. It was following the Japanese victory over China in 1895 that Kaiser Wilhelm II had had his notorious nightmare of a yellow peril, the drawing of which he sent to Nicholas II and which was widely published around Europe. But it was only after the defeat of Russia that the image of Japan became equated with the age-old fears of the enemy from the East and the Japanese were seen by many in Europe as a new yellow peril. Japan, it was argued, would throw off her thin veneer of Westernization and revert to a supposed Mongolian past to lead the Chinese against the West, launching a massive war of Orientals against Occidentals. A

German political commentator, Baron Von Falkenegg, expressed his fears as follows:

> The European powers should have realized in good time that the cunning, skilled and valiant Japanese people would soon be uttering the slogan 'Asia for the Asians' . . . As soon as the Mongolians were set in a belligerent direction, they knew no retreat, even when the bodies were piled as high as hills. Exactly like the Japanese. Here, as there, we find that uncanny, wild bravery, incomprehensible to the European mind, which sets value of the individual at naught . . . 'Asia for the Asians' has become the slogan in Japan, and is directed at all those Europeans who want to take political and commercial advantages in Asia.
> But for the Japanese, 'Asia for the Asians' has the obvious implication, 'Japan dominates Asia, and Asia dominates Europe.'[49]

Another writer, René Pinon, having remarked that the war re-awakened 'the notion of an external enemy – the yellows', continued:

> Whether one likes it or not, the 'yellow peril' has entered already into the imagination of the people, just as represented in the famous drawing of Kaiser Wilhelm II: in a setting of conflagration and carnage, Japanese and Chinese hordes spread out over all Europe, crushing under their feet the ruins of our capital cities and destroying our civilizations, grown anaemic due to the enjoyment of luxuries and corrupted by vanity of spirit.[50]

Such fears also found expression in bestselling novels like Emile Driant's *The Yellow Invasion* (written under the pseudonym, Capitaine Danrit, Paris, 3 vols., 1905; re-issued 1979) whose main theme was an attack on the West by the Chinese masses led by Japanese brains. These years also saw the first novels about a future war between Japan and the United States, most famous of which was 'General' Homer Lea's *The Valor of Ignorance* (1909).[51]

Some also thought that the real danger from the East lay in economic competition, as the French economist and editor of the well-known journal, *L'Économiste Européen*, Édouard Théry repeatedly warned:

The Yellow Peril . . . is the violent disrupture of the economic equilibrium at present in force in the great European industrial countries, a disrupture provoked by the rapid industrial and commercial awakening of an immense region with a population of 500 millions of inhabitants . . . and possessing natural resources . . . incomparably superior to those of all the European nations put together.[52]

It was felt that the Japanese were in no hurry because 'they will choose the field of action which suits them best, and they will lead the pack and stimulate the organization of the industrial victory of the Far East over the West using our capital, our machines and our methods'.[53] Even relative moderates like Pinon believed that 'the competition of yellow labour, which although it is not the imminent peril that it is sometimes painted, is none the less far from being imaginary . . . The victory of Japan over Russia will be the start of a new era for the yellow race, which, spurred on by the Japanese, will adopt all the procedures and tools of our civilization, resulting for Europe in economic disturbance which will singularly delay solutions to the great social problems.'[54]

Two generations later, a majority of Frenchmen questioned in a poll conducted in 1977 still said that they did not welcome Japan's industrial progress because of the strong competition to French industry![55]

At the turn of the century, there were even those who went so far as to suggest that the solution was to cut off Europe's trade with Japan, to boycott Japanese goods and refuse to export European goods to her.

Not all Europeans thought Japan was a danger. On the contrary, most serious commentators rejected the notion of a yellow invasion or industrial challenge as fanciful and some even warned the Japanese of the dangers of Western imperialism. The influential philosopher and prophet of Social Darwinism, Herbert Spencer, for example, had given confidential advice in 1892 (to be passed to Prime Minister Itō) that 'Japanese policy should be that of keeping Americans and Europeans *as much as possible at arm's length*. In presence of the more powerful races your position is one of chronic danger, and you should take every precaution to give as little foothold as possible to foreigners.'

At the time of the Russo-Japanese War, everyone who wanted for one reason or another the defeat of Russia, hoped for the victory of Japan. This was the case in countries such as Finland or Sweden where Russia was viewed as an aggressor. It was also true of the Anglo-Saxon countries where it soon became fashionable to explain Japan's victory in terms of the heroic virtues of the samurai as put forward, for example, in Nitobe Inazo's *Bushido, the Soul of Japan* (1899; 1905). It was one of the first of a long line of books by Japanese writers instrumental in shaping Western views of Japan.[56]

In France, which was allied to Russia, public opinion was against Japan. It was also hostile to Great Britain. A novel such as *The Yellow Invasion* is not only anti-Chinese and Japanese, it is also venomously anti-British. But even in France, socialists took the side of Japan. In a passage much quoted at the time, a character in Anatole France's *Sur la Pierre Blanche* argues for example:

What the Russians are paying for at this very moment in the seas of Japan and in the gorges of Manchuria is not just their avid and brutal policy in the Orient, it is the colonial policy of all the European powers . . . It would not appear to be the case, however, that the yellow peril terrifying European economists is comparable to the white peril hanging over Asia. The Chinese do not send to Paris, Berlin or St Petersburg missionaries to teach Christians *feng-shui* and cause general chaos in European affairs . . . Admiral Togo did not come with a dozen battleships to bombard the roadstead of Brest in order to help Japanese commerce in France . . . The armies of the Asiatic powers have not taken to Tokyo or Peking the paintings of the Louvre or the china of the Élysée.[57]

After the formation of the Anglo-Japanese alliance in 1902, Britons became fond of identifying their new ally as the 'Britain of Asia', and there was considerable sympathy for Japan, the small young country taking on and beating the huge Russian bear. Cartoons of 'Jap the giant killer' were popular. A British novelist, William Plomer, recalled catching sight of a Japanese battleship at a naval review off the Isle of Wight in about 1910.

'Look at the pretty flag, Billy,' somebody had said, 'The rising sun. That great ship belongs to the plucky little Japs who beat the Russians. Yes, they're our friends and perhaps someday you'll go and see their pretty country, where the houses are made of paper and the ladies wear chrysanthemums in their hair.'[58]

The year 1905 was widely accepted as marking the emergence of a new kind of colonial power, an Asian colonial power, and hence the end of unchallenged Western dominance and eventually the end of the European colonies in East Asia.[59]

Of the Western reactions to Japan's victories over Russia in 1904 and 1905, some proved to be wide of the mark, but others turned out to be not so far wrong.

Japan's militant nationalists in the 1930s did indeed attempt to lead a resurgence of Asian power against the West. They did succeed in driving the Europeans out of most of their Asian colonies. But what was not foreseen was that Japan would very quickly alienate most of the Asian peoples including the Chinese.

The view that proved most lasting was that Japan would become the leader of peaceful efforts of the Asian countries to modernize. As a contemporary put it:

Her [Japan's] new role may be described as that of the Schoolmaster of Asia. In other words, recent events would indicate that Japan will be the chief influence to modernize China, to awaken Korea, to help Siam, and even incongruous though it seems, to cooperate with Russia in making Eastern Siberia habitable and prosperous.[60]

Also correctly foreseen was that Japan would become an industrial power capable of competing with the West.

The fear that proved completely unfounded was the fear of a racial war of the 'yellows' against the 'whites'.

With the outbreak of the First World War, the attention of Europe was directed away from the Far East. After the war, the fears that Japan would lead China against the West were not revived, because Japan and China were almost continuously at war with each other, but the image of a Japanese economic peril repeatedly returned. Indeed during the Great Depression of 1929–32, to many in Europe the fears of Japanese competition based on cheap labour seemed to be only too justified. Denunciation of Japan reached a peak in the European press during these years as Japan alone of the industrial powers continued to expand her markets and to increase her exports. 'Swelling tide of yellow trade', 'unfair competition', 'social dumping', 'a new yellow peril', 'menace of a sharp inrush of Japanese goods', 'manipulation of the yen exchange rate', were some of the typical accusations made, particularly by spokesmen of labour-intensive light industries such as textiles, which were already non-competitive on world markets.

These were also the years when the label 'Made in Japan' on goods such as toys, bicycles, textiles, matches and so on became synonymous with cheap and unreliable.

As Japan industrialized it became fashionable for practically every European who ever wrote about her to point to the sharp contrasts in Japanese society between 'Western' elements and 'Eastern' elements. Many Japanese writers, too, referred to 'a dual mode of living – European outside . . . and Japanese at home . . . an amphibian mode of living'.[61] Kipling in his blunt way had applied this to the Japanese themselves when he said, 'The Jap isn't a native, and he isn't a Sahib either.'[62] Critics would often not only be disappointed at finding factory chimneys where they had hoped to find an unspoiled 'Oriental' land, but also suggest that the Western elements were only skin deep, a caricature of the West. They would therefore suggest that underneath the outer veneer, the Japanese himself was an untrustworthy Oriental. These prejudices have been extraordinarily persistent right to this day, even though they are based on a false dichotomy between 'East' and 'West', and even though Japan's modernization process has become sufficiently internalized for her to catch up and surpass in many respects most of the European economies.

The early 1930s were the years when the Japanese military began the conquest of China, drawing unanimous censure from the League of Nations in 1932. Japanese atrocities were widely condemned in the European press, particularly after the bombings of Shanghai in 1932 which were amongst the first scenes of warfare filmed by newsreel cameramen. Next came the rape of Nanking and the aerial bombardment of Canton in 1937:

If the Japan of today has learnt much, she has forgotten much. The levying without cause of 'totalitarian' war on China; the repeated bombings of populous and undefended cities with callous disregard for a hideous toll of innocent civilian lives – these actions are ugly blots on the scroll of chivalry from which the Japan of thirty years ago would have recoiled.[63]

But nobody in Europe seriously believed that Japan would ever attack the European colonies in Asia – after all, the Japanese were a charming, if occasionally slightly unpredictable, people. During the years 1920–40, there was only one bestseller on a Japanese theme in Europe. This was Arthur Waley's translation of the *Tale of Genji* which naturally reinforced the old image of Japan as a refined and exotic culture. About as far from the cockpit of a Zero fighter as Lady Murasaki from a typewriter.

Not only did the European powers underestimate the strength of their potential Asian enemy, but a probably more important reason for their total unpreparedness was the fatal illusion of their own power in Asia. 'Pride of race, contempt for other races, and an enervating century of security lay at the basis of these illusions,' a historian has written on the fall of Hong Kong and Malaya. His remarks could also be applied to the French in Indo-China and to the Dutch in Indonesia. 'Despite all the evidence from the Russo-Japanese war of 1905 onwards,' he continues, 'the British still regarded the Asians as inferiors, at once amusing and exasperating, and until 1941 few of them realized how strong Japan had become and how intent on establishing an Asian Empire which it did not propose to share with others.' As Winston Churchill put it in a speech to the British Parliament in April 1942, 'I frankly admit that the violence, fury, skill and might of Japan have far exceeded anything that we had been led to expect.' The Americans were no better prepared – like the Europeans they thought the Japanese were comical. The notion that they could shoot straight or pilot an aeroplane was regarded by most Americans, including General MacArthur in 1941, as simply preposterous.[64]

As the Japanese navy launched its attack on Pearl Harbour and as the Japanese armies descended with the speed of a tropical thunderstorm on the European colonial armies, and annexed or brought under their control all the European territories in East Asia, the old aesthetic image of Japan was temporarily replaced. The fighting was short but harsh, and soon the Japanese were invested with near demon-like qualities.

In an effort to explain the phenomenon of Japan at war, what might be called the 'conspiracy theory' of modern Japanese history gained wide currency at this time.

A popular expression of this theory appeared in Robert Standish's wartime novel *The Three Bamboos*, which links the fortunes of Japan since the mid nineteenth century to the plans of a great *zaibatsu* family to rebuild its own power and, at the same time, 'to make of Nippon the greatest and most powerful nation in the world'; 'to free Asia from the domination of foreigners' and 'to lead Japan to conquer the world'.

Five generations of Furenos, for this is the family name, work single-mindedly and secretly towards these aims. The first generation, young sons of an impoverished samurai family, are sent to Europe and America in the 1850s and 1860s 'to suck up knowledge about the West like octopuses'. Next they apply that knowledge to set up a vast industrial and commercial empire based on slave labour at home and quick money and intelligence derived from a pseudo-Buddhist spy network in China engaged in opium cultivation.

The family controls Japanese politicians with its own secret assassination team, 'the little flowers'. After the humiliation of the Triple Intervention of 1895, when Japan was forced to give back many of the concessions she had just won from China, the fictional Furenos decide that the three powers, Russia, Germany and France must be made to pay for this humiliation. Accordingly preparations are made for war with Russia which duly takes place a decade later. Next, while Germany is at war with England, German trade in Asia, German patents in Japan and German concessions in China and the Pacific are seized by Japan. Revenge on France has to wait until 1941 when the Japanese bring under their control the French administration in Indo-China. 'Having beaten the Russians, the white races – all of them, including the English', turn against Japan. The Furenos, who occasionally show their contempt for Westerners by mixing human excrement with the food served to their Western guests, dominate the small group of influential Japanese industrialists, officials and military who have secretly controlled all important decisions in Japan since the nineteenth century. So when rising tariff walls against 'the flood of cheap Japanese goods' in the 1930s forces the Furenos to sell at a loss, it is they who decide that the time has come to launch the last phase of the plan to conquer the world. Appropriately enough, the senior Fureno of the fifth generation is pictured piloting the first dive bomber at Pearl Harbor, which is navigated by his younger brother. The plane crashes.

The reader will readily identify a number of stereotypes in the 'conspiracy theory' of modern Japanese history, magnified to the point of absurdity in novels such as *The Three Bamboos*. One such stereotype which has continued in circulation long after the war is what has come to be called 'Japan Incorporated', the notion that behind a façade of democratic institutions and a powerless parliament, top Japanese government and business leaders are working (plotting) so closely together that Japan is directed like a monolithic corporation, the mass of whose workers, the ordinary citizens, docilely follow their orders. Behind a thin veneer of Westernization, in other words, there lurks a modern version of the old stereotype of 'Oriental despotism'.

In Germany during the war years, opportunism dictated that Nazi ideology be downplayed in the interests of *realpolitik*, and Japan was officially regarded as a fellow victim of the international Jewish conspiracy. When Hitler was asked if the alliance with Japan did not contradict Germany's racial principles, he replied, 'the essential aim is to win, and to that end we are quite ready to make an alliance with the devil himself'.

Already before the war in *Mein Kampf*, Hitler had expressed his views on Japan in terms as condescending as so much European commentary of the day. He wrote, for example, that Japan had only advanced because of Greek spirit and German technique, and reckoned that 'if beginning today all further Aryan influence on Japan should stop, assuming that Europe and America should perish, Japan's present rise in science and technology might continue for a short time; but even in a few years the well would dry up, the Japanese special character would gain, but the present culture would freeze and sink back into the slumber from which it was awakened seven decades ago by the wave of Aryan culture'. Hearing of Japan's initial successes in the Pacific War, he remarked, 'It means the loss of a whole continent, and one must regret it, for it's the white race which is the loser.' During the war he referred privately to the Japanese as 'little yellow Aryans' no better than 'half-lacquered monkeys'.[65]

Scenes of brutal and cruel behaviour of the Japanese at war became all too familiar and were later passed on to the next generation in novels such as Norman Mailer's *The Naked and the Dead* or films like *The Bridge over the River Kwai*. The kamikaze pilots at the end of the war reinforced the images of the Japanese as fanatical and inhuman 'Orientals' and as such, totally uncaring for human life. As a schoolboy in the mid 1950s I can just remember reading popular histories of Japanese war atrocities such as *The Knights of Bushido*; but many European businessmen at board level involved in Japanese market decisions today, as well as senior government officials, had direct experience of Japan at war in Southeast Asia. Their later attitudes towards Japan have inevitably been coloured by these early experiences.

In the nineteenth century *Madam Chrysanthemum* had symbolized the exotic image of Japan. To this was now added in the mid twentieth century the completely opposite image of a fanatically warlike, cruel and untrustworthy nation. Book titles such as *Pays de Mousmé! Pays de Guerre!*, *Cannoni e ciliegi in fiore*, or *The Chrysanthemum and the Sword*, sum up the attempt to blend the new perception of Japan with the old aesthetic image.[66]

In doing so Europeans were grafting onto Japan the age-old myth of the Orient as a mixture of extremes – the exotic and the crooked; the fabulous and the cruel.

5

Japan as a World Economic Power

Japan's growth as a military power was accompanied by industrial development, but it was only after the defeat in the Second World War and its rapid growth, or 'economic miracle', in the late 1950s and 1960s that she built up one of the largest economies in the world.

In Europe in the 1950s there was already a widespread apprehension, no doubt reflecting memories of the 1930s, that Japanese exports would flood European markets.

Such apprehensions seemed only to be confirmed as the Japanese economic miracle at the speed, and with the efficiency, of the new 'bullet' train overtook the European countries. In 1966 Japan's GNP overtook that of Italy, in 1967 that of the UK, and in 1968 that of France. In 1969 it was the turn of Germany to be overtaken.

The initial shock inspired fear and admiration, with fear predominating. The old image of Japan as an economic peril, which was derived from the fears of a yellow peril, or hordes of cheap labour attacking the industrial bastions of the West, was revived. At the same time, it was once again combined with the images of Japan at war, this time the images left over from the Pacific War. A flood of articles in the European press in the late 1960s warned of the ruthless aggressiveness of the Japanese in their 'military' quest for larger markets:

Should one imagine in the basement of a building in Tokyo, a group of mysterious people with enigmatic smiles, standing before a huge general staff table, placing Japanese flags on the capitals of Europe? This is to romanticise somewhat, but the truth, as it appeared in the course of our enquiry, is not so far. *Vision* interviewed the Ministry of International Trade and Industry in Tokyo (MITI) in the Occidental style, without useless circumlocutions: 'Have you somewhere here people who are directing a campaign for the economic conquest of Europe?' The MITI people replied, politely of course, for they are Japanese, that we were stupid. It is none the less clear, seeing through their flowery and delicate formulas, that direct investment in Europe is an essential aspect of their preoccupations.[67]

Time magazine in 1970 compared the Japanese salesmen to the 'warrior trader of the 14th century' and the 'soldier bureaucrat' of the Second World War. 'The difference is that the latter day *wakō* carries a *soroban* (abacus) instead of a sword and wears blue serge instead of the khaki of General Hideki Tojo's Imperial Army.' To the ambition of conquering world markets 'they bring a machine-like discipline, an ability to focus with fearful energy on the task at hand, an almost Teutonic thoroughness in all pursuits, whether business or pleasure'.[68]

The following year, Ralf Dahrendorf, the EC Commissioner for external relations at that time, warned the European Parliament that 'the harsh and sometimes emotional criticism of Japanese economic behaviour will already be invalid in a few years. [But] as with American protection, it may be true of the Japanese combination of isolation and ruthlessly aggressive economic policy that we have a few difficult years before us . . .'[69] A similar thought, phrased somewhat more directly, was attributed to a member of the Nixon Cabinet: 'The Japanese are still fighting the war, only now instead of a shooting war it is an economic war. Their immediate intention is to try to dominate the Pacific and then perhaps the world.'[70]

It would be hard to exaggerate the degree to which this sort of imagery is now automatically applied to Japanese business practices and businessmen. As an executive with fourteen years of experience in Asia put it in a typical letter to *Newsweek* in 1979: 'in business arrangements in most of the world, the only "good deals" are those that are fair to all parties involved. But the Japanese are not merely doing business – they are at war. In any war, you do not consider giving your enemy a "fair" or "reasonable" break.' Or listen to the Editor-in-Chief of *Le Monde*, who, when asked in June 1979 what image he held of the Japanese, replied: 'a powerful, dynamic, hard-working people . . . having come to admit that nothing can any longer be achieved through war, but knowing that economic competition, in a way, can perfectly mean war continued by another means'.[71]

Phrases such as 'business soldiers fighting outside the country in the trade war' also began to become popular in Japan herself at this time. They were copied from the Western press. As late as 1979, a Japanese executive could write in a paper intended for foreign readers: 'If you remember the special death corps on the sea and in the air in the last war of the Japanese army, the same thing still exists in the war of business. Everywhere is the *Tokutai* or death corps in Japanese firms.'[72]

As we have seen, as far as Europe and America are concerned, fears of Japanese trade competition began to be linked with Japanese military strength right from the time of Japan's first modern war, the defeat of the Qing empire in 1895. For example, an American magazine summed up the linkage in an article written in 1896 in words which have a very modern ring, 'Japan has entered upon a commercial war against the great industrial nations of the world with the same energy, earnestness, determination, and foresight, which characterized the war [with China] . . .'[73]

Over the last hundred years such remarks have been repeated every single time there has been a business recession in the West and every time Japan has launched an export drive or won a military victory. They show the basic fear that Japan is engaged in a perpetual struggle with the West, either by trade war or by military attack. It is one of the most lasting reactions to Japan and to the Japanese.

To appreciate this, one only has to look at the rash of books warning of the Japanese industrial and commercial threat which were published in Europe between 1969 and 1971, with titles such as *The Japanese Challenge*; *Japan: The Planned Aggression*; *The Japanese Threat*; *The Japanese Industrial Challenge*; *Japan:*

Monster or Model; *The Japanese Miracle and Peril*; *Stop the Japanese Now*.[74]

The new image of Japan itself which became current in the late 1960s and early 1970s was a complete reversal of the old aesthetic image: Japan now came to be seen as a country of 'economic animals', a phrase incidentally more widely heard in Japan than in Europe, despite General de Gaulle's remark comparing Prime Minister Ikeda to an electronic salesman. The Japanese were felt to be pursuing GNP growth at the expense of everything else, spreading pollution and spawning megalopoli. The admirers of the new Japan readily accepted the officially inspired, tourist-poster image of the 'bullet' train streaking past Mt Fuji. A combination of traditional aesthetics with modern efficiency or, as a German trades unionist put it, 'a symbiosis of Western technology and efficiency and Far Eastern charm'. What might be called *The Lotus and the Robot* image, to borrow the title of a popular book.[75] But for most Europeans a more lasting image was probably the sight of professional pushers cramming commuters into Tokyo's trains.

It was also felt that the polluted monster was directed by a super-efficient inter-locking elite of big business (the *zaibatsu*) and government often referred to as 'Japan Inc.'. Nobody stopped to ask themselves why, if 'Japan Inc.' really existed and was so efficient, it could have produced such a polluted and apparently joyless result. The notion of 'Japan Inc.', as I mentioned before, is more easily understood as an echo of the age-old European fear of 'Oriental despotism', a phrase first used by the ancient Greeks to describe the Persians. It is a negative image easily evoked at a time of war, and one which satisfies the emotional need to identify a single malific enemy, rather than face the complex reality of both one's own society, and the country to which such simplistic personifications are applied.

The various other elements of the 'Japan Inc.' image included a population grimly working with low salaries and without vacations; a single-minded and centrally directed concentration on export industries at the expense of housing and other social overheads; and a domestic market unfairly protected from foreign competition by complex and deliberate non-tariff barriers, and by petty, arrogant and capricious officials using opaque but effective 'administrative guidance' to build up Japanese industries and to keep foreign imports out.

The dreary images of an efficient, but polluted, economic monster were occasionally relieved by sudden flashes of fanatical violence or cruelty – the dramatic suicide of Mishima Yukio; helmeted students smashing professor's libraries; Red Army radicals massacring civilians at Lod airport; the grisly activities of 'the cannibal of the Bois de Boulogne'. Or, in a different vein, Japanese slaughter of dolphins and hunting of whales.

The overwhelming European response to the new Japanese industrial and commercial challenge which emerged in the late 1960s and early 1970s was negative. But a challenge can be accepted as well as rejected, the response may be sympathetic or it may be hostile. Indeed there has been a small but growing number of opinion-makers in Europe whose response to the new Japan has been sympathetic.

One of the foremost has been the London *Economist*, which as early as 1962 began to warn its readers that the Japanese 'could beat us competitively in a much wider field of industry than most people in Britain at present begin to imagine'.[76] This warning is similar to that made by the Federation of British Industries in 1934: 'it would be unwise to assume that the future export activities of Japan will be limited to cheap goods of low quality'.[77] Even further back, at the beginning of the century, Sir Henry Norman for example had made similar and equally unheeded observations. But since the early 1960s warnings of the competition to be expected from Japan have for the first time been accompanied by the novel advice that Europeans have something to learn from the Japanese economy. The *Economist* articles of 1962 are to my knowledge the first which examined the whole range of economic policy-making in Japan in an effort to draw lessons for the British economy. Ten years later in 1975 the *Economist*, taking its cue perhaps from Kahn's optimistic *The Emerging Japanese Superstate*, had become even more enthusiastic, and widened the field for Europeans to learn from Japan to include housing, culture, health care, transport and crime prevention.[78] In the British Parliament a Japan subcommittee began 'looking at Japanese industry, trying to find out if their methods, particularly in production and development, have lessons for British industry and to assess their success technically in world markets and to discover if we can find the reasons for it, taking into account the very different conditions, background and so on in the two countries'. In Belgium, the Minister of Economic Affairs called on his countrymen to become 'the Japanese of Europe' in order to get out of their economic difficulties.[79]

Studies and reports began to proliferate arguing that Japan's economic successes were due to hard work and to good planning. These reports were widely quoted in the serious European press. A book like Vogel's *Japan as Number One*, although not a bestseller in Europe, was sympathetically reviewed and read by the small elite which seeks to understand events outside Europe.

At a more popular level, recent years have also seen a spate of TV programmes on Japan all over Europe, many of which have succeeded not only in catching large audiences but also in being fairly balanced, such as the BBC–NHK joint-production entitled *The Shōgun Inheritance*.

Individual sectors and industries have also begun to look to their Japanese counterparts. In Britain, for example, the National Economic Development Council announced in 1979 a study on how to revitalize the television and hi-fi industries using Japanese technology. The study noted that the Japanese gained a substantial cost advantage mainly through the high level of investment in advanced and automated production technology. The study's findings were therefore contrary both to the old myth that the Japanese rely on cost-advantages gained through cheap labour, and to the newer myth that they rely on 'docile' labour. The study recommended that the best way of introducing the new technology would be to seek the active involvement of Japanese manufacturers by encouraging inward investment in addition to purchasing technological licences.

In France in 1978 a report commissioned by the President on a national strategy for information technology (*L'informatisation de la société*) recommended that France learn from Japan in responding to the new technologies. The report became a bestseller in France and has since been translated into English. Two years later, at the 1980 national convention of the French Patronat (Employers' Association), two thousand leading industrialists were urged to abandon West Germany and to turn to Japan as a model for technological innovation. A similar theme was developed by Servan-Schreiber in *The World Challenge*, in which Japan's rapidly developing new industrial structure, based on the application of information technologies to production, is held up as the wave of the future and the key to the solution of many of our current ills.

In America, a subcommittee of the House of Representatives, in its second full-scale report on trade with Japan in two years, reached the following conclusion: 'It has become increasingly clear to us, and to many businessmen dealing with Japan, that our trade problems result less and less from Japanese import barriers, and more and more from domestic American structured problems of competitiveness and quality. There are clearly lessons to be learnt from Japan.'[80]

In recent years, there has also been a growing interest in Japanese techniques of management, such as on-the-job training, lifetime employment, a seniority-based wage system, enterprise unions, long-term planning and, above all, total quality control ('QC circles'). Indeed, so far had this trend gone by the early 1980s that a new myth had begun to emerge, that of the omnipotence of Japanese management science. Although this trend was far more advanced in the United States than in Europe, nevertheless Japan Air Lines in 1981 found it worthwhile to organize special tours of Japanese plants for European businessmen. The airline reported that these tours were particularly popular among the Germans and the Dutch, followed by the Danes and the French. The British apparently were not so keen to go.

Closer to home, searching questions began to be asked about Japanese management in Europe. A number of studies (for example those conducted by the International Centre for Economics and Related Disciplines at the London School of Economics) began to show that Japanese consumer electronics factories in Britain obtained output levels more than twice as high as British companies and 50 per cent higher than US-owned producers operating in the UK. Such studies provided powerful support to those who argued that Japanese industrial successes were not based on some mysterious qualities specific to Japanese culture, but rather on Japanese management and 'organizational engineering' which were clearly effective in a non-Japanese environment.

One increasingly heard political articulation of the new awareness of Japan in Europe has been the suggestion that Japan represents such an important challenge that it can only be met by uniting and adopting similar strategies of technological innovation as those which have helped Japan capture world leadership in one industry after another.

Thus, Étienne Davignon, responsible in the EC Commission for industrial affairs, pointed out in a speech in September 1979 that the EC was not keeping pace in the electronic revolution with America and Japan. In an implicit comparison with Japan, he said that Europe tended to measure technological innovation in terms of jobs lost rather than in terms of the jobs it would create; an attitude typical of a society overtaken by age and making security its top priority. He ended his speech by urging a plan of action at the European level to update the Community's information technology industries, or otherwise vital new opportunities would be lost to Japan and America.

In the European car industry there has been some talk of a 'joint defence strategy' against the Japanese (or the Americans). Frequent tie-ups have taken place amongst European makers, often across national boundaries. The industry is split down the middle, however, as many makers have preferred to join first the Americans and then the Japanese, rather than unite against them. In some cases tie-ups have been agreed between Japanese and European makers for production in Europe (for example, Nissan and Alfa-Romeo or Honda and British Leyland). In other cases the Japanese makers, led by Nissan, have begun to set up their own manufacturing plants in Europe. The first steps have also been taken for distribution or manufacturing tie-ups in Japan (for example, British Leyland and Mitsui or Volkswagen and Nissan). Such arrangements were virtually unheard of, even as late as 1975, when the Japanese technological challenge in the car industry was still not taken very seriously in Europe, and when it was still the norm to dismiss Japanese cars as unsophisticated and poorly designed.

Other European industries have been quicker to turn to the Japanese, for example shipbuilding and steel which have for some time been modernizing their plants with new technology bought from Japan. There is also a growing tendency for all kinds of industrial tie-up, including joint manufacturing as well as marketing. Recent examples would be the Japan Victor Company's arrangement with Telefunken and Thorn (UK) to manufacture video consumer electronics in Europe. Matsushita and Bosch have also announced plans to jointly produce video tape recorders. Fujitsu-Fanuc computers have been distributed in Germany for some time and now Fujitsu plans to manufacture in Luxemburg. In the machine tools industry, one of the first Japanese companies to set up a joint venture in Europe was Makino Milling which contributed its new technology to the Hamburg firm of Heidenreich and Harbeck in 1978. Despite a growing number of Japanese manufacturing investments in Germany, most such investments are in other parts of Europe, notably Britain, where ailing industries, an English-language environment and government incentives have proved attractive to Japanese companies seeking to establish a manufacturing base in Europe.

Most recently, then, there are indications that after the initial shock and negative reaction to Japan's emergence as a world economic power in the late 1960s, at least some Europeans had begun to wake up and take note of the new challenge, stressing the need, for example, to learn from Japanese successes in technological innovation or industrial organization. European industries too had begun to see the need to reorganize in order to become more competitive and in increasing numbers were making their way to Japan to try and find out the secrets of Japanese success. A trend had also begun to develop for a wide variety of industrial tie-ups between European and Japanese companies.

Indeed so far had this new assessment gone by the early 1980s that some European comment was beginning to make Japan sound like an industrial Utopia where everything worked smoothly and none of the afflictions currently troubling Europe could be found. Given the past history of neglect and underestimation of Japan in Europe, it is perhaps inevitable that the 'discoverers' of the new Japan should seek to redress the balance by enthusiastically concentrating on all that appears to them best in Japan. For the time being theirs is still a minority view. But it may not long remain so as more and more people are becoming fascinated by Japan. Not only industrialists, but also fashion designers; not only museum directors, but also managers. The first signs of a many-sided Japan boom have begun to appear. If such a boom does come, then the pendulum will have swung from one extreme to the other in just over twenty years and Europeans will be as far as ever from a balanced understanding of Japan.

6

The Most Paradoxical People?

Recent European images of Japan were hastily formed following the shock of Japan's emergence as a world economic power, just at a period when European economic growth seemed to be slowing down. The new images, however, were simply derived from older ones, to which they have now been added. Thus, a European today is able to draw upon a fund of stereotypes inherited from the past. The fund is rich enough to hold both positive and negative images which are often contradictory, for contrariness is the basic Western image of Japan. Such images date from different periods of contact and perception. The public will use whichever one suits the mood of the day.

Very few Europeans have ever been to Japan or met a Japanese. Older generations will remember the unfavourable images of Japan during the Great Depression or Japan during the Pacific War. Younger generations are more likely to have had some direct experience with one or another manifestation of Japanese culture, usually such 'traditional' aspects as the martial arts, which are widespread in Europe, or Zen Buddhism. Ever since Kurosawa's *Rashōmon* caught the West by surprise at the Venice film festival of 1951, Japanese films, especially samurai films, have had a considerable following. Indeed Kurosawa has maintained his following for thirty years. In 1981 his *Kagemusha* received rave reviews in Europe, and a leading Italian fashion designer went so far as to base his collection for that autumn on 'Japanese' themes inspired by the film. Japanese literature has been extensively translated but little read. Perhaps the most famous author is Mishima Yukio, but more as the result of the publicity following his suicide than through a wide acquaintance with his writings. Japan is also represented by her impeccably styled consumer goods; no doubt these have done much to contradict the old view in Europe that the Japanese are producers of low-quality cheap exports. Today, amongst younger people it is quite possible that names such as Sony, Nikon, Honda, Nissan, Toyota and National Panasonic are as familiar, if not more so, than terms such as samurai, harakiri, bonsai, kamikaze, geisha and zen. Indeed much of the respect for modern Japan derives from the false assumption that Japanese industry and society are as efficient as the consumer durables which are produced for export to Europe.

If you ask the average European today what he associates Japan and the Japanese with, he will probably give you a confused picture of cherry blossoms and commuter trains; geisha girls and electronic salesmen. These are drawn from the aesthetic image and the crowded and polluted monster image; the erotic and the practical images; the lotus and the robot. On the whole his image will be positive but ill-formed. Thus the first comprehensive survey of European images of Japan, conducted as a public opinion poll in the winter of 1977 in England, France, West Germany, Italy and Belgium, found that in England, for example, one third of those polled thought Japan was either a Communist state or a despotism; more than 30 per cent in all five countries thought that Japan possessed atomic weapons and 50 per cent thought either that she possessed them or would acquire them. They also felt that Japanese salaries and social welfare were lower than in their own countries. As to Japan's international role they were critical, feeling she was too reactive, and that there was room for her to make positive contributions to the world economy, for example, by increasing development aid. In general, they were not convinced that Japan was reliable.

A follow-up to this poll was made five years later in 1982. Unfortunately the pollsters addressed themselves not to the general public, as they had done in the earlier poll, but to leaders of public opinion, so the two polls strictly speaking are not comparable.

Reflecting the better informed group polled, the 1982 poll reveals a more accurate image of Japan, which is seen primarily as a strong economic power deeply influenced by tradition, whose people are hard-working, efficient, co-operative and polite. A majority this time were aware that Japan has a democratic government and a policy of not possessing nuclear weapons, but most still thought that Japanese salaries and social security benefits were lower than in Europe. As to Japan's international role, a greater number in Germany, Italy and Belgium felt that Japan was pulling her weight, but in Britain, France and the Netherlands a majority still felt Japan should do more, for example, in extending aid to developing countries.[81]

Another survey found that the qualities associated with the Japanese people, in addition to groupism and discipline, were hard work, progressiveness, practicality, intelligence, courtesy and bravery.[82]

If there happens to be a wave of fear or dislike of Japan and the Japanese, which usually takes place when there is a recession in Europe or when there are tensions, such as trade frictions, the average European will readily evoke negative images inherited from a previous generation of cruel soldiers, violent suicides and ruthlessly unfair competitors. These associations are drawn from the war image merged with the tricky Oriental image. All the qualities normally attributed to the Japanese will then take on their negative aspects – 'efficient' becomes 'aggressive', 'group behaviour' becomes 'conformism', 'disciplined' becomes 'regimented', 'willingness to learn' becomes 'slavish imitation' and so on.

Faced with these sharply contrasted images of Japan, which are now part of the European inheritance, it is not uncommon for Europeans to conclude that the Japanese themselves must be unpredictable, if not incomprehensible:

> The Japanese are, to the highest degree, both aggressive and unaggressive, both militaristic and aesthetic, both insolent and polite, rigid and adaptable, submissive and resentful of being pushed around, loyal and treacherous, brave and timid, conservative and hospitable to new ways.[83]

Such apparently schizoid behaviour suggests the corollary, that in jumping incomprehensibly from one extreme to another, the Japanese must be emotional rather than rational (particularly as reason is felt to be pre-eminently a European characteristic). Indeed the view that the Japanese are schizophrenic, emotional and in the last resort, incomprehensible and unstable, has now attained the status of a self-perpetuating stereotype in its own right. It was a view which as we have seen was first expressed by the Jesuit missionaries in the sixteenth century. It was repeated in the nineteenth century by practically every European traveller or resident in Japan. All of whom would have heartily agreed with an American missionary, Miss Scidmore, that 'the Japanese are the enigma of this century; the most inscrutable, the most paradoxical of races'.[84] Even one of the best informed early Japanologists, Professor Chamberlain, could write on Japanese logic:

> One is apt to exclaim that Japanese logic is the very antipodes of European logic . . . Were it really so, action would be easy enough: one would simply have to go by the 'rule of contraries'. But no, that will not do either. The contradiction's only occasional, it only manifests itself sporadically and along certain – or uncertain – lines . . . the result is that the oldest resident . . . may still . . . be pulled up sharp, and forced to exclaim that all his experience does not yet suffice to probe the depths of the mental disposition of this fascinating but enigmatical race.[85]

This view is not simply that of a prejudiced nineteenth-century European professor. In 1979, Kimpei Shiba, a prize-winning Japanese journalist, who has written extensively explaining his country to foreigners, could still write that 'the Japanese are unquestionably amongst the most illogical and inconsistent people on earth'.[86] Another version of supposed Japanese illogicity is the frequently heard comment that the Japanese language is unfit for clear thought or the Japanese cannot think philosophically. Those making this observation do not explain how it is that technology and mathematics flourish in Japan.

Today newspapers refer as a matter of course to Japan, as 'the world's newest and least predictable economic super power'.[87]

If a distinguished Japanese journalist such as Shiba can still repeat the old stereotype of Japan as a strange upside-down land where paradoxes and contrasts confront one at every turn, then who can be surprised that popular writers such as Arthur Koestler conclude that 'all nations are bundles of contradictions, but *nowhere except in Japan* are the conflicting strands so neatly sorted out, and arranged on two mutually exclusive levels which alternate in taking control, and produce dual personalities in a dual culture as sharply defined as', and the reader should be able to guess the tired comparison Koestler chooses, 'as sharply defined as a Japanese colour print'.[88]

Each of the periods in which Europeans formed images of Japan have a number of points in common. The Europeans have consistently regarded themselves as teachers and the Japanese as imitators or learners. The first Europeans came as missionaries to teach the heathen, and in the nineteenth and early twentieth centuries they came as propagators of the secular faith of industrial progress and the political philosophy of the enlightenment to teach the backward. They had a 'mission civilisatrice' as the French put it. That attitude has persisted right to our own day. The following comment made by a well-known European expert on Japan in 1978 is not untypical: 'When it comes to evaluating the attitude of the Japanese toward any new technology, one could compare them to eager pupils looking up at us, their teachers.'[89]

Because of this sense of superiority the Europeans hardly took Japan seriously and made no effort to find out what was going on there. As a result they held subjective and out-of-date images of Japan.

The missionaries in the sixteenth century expected to find a heathen people, ignorant and primitive. Instead they found the Japanese to be highly civilized. In the nineteenth century, the aesthetic image of Japan was hopelessly inaccurate, even as it was being formed, and it proved a poor preparation for the emergence of Japan as a military power. This was the case for the Russians in 1904; astonishingly enough it proved the case again for the European colonial powers, a whole generation later, which apparently had learnt nothing, so totally did they overestimate their own strength and misread Japanese intentions in the years leading up to the surrender of Hong Kong, Malaya, Singapore, Burma, Vietnam and the Dutch East Indies in the early 1940s.

It was in the colonial and imperial period that Europe had its most intense contacts with Asia, including Japan. All sorts of prejudices were given full reign and matching images were formed. In the twentieth century, as Europe withdrew from Asia, contacts declined and there were therefore few opportunities to form fresh images, so the attitudes of colonial and imperial superiority towards an Oriental people and the images associated with those attitudes lived on unchallenged.

Perhaps this helps explain why in the 1970s the Europeans were caught by surprise by Japan's rapid economic growth and penetration of world markets. The reaction was based on the 1930s image of Japan as a cheap-labour, Asiatic country operating with an unfair advantage. Little or no attention had been paid to the gradual build-up of capital and technology intensive industries in Japan which were the main source of her new competitiveness. Had sufficient account been taken of what was going on in Japan in the 1950s and 1960s, it is just possible that Europeans might have been persuaded to take a leaf from Japan's book. At the very least there would have been less of a shock when Japan began scoring massive trade surpluses with Europe in the 1970s. But apparently the Europeans were still incapable of taking seriously the notion of an 'Oriental' industrial power. The old European self-view as teacher persisted and along with it the image of the Japanese as 'Orientals' and hence backward pupils, not worth taking very seriously.

Today, it is still not clear that the old attitudes have faded sufficiently for the Europeans to stop underestimating Japan and to start making an effort to find out what is going on there before being once again shocked into belated action.

There is still an extraordinary ignorance of Japan in Europe which compares most unfavourably with the widespread knowledge of Europe in Japan. This 'knowledge deficit' has led to a 'communications gap' between Europe and Japan just as alarming as Europe's massive trade deficit with her.

Before considering the effects of this communications gap on the trade relations between Europe and Japan, it is worth taking a look at the other side of the coin. What have the Japanese learnt about Europe? What advantage have they gained from this knowledge? Why is it that they have been able to form rather accurate images of Europe? What do they think of Europeans today?

PART II

The Cultural Museum:
Europe as Seen by the Japanese

7

Learning from Abroad

Immediately after the Tokyo Summit of advanced industrial countries in June 1979, I accompanied the President of the EC Commission, Roy Jenkins, to Haneda Airport where the late Prime Minister Ohira and members of his Cabinet were waiting to say good-bye. A military plane then flew us to Narita and within minutes of arriving the President had boarded his plane and left for the long return trip to Europe.

As so often during those six years, having seen off a visitor, I found myself in that reflective mood which comes to us all at such times, and in places such as railway stations or airports – the thresholds between the known and the unknown.

There had not been much time to eat that day, so feeling hungry I went to one of the airport restaurants (decorated in the 'French' style) and ordered dinner and a half bottle of white wine. As I waited for it to arrive, I thought back over the events of the previous days.

All the elaborate arrangements for the Summit had gone without a hitch, and because energy prices had once again just become the burning topic of the hour, it had also had substantial content. Despite the usual criticisms of weak Japanese chairmanship, it was generally agreed by the participants to have been one of the most successful in this series of Summits, if not the most successful so far. It also had a special significance for Japan. In the long struggle to catch up with and surpass the West, the Summit surely marked an important landmark. In a sense the holding of it in Tokyo, and the recognition for Japan's achievements which that implied, was long overdue. After all, Japan's GNP had

overtaken that of the European participants, Italy, England,
France and Germany, a decade earlier.

As I reflected in this way, I became aware that the wine waiter
had begun an elaborate ritual of preparations. I had ordered a half
bottle of white wine, which he brought in an ice bucket. This he
placed on the table. Then he stepped back and adjusted a white
napkin over his left arm and inspected the positioning of the
bucket. I was alone in the restaurant so I had no choice but to
follow these preparations. Besides, I was anxious to taste the
wine. Instead of opening it, however, the waiter stepped forward
and rearranged the position of the bucket on the table. Once more
he readjusted the napkin on his arm and once more he withdrew,
the better to survey the effect of the bucket on the table. Finally,
apparently pleased with what he saw, and now ready to take the
plunge, he stepped smartly to the table, discreetly withdrew the
bottle from the bucket, wiped it, grasped it in his left hand, and,
crouching over it, slowly twisted in the corkscrew. He was
apparently nervous. After all the self-conscious preparations,
what would happen if the cork disintegrated in the bottle? For-
tunately it did not. It came out whole, but before serving the wine,
the waiter placed the bottle back in the bucket, wiped the cork dry
and put it in a small silver platter before me. It was not a vintage
wine. By the time I took my first sip I was feeling in a state of mild
nervous tension.

What was it that had made the waiter so self-conscious? As a
boy I used often to sit in cafés in Paris mesmerized by the
unconscious ease with which the barman uncorked the bottle,
splashed the wine into the glasses, recorked the bottle and slid it
back down the 'zinc' to one of his fellows, all in one swift, deft set
of movements. Was it that the waiter at Narita felt nervous
uncorking 'imported grape wine' (for that was what it was called
on the wine list) in front of a foreigner? Probably not. The
so-called '*gaijin* complex' of the post-war period is largely a thing
of the past, especially among the younger generation. Or was it
that the waiter had not internalized the business of opening a
bottle of French wine, but had learnt how to do it step by step as
an alien ritual?

It is quite possible that the explanation is more matter of fact.

That the waiter, for example, had only just learnt his job, or that he had just been given a severe rocket by the manager of the restaurant, and was still feeling nervous as a result. One way or another he certainly felt under some form of pressure, whether internally or externally generated I shall never know.

The incident, though trivial, stuck in my mind for it was one more example of the extraordinary Japanese ability to learn all sorts of things from other peoples, often in the end surpassing their former teachers, yet remaining self-consciously nervous, performing a stylized ritual which sometimes comes near to being a caricature.

In that dreamy mood of relaxation in the airport restaurant after all the bustle and pomp of the Summit, I almost found myself comparing the immensely elaborate preparations leading up to its opening with the rituals of the wine waiter. Absurd thoughts indeed, for the Summit was an event of perhaps historic significance, but a waiter all tensed up over opening a bottle of French wine was in himself of no significance at all.

In the pages which follow I have traced the formation of Japanese images of Europe and Europeans in an effort to understand Japan's ability to learn from others and to comprehend the range of metaphor available to her as she contemplates Europe today. But also to try and understand how it is that having caught up with the West, the Japanese are apparently still rendered nervous by Western culture.

The Japanese have long since been accustomed to situating themselves on the cultural periphery of great powers: first China, then Europe, then America. They even developed a useful slogan to encapsulate the process. *Wakon Kansai* (Japanese spirit, Chinese techniques) during the period of learning from China, and *Wakon Yōsai* during the period of learning from Europe and America (Japanese spirit, Western techniques). Like all such simplistic dualisms, the slogan did not so much describe the reality of the learning process, as provide a comforting reassurance that no matter how much was brought in from abroad, there was always an essential core of integrity at home which retained its 'pure Japanese' character. This core of integrity could always be redefined as the need arose. The slogan legitimized the learning process which itself came to be regarded as one of the strong points of the national character.

Europeans, too, have at many periods of their history turned to other more advanced cultures for models and inspiration. But these cultures, notably Greece and Rome, were dead and could therefore be claimed as part of the 'European' past itself, not external to Europe. The pressures for change in the fourteenth and fifteenth centuries may have been largely external (Islam), but the cultural inspiration in the Renaissance was based on classical models which had long since come to be regarded as part of the European tradition itself. In the twentieth century America has been the greatest source of rejuvenation for Europe, as indeed it has also been for Japan. But America is an off-shoot of Europe and therefore less of an alien influence than it was for Japan.

There is a fundamental difference then between the conditions under which Europe and Japan have renewed themselves. For the Europeans it has usually been an internally generated process, even if triggered by external threats. For the Japanese in the nineteenth century, the necessity was to adopt an alien model and to adopt it at the point of a gun. Again in the twentieth century, another alien culture, the American, was adopted following the defeat of the Pacific War.

These differences were summed up by the great novelist Natsume Sōseki in terms which have become part of the language:

The enlightenment in the West . . . is inner-directed, while the enlightenment in modern Japan is outer-directed. By the phrase 'inner-directed' (*naihatsu-teki*) I mean spontaneous growth like the process by which a flower blossoms with its bud opening and its petals growing outward. By 'outer-directed' (*gaihatsu-teki*) I mean the moulding of a shape by means of external forces imposed from outside.[1]

If you have to learn a matter of life and death under strong external pressure, there is bound to be a sense of nervousness, if not downright panic.

So one of the traditional strong points of Japan has been a timely ability to learn from other cultures. Even if this meant situating herself psychologically on the periphery of those cultures, there was always a core of Japanese identity, jealously guarded as such mysteries tend to be, from the profane eye of the foreigner. Indeed the corollary of learning so effectively from abroad was the intensely strong feeling in Japan herself that she was utterly unique. This feeling more than made up for being situated, as it were, at the edge of a culture area, and for accepting the world view of the culture upon whose periphery she found herself.

There is a persuasive interpretation of the roots of Japanese individual behaviour by the psychiatrist Doi Takeo that holds that the fundamental characteristic of the Japanese is his desire, his need, to be loved (*amae*) by an understanding and respected parental or big brother figure on whom he can depend.[2] To extend Professor Doi's concept of the role of *amae* to Japan as a nation: in the past Japan felt not only unique but also isolated. In looking to China, to Europe and then to America as models she derived a sense of belonging. If Japan acted in consonance with the patterns laid down by these models she would win their approval and affection. Conversely the parental model figure was expected to play its role in extending understanding to Japan. Although there are signs, as we shall see, that Japan is beginning to break out of this role playing, nevertheless, even to this day, the pattern persists. For example, the government's aid programme is not seen primarily as an obligation to the recipient developing countries, but rather as an obligation to 'share the burden' with the other advanced countries in the West.[3] To take another example, it is not enough for individual Japanese artists to win the esteem and affection of the domestic audience, but they must seek recognition and awards from Europe and America. How else can one explain the often extraordinary lengths which writers such as Mishima or Kawabata have gone in order to try and win the Nobel prize for literature? And to the man in the street as well, the prize is like a first-class badge of foreign approval. Even politicians have been affected by this desire for foreign approbation, as the former Prime Minister Satō's single-minded pursuit of the Nobel peace prize attests.

In an earlier age, the entire government and elite of Tokyo succumbed to the craze for swallowtails and bustles and ballroom dancing in the Rokumeikan period as part of an all-out effort to win foreign approval. The irony has often been that these efforts have sometimes been rewarded with the opposite of the expected results. Westerners acted with indifference or even scorn and this inevitably led in Japan to a revulsion against the West.

Another important consequence of the habit of taking an external culture as a model has been that the Japanese have tended to hold over-idealistic images of the model culture. It was said at the time of the war with China in 1894–5 that many Japanese were shocked to find that China, whose culture had been revered for centuries, turned out to be a weak country riddled with corruption and racked with poverty. Esteem quickly turned to scorn.

Likewise, the image of Europe has often tended to be an ideal cultural image based on books rather than on observed realities. Time and again young Japanese would report their disappointment at finding that actual Europeans did not live up to the ideal qualities of freedom, humanism, love of truth or whatever qualities which they had associated with Europe and which they therefore expected Europeans to embody. Many preferred simply to hold to a sort of undifferentiated ideal image of 'the West' (*Seiyō*) rather than to try and adjust to the complex, confusing and inevitably disappointing flux which is Europe.

In line with the habit of identifying with the expected wishes of a parental figure, Japan has tended to see the world in terms of the model country of the day, whether America, Europe or China. In the 1970s it was often said that Japan still tended to accept an American map of the international scene. And having accepted it, Japan 'took for granted' American goodwill and therefore felt shock and disappointment when the Americans suddenly changed their world view without a moment's notice.

It was the same in the nineteenth century as Japan, with all the fervour of an aspirant member of a club, sought to adopt the European view of the world, including the European colonial view of the rest of Asia. She did so and was understandably hurt when the Europeans and Americans failed to fully acknowledge the fact.

Going even further back into history, we find the same pattern.

In the sixteenth and seventeenth centuries, when the first European merchants and missionaries arrived in Japan, they were regarded as outside the pale of civilization as defined in the Chinese world view, and dubbed 'southern barbarians' (*nanbanjin*). The term itself was originally Chinese.

Japanese tradition and the Chinese model prevailed: the Europeans with the exception of the Dutch were expelled. As we trace this and later contacts with the West, a second pattern begins to emerge: a zig-zag course between revulsion and attraction.

In the nineteenth century, it was a much more powerful Europe which came to trade and colonize in East Asia. Also China had entered into one of its long periods of decline. When these two tendencies became clearer, particularly after the immense shock of China's defeat at the hands of the British in the Opium War (1842), the Japanese gradually began to abandon those elements of their own tradition derived from China, as well as the centuries-old view of China as the centre of the civilized universe, and to turn to the West as a new model.

By the 'West', the Japanese, of course, understood Europe and America. And in Europe, interest which had been focused on the Dutch during the period of isolation, shifted to Britain, France and the newly emerging state of Prussia. Soon the Dutch joined the Spaniards and Portuguese in that limbo reserved for cultural contacts of a past age.

First the reaction was totally negative, then, on the old Chinese principle of 'know yourself, know your enemy', it became the overriding objective of patriotic Japanese from the mid nineteenth century onwards to learn the strong points of the West in order to catch up with it and to surpass it, and thereby defend their country, saving it from further encroachments and possible subjugation. The Japanese wanted to learn about the West, then, initially because they were convinced it was a dangerous threat to the country.

After the domestic political upheavals of the Meiji Restoration, Japan in the 1870s and 1880s entered into a feverish effort to adopt Western ways. This was the period of Europe's greatest influence. The copying of guns and armaments industries was no longer felt to be sufficient to build up a strong and powerful country. European institutions, laws, even ideas, were widely adopted. And soon there was the inevitable rejection.

In the twentieth century as Europe's role in the world declined, it was replaced by the United States as the model and guide for Japan, especially following the US victory over Japan in the Second World War.

Thereafter, Europe, with the possible exceptions of Switzerland, Sweden and Germany, joined the Dutch, the Spaniards and the Portuguese as models of a bygone age.

Glancing back rapidly over Japan's contacts with the West over the last five hundred years then, we detect a pattern of initial revulsion, followed by assimilation and then rejection.

An external presence or threat, particularly if it coincides with, or is in part the cause of, a major domestic social and political upheaval, is followed by a period of openness to Western ideas, including, in the nineteenth century and after, such novel ideas as individual liberty and parliamentary democracy. An idealized version of European culture is held at such times, and the China model, or the Asian roots of Japan, even Japanese tradition itself, are downplayed if not completely rejected.[4]

Next, often following a rebuff by the Western powers. Japan turns back to her own roots and to a militant nationalism. There is a spate of books seeking to define the nature of 'Japaneseness' at such times. The West is seen chiefly as a threat and the negative aspects of its culture are emphasized. Externally Japan stresses her role as the leader of Asia and in most recent times seeks a more active role there.

This pattern may be summarized chronologically as follows:

1543–1639 Superficial contact with the West
1639–1853 Country closed; traditionalistic reaction
1868–87 Opening to the West (Europe and the United States) ('dissociating from Asia', *Datsu-A ron*); individual liberty stressed
1887–1914 Nationalistic reaction; state power and Japanese

	tradition stressed; external adventures in Asia ('Asia is one', *Ajia ichi*)
1920s	Opening to the West (the United States and Europe); democracy and liberty stressed
1931–45	Nationalistic reaction; state power stressed; external adventures in Asia (Great East Asia Co-prosperity Sphere, *Dai Tōa Kyōeiken*)
1945–60	Opening to the West (the United States); individual liberty and parliamentary democracy stressed
1970s–80s	Development of a new self-confidence; search for a new role in Asia and in the world

Many other countries have followed a similar zig-zag course as they felt the pressures of external models from the West competing with their own traditions, but few have done so with the intensity experienced by the Japanese. Some of the reasons have already been suggested why this should be so. Some obvious ones remain to be added.

For a start Japan was in a unique position – she was the first Asian country to Westernize and there was therefore no clear pattern to follow. Secondly, there was an acute sense that time was running out and that the country for the first time since the Mongol invasion six hundred years previously was in grave danger. The Iwakura mission in the 1870s drew the conclusion that the West had taken fifty years to reach the stage of its development at that time. So Japan had a massive lead to catch up with – or be swallowed. Ever since that unpleasant realization Japan has been running feverishly to catch up, crowding social and economic changes which Europe had achieved in two centuries, into two or three generations. The results were dramatic, with every decade producing world headlines, as Japan pulled and pushed to win her place in the international system and to be accepted by the West. This remorseless climbing up the international status ladder has had its rewards. Today it has almost become second nature, like the motorist who automatically drives in the 'overtake' lane of a highway, regardless of whether or not there is other traffic on the road or coming up behind.

All countries are familiar with the stereotypes of youth as

questioning tradition, in the shape of the previous generation, and old age as sinking back into traditional patterns of thought and behaviour. But the speed of the switch-back process between the West and Japanese tradition in early modern Japan meant that the differences between the outlooks of different generations was unusually extreme; indeed within the course of the life of an individual the changes must have seemed totally confusing. People have often been torn between philosophical interest in the West and nationalistic imperatives, the desire to be modern and accepted by the West, yet at the same time to retain their identity as Japanese, even as the very definitions of what was acceptable in Western terms and of Japanese tradition were constantly changing. Small wonder that the term 'identity crisis' seems to have been coined to describe modern Japanese intelligentsia and that attitudes towards the West and Westerners have often been ambivalent.

In the past, as they looked to China, to Europe and then to America, it became second nature for the Japanese to see themselves in the role of a learner or student, the recipient of *amae*. It was easy to accept the self-image of the Chinese, the Europeans and the Americans, who all in their different ways, and for their different reasons, saw themselves as teachers. The foreigners on the other hand, by the same token, found it easy to adopt the Japanese self-view of student, which reinforced their own self-image as teacher.

One important and fruitful consequence of this pattern of role playing for Japan remains to be noted: the Japanese have learned ten times more about the Chinese, the Europeans and the Americans than any of these three peoples have ever learned about the Japanese. Japanese images of Europe therefore are based upon an astonishingly rich tradition of basic knowledge.

8

First Impressions

The Spanish and Portuguese missionaries and traders, who came to Japan in the sixteenth century, provided the first direct contacts between Japan and Europe.

They came from the south, from Macao or Luzon, and they were given the name 'southern barbarians' (*nanbanjin*). The phrase had been adopted from the Chinese, who used it to describe the non-Chinese people in the South China seas and the Indo-China peninsula. The first Japanese people to meet the *nanbanjin* had no clear idea where they came from originally. Typical was the daimyō of Kagoshima and his mother, who when they met Francis Xavier in 1549 probably thought that he was an itinerant priest propagating a new sect of Buddhism from India.[5]

Gradually as a more accurate idea of Europe took shape, the adjective '*nanban*' shifted to mean 'Southern Europe': it was widely used in such phrases as '*nanban* food' (e.g. tempura and *pan*, the Japanese for bread, derived from the Portuguese *pao*), '*nanban* wine', '*nanban* hats', '*nanban* paintings' and so on.

There were even from time to time what one might call '*nanban* booms'. Thus, when Xavier's successor, Valignano, was received by Hideyoshi in 1591 in Kyoto, his procession was said to have caused a great stir and longing for foreign exotica. Next year the same thing happened again when Hideyoshi set up his headquarters for the Korean campaign at Hizen near Nagasaki. There was an instant '*nanban* boom' throughout the army; both officers and men began sporting Portuguese clothes and trinkets and it became quite the fashion, at least for a short time, to wear amber balls, gold chains and buttons. Some even went so far as to experiment with eating eggs and beef.[6]

Was there a particular image of Europe associated with such booms? I think not. The *nanbanjin* were truly exotic – neither fitting Japanese tradition nor stemming from India or China. As such they naturally aroused considerable curiosity and sparked off a short craze for foreign exotica, which crazes are characteristically, but not exclusively, Japanese. There was a further and practical interest in the new arrivals. They brought with them arquebuses and canons. Their huge ocean-going vessels were novel and awe-inspiring. Their medicine too was potent. All these were more powerfully attractive than gold chains or amber balls, or Christianity, or even the *nanbanjin* themselves.

Eventually, fears that the missionaries were the vanguard of predatory soldiers from Europe, and fears of the subversive influence of Christianity itself, led to the exclusion of the *nanbanjin*, the proscription of Christianity and the final closing of the country to foreign intercourse in 1639.

Such fears are today almost totally forgotten, but the word *nanbanjin* still probably carries negative connotations.

Actual knowledge of the southern barbarians faded fast, and during the remainder of the seventeenth century the little that had been known and diffused about the *nanbanjin* was also forgotten. As one of the leading opponents of extreme Westernization in the Meiji period, Shiga Shigetaka, summed it up in an amusing comment strongly reminiscent of Voltaire's celebrated remarks on the results of Columbus's discovery of America,

after nearly a hundred years of Christianity and foreign intercourse, the only apparent results . . . were the adoption of gunpowder and firearms and weapons, the use of tobacco and the habit of smoking, the making of spongecake, the naturalization into the language of a few foreign words, and the introduction of new and strange forms of disease.[7]

The most vivid images today of those first far-off contacts between Europe and Japan are the intricate and brightly coloured screen paintings of southern barbarian themes – Portuguese and Spanish galleons in the harbour and tall strangers in exotic clothes disembarking – to trade, to convert or to conquer.

The first encounter with the Europeans sparked curiosity, mixed with anxiety, and it led eventually to a firm and complete rejection of the potentially dangerous foreigners, and an effort to purify and strengthen Japanese tradition itself, during a long period of introspection conducted behind closed doors. Not for the last time intellectuals busied themselves with elucidating the fundamentals of the Japanese tradition.

The next serious encounter with Europe and the West took place in the nineteenth century. The initial reaction then too was to completely reject Westerners and their 'barbarian' ways, but the conditions both within Japan and outside the country were very different in the nineteenth century from what they had been in the sixteenth century. Eventually it became clear that outright rejection of the West and continued closing of the country were impossible.

But this is to anticipate somewhat, because from the seventeenth to the nineteenth centuries when Japan was closed, not all contact with the West was lost. The court made efforts to keep itself informed about events in the world including in Europe, which knowledge it kept secret to itself. Also individual scholars studied from the Dutch and learned new perspectives and practical knowledge.

As part of the policy of closing the country (*sakoku*), not only were all foreigners forbidden to enter Japan, but also Japanese were forbidden to go abroad or to teach the Japanese language to foreigners. There was also a strictly enforced censorship on importation of Western books.

During the period of self-imposed isolation the only foreigners who had a limited intercourse with Japan were the Chinese and the Dutch, who were permitted to maintain small trading stations in Nagasaki. The Dutch won this privilege for their proclaimed lack of interest in propagating Christianity. During the next two centuries Westerners (the Dutch, and to a lesser extent the British) were called 'red-hairs' (*kōmōjin*) and Japanese public knowledge of Europe was limited to what a few enthusiasts of 'Dutch studies' (*Rangaku*) were able to glean through the haphazard mediation of the Dutch trading station and the officially appointed hereditary interpreters attached to it.[8]

No matter how strict the censorship on foreign affairs and knowledge, information did filter in. The thin edge of the wedge, as in so many other countries, was European medicine and astronomy, both of which proved themselves to be more effective than the traditional (Chinese) techniques which had been in use until then. Such Western sciences had an additional point in their favour: they were not political and they had no connection with Christianity. Furthermore it is worth recalling that doctors, along with Confucian scholars and Buddhist priests, were one of the three major intellectual professions in Tokugawa times. In general the doctors were the most pro-Western, while the Confucian scholars, for the obvious reason that they saw their rice bowls threatened, were the most anti-Western.

From at least the early years of the eighteenth century, the Shōguns had retained amongst their physicians practitioners of 'Dutch medicine', usually specializing in surgery, the internal medicine being conducted by practitioners of Chinese medicine. How much these doctors actually knew is open to question, since no work of Western medicine had been translated at that time into Japanese. But already two court doctors in the mid eighteenth century had observed dissections and noted that the traditional Chinese manuals of anatomy bore no relation to their actual observations. To justify to themselves this discrepancy they concluded that Japanese were anatomically different from Chinese. A striking example of the tyranny of inherited perceptions! It was not until the 1770s that by a series of accidents a Japanese practitioner of Dutch medicine was able to compare a Dutch illustrated manual of anatomy (the *Ontleedkundige Tafelen*, 1731) with observations made at a dissection.

The story is extremely interesting and I shall tell it in detail for it symbolizes the beginnings of a massive shift: the disenchantment with China and the turning towards Europe. A shift that was at the very heart of Japanese cultural dilemmas for most of the nineteenth century.

It was in 1771 that a medical practitioner, Sugita Genpaku, attended the dissection of the body of an executed female criminal with the nickname 'green tea hag' (*aocha baba*). Sugita and his other friends present were unable to identify the lady's organs with those which were listed in the old Chinese medical text-books. On the other hand, when they compared her organs with those illustrated in the charts in the *Ontleedkundige Tafelen*, they were amazed to find perfect agreement between the two. So, the following day, the group of friends decided to translate the work into Japanese, no easy undertaking since they had only a slight knowledge of Dutch and no dictionary. 'After two or three years' hard work and as we gradually learned how to deal with it, we began to find pleasure in it like chewing on a sugar cane and tasting its mellowness. We also came to realize what wrong ideas we had been fettered to for many long years in the past.' Writing of his own motivation, Sugita recorded in 1803, 'All I wanted was to show somehow to the people that the real structure of the human body was different from the one described in Chinese books.'[9]

The scholars of Dutch learning, the *Rangaku* scholars such as Sugita, concentrated their efforts mainly on European medicine as well as on other practical sciences such as astronomy, navigation, geography, natural history, physics and mathematics.

There was also something of a 'Dutch boom' at the end of the eighteenth century; in the words of Sugita, 'people somehow began to be enamoured of anything Dutch. They would treasure imported vessels and other curious things. A dilettante, if worthy of the title, never failed to have a collection, large or small, of Dutch things . . .' These included barometers, thermometers, Leyden jars, hydrometers, magic lanterns, sunglasses, megaphones, timepieces, telescopes, glass handiworks and numerous other objects. 'People wondered at their delicate workmanship and the subtlety of their mechanism. People swarmed every spring around the hotel where the Dutch party was staying [in Edo for the annual visit to the Shōgun's Court].'[10]

One is reminded of the '*nanban* boom' of the sixteenth century and the later crazes for Western 'exotica' in the nineteenth century or the craze for Japonaiserie in Europe in the 1870s.

We have already seen that contact with European medicine and astronomy led to a certain amount of questioning of traditional learning of Chinese origin. In the late eighteenth and early nineteenth centuries, some of the *Rangaku* scholars even began to dispute China's claim to be the centre of world culture and model for Japan. They did so by asserting the greater age of Europe (citing ancient Egypt). The picture they painted of Europe was as idealistic as the European *philosophes* were painting of China at the same time. And for the same reasons. A conveniently distant and little known culture was held up as possessing those features which the writer wished to see introduced into his own country. In other words, just as the European *philosophes* used China as a supposedly 'objective co-relative' with which to belabour obscurantism at home, so the *Rangaku* scholars used Europe.[11]

Several of the *Rangaku* scholars were truly remarkable men who advocated policies far in advance of their age. Some of them paid with their lives, for example the thirty-eight people implicated in the so-called 'Siebold incident', who were executed in 1828 for having passed maps and other information about Japan to a foreigner. Some pursued their studies along unexpected lines. Shiba Kōkan (1747–1818) and others, for example, studied Western techniques for creating the illusion of space by the use of shadow and relief and perspectival lines leading into the back of the composition. Their paintings had a considerable influence on Hokusai and the early *ukiyo-e* print makers. Thus in the nineteenth century when French painters 'discovered' the Japanese print, they were no doubt unconsciously drawn to a form of Japanese art which had in part already been influenced by Western perspective.[12]

Amongst the population at large, Westerners were regarded as exotic, if not peculiar. Even the word 'Oranda' (Dutch) had long since evoked the sense 'eccentric' or 'odd' as in the charming little verse of Sōin, who on a visit to Nagasaki towards the close of the seventeenth century wrote: 'Is that Dutch writing? Across the heaven stretch a line of wild geese.'[13]

In the nineteenth century as news of the Western advance towards East Asia began to reach Japan, and as European, Russian and American ships, and sometimes small fleets, began to cruise off Japanese waters, fear, dislike and even hatred of Western 'barbarians' and Western studies began to mount. A warning by a conservative scholar, Aizawa Seishisai, was made in 1825:

Recently, there has appeared what is known as Dutch Studies, which had its inception among our official interpreters at Nagasaki. It has been concerned primarily with the reading and writing of Dutch, and there is nothing harmful about it. However, these students, who make a living by passing on whatever they hear, have been taken in by the vaunted theories of the Western foreigners. They enthusiastically extol these theories, some going so far as to publish books about them in the hope of transforming our civilized way of life into that of the barbarians. And the weakness of some for novel gadgets and rare medicines, which delight the eye and enthrall the heart, have led many to admire foreign ways. If someday the treacherous foreigner should take advantage of this situation and lure ignorant people to his ways, our people will adopt such practices as eating dogs and sheep and wearing woollen clothing. And no one will be able to stop it. We must not permit the frost to turn to hard ice. We must become fully aware of its harmful and weakening effects and make an effort to check it. Now the Western foreigners, spurred by the desire to wreak havoc upon us, are daily prying into our territorial waters. And within our own domain evil teachings flourish in a hundred subtle ways. It is like nurturing barbarians within our own country.[14]

Fear and suspicion of Europe, particularly England, redoubled following the Opium War (1840–42) in which China was defeated by the British. The image of China, the age-old model for Japan, also suffered a heavy blow as a result of the war. Many Confucians who made their living by expounding Chinese learning hated the West, but could only express an impotent fury, like Shionoya Tōin (1810–67), who described Western writing as

confused and irregular, wriggling like snakes or larvae of mosquitos. The straight ones are like dog's teeth, the round ones are like worms. The crooked ones are like the forelegs of a mantis, the stretched ones are like the slime left by the snails. They resemble dried bones or decaying skulls, rotten bellies of dead snakes or parched vipers.[15]

Others, while just as anti-foreign as Shionoya or Aizawa, nevertheless recognized the practical necessity of learning from one's enemies, or as one statesman put it, 'the necessity of defence against the barbarians requires that we know them and know ourselves; there is no other way to know them than through Dutch learning'.[16] Many drew a distinction between the Dutch, whom they could learn from, and even admire, and the English who were regarded as intrepid, crafty and calculating with a national character deeply rooted in militarism. All would have agreed that the barbarians (*banjin*, for that was what Westerners were now called) were crafty, fox-like and on the lookout to seize Japan.[17] In the popular mind it was even rumoured that the Westerners concealed bushy tails in their pants and urinated like dogs.

On the eve of the arrival of Commodore Perry's 'black ships' in Yedo Bay in 1853, despite the fear and suspicion of the West, or perhaps because of it, not only did the Japanese know far more about Europe than the Europeans knew about Japan, but they had also made themselves better informed about Europe than any other non-Western people. There is therefore a remarkable contrast between the enthusiasm and effectiveness of the early Japanese students of the West, the *Rangaku* scholars, as well as government efforts to gather intelligence about the West, and the almost total indifference of the Europeans, even in the shape of the Dutch, towards Japan. It is a contrast which we shall find repeated again and again.

The demands of Commodore Perry that Japan open her doors to foreign trade and thereby bring to an end the two-century-old Tokugawa policy of isolation were soon known throughout the country: 'the appearance of the American fleet in Yedo had already made its impression on every remote town in Japan', as one of the reformers later remembered of the year 1854, and 'the problem of national defence and modern gunnery had become the foremost interest of samurai'.[18]

Two consecutive reactions to the foreigner may be observed in these years: complete rejection or partial assimilation. Each reaction was grounded on a different domestic political programme.

At first the debate divided between those who advocated keeping the country closed and expelling the barbarians completely ('reverence to the Emperor and expel the barbarians,' *sonnō jōi*), and those who felt that the only way to make the country strong enough to resist foreign pressures was to open it partially to learn Western science and military technology while maintaining traditional values ('Japanese spirit, Western techniques', *Wakon Yōsai*). This second formulation is notable for fitting snugly into one of the basic stereotypes of each other shared by both East and West: the East is spiritual, the West material. There were precedents for such a dualism in Confucian thinking and in the Japanese tradition which explicitly sanctioned adopting and making use of the strong points of other countries. The old phrase *Wakon Kansai* was easily adapted to *Wakon Yōsai*. The formulation was a useful transitional one, allowing those who propounded it to maintain their pride in adverse circumstances and at the same time to justify extensive borrowing from the West. But the rigid dualism which it implied very soon proved impossible to maintain. Eventually, after 1868, it was to be temporarily replaced by a third option; imperial restoration coupled with out and out Westernization (*sonnō kaikoku*).

As Western pressure mounted in the 1850s and 1860s, it began to look increasingly impractical simply to keep Japan closed. Despite waves of anti-foreign violence, and resentment at the bullying and the arrogant behaviour of the foreign envoys, the government had little option but partially to open the country. In 1854, it signed a treaty with Perry. Immediate efforts were made to learn more about the new enemies. An Institute of Barbarian Letters was set up in 1856 to train interpreters and make translations, and seven diplomatic-cum-study missions were sent to the United States and Europe between 1860 and 1867. Extensive records of these missions were kept, both public and private, and they afford a fascinating insight into Japanese attitudes towards the West at that time.

The first mission abroad, that to the USA in 1860, was astonished to find how politely the foreigners treated them, whereas in Japan, 'seven or eight out of ten people think of Europeans as dogs and horses. Some even have killed them . . .'[19] People in the wave of anti-foreignism in Japan in the 1860s 'simply hated the foreigners because all foreigners were "impure", men who should not be permitted to tread the sacred soil of Japan'.[20]

Fukuzawa Yukichi, who later became one of the leading proponents of out and out Westernization, managed to get on to no less than three of the Bakufu diplomatic missions to Europe and America. Recalling the atmosphere in his hometown of Nakatsu in Kyushu in the 1850s, he later wrote, 'All the men in town, including my near relatives, hated anything Western . . .', adding that 'it was still the age of Chinese studies and anything Western was to be frowned upon. But since the Perry expedition, one subject in the culture of the West, the gunnery, came to be recognized as a necessity. This was one way of escape to study the civilization of the West.'[21]

Fukuzawa made his escape from the stifling atmosphere of his lower samurai family and eventually studied Dutch and medicine in Osaka. There he learnt much the same lesson as Sugita Genpaku had learnt three generations before him, that in order for Japan to advance, she would first have to throw off the influence of China, or, as he put it in a description of his student days: 'The only subject that bore our constant attack was Chinese medicine. And by hating Chinese medicine so thoroughly we came to dislike everything that had any connection with Chinese culture. Our general opinion was that we should rid our country of the influence of the Chinese altogether.'[22] A contemporary who stopped in Hong Kong in 1863, on the way back from one of the Bakufu missions to Europe, reached the same conclusions for different, but typical, reasons: 'They [the Chinese] are all rude and deceitful . . . After having been a very great country, they are now the slaves of the English barbarians, who beat and drive them out.'[23]

For Fukuzawa, and others like him, China was to be replaced by 'the West'. And the West meant for them not just guns and scientific inventions and industrial machinery but different social customs and ways of thinking. After his third trip abroad, Fukuzawa wrote a short book called *Conditions in the West* (*Seiyō jijō*, 1886). It was the first book on the West which attempted to explain in simple language what the West was really like to live in. The book was modern Japan's first bestseller: some 250,000 copies were sold in the year of publication alone. Fukuzawa's reputation was made and within a few years, after the Meiji Restoration in 1868, Japan entered into a frenzy of out and out Westernization.

9

Out and Out Westernization

After the Meiji Restoration in 1868, the state launched the policy of 'reverence the Emperor, open the country' (*sonnō kaikoku*) and inaugurated a period of rapid Westernization with the aim of completely renovating Japan's government and economy along Western lines in order to catch up with Europe and America, particularly in military power. Between 1868 and 1900, some 2,400 foreign experts, the largest number from Britain, were invited to work in Japan as advisers to the new government ministries, including the armed forces, and as teachers in the new schools. In 1875 there were about five hundred such experts. By 1885 their numbers had declined to less than a hundred. Large study missions and dozens of students a year were also sent to the West by the government. Many of the students on their return to Japan became prominent in their different fields and from that day to this returned students have acted as the main body of mediators introducing Europe to Japan. The practice of sending hundreds of students abroad reached a peak in the 1920s. Today young men and women are sent abroad by their company as well as by the government, or by their university, but many thousands more go under their own steam.

For a brief time in the 1870s and 1880s the imitation of European manners became all the rage in the new capital of Tokyo. European influence on Japan reached its height at this time. 'Foreign countries are not only novel and exotic for us Japanese,' wrote Fukuzawa in 1875, 'everything we see and hear about these cultures is strange and mysterious . . . a blazing brand has been thrust into ice-cold water. Not only are ripples and swells ruffling the surface of men's minds, but a massive upheaval is being stirred up at the very depths of their souls.'[24]

The urge to catch up with the West was inspired by the fear of being overcome by the Western powers. Another motive was the desire to wipe out the shame of the unequal treaties by which foreigners in the Treaty Ports enjoyed extra-territoriality and the Japanese government had no tariff autonomy. To show, in other words, that Japan too was a modern (Western) civilized state which should be treated as an equal. Many ardent Westernizers were also no doubt influenced by their own rapid advancement on the basis of their knowledge of the West. Nor should one underestimate the attractiveness in themselves of such new ideas as 'freedom'. J. S. Mill's *On Liberty* was a bestseller in 1872. Political ideas were also introduced through popular translations of novels such as Disraeli's *Coningsby* or Bulwer-Lytton's *Ernest Maltravers*. During these years 'Magna Carta was circulated in facsimile reprints; the name of Rousseau was repeated as if it were a saviour; Patrick Henry was well known to many, and his words, "Give me liberty, or give me death", became a slogan.'[25]

All the nine 'bestsellers' between 1866 and 1878 were translations of Western works or books about the West.

1866	Fukuzawa Yukichi	*Conditions in the West*
1871	Samuel Smiles	*Self-Help*
1872	Fukuzawa Yukichi	*The Encouragement of Learning* (1872–84)
	J. S. Mill	*On Liberty*
1875	Fukuzawa Yukichi	*An Outline of a Theory of Civilization*
1877	Taguchi Ukichi	*A Short History of the Opening of Japan* (1877–82)
1878	Jules Verne	*Around the World in Eighty Days* (1878–80)
	Bulwer-Lytton	*Ernest Maltravers*

The list also shows the extraordinary influence of Fukuzawa, indeed works about the West at this time were known popularly as 'Fukuzawa books' (*Fukuzawa-bon*). His *The Encouragement of*

Learning appeared in seventeen parts over the years 1872–84. Some 200,000 copies of each part were printed and sold, making a total sale of 3,400,000 copies!

By far the most popular of Western books during the Meiji period was Samuel Smiles's *Self-Help* which argued that the qualities needed to get ahead in industrial society were not rank or status, but thrift, hard work and individual self-reliance. Smiles's teaching was thoroughly absorbed in Japan and has remained influential long after it appears to have been abandoned in Europe.[26]

The desire to learn about and to emulate the West was not limited to government officials and intellectuals. It was also matched by a wave of popular enthusiasm and curiosity stretching down to the illiterate, as the following excerpt by the contemporary writer Hattori Busshō (1842–1908) indicates:

The Western Peep Show

The viewing parlours are for the most part small painted shacks, the fronts of which have been given a hasty coat of whitewash. The rear, however, is neglected, suggesting nothing so much as a slattern who powders her face but leaves her back dirty. Some of these parlours are several stories tall, and the wooden boards with which they are built are painted to resemble stone, exactly like the entrance to some quack doctor's residence. Inside the building, at intervals several feet apart, are arranged a number of machines, and one goes from one machine to another peeping at its display. The front of the machine has eyes like a giant snake, each of which neatly fits the two human eyes. The viewer peeps at the world as through the eye of a needle, and the cost is a mere one sen. Some machines contain pictures of the scenery of countries all over the world; others are of completely imaginary subjects: the steel bridge of London is longer than a rainbow; the palace of Paris is taller than the clouds. An enraged Russian general pulls out a soldier's whiskers; a recumbent Italian lady kisses her dog. They have bought an American conflagration to sell us; they have wrapped up a German war to open here. Warships push through the waves in droves; merchant ships enter port in a forest of masts. A steam engine climbs a mountain; a balloon flies in the sky. Seated one may contemplate the Cape of Good Hope, lying down one may gaze at the Mediterranean . . . You look at a picture of a museum and despise the pawnshop next door; you peep at a great hospital and lament the headaches of others. As the spectator approaches the last peep show he becomes increasingly aware how cheap the admission price has been.[27]

In these years the wearing of Western clothes and the sporting of Western hairstyles was taken as a sign of cultural openness. Just as in the sixteenth century, it was the army which first switched to a Western uniform. Next the government bureaucracy and the Court adopted Western clothes. Controversy raged. Some argued that Western clothes should be for practical use, while Japanese dress should be reserved for aesthetic delights, thereby making a sartorial application of the slogan 'Japanese spirit, Western techniques'. Even today this reasoning is often advanced to explain why men and women wear kimonos outside their place of work – men at home, and women away from home. Others pointed out with some justification in those days of bustles and stays that Western clothes were impractical, unhygienic and expensive.

Even the Prime Minister, Itō Hirobumi, held definite views on the subject, as the German doctor, Erwin Baelz, recorded in his diary in 1904:

When, a long while ago, Itō informed me that European dress was to be introduced at the Japanese court, I earnestly advised against the step, on the ground that European clothing was unsuited to the Japanese bodily structure, and especially that the corset would be most unwholesome for Japanese women. Hygiene apart, I said, from the cultural and aesthetic standpoint the proposed change was simply impossible. Itō smiled and replied: 'My dear Baelz, you don't in the least understand the requirements of high politics. All that you say may be perfectly sound, but so long as our ladies continue to appear in Japanese dress they will be regarded as mere dolls or bric-à-brac.'[28]

Itō's remark has an authentic ring. Behind the good humour is the very real sensitivity as to how foreigners regarded the Japanese and their attempts to conform to Western ways. As part of its policy to revoke the unequal treaties the government sought to convince the Western powers that Japan was not a backward Oriental country, but a modern power with a constitution (modelled on that of Bismark's Prussia), a legal code (modelled on the French Code), an up-to-date school system (part German, part American) and an army (German) and navy (British). And as Itō pointed out, clothes too played their part in this effort.

This purposeful and unique approach to the West, an eclectic choice of the best models available from the different countries, tended to leave the Japanese, especially in the early Meiji period, with an over-theoretical and over-idealistic image of Europe. The image was based on book learning and elite study missions which in their reports very naturally concentrated on the rationale of institutions in Europe, rather on their actual functioning. Take this description of the roots of Western success by Fukuzawa (which incidentally sounds very much like the sort of thing said by Europeans about Japan today): 'The citizens of the West are not all intelligent. However, most of what they achieve through concerted group action proves to be the product of intelligent men. The internal affairs of these countries are all agreed upon by these groups. The governments are based on group consensus . . . Westerners are intellectually vital, are personally well-disciplined and have patterned and orderly social relations.'[29]

For the intellectuals of the Japanese enlightenment, Europe was a desirable collection of cultural assets representing 'civilization' and 'strength'. It was not an actual congeries of conflicting countries each packed with its own weaknesses and contradictions. The early Meiji image of Europe as the source of light, of civilization, and above all of high culture, has been extraordinarily pervasive, and it continues as a powerful positive image right to the present day.

Another image of Europe, which was formed during the Meiji period and has continued to the present, was derived from the image of abroad as the perfect setting for adventure and for romance. Abroad was a region of pure otherness where ordinary Japanese rules did not apply. Most of the Japanese going to Europe or America were young and single. Fukuzawa tells the story of how at the age of twenty-five, he secured a photograph of himself with an American girl during the first Bakufu mission to America. It was in fact the photographer's daughter and when he showed the prized souvenir to his shipmates they were envious. But it was too late by then for them to get themselves photographed with a white girl using the same trick![30]

Some of those who went to Europe and America later wrote of

their affairs: the surgeon-author Mori Ōgai's 'The Dancer' comes to mind. His flaxen-haired German heroine with her sad blue questioning eyes became for generations of Japanese the ideal type of Western woman. The early Western-style painters, many of whom studied in Paris, were also fascinated by European girls whom they never tired of painting.

Back in Japan, for the majority unable to make the long trip to the West, it was also foreign women who inspired immense curiosity. Hattori Busshō describes it in his story 'The Western Peep Show', quoted earlier:

> In the last show, the Goddess of Beauty lies naked in bed. Her skin is pure white, except for a small black mole under her navel. It is unfortunate that she has one leg lifted, and we cannot admire what lies within. In another scene we regret that only half the body is exposed and we cannot see the behind; in still another we lament that though face to face we cannot kiss the lips. This marvel among marvels, novelty among novelties, is quite capable of startling the eyes of rustics and untutored individuals.

Then as now publishers knew the value of a good book title. They also knew what interested their readers. A very proper Victorian 'political romance' like Bulwer-Lytton's *Ernest Maltravers*, a bestseller in 1878 in Japan, was sold under the translated title 'Strange Stories from Europe: Pornographic Tales from the Red-Light Districts' (*Ōshū kiji, karyū shunwa*).

Today Europe seems to have become fixed in the Japanese mind as an ideal setting for romantic affairs combining eroticism with culture. Whether this is because of the influence of the French romantic image, the reputation of Nordic girls or Italian men as 'Latin lovers', I do not know. Sex hotels in Japan are more often than not decorated in what might be termed 'the high French boudoir style' and a well-known manufacturer of Western-style beds chose the company name of 'France Bed'. During one visit to the provinces I was struck that the main attraction of the live sex show was the performance of the sex act by a Japanese boy with a Swedish girl. After it was over, the girl presented herself for inspection in a manner which had been denied the viewers of Hattori's peep show. It would be easy to lengthen the list . . .

In the previous chapter we saw that the European erotic image of Japan assumed central importance with the popularity of the Chrysanthemum theme. It beclouded a more balanced image of Japan for half a century and it still exerts a powerful attraction today. The Japanese erotic image of Europe on the other hand never played a central role, it merely enlivened the more serious images of Europe as a source of higher culture.

The headlong pursuit of Western ways and the desire for Western approval in those far-off days of early Meiji led the government in unexpected directions. One was to sponsor elaborate balls in the specially constructed Rokumeikan, which we have already come across in the incredulous and sneering descriptions of Pierre Loti. To the Westerner, Loti, the Rokumeikan was boring because there was nothing 'Oriental' or exotic about it. The Japanese in Western swallowtails appeared ridiculous to him. Only the Chinese at the ball in their traditional costumes won his admiration because they seemed authentically 'Oriental'. Seen through Japanese eyes, however, things would have appeared very differently, and indeed this is the theme of Akutagawa Ryūnosuke's short story 'The Ball'. The heroine, Akiko, recounts how years before as a young girl her father had taken her to a ball at the Rokumeikan where she had been asked to dance by a young French naval officer (Loti). To her the ball was a magical and exotic event because it was just what she imagined a Parisian ball would be like. Only the Chinese officials appeared to her as ridiculous, with their fat bellies and long pig-tails hanging down their backs. When Loti looked at the Japanese women at the ball he saw their clumsy efforts to dance. Akiko on the other hand drew the opposite conclusion from Loti's glances: 'the naval officer was watching her every movement. This simply showed how much interest this foreigner, unaccustomed to Japan, took in her vivacious dancing.'[31]

And the partners in this semi-fictional, but emotionally real contact, sailed on in their lives, both mercifully ignorant, one hopes, of the impressions which each had created in the heart of the other.

10

Disillusion

There was a contradiction in the movement for out and out Westernization: it was not possible to establish Japan as a Western state simply by adopting Western civilization. Nationalism too was needed, but nationalism implied an indigenous culture and national essence peculiar to Japan and the rejection of increasingly aggressive Western efforts to control Japan. Under these conditions it became virtually impossible to advocate out and out Westernization while remaining a patriot.

The trigger which eventually sparked a revulsion from Westernization was the failure to secure Western respect for Japan's efforts to 'civilize' herself, which came to a political head in the breakdown of efforts to negotiate the revocation of the unequal treaties in 1887. Societies sprang up dedicated to combating the loss of national identity and to opposing 'Europeanization'. Soon Japan turned back to her own traditions and towards a militant nationalism. In cultural circles the search for the essence of the Japanese tradition began once again, and the spate of translations of Western works declined.

Even without the shock of the failure of treaty revision, the extraordinary speed of the adoption of Western institutions and manners, a speed which sometimes led to indiscriminate borrowing, would probably have produced a revulsion sooner or later.

There were other factors making for disillusion with Europe. As more people travelled, there was a growing awareness by the 1880s of a gap between the idealized vision of Europe, derived from book reading, and actual realities, a lesson which was all too often reinforced by the racialist treatment which many individuals encountered, or felt they had encountered, during their stay overseas.

The novelist Natsume Sōseki's case from a few years later was no doubt particularly extreme:

> The two years I spent in London were the most unpleasant two years in my life. Among English gentlemen, I lived miserably like a lost dog in a pack of wolves.[32]

Nakae Chōmin, one of the founders of Japanese socialism, wrote in an 1882 newspaper article on his return from a trip to Europe:

> The British in Port Said and the French in Saigon are extremely arrogant, treating the Turks and Indians almost as dogs and pigs . . . The Europeans, who call themselves civilized people, consistently behave like that.[33]

Individual differences began to be noted: 'Where is the essence of the West in the countries of Europe and America?' asked the aesthete Okakura Tenshin after a trip to Europe in 1887. 'All these countries have different systems; what is right in one country is wrong in the rest; religion, customs, morals – there is no common agreement on any of these. Europe is discussed in a general way, and this sounds splendid; the question remains, where in reality does what is called "Europe" exist!'[34] The question remains valid today.

Tokutomi Sōho one of the most influential journalists and opinion leaders of the day, made an increasingly common objection, already voiced by Itō in his conversation with Baelz: 'these foreigners regard Japan as the world's playground, a museum . . . They pay their admission and enter because there are so many strange, weird things to see . . .'[35]

A few years later Chamberlain remarked that 'the travelled Japanese consider our three most prominent characteristics to be dirt, laziness and superstition'.[36] The view that Europeans were dirty dates back to the sixteenth century, when the first Europeans to arrive in Japan were observed to eat with their fingers rather than with chopsticks. The old phrase for Westerners, 'hairy bastards' (*ketojin*), also obviously implies that they are 'dirty'.

The political disappointment of 1887 was soon followed by the major disillusionment of the triple intervention of 1895.

Since the Japanese government had scrupulously followed the Western model of concluding a war with China by acquiring a sphere of interest in that country, all according to the norms of international law, there was severe criticism of the West. The following is a fairly typical later comment (made in the more outspoken 1930s) on the triple intervention, 'Japan has perceived that the Western saying "Honesty is the best policy" is applicable only among individuals. The discovery was made when three international hijackers, Russia, Germany and France, browbeat Japan into relinquishing the legitimate result of her war with China . . . The Manchurian incident may be taken as Japan's formal notice to the powers that she is fed up with the peculiar type of fair play practised by the whites in their association with the non-white races.'[37]

The pattern of Japan playing 'the rules of the game' yet not being accepted fully as a 'member of the club' by the Western powers was to be repeated many times over the next decades.

The turning away from the West in the late 1880s and 1890s and the search for a new national identity, for a specifically Japanese national essence, soon became engulfed in a torrent of jingoism during the Sino-Japanese War. One of the first popular novels depicting a war between Japan and the West was serialized in a Tokyo newspaper in 1895. The high point of the novel, *Asahi Zakura* by Murai Gensai, is the bombardment by a Japanese fleet, which has sailed up the River Thames, of London Bridge!

Even out and out Westernizers like Fukuzawa or Tokutomi revelled in the war against China. Characteristically, however, they still seem to have been very concerned with correcting the false Western image of Japan as the 'world's playground': to be concerned that is with being accepted and respected by the West. But the concomitant of 'measuring up' to the West was unfortunately 'looking down' on the East. Contempt for the 'Chinks' (*chanchan, chankorō* or *tombi*) and other 'Asiatics' now became openly the vogue. Thus a show of force in Korea or China seemed an appropriate way of demonstrating to the West that Japan had effectively Westernized and was no longer in the same league as other Oriental countries. 'On the whole,' wrote Fukuzawa in 1899, 'I see the country well on the road to advancement. One of the tangible results was to be seen a few years ago in our victorious war with China, which was the result of perfect cooperation between the government and the people . . . in the heat of the moment I could hardly refrain from rising up in delight.'[38]

The first results of the new-found power began to bear fruit at the turn of the century. Japan successfully renegotiated her unequal treaties with the Western powers in 1894 (full tariff autonomy followed in 1911). Colonies were also acquired – Taiwan in 1895 (a mere decade after the French defeated the Chinese in Vietnam in 1884), and Korea in 1910. China had not only been forced to cede Taiwan but also to extend most-favoured nation treatment to Japan.

In 1901 Japanese troops fought alongside the allied powers at the siege of Peking. Finally the Japanese resoundingly defeated Russia in the Russo-Japanese War (1904–5). It was the first victory of an Asian country over a Western power in modern times.

The mood in Japan was exultant, but tinged with doubts as to what the West would think. As Mori Ōgai put it:

> Win the war,
> And Japan will be denounced as a Yellow Peril.
> Lose it,
> And she will be branded as a barbaric land.

In the event, although winning the war did arouse fears of Japan in the West, the irony was that Japan gained far more attention and respect from the European powers and America by her defeat of China and even more so by the victories over Russia, than by all her efforts to adopt Western civilized ways. As Okakura Tenshin remarked, 'The average Westerner . . . was wont to regard Japan as barbarous while she indulged in the gentle arts of peace: he calls her civilized since she began to commit wholesale slaughter on Manchurian battlefields.'[39] The official victor of Port Arthur,

Nogi Maresuke, made a triumphal tour in Europe and was decorated by the governments of Prussia, France and Great Britain.

Despite Japan's recognition by the Western powers, discrimination continued, eventually with the disastrous result of encouraging Japan to go down the road which led from the Sino-Japanese War of 1895 to the Manchurian incident in 1931. First there were the exclusion bills in the United States, then Versailles in 1919, when Japan's initiative for a clause on racial equality was rebuffed by the US and Britain. Many individuals too had suffered personal discrimination of one form or another in the United States or in Europe. The more Japan shifted to 'Pan-Asianism', the more the image of Europe declined. There were other reasons too. The First World War demonstrated that Europe as the home of liberty and enlightenment was a patently false image. The defeat of Germany also meant the collapse of one of Japan's most respected models during the Meiji period.

Further disillusion with Europe came when, after the War, the Europeans themselves began talking of decline.

'Europe is sick, perhaps dying,' said Anatole France, and many Japanese would have agreed, particularly as the corollary of the decline of the West was felt by many to be the rise of the East under the leadership of Japan. Marxist critiques of Western bourgeois society at this time found a willing ear in Japan. Spengler's *Decline of the West* too was rapidly translated into Japanese and met with a not unappreciative audience. It has sold steadily since the appearance of volume 1 in 1925 at the rate of about a thousand copies a year and is currently available in six or seven different complete editions.

In this climate of opinion, and with the development of socialism, people who went to Europe began to notice unfavourable things, and not only notice them, but to give more emphasis to them on their return to Japan than they had done in the past. One of the earliest was Kawakami Hajime, whose *Tales of Poverty* (1917) contained graphic descriptions of the slums and suffering in the cities of Europe in the years leading up to the First World War. It became an instant bestseller. He wrote:

Although England, America, Germany and France and many others are rich countries, their people are very poor. It is surprising that in these civilized countries there are so many people who are poor.[40]

Kawakami was by no means the only young intellectual who went to study in Europe and found unpleasant smells where others had found heady perfumes. Books like Ikemoto Kimio's *Tales of French Villages* (1934) contained graphic descriptions of the squalor and backwardness of French country life, where he discovered to his surprise toilets and baths were virtually unheard of.

In the 1930s there was growing dissatisfaction with Europe, triggered by the negative images evoked by the trade frictions during the Great Depression at the start of the decade, and encouraged by the wave of anti-Westernism and rumours of war at the end of the decade. This is reflected even in the work of a non-political writer such as Mushanokoji Saneatsu whose novel *Love and Death* (1939) gives an insight into the popular sentiments of those days.

At a farewell party given for the chief protagonist of the novel on the eve of his departure for Paris, a friend says:

I was the first to urge Muraoka to go to Paris. Thousands and ten thousands have gone and will continue to go. But Paris is the cultural centre of the world today. I would like to have him learn from his trip how frivolous the world really is. What I got from the literature course in Tokyo Imperial University in the way of knowledge I could have got by reading a single volume, but an important thing I did get was a point of view which spares me from being the least bit impressed by the reputation of that most noble seat of learning. That point of view, I might say, has given me awareness and self-confidence. From the standpoint of knowledge, one would be better off reading a book than going to Europe or Paris. But the awareness that Europe or Paris are frivolous places is something one can get only by going to the West. And that, I maintain, is not at all an insignificant possession. Paris is not the centre of the world; it is wherever we happen to be standing. Let us think about the fact that the earth is round. For us the centre of the earth is Tokyo. To live decently is the most important thing for all of us. But until we have seen Paris we remain in awe of Paris.

These deliberately anti-Romantic and somewhat chauvinistic words make the same point as Paul Valéry, but the other way around. Valéry's advice was that if you wish to maintain your illusions about the Orient, it is better not to go there. Muraoka's friend is saying, if you want to destroy your illusions about the West, the best way is to go there. Generations of Orientalists in Europe have preferred Valéry's advice. Arthur Waley, for example, perhaps the most famous British Orientalist and translator of Chinese and Japanese literature in the twentieth century, never once visited either China or Japan. It was said that he preferred to avoid confronting the ideal image he held of them based on the classic texts, with what he feared would be the humdrum realities of present-day life. He preferred to live with his illusions. He preferred not to betray his dreams. In 1964 when I first went to China, I was seriously advised by my professor that if I wished to continue my career as a sinologist, I was wasting my time going there! Advice exactly the opposite of Muraoka's cynical friend.

After arriving in Paris, Muraoka writes home that,

> Wherever one goes one sees only Occidentals . . . somehow I have the feeling that we are looked down upon . . . A solitary Japanese among a group of Occidentals is hardly an imposing figure. This is due to a large extent to our not being suited to Western style clothes, but even if we try to make something of the colour of our skin and our physique, we still have very little to boast about. Nevertheless, I am confident that from the standpoint of spiritual power and intelligence we are not in the least inferior. The majority of Europeans love pleasure too much. Few of them have any faith in a future life. For the most part they live idly from day to day.

These thoughts contain many of the most common stereotypes held by Japanese about Europeans which we have already come across several times. The Japanese may be physically inferior, but they are spiritually superior. The Europeans are self-indulgent and lazy. 'They are,' he continues, 'for the most part satisfied with their own culture. They show by their expression that they feel no need to be interested in anything beyond it.'

Muraoka writes much on the paintings and statues and art which he sees in Europe, but he also asserts the equal value of

Japanese art. Finally, on the eve of his departure from Europe he sums it all up:

> As an Oriental travelling around in Europe I have had to endure a great deal.
>
> It's because of the way things are between the East and the West. I believe that we Orientals still have much to learn from the West.
>
> But I feel also that there are a great many things about the East that we should try to teach the West . . . Feeling as I do, I have never forgot my manners or lost my good will toward them, but I have seen no special reason for flattering them. But what a lot of silly tensions I will be relieved of when I get back to Japan! Being aware always that one is a foreigner among foreigners wherever one goes doesn't make for peace of mind.[41]

I fully sympathize with many of the feelings of 'Muraoka', having once spent a year as a minority of one in a totally alien surrounding. Because you look different you think everybody is watching you. You begin to feel nervous, you suspect that every time a dog barks, he is barking at you and that every laugh is pointed in your direction. You long for the anonymity which only a return to your own people can offer. Sōseki felt this isolation and paranoia so strongly in London that he had a nervous breakdown. Muraoka felt the same in Paris. But such feelings are not always the result of a hostile environment. The fact that Sōseki was apparently unable to have a successful liaison with an English girl may have contributed to his misery. The fact that Muraoka confesses that he could not speak a word of French before going to Paris and made no effort to learn it when he got there, no doubt made it difficult for him to break out of his isolation.

Anybody who has had to live in a totally alien environment will know what the fictional Muraoka is saying in his letters home. Indeed many of his comments had been made by Japanese visitors to Europe in the nineteenth century and are often still echoed today. Only today the contrast between Japan and Europe, between being Japanese and European, is likely to be less strongly felt. And the chauvinistic tone of the 1930s is now muted, if not wholly a thing of the past.

The final stage in the rejection of the West was reached during the years when Japan sought to become 'the Light of the Greater

East Asia . . . and ultimately the Light of the World'. The commentary on the Imperial Declaration of War which sold more than three million copies continued,

> To speak the truth, the various races of East Asia look upon the British and Americans as superior to the Nippon race. They look upon Britain and the United States as more powerful nations than Nippon. Therefore we must show our real strength before all our fellow-races of East Asia. We must show them an object lesson. It is not a lesson in words. It should be a lesson in facts. In other words, before we can expel the Anglo-Saxons and make them remove all their traces from East Asia, we must annihilate them.[42]

During this period when Japanese intellectuals felt they had a mission to throw off Western influence and liberate their fellow Asians, the official image of Germany and Italy was naturally a favourable one. A biography of Mussolini was a bestseller in 1928 and a suitably bowdlerized translation of Hitler's *Mein Kampf* became a bestseller in 1940. Unofficially, the Germans came to be disliked during the war for their arrogance, and Hitler's views on Japan and the Asians were widely known. Not even the army was particularly pro-German.

The official enemies were, of course, the allied powers in the Pacific theatre, the 'diabolical Americans and British' (*kichiku Bei-Ei*).

They were government-inspired attempts to expel Western influence. But they stood little chance of success. For a start, there was no longer any clear or meaningful distinction between East and West. Four generations had absorbed Western ways since the early Meiji and a new amalgam had developed which could no longer be separated into such simplistic divisions as 'Japanese' or 'Western'. Secondly, the Germans, Italians and Vichy French were allies of Japan. Their culture therefore could not be rejected out of hand. The censors were left with the impossible task not only of trying to cut out the Western elements from Japanese culture, but also of trying to isolate the Anglo-Saxon elements from it. Yet even such a basic element of that culture, the English language, was an essential tool for governing the Great East Asia Co-prosperity Sphere. Despite efforts to limit the teaching of

English, it continued to be taught in the schools. The censors exercised their negative function: there was, for example, a ban on British and American music, especially jazz. But it was ineffective because in the long run, as such bans tend to be, it was practically unenforceable.[43]

There were two Western bestsellers between 1939 and 1945 apart from Hitler's *Mein Kampf* and Maurois's *Why France Fell*; both were non-political books by Hogben, popularizing mathematics and science, a reminder perhaps that it was European sciences which had breached the tough walls of Tokugawa seclusion. A reminder too that a modern state cannot function without science and technology, those powerful bridges linking East and West.

Many years after the end of the Pacific War, a well-known authority on Europe, Professor Aida Yūji, described how he came to be disillusioned with the Europeans and to discover the 'limits of European humanism'. At the end of the war, he had worked as a surrendered soldier for two years in Burma and found that the English did not physically maltreat him, but apparently regarded him as sub-human. They treated the Japanese in the same way they treated the Indians – coldly.

It seems that each generation in turn since the Meiji had to learn in its own way the vast distance between its ideal images of Europe and what it perceived as European realities. And at regular intervals, coinciding with nationalism at home and the turning away from the West abroad, the assertion of Japanese self-confidence involved the deflation of the European image – 'until we have seen Paris we remain in awe of Paris'.

Today more than ever Japanese tourists are flocking to the French capital.

11

Europe as a Cultural Museum

Defeat in the Pacific War led to Japan's second period of rapid and massive assimilation from the West. Only this time it was the United States which was the model, not Europe.

For about ten years, from 1945 to 1955, Japan's institutions were re-cast in an American mould and an entire generation turned to the United States as the ultimate source of wisdom in every sphere from clothing styles to business management. Bit by bit, economic recovery followed by rapid growth led to the gradual weaning from the American tutelage. By the late 1960s the Japanese were just beginning to be aware of their new affluence and the fact that their economy had not only caught up with the West, but in some cases had overtaken the old models of the nineteenth century – Italy, France, England and even Germany. Herman Kahn's *The Emerging Japanese Superstate*, published in 1970 with sales-catching exaggeration, trumpeted an American's view of Japan's new importance. The book sold extremely well in Japan as do most books, such as Vogel's *Japan as Number One*, which suggest that she has finally caught up with the West. Unfortunately few pause to consider why such books sell so very much better in Japan than in the West.

Despite the signs of a new confidence in Japan and the gradual disenchantment with the United States from the 1960s onwards, US influence still remains paramount on all generations today.

Changing Japanese attitudes towards the West and towards Europe can be traced through the polls and surveys of attitudes towards foreign countries which have been taken since the 1950s.

Before the Pacific War, the countries of Western Europe were probably the most popular. After the war they were surpassed by America. From about the mid 1960s the pattern changed again with a more diversified range of countries, usually led by Switzerland, being picked as favourites.[44]

Today, European countries are regarded as a source of high culture, rather like a good museum and, in this sense, perhaps superior to Japan. But in other respects such as economic development, knowledge or the will to work, since the 1970s, only Switzerland, Sweden and Germany are felt to be superior to Japan.

Switzerland has been regarded as the home of idealized liberty since the Meiji period. Today it is felt to be a model of neutrality as well as clean, neat and, although small, thanks to the hard work of its citizens, rich – all qualities held in high regard in Japan. Sweden, too, has made a success of neutrality and it is small and rich; in addition it is esteemed for its women and its welfare state. Its active third-world policies are conveniently ignored. Germany has been admired ever since the formidable impression of strength as a newcomer which it made on Japan following the victory of Prussia over France in 1870. Germany too was a model and inspiration for three key professions in the modernization process – the army, medicine and the law (as well as academic philosophy). Moreover, since the Pacific War, Germany, like Japan, has had to make its way quietly in the world. Its economic management has been held up as a model for Japan's planners too.

In admiring all three countries, the Japanese are no doubt unconsciously gratified by identifying qualities which they are pleased to associate with themselves. There is, in other words, an element of self-identification, particularly in the case of Germany, whose experience both as a newcomer in the nineteenth century, and as one of the defeated powers after the Pacific War, have been not dissimilar to Japan's.[45]

Moving now from perceptions of individually esteemed European countries, to perceptions of the EC as a whole, an opinion poll conducted in March 1979 revealed awareness of the acronym 'EC', and a fairly accurate knowledge of the EC's economic aims.

Most were able to name the four largest countries in the EC, but very few could name the five smaller ones. One quarter of those polled were unable to name even one member country. A majority did not know that the EC produces more goods than Japan. As might be expected, knowledge of the EC was highest amongst those below thirty years old.[46]

Turning to Japanese attitudes towards 'foreigners' as opposed to foreign countries, it is worth recalling that the word 'foreigner' (*gaijin*) still carries the connotation 'white man' (*hakujin*) and usually excludes Chinese and Southeast Asians as well as Africans and black Americans. There is the story of a Southeast Asian student who had telephoned a Japanese landlady for an apartment, presumably in heavily accented Japanese, because when he presented himself at her door, she refused to rent it to him, saying that she had just promised it to a *gaijin* on the telephone!

A survey conducted by the Prime Minister's office in 1980 showed that 64 per cent of those polled wanted to have nothing to do with foreigners and that only 'one out of every four Japanese either associates with foreigners or wishes to associate with them'. Thirty-eight per cent of the respondents said they would not allow their children, brothers or sisters to marry a foreigner. The findings of an earlier poll showed that amongst the minority of Japanese girls who wished to marry a foreigner, a European professor or businessman was felt to be the least objectionable of foreign marriage partners. No doubt a sign of the residual high esteem in which Europeans were held in the 1960s when this second poll was conducted.[47]

Actual Japanese images of Europeans tend to be as stereotyped as European images of Japanese. But they are on the whole formed from very positive stereotypes. One survey found that a majority of Japanese felt that North Europeans were 'cold', while South Europeans were 'hot'. This reminds one of Aristotle's view that the Northern races were spirited and the Southern ones were civilized – although as a Greek, he added that it was the Greeks alone who were both spirited and civilized. Today the Japanese might well be tempted to add that it is they alone who combine the best of East and West, *Wakon Wasai*, to take the title of a recent book by Kimura Shosaburō.

Another poll, done in 1967, showed that a majority thought of the English as courteous (and next as conservative, cold and reasonable); the Germans as scientific (and next as argumentative, reasonable and outstandingly able); the French as artistic (and next as vivacious, individualistic and affable); and the Italians as vivacious (and next as artistic, affable and emotional).[48] My own experience, as I mentioned earlier, suggests that this survey is absolutely correct, at least in respect to one European country, for on introducing myself as an Englishman, the reaction of ordinary Japanese was invariably the same: 'Oh, the Englishmen are gentlemen, aren't they?'

Various other similar 'national character' stereotypes are applied to the Europeans. The Germans, for example, are popularly regarded as prudent, earnest, efficient, diligent, thrifty and orderly people who eat potatoes and sausages and drink beer. Such formulations are more often than not identical to the view about Europeans held by themselves and by other peoples. I could find nothing specifically Japanese in them. One witty formulation is credited to the late Professor Ryū Shintarō: 'Germans consider then run; Italians run without reflection; the British run while thinking . . .' and the Professor added, in line with the common European view of the Japanese as emotional, 'Japanese run, then think.'

The post-war bestsellers list is another useful index, not only of popular interests and reading habits, but also of the sort of things found attractive about Europe and America by Japanese readers.

TRANSLATED WESTERN BOOKS OR BOOKS ABOUT THE WEST ON THE
JAPANESE BESTSELLERS LIST 1946–81

Year	Ranking (out of ten)	Author	Title
1946	5	Sartre	La Nausée
	6	Van de Velde	Le Mariage Parfait (sex manual)
	7	Gide	Intervues Imaginaires
	8	Remarque	Arc de Triomphe

Year	Ranking (out of ten)	Author	Title
1947	3	Remarque	Arc de Triomphe
	7	Eva Curie	Life of Madame Curie
	9	Van de Velde	Le Mariage Parfait (sex manual)
1948	4	Dostoevsky	Crime and Punishment
	5	Remarque	Arc de Triomphe
1949	2	Mitchell	Gone with the Wind
1950	3	Mitchell	Gone with the Wind
	5	Lawrence	Lady Chatterley's Lover
	6	Mailer	The Naked and the Dead
1952	3	Gain	Japan Diary
	10	Rolland	Jean Christophe, 1
1953	1	Anne Frank	Diary of a Young Girl
	2	Simone de Beauvoir	The Second Sex, 3
	5	Simone de Beauvoir	The Second Sex, 1
	10	Rolland	Jean Christophe, 3
1954	2	Mrs Rosenberg	Love Overtakes Death
1956	7	Viktor Frankl	Ein Pswsholg erlebt das Konzentrationslager
1957	9	Lobsan Rampa	The Third Eye
1958	8		World Literature for Young Girls
1959	4	Pasternak	Doctor Zhivago
1961	1	Iwata	How to Strengthen Your English
	2	Oda	Let's Look at Whatever Comes Along
1962	2	Joy Adamson	Born Free
	7	Watanabe	How to Learn Foreign Languages
	8	Joy Adamson	Forever Free
1963	5	Dostoevsky	Crime and Punishment
	7	Joy Adamson	My Elsa
1966	7	Tolstoy	War and Peace
1967	7	De Bono	New Thinking – the Use of Lateral Thinking in the Generation of New Ideas
	10	Drucker	The Age of Discontinuity

Year	Ranking (out of ten)	Author	Title
1971	1	Ben-Dasan	The Japanese and the Jews
	3	Segal	Love Story
1974	1	Burke	Jonathan Seagull
	2	Goto Tsutomu	Prophecies of Nostradamus
	9	Braty	Exorcist
1975	3	Harold	Sight without Glasses
	5	Solzhenitsyn	Gulag Archipelago
	6	Perliz	The Bermuda Triangle
	8	Taylor	Black Holes: The End of the Universe
1976	10	Fukada	New Conditions in the West
1977	2	Haley	Roots
1978	2	Galbraith	The Age of Uncertainty
1979	5	Vogel	Japan as Number One
	8	McWhirter	The Guinness Book of Records
1980	5	Forsyth	Devil's Alternative
	8	Clavell	Shōgun
1981	5	Goto	Nostradamus, 3
	10	Sagan	Cosmos

Source: Publisher's Annual (Shuppan nenkan), Tokyo, 1982.

The first thing which strikes one about this list is the large number of translated foreign books or books about foreign countries. There were only seven years between 1946 and 1981 when there were no such books on the list.

Next, European books appeared most frequently on the list in the 1940s and early 1950s. Since then they have been largely replaced by American books.

The European bestsellers in Japan just after the war reflect the lifting of the wartime censorship and the continuation of pre-war trends. Remarque and Madame Curie had been on the bestseller list just prior to the war.

The titles also reflect the mood of the day. The sense of desolation, isolation and disorientation of Sartre's *La Nausée* as well as Dostoevsky's *Crime and Punishment* made them bestsellers in Europe at this time too. For students in particular there was an obvious element of self-identification. French books are much in evidence, reflecting the old association of France and culture. Sex is also there; it is perhaps not surprising in those years of the post-war babyboom to find a French sex manual (Van de Velde) two years running as a bestseller. And *Lady Chatterley's Lover* or *The Second Sex* also presumably owed their popularity to the erotic image of Europe. Remarque's *Arc de Triomphe* is a sentimental story with a timely theme of international love overcoming national hostilities. Remarque, like Romain Rolland, was popular in Japan at this time because of his opposition to war. The film version of *Arc de Triomphe* (1948) starring Ingrid Bergman and Charles Boyer was released in Japan in the same year which perhaps contributed to its extraordinary success, although in those far-off days it was usually the film which followed the bestseller and not vice versa.

To sum up, Europe's image as a source of high culture was still strong in the post-war years. The erotic image too was very much in evidence, but Europe as a source of practical knowledge, so clearly reflected in the translated titles of earlier ages, including bestsellers, is hardly represented at all.

In the 1960s and 1970s the post-war generation turned to America and most bestsellers were now American. These same books were also bestsellers in America and Europe. Either they were about American management methods or they reflected the global homogenized, youth culture which emerged in the 1960s. Largely American, coinciding with the spread of hamburger and coke, wash-and-wear pants and jeans, rock, pop and disco-sound, it found its most characteristic and influential expression in movies, television and cassette and video tapes. Most of the foreign books on the bestseller lists of the last twenty years owed their popularity to the advertising which they gained as films either in the cinema or on television. Thus Tolstoy's panoramic *War and Peace* replaced Dostoevsky's introspective *Crime and Punishment* as a bestseller, not only because it suited the more brash mood of the day, but also because it suited the popular cinema better. It hit the bestseller list in the same year as the release in Japan of Bondachuk's spectacular: the film helped sell the book. This was also true of the only other European best-sellers of the 1960s, Joy Adamson's books about Elsa the lion cub which were made into films and became box-office hits in Japan. This applies as well to Haley's *Roots* as to Galbraith's *Age of Uncertainty*, to Clavell's *Shōgun* or to Sagan's *Cosmos*, all of which gained or consolidated their bestseller status thanks to television. Europe with its image of a high or elite culture was usually not in this league. There have been very few European bestsellers in Japan over the last twenty years.

In line with the view of Europe as a historic source of high culture, European goods are felt to be especially 'high class' and they are still referred to by the old phrase: 'goods which come by ship' (*hakurai hin*). The phrase is applied to luxury goods which come mainly from Europe. It was first used of the luxury goods imported by the Dutch and Chinese during the Edo period. Today, particularly France is the captive of her cultural image (over 50 per cent of her exports to Japan are consumer goods such as haute couture or perfumes). Because the Japanese regard Europe as a source of high culture, and by implication a source of expensive luxury goods, roughly 40 per cent of European sales in Japan are characterized by small volume turnover of consumer goods at exceedingly high prices. It is almost as if European imports were regarded as a sort of expensive garnish to com-plement the basic fare of Japanese industrial products.

The delight in European consumer goods as status symbols began somewhat indiscriminately in the Meiji period, as the following satirical comments on a 'beefeater' or Westernizer of those days illustrates:

His hair, not having been cut some hundred days, is long and flowing – in the foreign style. Naturally enough, he uses the scent called Eau de Cologne to give a sheen to his hair. He wears a padded silken kimono beneath which a calico undergarment is visible. By his side is his Western style umbrella covered in Gingham. From time to time he removes from his sleeve with a painfully contrived gesture a cheap watch, and consults the time.[49]

The practice continued in the 1930s:

> It is not at all odd to see a Japanese in the native costume wearing a wooden undershirt made of material brought from Australia and an informal *hakama* made of serge imported from Bradford, covering himself meanwhile with an Inverness made of cloth produced in America. He is also likely to have a wristwatch made in Switzerland, a snakewood cane from the South Seas and a package of Turkish cigarettes accompanied by an American lighter. If it is cold he may be protecting his neck with a scarf bearing the mark of a well-known Parisian haberdasher and his hands with a pair of gloves of Italian make.[50]

Today, when Europeans complain of the unwillingness of Japan to import from Europe, it is common for elderly Japanese politicians and businessmen to counter the complaint by offering you a glass of 'Old Parr' Scotch whisky and by pointing to their Savile Row suit (*Sebirō*, in Japanese), their Cardin neck tie, their Mont Blanc fountain pen and their Gucci loafers as demonstration of Japan's willingness to buy from Europe!

Apart from a residual esteem for Europe, particularly European historic culture, there is a conviction in Japan that Europeans are suffering from a disease – they appear to have lost the habit of work and to have become ever more inward-looking as they are faced with intractable problems of democratic ungovernability, regional separatism, ageing populations, overcostly social welfare systems, soaring unemployment, labour unrest, inflation and industries which are unable to compete on world markets.

It is widely felt that Europeans are arrogant and self-indulgent.

In short, far from being a model for Japan, as it was one hundred years ago, Europe (with the possible exception of Germany) has now become something of a negative example when it is considered at all, or else merely irrelevant. In line with this feeling, a poll which has been taken every five years since 1958 reveals that the only peoples which the Japanese have thought of as growing increasingly excellent since the mid-1950s are the Japanese themselves, the Chinese and the Jews. All the others, including the Europeans, are felt to be declining.[51] 'If we persist in comparing ourselves with England, we run the risk of slipping easily into a comfortable feeling of self-complacency,' wrote an unusually outspoken young Japanese intellectual recently. The same writer criticizes the 'well-worn cliché' held by Japanese intellectuals 'ever since the Meiji Restoration' that 'Japan is backward and foreign countries are advanced.'

In the new mood of impatience with the West, he also refers to those Japanese intellectuals who act as mediators with the West as 'sellers of imported merchandise'. He quotes approvingly the author of a recent bestselling book about Europe as saying, 'in England, it is impossible for the lower classes, and indeed for most middle-class families, to provide their children with a decent supper', but adds that 'this is not only true in England, a country that is in the process of collapse and disintegration. In Europe and America generally, people must make do with very little to eat.'[52]

Lest anyone think that such views are limited to the younger generation let him listen to a senior official of the Ministry of International Trade and Industry, who said in a characteristically frank interview (not intended for foreign consumption), 'I think that the cause of the decline of West Europe is to be found in Europe itself. They do not like to think so [laughter] . . . Europe woke up in the morning to find that the Rising-Sun flag had been raised overnight in the area which it regards as its own traditional sphere of influence . . . its own "Greater Europe Co-Prosperity Sphere".' Later in the same interview he expressed a commonly held view of Japan's trade problems with Europe: 'Japan's competitive power is overwhelmingly great. If we compare it to a golf match, Japan's handicap is single while that of Europe is 25 or 26.'[53]

In terms of Japanese priorities in international relations Europe is invariably placed low. Despite this and despite the widely held view that Europe is declining politically, economically and socially – that it is suffering from a disease from whose contamination Japan should immunize herself – there are specialized groups who continue to regard Europe as a model. The Japanese Trade Unions, for example, gaze with envy at the far greater power held by their brothers in Europe. Europe's welfare systems too are sometimes held up as an example of what can be achieved in this direction.

But above all, Europe is regarded as a cultural museum. I first realized this as a research student in America in the 1960s, when Japanese friends would show me their European vacation photographs. Again and again I found myself confronting photos of the grave of Balzac, Shakespeare's tomb or Goethe's birthplace. So, much later, when I read memoirs and travel accounts of Japanese who visited Europe, I was well prepared for the fact that the first place they went to was the Pantheon or Westminster Abbey, there to gaze at the busts of long-dead European philosophers and poets.

Today Europe is a major attraction for Japanese tourists and honeymoon couples. And who can be in the least bit surprised? For Europe offers to the Japanese visitor those jewels of the tourist trade – cultural monuments, good shopping and exotic sex – all at reasonable prices and all set in an elegant stagnation.

Between 1950 and 1970, 2,300 travelogues were published in Japan and most of them catered to the boom in tourism to Europe. In 1980 between two and three hundred thousand Japanese tourists visited each of the main countries in Western Europe (Italy, France, Germany, Switzerland and England were the most popular, in that order). This was more than went to the Mainland US (although hundreds of thousands more Japanese visited Guam or Hawaii).[54]

The combination of high culture, haute couture and low life which Europe offers the Japanese tourist was apparently particularly appealing to Japanese honeymoon couples: only 100 visited Europe in 1970, but 27,000 went in 1980. This boom owed a lot to the higher yen, but that could have been spent elsewhere too. The fact remains that no less than 11 per cent of all Japanese overseas honeymooners went to Europe in 1980 compared with 42 per cent to Hawaii, 16 per cent to Guam and 12 per cent to the mainland US.[55]

In addition to its magnificent tourist attractions, Europe still remains Japan's fourth most important export market after Southeast Asia, North America and the Middle East. For this reason alone it is considered worth a great deal of study and marketing efforts. Reflecting this, the only bestseller about Europe published in Japan since 1963 consists of anecdotes relating the quaint native customs in Europe and how they affect the Japanese 'business warriors' stationed there. If the book had a serious purpose, presumably it was to assist its readers in understanding the difficulties they might be expected to encounter with the local population.[56]

12

The Dawning of a New Age
in Japan?

Recent years have seen the dawning of a new age in Japan with the search for a new identity at home, balanced by the first tentative budding of a new self-confidence abroad.

By the early 1970s, the long-term objective of catching up with and surpassing the West had largely been achieved, at least in economic terms. Then, just at the moment when the realization of this achievement was registering, there was a hiatus; the goal of economic growth itself began to be questioned and the Japanese began to see themselves as 'economic animals' pursuing 'Gross National Pollution'.

The oil shock of 1973 rapidly put an end to this self-questioning, as Japan, like all the rest of the industrialized world, rushed to cope with stagflation at home and declining demand for her exports in traditional markets abroad. She got over these difficulties faster than any other major economy, including the United States. Again at the time of the second oil shock in 1979–80, she reacted with remarkable resilience. The comparatively quick recovery from the first oil shock and the swift adjustment to the second, both contributed largely to the new self-confidence in Japan.

These were also years when the second great period of assimilation from the West had long since ended and the cycle, as so often in the past, had shifted to an internal search to redefine 'Japaneseness', a turning back to Japanese roots. The search took many forms. There was a boom in books about the Japanese, sparked off in 1971 by a bestseller comparing the Japanese to the Jews – another brilliant but only half-recognized people. The polls began to register signs of a swing back towards such traditional

'Japanese' values as filial piety (*oyakōko*); gratitude, or repayment of kindness (*ongaeshi*); living in harmony with nature, and a growing elevation of conformism at the expense of individual freedoms.[57]

A glimpse into the thoughts of the younger generation is provided by the number-one pop song in the summer of 1979, Sada Masashi's 'Your Husband and Master Proclaims' whose lyrics included such 'traditional' injunctions as, 'before you become my bride, hear this, you will not go to bed before I do, you will not get up after I do; cook nothing but good meals and always look pretty, and keep quiet and follow behind me'. The song stirred up something of a controversy, but the popular press reported a deluge of letters in support of it!

I do not believe that the occasional evocation of Japanese roots represents the first signs of a shift towards nationalism or narrow traditionalism. I doubt very much whether the younger generation would want to make a sharp dividing line between 'traditional' and 'modern' or between 'Japanese' and 'Western' even if they were able to. The huge gap between the villages (seat of traditional Japanese values) and the cities (seat of modern Western values), which formed the social basis of militant nationalism in the 1930s, no longer exists today. 85 per cent of the population is urban and 'modern'.[58] Young people today have a much more homogenized culture than that of any previous generation and they are accustomed to picking and choosing from many sources, including Japanese tradition, which is itself, just as in other countries, constantly being redefined.

The new feeling of confidence, often going hand in hand with a new appreciation of tradition, was felt strongly by the generation born after 1955. They had no memories of the Pacific War, and the first events which made an impression on them were the signs of Japan's post-war successes – the Tokyo Olympics, Expo and a flood of high-quality consumer goods, all made in Japan. These were also the years when the image of America (as opposed to American culture) was declining fast, no doubt in part as the result of the scenes of domestic violence there mingled with the pictures of the brutal war in Vietnam which appeared constantly on the TV screens of their childhood.

A not unrepresentative book from the elite members of this generation is the novel *Somewhat Like Crystal*, which sold over a million copies in 1981. For its author, Tanaka Yasuo, a 24-year-old university student at the time, the 'crystal' or 'cool' generation is rich, apolitical and drifts with no particular effort or interest from one pleasurable experience to the next. The members of the 'crystal generation' express their individuality by the famous name clothes they wear and the brand-name goods they buy. What sort of impact this generation will eventually have on Japanese values such as frugality and hard work remains to be seen.

Externally there were powerful pressures on Japan to reduce her dependence on the US and stand on her own feet. The post-war period drew to a close in the late 1960s and early 1970s amidst uncertainties in the international political and economic environment dramatized by the 'Nixon shock', by the President's surprise visit to China, and by the US withdrawal from Vietnam which seemed to mark the beginning of a larger US pullout from Asia. These were also the years which saw the extension of Soviet power all over the globe including in the Pacific and around Japan, marking the termination of a clear US military supremacy. Under these conditions, there was a growing recognition of the necessity to strengthen the Japanese defence forces.

There has also been a renewed interest in seeking closer ties with the countries around Japan in the Asia-Pacific region. The most important change was the normalization of relations with China which touched off something of a 'China boom' in Japan. It was partly stimulated by relief that the abnormal circumstances which had kept the two countries apart for so long were now over, but also by the prospects, often exaggerated, of huge new markets opening up just when the West was filled with the sour grapes of protectionism. The bubble of false expectations was only pricked when the Chinese unilaterally postponed Japanese contracts in China in spring 1979 and, if that was not enough, did the same again in early 1981.

Closer links with Southeast Asia were somewhat prematurely sought by Prime Minister Tanaka during a tour of the area in 1974 which was marred by anti-Japanese riots. This unfortunate episode was soon set right by his successor, Mr Fukuda, who toured the ASEAN countries in August 1977 with generous promises of aid and investments.

The re-emphasis on links with East Asia was taken a step further by Prime Minister Ohira when he gave his support to the idea of a loose form of economic and cultural co-operation between the countries of the Pacific basin. During a visit to Australia and New Zealand in January 1980 he made a point of stressing the idea of a Pacific community with those countries at its southern rim and Japan to the north.

The following year, in January 1981, the new Prime Minister, Mr Suzuki, emphasized the importance which Japan attached to the region by making his first trip overseas to the ASEAN countries.

Even though the ties, especially the economic ties, between Japan and the other countries of the Pacific region are now much closer than ever before, it is highly unlikely that we shall see in this century the emergence of a tightly organized Pacific community. The political systems, economies and cultures there are just too heterogeneous. Also bitter memories of the war are still not far from the surface, as witness the angry reactions throughout East and Southeast Asia in 1982 to the revision of Japan's history textbooks in order to downplay her wartime attack on the region by describing it as an 'advance' rather than as an 'invasion'. Like Germany in Europe, too hasty a Japanese assumption of leadership in the region could easily awaken the fears and resentments of the past.

Nevertheless, not wishing to be isolated and often faced with regional blocs in other parts of the world, Japan has a clear interest in strengthening her relations with the countries around her. All the more so because the region is rich in food and raw materials including oil. Not negligible considerations when other sources of supply are either endangered by unstable political conditions or made even more expensive than they have become by spiralling transport costs over the long sea-lanes.

The region too has other important attractions besides its raw materials and food.

The rapid development of newly industrializing countries, such as South Korea, Taiwan, Singapore and Hong Kong, has already led to a closer integration of their economies with Japan. The continued shift of North American wealth based on new technologically advanced industries to the Pacific coast means that the US now does as much trade across the Pacific as across the Atlantic. Huge flows of US and Japanese trade, aid and investments into the region have contributed to make it one of the biggest and most rapidly developing growth areas in the world. Indeed by the end of this century the balance of world economic gravity will probably have moved from the Atlantic to the Pacific.

Japan's own economic development has been one of the main stimuli to these changes. Japan will also be one of its main beneficiaries.

Not the least of the attractions of the Pacific concept is that emphasis on greater regional integration no longer necessarily implies a weakening of Japan's links with the West. On the contrary, it is one of several distinguishing features of the new age that the old sharp dichotomy between 'East' and 'West' is less real than ever before. Both East and West have fragmented, here and there to coalesce into new combinations, or to be absorbed into the new homogenized global culture. Nowhere is this seen more clearly than in the Asia-Pacific region itself, whose dynamism today derives precisely from the successful blending of many cultural traditions, including some of the best elements from both East and West. It is too late now to switch the clock back to the days of the Meiji intellectuals, even if anybody wanted to, when it was possible to envisage a stark choice between two mutually exclusive categories, 'East' and 'West'; between 'dissociating from Asia' or 'putting Asia first'.

Another distinguishing characteristic of the new age is that it is an age without a model for Japan. Having caught up with the West, it is no longer possible to turn to a single 'parental' culture. Eventually this is going to have profound implications for Japan's role in the world, including her relations with China and Europe. In the nineteenth century, the opening to the West was preceded and accompanied by a turning away from China. In the twentieth century, the same happened to Europe, which, as we have seen, was relegated to a sort of cultural limbo reserved for models of a previous age – safely tucked away in an aura of 'high-class' nostalgia.

But now that Japan has caught up with the West, at least in the GNP growth stakes, the driving need to climb the international status ladder has diminished and it is time to look around. There is the possibility of an eclectic appreciation of whatever is of value throughout the world. A more realistic appraisal of other cultures becomes possible, including a fresh look at old models such as China or Europe. No longer threatened by them, and therefore able to understand with greater detachment their strengths and to sympathize with tolerance their weaknesses, it is possible for Japan for the first time to enter into more balanced relations with them, communicating through all sorts of channels, in a genuine and mutually beneficial dialogue.

The very fact that Japan has caught up also means that Japan herself will more and more come to be regarded as a model for other countries. She will be under great pressure to articulate visions based on her own experience to pass on to other nations (and not only the late-developing ones) and to contribute to the enlightenment of other peoples, both in the West as well as in the East. This will pose a tremendous challenge to new generations in Japan who will have to change past habits ingrained over centuries. No longer will Japan be able to situate herself on the cultural periphery of a great power, but she will herself have to act as a source of culture for others. Nor will the colonial pattern of absorbing culture from 'above' and passing it on to those 'below' be possible. Instead she will have to develop a new noblesse oblige to go with the new self-confidence, and enter into a genuine dialogue with all other peoples. Under these conditions the Japanese will no longer be rendered nervous by Western culture.

Just how Japan will act out and articulate her role on the world stage remains to be seen. Fundamental new departures will probably not be taken until the generation whose most important political experience was defeat in the Pacific War has passed away.

PART III

Open Markets
and Double-Bolted Doors

13

Europe's Decline in Asia and the Rise of Japan

For both Europe and Japan their direct political relations with each other are less important today than they were at the beginning of the century. The nature of their economic relations too has changed greatly.

In 1910, Great Britain, France, Germany, Holland and Russia were all colonial powers in Asia with extensive territories in the countries which are Japan's neighbours and which were the sources of raw materials for her new industries. In addition Japan had just become active as a colonial power. The international relations of East Asia at this time were therefore inevitably chiefly concerned with the direct rivalries and shifting alliances of the Great Powers, including the new member of the club – Japan.

Largely as a result of the rapid growth of the Japanese colonial empire and the weakening of Europe in two world wars, one by one the European powers were defeated by the Japanese in Asia. First the staggering defeat of the Russians in 1905. Next the Germans were forced to withdraw from Shandong in 1914 as well as from the last of their Pacific possessions. A generation later, the British and Dutch were caught completely by surprise and defeated in their colonies in Southeast Asia in 1941 and 1942, at which time the French administration in Indo-China was also brought under Japanese control.

The story of the rise of Japan as a power in East Asia and the simultaneous decline of Europe in the region is an interesting one, but it is well enough known for there to be no need to repeat it here. Since before the First World War the Japanese had been encouraging Asian nationalists to overthrow 'white imperialism' and preaching 'Asia for the Asians'. But it was only after 1931 and during the Pacific War that the enemies of the Asian nationalists and the Japanese became for a short while identical. The Japanese trained anti-colonial armies in all the European Asian colonies, and they also deliberately recruited from strata who had not served under the previous colonial regimes. These newly trained elites were frequently the future leaders of the Asian independence movements. Thus not only was the myth of colonial omnipotence exposed during the Pacific War by the rapid defeat of European armies by Japan, but Asian nationalist and revolutionary movements were given effective military training and discipline by the Japanese.

All the European colonial powers attempted to return to their previous colonies in Asia after the war but with little or no success. The Russians alone maintained vast portions of their nineteenth-century acquisitions and in some cases even extended the borders of their Asian empire.

Today the map of East Asia and the Pacific region shows the European presence in only one or two exceptional or marginal areas: in Hong Kong or Tahiti.

The decline of direct European interests in East Asia between about 1910 and the present day is clearly shown in Maps 1 and 2.

Today in Europe, amongst the decision-making elite, there are still memories of the Pacific War. Memories which will presumably only fade with the passing away of the generation whose first impressions of Japan were formed at this time.

The defeat of the European colonial powers by the forces of Asian independence after the war led to a gradual European psychological withdrawal, and to a decline in European political and economic involvement in the region. This is in marked contrast to Japan which, although adopting a low posture in international politics and remaining in the background during the wars and upheavals in Asia in the 1950s and 1960s, nevertheless continued to consolidate her economic ties with the region until by the 1970s she was the main source of trade, aid and investment for many Asian countries, especially in East and Southeast Asia.

Anyone who travelled in the region in the early 1960s and again in more recent years will have noticed the strikingly visible signs of

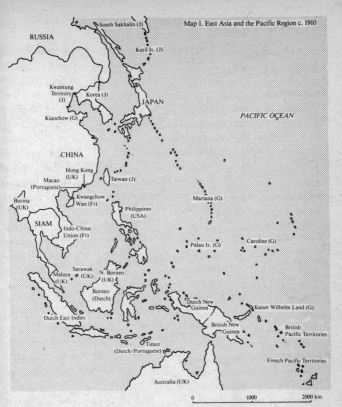

Map 1. East Asia and the Pacific Region c. 1910

Hong Kong (leased to UK 1841; 1860; 1898)

Kwantung Territory (leased to Japan 1905–45)

Korea (J)

Kuril Is. (J)

South Sakhalin (J)

Taiwan (J)

Kiaochow (leased to Germany 1898–1919)

Kwangchow Wan (leased to France 1898–1945)

Macao (Portuguese)

Indo-China Union (Fr) (Tonkin, Annam, Cochinchina, Laos, Cambodia)

Burma (UK)

Malaya (UK)

Dutch East Indies (Indonesia)

Sarawak (UK)

Borneo (Dutch)

N. Borneo (UK)

Philippines (USA)

Timor (Dutch/Portuguese)

Dutch New Guinea

British New Guinea (Papua)

Kaiser Wilhelm Land (German)

Palau Is. (German)

Caroline (German)

Mariana (German)

French Pacific Territories

British Pacific Territories

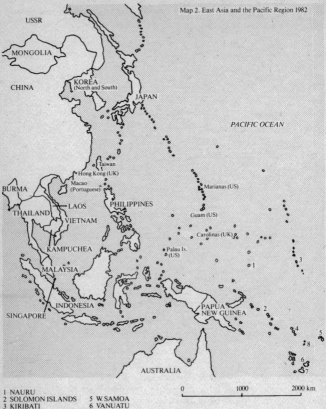

Map 2. East Asia and the Pacific Region 1982

1 NAURU
2 SOLOMON ISLANDS
3 KIRIBATI
4 TUVALU
5 W. SAMOA
6 VANUATU
7 FIJI

0   1000   2000 km

Note: In 1982, the situation was the reverse of what it had been in 1910. Then there
had been only four sovereign states in the region. Now there are two dozen and only
a handful of dependent territories.

British dependent territory:
Hong Kong

French overseas territories:
French Polynesia
New Caledonia
Wallis and Futuna

Portuguese territory:
Macao

US trust territory of the Pacific Islands
Palau Is.
Carolinas
Marianas
Guam

Soviet possessions:
Sakhalin
Kuril Is.

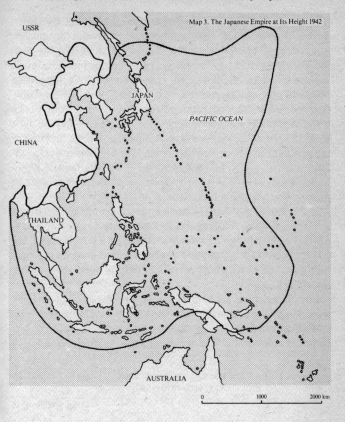

Map 3. The Japanese Empire at Its Height 1942

USSR

CHINA

JAPAN

PACIFIC OCEAN

THAILAND

AUSTRALIA

0   1000   2000 km

the replacement of Europe – first by the US and then by Japan. Today, over the whole region in both the towns and the villages, practically everything that moves on powered wheels, the cars, the trucks, the tractors, the motorcycles, even the bicycles, as well as the neon lights, the radios, the stereos and the TVs, the sewing machines, the clocks and the watches and all the other visible paraphernalia of modern life are made in Japan. Not, as they once were, in Europe. And these consumer durables are but the most striking signs of the massive flow of Japanese exports and investments which now pour into the region. The only European goods tend increasingly to be limited to snob symbols for the rich – Mercedes Benz or BMW cars; expensive low-volume exports. A pattern which is also reflected in European exports to Japan.

In line with these changes, the number of European expatriates in the main Asian business centres has declined. Their place is now taken by a far greater number of Japanese businessmen, not settling down to a comfortable 'expat' life as did the Europeans, but posted there for short periods of two or three years before returning home.

The diminishing economic role of Europe in Asia and the increasingly important role of Japan can be seen in the following tables (statistics for the EC as a whole are given, since the EC countries conduct the bulk of Europe's trade with Asia):

Table 1. The EC (Nine Countries) and Japan's Trade with Asia
(1960, 1970, 1980)

Unit = billion US$

	EC exports	Japan's exports	EC imports	Japan's imports
1960	2.7	1.2	2.3	0.9
1970	3.6	5.1	3.1	3.2
1980	21.2	36.5	28.0	36.3

Note: Asia includes all countries on the Asian Continent and in South, Southeast and East Asia except the Middle East and Japan.

Sources: EC, 1960 and 1970: OECD Statistics of Foreign Trade, Series A, 1980: Eurostat. Japan, 1960, 1970 and 1980: Ministry of Finance, Tokyo.

In 1960, the EC still had more than twice the volume of trade with Asia than did Japan. But by 1970 Japan had overtaken the nine countries of the EC in both exports and imports to Asia for the first time in modern history, except for during the world wars. The trend continued in the 1970s and by 1980 the total volume of Japan's trade with Asia was one-and-a-half times larger than that of the EC.

Seventy per cent of Japan's official development assistance in recent years has gone to Asia. The amounts increased rapidly until by 1978 Japan's aid to Asia had overtaken that of the USA and reached 80 per cent of that given by the EC countries.

As far as investments go, by 1980 Japan had three to four times more invested in South Korea, Taiwan, Indonesia, the Philippines and Thailand than did all the countries of the EC. In Hong Kong, Japan had one-and-a-half times more invested than the EC and in Malaysia slightly more. Only in Singapore did Japan have less invested than the EC.

This is not the place to enter into a more detailed discussion of the trade flows, the quality of the aid or the nature of the different investments. I cite these statistics here merely as indications of the relatively small economic role of Europe in the area compared with the past, and the relatively large role now played there by Japan. This point is crucial to the understanding of the trade frictions of the 1970s and the emerging pattern of regional alignments in the 1980s.

Turning to China, a country and a market which has long been

Table 2. Aid to Asia (1977–80)

Unit = billion US $

	1977	1978	1979	1980
EC (9)	0.870	1.153	1.561	1.932
USA	0.549	0.760	0.613	0.665
Japan	0.539	0.929	1.343	1.521

Note: See Note to Table 1.
Source: OECD (DAC) returns of members.

considered important in Europe, we find the same story; Japan
does far more business with China than all the European countries
put together. Today this causes no particular surprise, but at the
turn of the century the very possibility of the Japanese entering
into competition with the Europeans, who held a predominant
position in China, gave rise to the first wave of fear of a 'yellow
peril' of Chinese brawn led by Japanese brain threatening the
West either with military force or with cheap exports. Such fears
have all but been forgotten and it is now not uncommon to refer to
the twenty-first century as a 'Pacific century', in the same way that
the nineteenth and twentieth centuries were 'Atlantic centuries'.

Only the Soviet Union in retaining many of its nineteenth-
century acquisitions seems also to have retained many nineteenth-
century attitudes, including the old fears of a 'yellow peril'. Thus it
was the Soviet Union which was the only Western country to greet
the signing of the Japan–China Treaty of Peace and Friendship
in 1978 with warnings of the dangers that this implied for the rest
of the world.

The current weakness of Europe's relations with Japan is shown
in the diagram (see page 153) which sums up the relations between
Europe, Japan and the USA.

While Japan and Europe both have cultural, political, security
and economic interests linking them with the USA and the USA
with them, the weak side of the triangle is the Japan–Europe side.
Not only is there no direct political or security linkage, but also
Europe's 'economic impulse' towards Asia and Japan has grown
far weaker (see dotted arrow) than Japan's 'economic impulse'
towards Europe and its neighbouring regions. Likewise Europe's
cultural influence over Japan is today greatly diminished.

This is in direct contrast to the situation one hundred years ago
when Europe was clearly much more powerful than Japan. Then
it seemed only natural for the Europeans to teach and for the
Japanese to learn. Today the roles are reversed. For a start,
European involvement in Asia, especially during the nineteenth
century, now seems merely a one-time intervention in the full
sweep of Asian history. In many ways the situation today has
reverted to pre-nineteenth-century patterns: China is again united, Japan is vastly strengthened and the European presence in

Relations between Europe, Japan and the USA,
including spheres closest to them

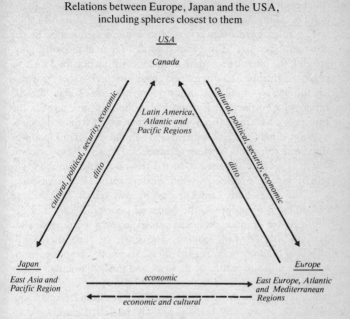

Asia is once more marginal. In line with these changes it is only natural that European trade with East Asia is less important to many countries there than it was in the nineteenth century. Indeed in several cases, including Japan, there has been a reversion to the old pattern of the European trade as a luxury trade. The difference is that this time round, Japan is an increasingly serious trade rival, not only in third markets in Asia, as she was already at the beginning of the twentieth century, but also in the United States and in markets throughout the world, including in Europe's backyard and in Europe itself.

One hundred years ago it was the Japanese complaining of sudden influxes of European goods disrupting domestic industries. Today the boot is on the other foot and it is the turn of the Europeans and Americans to plead with the Japanese to restrain their exports. The only difference is that today the Japanese do not send gunboats to keep the European markets open, as was the practice in the nineteenth century, when Europeans were in the habit of taking Japanese protectionist moves as a *casus belli*.

The roles have been reversed in other spheres too. In the nineteenth century, Europeans regarded Japan as an exotic playground, the ultimate in sophisticated tourism, while the Japanese regarded Europe as a disciplined group-oriented society possessing the secrets of efficient industrial production. Today, it is the Japanese who flock to Europe for exotic tourism and it is the Europeans who increasingly regard Japan as a disciplined society with amazingly efficient industries. Then the slogan in Japan was 'Japanese spirit and Western techniques' (*Wakon Yōsai*). Now it would make as much sense to turn it around and for Europeans to talk of 'Japanese techniques and Western spirit' (*Wasai Yōkon*).

In the nineteenth century, Europe was felt to be the very embodiment of progress, the home of political liberty and the world centre of innovation and new ideas. In a word, powerful, dynamic and outward-looking. The East, on the other hand, including Japan, was regarded as stagnant, despotic, non-scientific and superstitious, as weak and inward-looking. Today most of these simplistic contrasts have been stood on their head: political liberty has been extinguished repeatedly in Europe in the twentieth century by fascism and by Marxist-Leninist dictatorships. On the other hand, here and there in Asia, notably in Japan, liberty has taken root. Today Europe is no longer the world centre of new ideas and of the natural sciences, and in social and economic organization, it is often Europe which seems slow to change and parts of Asia which seem dynamic. The wheels of capitalism hum with energy in Japan (or in Singapore or in South Korea), where in Europe they merely tick over. This is of course seen in the much higher rates of GNP growth in these countries than in Europe. So high in fact that by the end of this century they will have a greater share of world exports and a larger share of global GNP than all the countries of the EC put together.

The contrasts between Japan and the Asian growth centres, on the one hand, and Europe, on the other, can also be sensed at the more impressionistic level. People walk slower in London or Paris than they do in Tokyo or in Singapore. It is often hard to escape the feeling that Europe has become the home of an elegant stagnation, while Japan and the other Asian countries following her lead throb with a fresh dynamism.

If the withdrawal of Europe from Asia has inevitably meant that direct political and security relations with Japan are fewer today than at the beginning of the century, the growth of Japan as one of the world's largest economic powers since the war has introduced new forms of interaction with Europe.

Firstly, these are indirect and concerned with multilateral economic issues rather than with the politics of national security. Europe and Japan share many values in common, they also face many of the same problems; the need to maintain their independence in a world of superpowers; the need for access to raw materials and energy supplies as well as access to export markets. In seeking solutions to these problems they are objective allies. They have a shared interest in maintaining an open trading system even if they compete strongly within that system.

Secondly, just at a time when European interests moved away from Asia and the predominant economic position of the USA vis-à-vis both Europe and Japan has been undermined, Japan's increasingly large role in the world economy has meant that her interests have moved closer to Europe and America. This shift in spheres of action has been the principal cause of friction, mainly of an economic and commercial nature, in the bilateral relations between Japan and Europe, as well as between Japan and the USA.

It is one of the main themes of this book that these long-run shifts in economic and political roles have not yet been accompanied by a corresponding adjustment of either Europe's or Japan's views of each other. Old images have persisted, thereby impeding communications and exacerbating trade frictions

These frictions have usually occurred when a decline in domestic demand in Japan leading to strong pressures to export coincides with a downturn of the business cycle in Europe, especially in labour-intensive industries. Reflecting a previous negative balance of payments, the yen at such times tends to be undervalued, thus giving Japan's exports an added advantage. The knife has been given an added twist if, in addition to scoring surpluses in trade with Europe, the Japanese balance of payments has moved into the black while her partners are still in the red. It happened during the Great Depression of 1929–32 and again during the 1970s when massive rises in the price of oil and other raw materials created a sharp new stimulus for Japan to export. Indeed the oil shocks of 1973 and 1979 triggered huge Japanese export booms which led directly to trade frictions with both Europe and America.

There are of course many other reasons why trade frictions have broken out between Japan and Europe. One conditioning factor is that both partners are poor in natural resources so that their trade is almost entirely in industrial goods. This is in striking contrast to Japan's trade with other major regions of the world – North and South America, Australasia, the Middle East, China or Southeast Asia for example – all of which regions include raw materials as an important element of their exports to Japan, with the result that the pattern of their trade with her is far more complementary than that of Europe's. Today Europe and Japan are in direct competition with each other.

And the nature of the competition has changed very rapidly; in the early days Japan's advantage in industries such as textiles lay in her cheap labour. Competition was primarily price competition. More recently, however, as Japan has developed her capital-intensive and knowledge-intensive industries, her comparative advantage has been in technology and efficiency, not in cheap labour. So competition today is less in price than it is in quality. The reaction in Europe to the latest Japanese challenge was often inadequate, geared more to the previous age when cheap exports from Japan were the problem. Insufficient efforts were made to meet the challenge by restructuring industries and by adopting new technologies.

A positive reaction was no doubt made that much more difficult by the fact that Japan's export drives, which built up very swiftly, were often concentrated precisely in those European industries which were for one reason or another already in decline and therefore suffering from high levels of unemployment. Moreover, these industries numbered some of the largest in the entire economy – steel, shipbuilding, cars, bearings, electronics. The very core of the industrial economy seemed threatened and political lobbies were quickly aroused. Japan was accused of operating with all kinds of unfair advantage, of keeping her own market closed and of exporting unemployment.

The most recent Japanese export drives have also come at a period when the principal economies of the world are far more tightly interconnected than ever before, but when the expansion of world trade and economic growth has slowed down and the floating exchange-rate system has been less and less effective in contributing to balance of payments adjustments. If one country recovers faster from recession than the others, it is then all too easy for that country to be seen as recovering at the expense of the others, especially if its recovery is based on exports. To make matters worse, in many European countries inflation, high levels of unemployment and falling productivity have become the norm.

Under these conditions timely restructuring of industries and development of strategies to cope with the Japanese challenge have been that much harder – instead there have been continual outbursts of trade frictions, on and off throughout the 1970s, and again, after the second oil shock, at the opening of the 1980s.

Before examining these in greater detail, it is perhaps worth taking a quick look at the steps by which Japan turned the tables on Europe and reversed her trading relationship with the West from one of almost total submission to one of something approaching dominance today.

14

Early Days

Trade relations between Europe and Japan have been unequal and unbalanced since the first trade treaties in 1866. For a hundred years they were unbalanced in Europe's favour, except during the two world wars. During all this time Japan had large deficits with Europe. After 1968 however the trade balance for the first time in history began moving steadily in Japan's favour.

The trade relations were unequal in the early days in the sense that Japan, although never becoming a colony, did sign unequal treaties which allowed *inter alia* extra-territoriality for foreign nations and denied Japan an independent commercial policy. Thus the government had no tariff autonomy and the duties on European imports were fixed at a uniformly low rate for almost fifty years from 1866 to 1911. In addition, Japan was obliged to accord most-favoured nation treatment to all foreign powers, without reciprocal treatment to Japan by them.

The trade itself has also been unequal in the sense that Europe has been a much more important source of supplies and market for Japan than Japan has been for Europe. This situation continues today, although Europe is a far less important trading partner for Japan than it was a hundred years ago.

From the Meiji Restoration (1868) to the First World War, Europe, chiefly Great Britain, was Japan's main supplier of modern goods, from munitions, factories and machines to textiles and cotton goods. In some years upwards of 70 per cent of all Japan's imports came from five European countries (Great Britain, France, Germany, Belgium and Italy). These were also the years when European exporters benefited from especially low tariffs. As a contemporary Japanese observer put it in 1890: 'The evils that Japan has suffered on account of her contact with European people does not so much consist in the overthrow of some of her old industries, by the free and sudden influx of foreign goods, as in her inability, on account of the treaties, to derive a revenue from that importation.'[1]

The trend was for a gradual shift to other suppliers, but it was not until 1915 that the United States exported more to Japan than the European countries (see Table 3). Europe was also Japan's major export market, principally for raw silk, tea and rice until the 1880s and 1890s, when the United States achieved that position.

In contrast to Europe's importance in Japan's trade during this early period, less than 1 per cent of Europe's imports came from Japan, while at the most Japan absorbed no more than 2.5 per cent of Europe's exports. In other words the trade relations were typical of those between a developed region and an under-developed country. Not only in the nature of the goods exchanged, but also in the different degree of importance attached to the trade by each partner. To Japan it was vital; to Europe it was marginal. The difference in the size of the bilateral trade in the total trade of each partner goes a long way to help explain the indifference of most Europeans towards the Japanese market, an indifference which has largely continued to this day.

In Europe there were many who would have agreed with Adam Smith's optimistic judgement that China was 'perhaps in extent not much inferior to the market of all the different countries of Europe put together'.[2] Nobody felt the same about Japan, particularly as the Japanese were already developing a domestic manufacturing industry (led by textiles) capable of competing with Europe.

Already long before the Meiji Restoration one of the scholars of Dutch learning, Honda Toshiaki (1744–1821), had outlined a basic mercantilist plan for his country:

As part of a national policy, every effort should be made to promote the production in this country of articles that are of as fine manufacture as possible. If such efforts are made, individual industries will be encouraged, and attempts to improve the quality of Japanese products will follow. In that way many articles famed for their excellence will be produced in this country. This will help us gain profit when trading with foreign nations.[3]

Honda was well ahead of his time and mercantilism made little impression on his countrymen until the Meiji period, but from then on it was to have great influence on Japanese policy makers as they sought to win back control of Japan's trade from foreign hands and as they pursued the aim of catching up with the West and 'excelling the nations of the whole world'.[4]

Protectionism as a means of enabling Japan's industries to grow was first extensively aired during the debate over treaty reform in the 1870s and 1880s.[5]

Cromwell and Colbert were praised as 'extraordinary men and the fathers of protection' who had laid the ground for the wealth and prosperity of England and France. It was observed that 'even England initially followed mercantile theories . . . only much later did Adam Smith advocate free trade . . . only when England was prosperous and strong did she move to free trade'. Therefore, looking into the future, 'if we reach the point some years hence where the trade and industry of our people both surpass that of foreigners and where there is no wastage of our human and soil resources, the time will perhaps have come when we too may adopt free trade'.[6]

Herbert Spencer's advice, to be passed to Prime Minister Itō in 1892, was very much in line with this thinking:

The Japanese policy should . . . be of *keeping Americans and Europeans as much as possible at arm's length* . . . It seems to me that the only forms of intercourse which you may with advantage permit are those which are indispensable for the exchange of commodities – importation and exportation of physical and mental products. Apparently you are proposing by revision of the treaty with the powers of Europe and America 'to open the whole Empire to foreigners and foreign capital'. I regret this as a fatal policy. If you wish to see what is likely to happen, study the history of India . . .

There should be, not only a prohibition of foreign persons to hold property in land, but also a refusal to give them leases, and a permission only to reside as annual tenants . . .

. . . prohibit to foreigners the working of mines owned or worked by the
Government.
. . . keep the coasting trade in your own hands and forbid foreigners to
engage in it . . .
The distribution of commodities brought to Japan from other places may
be properly left to the Japanese themselves, and should be denied to
foreigners . . .
. . . respecting the intermarriage of foreigners and Japanese . . . it should
be positively forbidden.[7]

The governments of Japan did pursue mercantilist policies,
including policies of import substitution, from that day on, so
successfully that when trade liberalization finally started to come
in the 1960s, many foreign observers, perhaps understandably,
continued to believe that Japan was only a partially opened
market.

Expatriate European businessmen in those far-off nineteenth-
century days complained bitterly. Echoes of some of their complaints are still heard even today. The following summary, for
example, was contained in a European guide to Japan first
published in 1890, which is still in print and on sale in every hotel
in Japan catering to foreign visitors.

European bankers and merchants in Japan . . . complain it is true, not
so much of actual, wilful dishonesty – though of that too, they affirm there
is plenty – as of pettiness, constant shilly-shallying, unbusinesslikeness
almost passing belief. Japan, the globetrotter's paradise, is also the grave
of the merchant's hopes.[8]

Another early complaint, this time from 1892, has also been
repeated from that day to this:

In commercial matters the Japanese have exhibited their imitativeness
in the most extraordinary degree. Almost everything they have once
bought, from beer to bayonets and from straw hats to heavy ordnance,
they have since learned to make for themselves. There is hardly a
well-known European trademark that you do not find fraudulently imitated in Japan . . .[9]

It was not all complaints however. Observers pointed out some

Table 3. Per Cent Share of Japan's Exports and Imports with Nine European Countries and with the USA (1873–1981)

	Japan's Exports				Japan's Imports				Cover ratio with nine European countries (percentage)
	Per cent share to nine European countries	Rank	Per cent share to USA	Rank	Per cent share from nine European countries	Rank	Per cent share from USA	Rank	
1873	51.9	1st	19.5	3rd	58.5	1st	3.6	3rd	67
1878	38.8	1st	22.5	3rd	74.2	1st	8.3	3rd	52
1883	41.8	1st	37.1	2nd	58.0	1st	11.2	3rd	91
1888	38.9	1st	35.5	2nd	59.7	1st	8.6	4th	63
1893	31.7	1st	31.5	2nd	44.9	1st	6.9	6th	70
1898	20.7	2nd	29.1	1st	36.1	1st	14.4	3rd	34
1900	21.0	2nd	26.5	1st	41.1	1st	21.8	2nd	35
1905	16.7	3rd	29.2	2nd	35.9	1st	21.3	2nd	31
1910	22.5	2nd	31.3	1st	33.4	1st	11.8	4th	66
1915	16.1	3rd	28.8	1st	13.0	4th	19.3	2nd	166
1920	9.8	4th	29.0	1st	13.1	3rd	41.6	1st	69
1925	6.2	4th	43.6	1st	11.9	3rd	25.8	1st	47

1930	8.0	34.4	4th	15.3	1st	28.6	2nd	1st	50
1933	9.0	26.4	4th	11.7	1st	22.4	2nd	1st	90
1938	8.7	15.8	5th	10.3	2nd	34.4	3rd	1st	85
1949	11.1	18.1	3rd	3.0	1st	62.2	3rd	1st	122
1953	7.2	17.8	4th	6.5	1st	31.4	3rd	1st	58
1955	7.6	22.3	2nd	5.5	1st	31.2	3rd	1st	114
1960	7.8	27.2	2nd	7.0	1st	34.6	3rd	1st	101
1965	8.8	29.3	2nd	7.0	1st	29.0	2nd	1st	130
1970	9.6	30.7	2nd	8.2	1st	29.4	2nd	1st	120
1973	11.9	25.6	2nd	8.3	1st	24.2	3rd	1st	138
1974	10.7	23.0	2nd	6.4	1st	20.4	6th	1st	150
1975	10.2	20.0	2nd	5.8	1st	20.1	6th	1st	168
1976	10.8	23.3	2nd	5.6	1st	18.2	6th	1st	200
1977	10.9	24.5	2nd	5.9	1st	17.5	6th	1st	208
1978	11.4	25.4	2nd	7.7	1st	18.6	3rd	1st	183
1979	12.3	25.6	2nd	6.8	1st	18.4	4th	1st	168
1980	12.8	24.2	2nd	5.6	1st	17.3	4th	1st	212
1981	12.4	25.3	2nd	6.0	1st	17.6	4th	1st	221

Note: Cover ratio equals the percentage of exports over imports. The years 1873 and 1878 are based on Japan's trade with the UK, France, Germany, Italy, Holland and Belgium (*Source:* calculated from Ishibashi Tanzan, *The Foreign Trade of Japan*, Tokyo, 1935). From 1883 to 1930 the figures show Japan's trade with these countries as well as Denmark and from 1935 onwards Ireland and Luxemburg are also included: from 1981, Greece is also included. The source for 1883 to 1981 is the Ministry of Finance, Tokyo, Exports, FOB; Imports, CIF.

hard facts about Japanese business successes as well as some of the
long-range consequences of Japan's industrialization.

Sir Henry Norman, for example, the English traveller, journalist and expert on the Far East, wrote in 1895 that Japan had
become a first-class power because of her army and the defeat of
China, and he continued:

> The second aspect, under which the progress of Japan is of great interest
> to Western nations, is that of a rival in manufactures. This is a far more
> serious question, especially to Great Britain, than is yet generally under-
> stood. The truth is that our manufactures are actually being driven out of
> many markets of the East by the Japanese, and that the most competent
> observers prophesy the rapid development of this process.

Sir Henry went on to quote a certain Mr Gubbins of the British
Legation in Tokyo who had written in a report on industries such
as cotton, watch-making and match-making, 'so far as the Eastern
market is concerned, no country can any longer compete with
Japan'. Sir Henry also quotes another British official, a Mr Hunt
stationed in Pusan in Korea, who had reported to London that:

> While the great bulk of the piece goods and metals sold in Pusan are of
> European origin, principally British, the fact should not be overlooked
> that Japan, by carefully studying arising needs, and supplying articles
> suitable to the tastes and means of Koreans and her Pusan colonists, is able
> to compete, more successfully each year, with almost all the goods of
> European manufacture.[10]

Mr Hunt's analysis was simple, but it retains its validity to this
day.

In Part I, we saw that Japan's victory over the Qing Empire in
1895 had already touched off a fear of a new 'economic yellow
peril'. Some even began speculating that the centre of world
power was moving to the Pacific. Sir Henry was one of them:
'under [the Mikado] the dreams of the supremacy of the yellow
race in Europe, Asia and even Africa . . . would be no longer
mere nightmares. Instead of speculating as to whether England or
Germany or Russia is to be the next world's ruler, we might have
to learn that Japan was on its way to that position.'[11]

But most people in Europe were hardly aware that the lesson

existed. In Britain, which conducted the lion's share of Europe's trade with Japan until overtaken by Germany in 1929, a contemporary complained that:

Japan's material and industrial progress since 1890 has been even more marked than that which she has shown in military and constitutional affairs, though even to this day what she has achieved in this respect meets but with scant recognition among the manufacturers and merchants of Great Britain, who have failed alike to recognize the already great and always growing importance of Japan as a market for their own products or the possibility of her becoming a formidable competitor with them, not only in the Far East, but even in Australia and India.[12]

In the years to come Europeans were to prove much more concerned about Japanese competition in third markets and in Europe itself than about their failure to penetrate the Japanese market, which had early acquired the reputation of being 'the grave of the merchant's hopes'.

As a result of the First World War, Europe was unable to maintain its exports to Japan and the United States became Japan's main supplier. Europe's trade with Japan moved into deficit for the first time (see Table 3). Japan was far from the active theatres of the war and her industries had reached a stage where they were able to take advantage of markets which the European countries were unable to supply because of war – in Asia or Africa, for example. For the first time in modern history Japan began scoring large trade surpluses and, also for the first time, most of her external trade now came to be conducted by Japanese companies.

After the war, although Europe never regained the central role it had played in Japan's modernization, it still continued to be a major trading partner for Japan.

Bit by bit as Japan built up her light industries and began to expand her exports to world markets, the warnings and complaints grew in Europe. Many of them echoed the remarks already quoted, or observations such as that made by the American historian, Brooks Adams, at the end of the nineteenth century:

Even now factories can be equipped almost as easily in India, Japan and China, as in Lancashire or Massachusetts, and the products of the cheapest labour can be sold more advantageously in European capitals than those of Tyre and Alexandria were in Rome under the Antonines.[13]

For those who did not take quite such a long historical view of the newly industrializing countries of that day as Brooks Adams, there was also the recent memory of the rise of Germany as an exporter of manufactured goods towards the end of the nineteenth century. At that time too there had been accusations against the Germans, mainly from the British, of low wages and dumping; of state subsidies and of stealing of patents and fraudulent imitation of trademarks.

Denunciation of Japan's supposedly unfair trading practices reached a peak at the time of the Great Depression in the early 1930s, when Japan alone of the industrial powers was able to increase her exports (two thirds of which were textiles and raw silk). The most vociferous lobbies calling for the closing of European and colonial markets to Japanese exports were formed by labour-intensive light industries, for example, the textiles of Lancashire, Lyons or Krefeld, which were already non-competitive on world markets and saw themselves dethroned by the Japanese from a hundred-year position of world supremacy.

By no means all voices in Europe were turned against Japan however. A study group in Paris produced an eminently fair-minded report amongst whose conclusions were that the Japanese were not practising dumping and that Japanese industry produced well-made goods at reasonable prices. If Japan had lower wages than in Europe this was because the Japanese were used to a less lavish style of life.[14] In England, the Federation of British Industries (FBI) sent a delegation to Japan in 1934 which reported with equal fairmindedness on its return that Japanese industry had benefited from the depreciation of the yen, lack of domestic inflation and the absence of an organized movement demanding increased wages. It rejected the notion of 'sweated labour', although noting the very poor conditions in the traditional sector of Japanese industry, which sector it concluded should be held responsible for generating a good deal of the domestic competition which had led to the fierce pressures to export. The vital role of government was noted. The report also drew attention to the high productivity of Japanese industry and warned that 'it would be unwise to assume that the future export activities of Japan will be limited to cheap goods of low quality'.

In its recommendations the FBI rejected protective measures whose outcome would be a trade war beneficial to no one and suggested instead:

A means of co-operation between British and Japanese industry . . . There are many different ways in which such co-operation might be realised. It might be by conscious directional control of exports; by means of a division of markets upon a percentage or some other quantitative basis; by some similar agreement on a territorial basis; by mutual action to develop in co-operation some of the more backward markets of the world; by agreements as to the level of export prices; by some rationalization of production according to type and quality; or by joint manufacturing activities.[15]

The report did not enter into further detail on industrial co-operation, recognizing that this should be the work of the FBI and the Japan Economic Federation Committees set up in London and Tokyo, and also that no general principle could be laid down which would suit all cases. Therefore it was felt that each industry should be left to decide for itself whether it wished to attempt to reach an understanding with its corresponding industry in Japan.

Given the economic depression in Europe and the popular outcry against Japan, such reasonable voices went unheeded. It became politically expedient to follow the pack and Japan was the obvious scapegoat. Discriminatory quotas and high tariffs were set whose effect was to gradually close European and colonial markets to Japanese goods. The Japanese reaction was to concentrate on markets closer to home. In 1916, Korea, Formosa and Manchuria took 16 per cent of Japan's exports. By 1937 this had risen to 38 per cent.

These years of rejection by the West and the closing of its markets to Japanese goods saw an ideological 'return to the East' in Japan, whose hallmark was a militant anti-Western Pan-Asianism. Indeed the war in north China was frequently justified as a legitimate search by Japan for new markets to replace those closed to her by Western protectionism.[16]

It was felt that Japan had been unfairly picked on, in the words of a Ministry of War pamphlet of 1934: 'countries suffering economic stagnation and anxiety concerning the international situation are jealous of the Empire's foreign trade expansion and her growing political power'.[17] It was pointed out that Japan had only been practising what she had had to learn by force from the West, namely free trade. The Japanese, it was claimed, had been able to rationalize their industries with new equipment because of the co-operation of the workers, which co-operation was notably lacking in Europe. Moreover, Japanese labour was frugal and worked hard while in the West 'labour aims at working the shortest possible hours, doing the minimum amount of work and getting the highest possible wage'. With some justification a Japanese official writing in a 'non-official' capacity observed in 1934:

Eighty years ago, Japan was compelled to open her door to Europe and America. Small-scale industries of Japan could not stand the competition of Western goods which were produced with superior machinery. Consequently they all ceased to exist. That is history. Japan was then told that free trade was a means whereby the common welfare of mankind was promoted. By discarding industries which did not suit her and by concentrating on those best suited to her, she has now attained that stage where some of her industries are superior to those of the old industrial countries. As soon as she begins competing with them, she is condemned in the name of humanity.[18]

Many of the arguments used on both sides not only had a pedigree stretching back to the turn of the century, but they were also to be repeated in the post-war period and again after the oil shocks in the 1970s and 1980s.

But one difference between the situation in the 1930s and today is that at that time both Britain and France had the option vis-à-vis their domestic industrial lobbies to reserve their Asian possessions as a privileged export area. Britain in addition had a preferential relation with Commonwealth countries such as Australia, New Zealand and Canada. A position which she does not have today when at least two of them do more trade with Japan than they do either with her or with the entire EC.

It took a number of years after the Pacific War for trade to recover to prewar levels. For most of Japan's European trading partners this had been achieved by the mid 1950s, at which time there was also a return to the old unbalanced pattern of a large European surplus.

In 1955 Japan entered the General Agreement on Tariffs and Trade (GATT), but several of the European countries refused to extend most-favoured nation treatment to her (in other words they invoked GATT Article XXXV).

The issue was widely followed in Japan. On a visit there at this time, the executive secretary of the GATT was reported to have encountered a taxi driver in a remote provincial town who, upon learning that his passenger was a GATT official from Geneva, immediately exclaimed, 'Ah, that Article XXXV!'

Japan's trade policy was therefore directed towards concluding individual trade agreements which sought to dismantle residual protectionist instruments such as discriminatory quantitative restrictions against her exports.

The problem was that the old fears of Japan flooding European markets with cheap goods were still very much alive and it was for this reason that import restrictions had been set up even before Japanese imports had started arriving. It was also noted that the Japanese market itself was securely closed to European exports. Only by about the time when Japan was admitted as a full member of OECD (in 1964) was it that most of the European countries agreed to dis-invoke Article XXXV, and to dismantle discriminatory quantitative restrictions against her. Even so, several countries still insisted as a quid pro quo on having a safeguard clause included in their trade agreements with Japan entitling them to take unilateral measures to stop Japanese imports in case of 'emergency'.

Today the number of discriminatory quantitative restrictions has been greatly reduced, but their continued existence is still regarded in resource-poor Japan, ever sensitive to such discriminations, as psychologically offensive, a stumbling-block to improving EC–Japan relations.[19]

Table 4. The EC (Eur 9) and Japan: World Trade and Bilateral Trade
(1960–70)

Unit = billion US $

		1960		1970
Extra EC (Eur 9)	Imports	28.7	×2	57.4
World trade	Exports	25.9	×2.1	55.7
Japan's world trade	Imports	4.5	×4.2	18.9
	Exports	4.1	×4.8	19.3
EC trade with Japan	Imports	0.3	×5.9	1.7
	Exports	0.3	×4.7	1.4

Source: Eurostat and Ministry of Finance, Tokyo; Exports FOB, Imports CIF.

During the 1960s, Japan's world trade was growing at about twice the speed of that of Europe. The bilateral trade between Europe and Japan was more or less in balance over the decade however, with Europe's exports to Japan growing at about the same speed as its imports from Japan. The trade was not very large but it was increasing rapidly.

The main concern in Europe at the time continued to be the defensive effort to prevent sudden concentrations or influxes of Japanese imports into the European market in certain 'sensitive' sectors such as cotton textiles, ceramics, shoes, umbrellas, cutlery, and then at the end of the decade, cameras, bearings and steel. There were also criticisms of Japan's rapidly growing share of the world shipbuilding market. Several of these items, notably the bigger ones such as steel, ships and bearings, were still problem sectors ten to fifteen years later. In other words the modernization and restructuring of these European industries to meet the Japanese challenge had either been too slow, or, in some cases, had not taken place at all.

The EC Commission *Bulletin* of December 1969 noted that although Japan 'had still been a feudal country one hundred years ago' she had become the third greatest economic power in the world. The reasons for this expansion, it continued, were that 'the population is characterized by its discipline, its enthusiasm for work, its sobriety and its capacity for adaptation'. Also the government had followed an active policy of expansion and channelled investments into knowledge-intensive industry since the war in preference to encouraging private consumption. Private industry 'combined patriarchal principles with modern management in a rational organization of production'. The article concluded that because Japan appeared to wish to diversify its exports from too great a dependence on the USA, and because the Japanese market offered excellent opportunities for European exporters, there was very considerable interest in concluding an EC–Japan trade agreement. The article noted that it would be necessary for the Japanese to open up their market to European exports and investments by dismantling tariff and non-tariff barriers. The European Parliament also produced a long document on relations with Japan at this time which reached the same conclusions.[20] Neither of these policy papers made much impact either in Europe or in Japan, but ten years later, when the EC Commission produced a very similar analysis, using somewhat more colourful language, it was, as we shall see, to produce an uproar in Japan.

Continuing efforts were made to put the Community house in order in the 1960s, chiefly by seeking to co-ordinate member states' trade negotiations with Japan by means of prior consultation.[21]

Some progress was also made towards the harmonizing of the member states' import regimes, but there was no success in the EC Commission's attempt to secure a mandate from the member states to negotiate a Community trade agreement with Japan until 1970 when negotiations were finally opened. They soon broke down.

The problem was the old one: the European countries' fear of Japan's exports led them to seek a Community-wide safeguard clause in any agreement with Japan. At the same time they also sought assurances that the Japanese market, which was kept securely shut at this time, would be fully opened to their exports. The Japanese authorities, on the other hand, while seeking the dismantling of the remaining discriminatory quantitative restrictions applied against Japanese exports to Europe, did not wish to conclude an agreement containing a Community-wide safeguard clause. And that is where the problem still rests today despite unsuccessful EC Commission efforts to secure a mandate from the member states to reopen negotiations in 1980.

By the end of the 1960s, Japan's balance of trade was growing so fast that her trading partners feared a serious dislocation of the international trading system, not to speak of the rapid unbalancing of their own bilateral trade with Japan. In 1971 Japan scored her highest balance of payments surplus in history. Not for the first time Europeans were taken by surprise and took note of Japan only when they were forced to.

European politicians began to visit Tokyo, such as British Prime Minister Heath in 1972, to register their concern; a wave of protectionist sentiment was touched off and Japan was accused of dumping and subsidizing exports. Ralf Dahrendorf, the EC external relations commissioner of the time, only voiced a widespread European view when he pointed out that 'in Japan protectionism is traditional', and he called for closer relations between the EC and Japan and the further opening of the Japanese market to EC exports, as necessary moves to stop a chain reaction leading to world-wide protectionism.[22]

The measures taken by the Japanese authorities in 1971 and 1972, under very strong American and European pressure to rectify the balance of payments surplus and to open the Japanese market, need not detain us here. Suffice it to say that they were effective in the short run, but quickly rendered out of date by the rapid shifts in the world economic scene in 1973, which rang down the curtain on Act 1 of the post-war Japan–US and Japan–Europe trade frictions

15

Japan Catches Up

The breakdown of the international monetary system in the early 1970s and the huge increase in the prices of raw materials, highlighted by the dramatic rise in the price of oil after 1973, effectively brought to an end the post-war period. Growth in the industrial countries declined sharply and in many cases became negative. Most experienced massive inflation. These changes were accompanied by a revulsion from previous goals of economic growth and a running chorus of wry or alarmist talk of 'Gross National Pollution' or the 'limits to growth'. It was in these years that the novel *Japan Sinks* hit the bestseller list in Tokyo.

The immediate way out for resource-poor trading nations, such as the European countries and Japan, became 'export or perish' and competition between them became much sharper than ever before. Despite the measures taken by the Japanese authorities to open the Japanese market to foreign imports in 1971 and 1972, the European deficit with Japan continued to grow as Japan entered into one of her biggest export drives of modern times.

It soon became evident that partly through good planning and official encouragement of new industries, partly through large investments in new plant and equipment, and partly through luck, Japan in the 1960s had better prepared her economy to meet the needs of new export markets in the 1970s than had Europe. This was reflected in the more lively global export performance of Japan than the European Community during the 1970s.

Between 1970 and 1980, in current dollar terms, Japan's exports to the world increased seven times, while her exports to the Community increased ten times. In contrast the Nine's exports to the world and to Japan both increased by only about five times.

The Community's imports from Japan continued to grow at nearly twice the speed of its imports from the world. In contrast Japan's exports to the Community grew faster than her world exports while imports from the Community grew slower than her world imports.

The result was that throughout these years Japan had an ever larger trade surplus with the EC, thus reversing the historic pattern of a deficit with Europe for the first time in a hundred years.

Since the Meiji period Japanese leaders had pursued the aim of 'excelling the nations of the whole world'. By the early 1970s, at least insofar as trade with Europe was concerned, Japan had caught up.

She had caught up not only in the sense that she had now a large and growing trade surplus with Europe, but also instead of importing manufactured goods and exporting raw materials and light industrial goods as she had done up to about 1955 in her trade with Europe, more than 90 per cent of her exports to Europe were now manufactured goods. Moreover, even as late as 1960, 55 per cent of her manufactured goods exports to the EC (which is symptomatic of her trade with Western Europe as a whole) were from labour-intensive industries such as leather or textiles. By

Table 5. The EC (Eur 9) and Japan: World Trade and Bilateral Trade
(1970–80)

Unit = billion US $

		1970	1980
Extra EC (Eur 9)	Imports to EC	59.4 × 6.4	378.2
World trade	Exports to world	55.7 × 5.6	312.6
Japan's world trade	Imports	18.9 × 7.4	140.5
	Exports	19.3 × 6.7	129.8
EC trade with Japan	Imports to EC	1.7 × 10.3	17.4
	Exports to Japan	1.4 × 4.5	6.3

Source: Eurostat and Ministry of Finance, Japan; Exports FOB, Imports CIF.

1976 this share had fallen to 8 per cent. Her exports of goods such as steel, ships, cars and household electronics which required skilled labour and considerable capital inputs rose from a 14 per cent share to a 54 per cent share between 1955 and 1976. During the same period her knowledge-intensive exports to the EC such as general machinery, pharmaceuticals, telecommunications etc. rose from a 4 per cent to a 24 per cent share. In other words, reflecting the changes in Japanese industrial structure in the 1950s and 1960s, there had been a continuing shift away from light industrial exports to heavy industrial goods, and then from these to knowledge-intensive exports. Instead of challenging Europe in labour-intensive or low value-added industries as she had done in earlier decades, Japan was now competing successfully with some of Europe's largest and most prestigious industries.

The converse trend is seen in the EC's exports to Japan, where increasingly it is the labour-intensive industrial and luxury consumer goods which alone can find a market, while exports of basic intermediate and capital goods have declined in importance since the mid-1960s.[23]

Another remarkable change in EC–Japan trade is that in the past, as we have seen, it accounted for a huge share of Japan's total trade and a tiny share of Europe's trade, making it axiomatic that Japan needed Europe far more than Europe needed Japan. In recent years, however, only about 5 per cent to 6 per cent of Japan's total imports came from the EC, which is roughly comparable to the 4 per cent to 5 per cent of the EC's imports which came from Japan, making Japan the EC's fourth main supplier after the US, Saudi Arabia and Switzerland. As an export market, however, the EC still remains more important for Japan than Japan is for the EC (12 per cent of Japan's exports went to the EC, making it her third largest regional market in 1981. By contrast, only 2 per cent of the EC's exports went to Japan, which was only its twelfth largest market in that year).

For most of the 1970s, the Europeans were thrown on the defensive and could only request the Japanese to co-operate by restricting their exports. Voluntary export restraints by Japanese producers (known as 'orderly marketing agreements') were negotiated either by industries, by governments or by the EC Commission. They covered a very large part of the total of Japanese exports to the European Community – radios, tape-recorders, television tubes, steel and cars were under more or less constant limitation of one kind or another throughout the decade. In the ship sector Japan was persuaded to raise her prices and institute capacity cutbacks. But even after these were implemented she managed to maintain 40 per cent to 50 per cent of the world order book for new ships. Bearings were the object of three dumping investigations which led to the Japanese makers increasing their export prices and eventually to setting up factories in Europe. But here too there was no decrease in sales. On the contrary, they continued to boom.

The large number of orderly marketing agreements (all of which lay outside the GATT), the fact that the European countries with safeguard clauses in their bilateral treaties with Japan have almost never invoked them, and the small number of anti-dumping actions against Japanese exports in the 1970s, all suggest that the policy tools for regulating international trade of the post-war era, which were designed to deal with unfair trading practices, were simply inappropriate to meet the challenge posed by industries which gained their advantage through greater technological sophistication and the superior quality, marketing and after-sales service of their products.

The best the Europeans could do was to seek a breathing space to enable their industries to restructure in order to be able more effectively to meet the competition from Japan. The trouble was that too often the breathing space was not used to restructure or to improve the productivity of European industries, which seemed either unable to appreciate the nature of the challenge facing them or unable to adapt. The decline of the textiles industry was followed by shipbuilding, which in turn was followed by steel. In some European countries home electronics and the automobile industry had begun to falter already in the mid 1970s.

The decline of such key industries in the European Community, many of which employ millions of workers, produced a highly charged atmosphere in which scapegoats were sought. Domestically the blame was laid on the trade unions or on management, or on the welfare state. Abroad, the obvious candidate for scapegoat was the country whose export industries were so successfully cutting a swathe into European and world markets, namely Japan.

In an effort to head off the protectionist pressures which so easily build up in this kind of atmosphere, the EC Commission repeatedly emphasized the necessity of increasing access to the Japanese market for European exporters.

A shift in other words from a defensive to an active policy. One way of achieving this was to lower tariffs. An exercise conducted in the Kennedy and Tokyo rounds of the multilateral trade negotiations in Geneva. Another approach, in consultation with the Japanese authorities, was to remove difficulties encountered on the Japanese market other than those presented by high tariffs.

Such 'non-tariff' barriers (NTBs) usually involved Japanese government regulations covering health, safety, industrial or environmental standards and customs procedures which were considered to be a real hindrance by European and other exporters, who complained of high costs and long delays.

In order to remove such barriers, the EC Commission sat down with the Japanese authorities, usually in Tokyo, and held talks on NTBs, the list of which gives some idea of the broad scope of the topics covered:

automobile type approval procedures and postponement of exhaust emission regulations;
agricultural processed foodstuffs;
pharmaceutical, chemical and agro-chemical testing standards;
diesel engine tests;
the banking sector;
standards for household appliances and cosmetics;
trademarks;
phytosanitary regulations;
electrical and gas appliance standards;
sanitary fittings standards.

One of the main NTBs dealt with before the outbreak of the EC–Japan trade frictions in October 1976 was the question of testing for automobile type approvals, which were felt to be more cumbersome in Japan than in the EC, and the introduction of stringent new Japanese emission regulations. The background to the EC–Japan car problem is similar to that in many other industries: overwhelming Japanese strength on her domestic market followed by a very rapid expansion on world markets, including the EC. This expansion coincided with and in part contributed to a decline of the European industry, which with increasing success called for protection against Japanese imports. Twenty years ago, the Japanese automobile industry was nurtured on the domestic market and grew very rapidly from a production of 400,000 units in 1963 to 4.4 million units in 1973, to 7.0 million units in 1980. Imports in the early part of this period were blocked by high tariffs. In 1963 Japan imported only 9,000 foreign cars. In 1973 the figure had risen to a mere 37,000. Automobile imports were liberated in the early 1970s, but by then the costs of entering the market were so high, and the domestic competition was so strong, that foreign makers did not consider it worth making the effort. In 1981 imports of foreign cars into Japan were not much higher, at 46,000 units, than they had been in 1973.

By 1980, thanks to a timely adaptation of their industry to producing reliable energy-saving cars, the Japanese had become the world's number one manufacturer and exporter of cars. Another record was broken: in 1981 only one car was imported for every ninety-five cars exported (compare the EC with 1.4 cars imported for every car exported and the US with four cars imported for every car exported).

Japanese wages in the car industry were above the European average by 1980 but about 10 per cent below those of German car workers. The Japanese workers also worked longer hours, were less frequently absent and took fewer paid holidays. Most important of all, investment in advanced technology and huge production runs contributed to the much higher productivity of the Japanese car industry compared with that of Europe or America. As a result the ex-factory price of Japanese cars was not nearly as high as comparable European and American models.

While the Japanese industry was gaining its lead in the 1970s, the European industry was already in decline. European car exports to the world declined by 30 per cent between 1970 and 1980 largely because they could not compete with Japanese exports. This trend was very striking on the North American market. In 1970, European makers had a 68 per cent share of the foreign car market there while the Japanese had only 28 per cent. By 1980 the tables were turned: the Japanese makers took a 76 per cent share compared with a European share of 21 per cent. The same was true of other markets around the globe including the Far East. There the European share fell from 34 per cent in 1970 to 20 per cent in 1980 while the Japanese share increased from 58 per cent to 70 per cent over the same period.

Given this background it is not hard to guess the trend in the EC–Japan bilateral trade in automobiles which is neatly summed up in the following table (Table 6).

Table 6. EC (Eur 9)–Japan Bilateral Automobile Trade (1970–81)
(Number, percentage)

	Registration in the EC of passenger cars imported from Japan	Japan's market share in EC (total registrations)	Registration in Japan of passenger cars imported from the EC	EC's market share in Japan (total registrations)
1970	31,923	0.6	11,313	0.7
1971	52,328	0.9	12,718	0.7
1972	90,286	1.5	17,578	0.8
1973	229,522	2.9	20,525	0.8
1974	218,624	3.3	24,855	1.2
1975	313,645	4.6	25,842	1.0
1976	402,139	5.2	25,318	1.1
1977	467,896	6.8	25,903	1.1
1978	511,422	6.0	34,626	1.3
1979	585,824	7.9	41,586	1.5
1980	756,000	11.1	32,500	1.1
1981	700,000	8.3	29,412	1.0

Source: Japanese passenger cars registered in Europe: The Japan Automobile Manufacturers' Association.
EC passenger cars registered in Japan: The Japan Automobile Importers' Association.

In 1970, 32,000 Japanese cars were registered in the EC. By 1980 this had risen to 756,000. From having a market share of 0.6 per cent in 1970, she had now achieved a market share of 11 per cent. The increase had been earlier in the decade for countries like England whose automobile industry was already in decline, or for those countries like Denmark or Ireland with no domestic car industry of their own. The cracking of the tougher nut of the German market came at the very end of the decade and the beginning of the 1980s.

In 1981, as a result of Japanese voluntary restraint, the registration of Japanese cars in the EC declined slightly for the first time in a decade, as also did Japan's market share.

Over the same period, the EC's share of the Japanese automobile market, which had been roughly comparable to Japan's share of the EC market in 1970 at 0.7 per cent, had risen to only 1.0 per cent by 1981, in which year only 29,412 European cars were sold in Japan compared with the 700,000 Japanese cars sold in the EC. The importance of automobile exports for Japan may be appreciated by the fact that in 1981 they accounted for no less than 15 per cent of her total exports to the EC, amounting to 2.8 billion dollars (compared with the value of the EC's car exports to Japan of 271 million dollars which was only 3 per cent of its total exports to Japan).

Automobile makers in Europe referred quite openly to the fact that Japan's markets were closed in the 1950s and 1960s, and to the overwhelmingly strong position of the Japanese auto industry in the 1970s in its own domestic market, as the main reasons making it not worthwhile to make the effort to export cars to Japan.

Meanwhile, in Italy imports of Japanese cars were limited throughout the decade to 2,200 a year by a government import quota, and in other parts of Europe there were calls from both management and the unions to cut back imports of Japanese cars. By the end of the 1970s Japanese imports were limited to approximately a 10 per cent share of the British market and a 3 per cent share of the French market.

It was against this background that the EC Commission proposed already in 1975 that the automobile trade problems with

Japan be made a Community issue, and that the stress be placed on increasing European car exports to Japan, rather than cutting off Japanese car exports to Europe. If it could be convincingly shown for once and all that the Japanese market was fully open, then the European manufacturers might be persuaded to adopt an effective sales policy to Japan.

The problems had already been discussed with the Japanese authorities at member state level, principally by the Germans and British, but they had been largely unsuccessful in their efforts to persuade the Japanese Transport Ministry to speed up and simplify the inspection of foreign cars, and also to grant a grace period for imported European cars before the application of the new exhaust emission regulations.

The issue was indeed made a Community one in autumn 1975, and following EC–Japan specialist consultations in Tokyo in May 1976 and in January 1977, eventually the Japanese authorities did recognize that there was a problem of reciprocity of market access, and they agreed that type-approval tests for European cars for export to Japan could be carried out in Europe and that foreign cars would be allowed a three-year grace period in which to meet the new exhaust emission regulations which were due to come into force on 1 April 1978.

The various efforts both to avoid difficulties caused in Europe in sensitive sectors by the sudden influx of Japanese goods and also to improve access to the Japanese market by removing non-tariff barriers were no doubt useful and necessary steps to keep the trade between Europe and Japan operating smoothly, and hopefully in the latter case to allay suspicions on the European side that the Japanese market was not fully open. The trouble was that despite these efforts by European and Japanese officials and industrialists, the results by their very nature were not calculated to be dramatic. The trade effects of removing NTBs could never be immediate and they could rarely hope to be more than significant at the margin.

Over the years considerable progress was made in some sectors. Cars have already been mentioned; successful efforts were also made to bring Japanese chemical and pharmaceutical tests more in line with international practice, and thereby to accord to

European exporters similar conditions of market entry as enjoyed by Japanese exporters to Europe.

Even those most wildly optimistic on the European side, however, never believed that the gradual removal of NTBs would fundamentally change the bilateral trade balance. Nobody believed that the further opening of the Japanese market would automatically lead to an export boom to Japan, because the market, as we shall see in a moment, was by the 1970s, for structural reasons, only able to absorb a limited amount of manufactured imports. Moreover, by the time that it was liberalized, it was often just too competitive. In fact the opening of the Japanese market coincided with the enormous increases of Japan's trade surpluses, which were therefore clearly not the result of a closed domestic market, but the fruit of a successful Japanese export drive.

To take the case of cars again, even after the improved access to the Japanese market negotiated in 1976–7, and even after the reduction of the Japanese import tariff to zero in 1978, European car exports to Japan hardly increased at all. On the other hand, Japanese cars continued to make ever deeper inroads on the European markets, including that of Germany, the last country in the EC with an automobile industry whose market remained unrestricted at the end of the 1970s. The Japanese share of the German market rose from about 4 per cent in 1978 to 10 per cent in 1980, even though the German market was shrinking in that year. As in the case of ships, bearings and electronics, the pressure on the Germans, usually the most ardent supporters of free trade, was sufficient to make them hesitate, if not actually to lend their weight to the growing chorus calling for protection against Japanese imports.

At bi-annual talks with the Japanese authorities from 1973 onwards, and at every other occasion, the EC Commission would repeat the warnings of the danger of protectionism in Europe, and state the grave concern over the trend for the EC's deficit with Japan to grow every year. Many Europeans also observed that in the last resort Japan needed the European market more than Europe needed the Japanese market. So Japanese companies

Unit: million US$

Year	Exports	Percentage of total EC extra exports	Japan ranked as export market for the EC	Imports	Percentage of total EC extra imports	Japan ranked amongst EC supplier countries	Balance	Percentage change over previous year	Cover ratio
1960	296	1.1	23rd	304	1.1	26th	− 8	–	97
1963	512	1.8	14th	510	1.5	18th	+ 2	–	100
1965	506	1.4	15th	725	1.8	14th	− 219	–	70
1966	628	1.7	12th	809	1.9	14th	− 181	− 17	78
1967	853	2.1	10th	849	2.0	14th	+ 4	c.t.	100
1968	904	2.1	11th	988	2.1	11th	− 84	c.t.	91
1969	1,086	2.2	11th	1,212	2.3	8th	− 126	+ 50	90
1970	1,384	2.5	11th	1,650	2.8	6th	− 266	+111	84
1971	1,403	2.2	11th	2,191	3.4	7th	− 788	+196	64
1972	1,673	2.3	10th	2,977	4.0	5th	− 1,304	+ 65	56
1973	2,840	2.9	6th	4,187	4.0	5th	− 1,347	+ 3	68
1974	3,303	2.4	10th	5,219	3.3	7th	− 1,916	+ 42	63
1975	2,763	1.8	16th	5,988	3.8	6th	− 3,225	+ 68	46
1976	3,043	1.9	15th	7,154	4.0	6th	− 4,111	+ 27	43
1977	3,529	1.9	13th	8,751	4.5	5th	− 5,222	+ 27	40
1978	4,748	2.1	11th	11,102	4.9	4th	− 6,354	+ 22	43
1979	6,347	2.4	8th	13,421	4.4	5th	− 7,074	+ 11	47
1980	6,364	2.1	12th	18,554	4.9	4th	− 12,190	+ 72	34
1981	6,262	2.1	12th	17,366	5.1	4th	− 11,104	− 9	36

Note: c.t. stands for change of trend (surplus–deficit).
Source: Eurostat, Exports FOB, Imports CIF. Greece is included for 1981.

were well advised to moderate their exports to Europe in order to avoid killing the goose which laid the golden eggs by triggering a wave of protectionism leading to the closing of European markets. In response, the Japanese side would repeat over and over again that it was wrong to look at bilateral balances. We lived in a multilateral world. What you lost on the roundabouts you gained on the swings. In most years the EC had a surplus with Switzerland and Austria larger than its deficit with Japan. Privately many Japanese added that Japan was in an especially vulnerable position because her dependence on imported energy was much greater than in Europe. Therefore Japan needed surpluses with Europe and the US to make up for her huge deficits with the Middle East.

Her negotiators also pointed out that the current balance (which includes 'invisible' payments such as transport, insurance and tourism) was a fairer yardstick for judging the bilateral economic relation than the trade balance because Japan usually has deficits in the 'invisible' account with the EC. Later, when Japan's current account surplus moved further and further into the black, and the US and the EC requested Japan to adjust her international balance of payments, this argument was changed, and Japan's trading partners were told that the 'basic' balance (which includes capital movements) was the only fair yardstick with which to measure a country's fulfilment of its international obligations.

To these lessons in basic economics, the EC would counter by drawing attention to the trend for its trade deficit with Japan to grow, against a background of stagflation and slow economic recovery, much slower in Europe than in Japan. Unemployment was a political problem and, while it might be theoretically correct from an economist's point of view to include invisible payments, even if both sides could agree on the statistics (which they have been unable to do to this day), to jobless shipyard workers, for example, often concentrated in single electoral districts, this was hardly a very convincing argument. In other words, the problem was fundamentally a political one. And it was made that much more urgent in that at least three of the sectors in which Japan's exports had made the fastest inroads were the most strike-prone in several European countries – ships, steel and cars. As these rather formalistic exchanges took place each year, the EC's deficit with Japan rose another billion dollars, and each year the chances of a violent storm seemed more likely.

Participating in these talks became increasingly frustrating; it seemed that the Japanese were unwilling or incapable of taking prior action to cope with the storm, the signs of which became ever more obvious. Eventually action came only after the storm had broken.

In 1975, Japan had a small global deficit but a large surplus with the EC, which from 1975 onwards was not selling half as much to Japan as it bought from her. Towards the end of the year rumours were carried in the Japanese press that the EC 'appears to be moving towards curbing imports of principal industrial products, such as textiles, steel, electronics, ships and automobiles, from Japan'.[24] But the rumours soon died away.

16

Trade Frictions in the
Late 1970s and Early 1980s

Eventually the storm broke, and this is how it happened: in the early autumn of 1976, it became only too clear in Europe that unemployment would be up again, not least in labour-intensive industries such as steel, shipbuilding and automobiles, all of which were faced by powerful and effective competition from Japan. It also became clear that the EC's global trade deficit was going to be as large as it had been in 1974, the year after the oil shock. The global current account was also going deeply into the red. At the same time it was observed that Japan showed every sign of continuing her strong recovery from the oil shock, and that once again she would have a reasonably high GNP growth, as well as moving into the black in her global current account and trade balances. These changes had not yet translated through to the exchange rates, so the yen was still relatively cheap, giving Japanese exports a considerable price advantage. Unemployment in Japan was much lower than in the EC, even when the problem of the different basis of Japanese unemployment statistics was taken into account. Finally, it was observed that the EC would score its largest trade deficit in history with Japan. This situation in early autumn 1976 and the trend lines leading up to it are shown in Tables 8 and 9.

Headlines such as 'Is Japan Playing Fair?', 'The Strategy of Invasion' or 'Japan is Back' began appearing in the European and American press. On 11 October, I was quoted in *Newsweek* as saying what my authorities had been saying for a number of years: 'We view the present imbalance with grave concern. It can't go on much longer.'[25]

Table 8. GDP Growth, Unemployment and Balance of Payments of the EC (1973–81)

	GDP growth (real) (percentage)	Unemployment (percentage of workforce)	Current balance (bil $)	Trade balance (bil $)	Trade balance with Japan (bil $)	Percentage increase of EC trade deficit with Japan	Cover ratio (exports as percentage of imports)
1973	+5.9	2.5	+ 1.33	− 4.5	− 1.3	+ 3	68
1974	+1.8	2.9	−11.3	−19.8	− 1.9	+42	63
1975	−1.1	4.3	− 0.7	− 5.3	− 3.2	+68	46
1976	+5.1	4.9	− 5.5	−17.8	− 4.1	+27	43
1977	+2.3	5.3	+ 2.5	− 8.2	− 5.2	+27	40
1978	+3.2	5.5	+17.1	− 3.2	− 6.4	+22	43
1979	+3.4	5.6	−12.6	−28.5	− 7.0	+11	47
1980	+1.4	6.2	−40.8	−61.6	−12.2	+72	34
1981	−0.5	7.9	−15.6	−37.9	−11.1	− 9	36

Source: Eurostat. Exports FOB, Imports CIF.

Table 9. GNP Growth, Unemployment and Balance of Payments of Japan (1973–81)

	GNP growth (real) (percentage)	Unemployment (percentage of workforce)	Current balance IMF basis (bil $)	Trade balance (bil $)	Trade balance with EC (bil $)	Percentage increase of Japan's surplus with EC	Cover ratio (exports as percentage of imports)
1973	+10.0	1.3	− 0.1	− 1.4	+ 1.2	− 9	138
1974	− 0.5	1.4	− 4.7	− 6.6	+ 2.0	+62	150
1975	+ 1.4	1.9	− 0.7	− 2.1	+ 2.3	+16	168
1976	+ 6.5	2.0	+ 3.7	+ 2.4	+ 3.6	+57	200
1977	+ 5.4	2.0	+10.9	+ 9.7	+ 4.5	+26	208
1978	+ 5.6	2.2	+16.5	+18.2	+ 5.0	+11	183
1979	+ 6.0	2.1	− 8.8	− 7.6	+ 5.1	+ 2	168
1980	+ 5.5	2.0	−10.8	−10.7	+ 8.8	+73	212
1981	+ 2.9	2.2	+ 4.7	+ 8.7	+10.3	+11	221

Source: GNP, Unemployment: Economic Planning Agency, Tokyo. Current Balance: The Bank of Japan. Trade Balance: The Ministry of Finance, Tokyo. Exports FOB. Imports CIF.

And indeed it did not. On 26 October Mr Doko Toshio, President of the Federation of Economic Organizations (Keidanren), and as such the single most powerful industrialist in Japan, led a mission of Japanese industrial leaders to Europe. They were confronted with bitter criticisms of Japan's trade surpluses wherever they went, in London, Paris, Brussels, and, to their surprise, in Bonn. These criticisms centred on Japan's exports in five 'problem sectors': steel, ships, home electronics, bearings and cars. Not exactly new problem areas!

The point was reiterated that Japan had developed her exports to Europe in these five sectors too rapidly and without apparently welcoming similar imports into Japan, to which the enormously increased European trade deficit with Japan so far that year appeared so eloquently to testify.

The problem had become a 'hot' one in Europe, not only for economic reasons, but also for various political reasons. The Hamburg shipyards, for example, were losing business and unemployment was rising rapidly there. Hamburg was the German Chancellor's electoral base. In England the left wing of the Labour Party and the trade unions were putting pressure on Prime Minister Callaghan unilaterally to close the British market to foreign imports and to 'save British jobs'. The most rapidly expanding imports into England were from Japan at that time and they were concentrated in highly visible sectors such as cars.

Mr Doko was rumoured to have been caught by surprise by the vehemence of the European criticisms, and also by the pettiness and misinformation revealed in some of the complaints. He was apparently nettled by the fact that his briefings from Japanese official agencies before leaving for the trip had insufficiently alerted him as to what to expect. At any rate, on his return to Tokyo, he moved swiftly. For months he had been expressing the desire of big business that the government adopt reflationary policies. Now he added the persuasive argument of foreign pressure. On 8 November he called on Prime Minister Miki and informed him that industry would do its part in solving the urgent problem with the Europeans by seeking to curb exports in the five problem sectors. This commitment was made somewhat more easy by the fact that export restraint was already being exercised in three of the sectors – steel, electronics and cars. Here only fine-tuning was necessary. Ships and bearings were to prove slightly more difficult. The government too, Mr Doko insisted, would have to do its part in responding to this dangerous external pressure by adopting reflationary measures. In stressing the gravity of the problem, he suggested that Mr Miki take the matter up in Cabinet rather than deal with it at sub-Cabinet or single-ministry level. The Prime Minister promised to co-operate along these lines.

Industry moved rapidly to placate the Europeans by strengthening voluntary export restraint in the five 'problem sectors'; by setting up study groups and by planning to send 'import promotion' missions to Europe. Steps were also taken to set up a special centre to help industrially advanced countries to export their finished products to Japan. (This centre, the Manufactured Imports Promotion Organization, was eventually opened in early 1978.) The government also announced that it would make a number of tariff cuts in advance of the programme agreed in the Tokyo round of multilateral trade negotiations.

Overnight, thanks to the 'Doko shock' the EC–Japan trade problem had become publicly recognized in Japan and it also began to receive a lot of attention in Europe. From November 1976 onwards, the European Council of Heads of State and Government, which in practice has become the highest decision-making body in the EC, included the question of trade relations with Japan on its agenda as it has done at almost every meeting since then. The media also immediately took up the EC–Japan trade problems in a big way and began talking of trade frictions or even trade war.

I have described in some detail the background and events leading up to the first round of post-oil-shock EC–Japan trade frictions because they set the tone for the following years.

Since that autumn of 1976 the EC and Japan went through bouts of trade frictions, usually coinciding with spring and autumn, which are the busy seasons in the international, political and bureaucratic calendar. The rhythm was somewhat complicated by the United States which could not allow the EC to 'steal a march' and win concessions from Japan ahead of them. So naturally enough the US soon followed the EC, coming in with all sorts of demands in July 1977, and intensifying the pressure that autumn. Japan was bound to provide concessions to Washington which included, in the first instance, the setting up of numerous joint study committees.

At which the EC in turn, not wishing to be left out, came back to Tokyo with further demands, including the setting up of numerous joint study committees.

Then the US negotiated a joint communiqué early in 1978, at which the EC (again very naturally) demanded a joint communiqué (March 1978).

Next, in the long period leading up to the Tokyo Summit of June 1979, the US, starting in the winter of December 1978, sought to put further pressure on Japan, which was quickly followed by the EC. So intense did this strange rivalry become that each time a Japanese negotiator visited Washington, he was put under strong pressure also to visit Brussels and vice versa. Japan's other trading partners all tried to get into the act but with little or no success.

Then, after a cooling-off period following the Tokyo Summit, trade frictions between Europe and Japan broke out once again in 1980. The circumstances were very similar to those surrounding the earlier outbreak in 1976.

In the first place, the European economies were already set for a downturn in the business cycle when they were hit by the oil shock of 1979. The 150 per cent rise in the price of oil accelerated the downward trend. By the spring of 1980 it was clear that unemployment and inflation were going to be higher in 1980 than in 1979, GNP growth was going to be much lower, and there was going to be a huge deficit in the balance of payments.

The effects of the second oil shock on the Japanese economy, on the other hand, was to stimulate an export boom which had already been in the making thanks to weak domestic demand and a large deficit in the Japanese balance of payments in 1979 which had led to a cheap yen. By the spring of 1980 it was clear that this was once again going to be an export-led growth year for Japan which found herself rising to the peak of her current business cycle – just as the Europeans and Americans were moving to the trough of theirs. Indeed the Japanese GNP grew three times faster than the European in 1980, unemployment was a third as high, inflation was much lower, and the current account deficit with the world of 10.8 billion dollars was by coincidence about the size of Japan's record high trade surplus with the EC of 8.8 billion dollars (see Tables 8 and 9).

By May 1980 the warning signs in Europe were out. Europe's bilateral deficit with Japan was all set to achieve yet another historic leap upwards, rising by as much as 40–50 per cent over the 1979 deficit. At the same time, to add salt to the wound, it was observed that the US deficit with Japan was not increasing at anything like the same rate. As so often on previous occasions Japanese exports to Europe were highly concentrated on a limited number of sectors which were already in trouble of one kind or another. The list of such 'sensitive' sectors included not only the old favourites such as ships, televisions, bearings and cars, but also one or two newcomers such as machine tools and computers. Another new element was that the most rapid build-up of Japanese exports of cars and televisions was to the German market. This was no coincidence, for by 1980, the German market was the only major market left in Europe to which access for these goods was still unrestricted.

Reaction was predictable. In the European press there was the usual talk of Japan conducting a trade war, although it is arguable that the press comment this time round contained less emotional criticism of Japan and more understanding that the problem was in part caused by the lack of competitiveness of European industries. In the French press, to take one example, out of 130 articles appearing in August and September 1980 on the subject of Japanese car exports, 40 per cent had factual or positive headlines. The remaining 60 per cent were emotionally hostile using expressions such as 'Japanese menace' (10 per cent of all the articles); 'Yellow peril' (10 per cent of all the articles); 'Japanese invasion'; 'Untrustworthy competitors'; 'The number one enemy' and so on and so forth. The background in this particular case was not Japanese inroads on the French car market. There Japanese imports had long since been limited by the government to a 3 per cent share. Rather it was the fact that Japan took nearly 50 per cent of the car market in Francophone North Africa in 1980, and for the first time ever began outselling French makers on European markets including on the huge and important German market.

Calls for protection against Japanese imports intensified and they began to be heard in Germany, traditionally the staunchest backer of free trade in the European Community.

In the summer of 1980, the EC Commission tabled new proposals to the Council of Ministers to negotiate an EC–Japan trade agreement. This was to be based on a phasing out of the residual quantitative restrictions against Japanese imports left over from the 1950s (on items such as honey and horses) in return for Japanese export restraints in key sectors (including a few, such as televisions or cars into Italy, which were covered by the old restrictions). The proposals however were not acceptable, mainly to Italy and France supported by the United Kingdom, who were not prepared to give up their restrictions against Japanese imports. So in the autumn, the Commission tabled a tougher set of proposals for a common Community approach towards Japan. These were accepted by the Council of Ministers. Japan was warned that steps toward a forward-looking dialogue, including further liberalization of each other's markets and industrial cooperation, could only be envisaged if Japan cut back her exports to the EC. In addition the government was called upon to let the yen revalue and to make a commitment to the policy of increasing imports into Japan from Europe as well as increasing the share of manufactured goods in total imports. Greater facilities for European investments and banking were requested, while on the European side it was recognized that progress would have to be made in persuading industries to adopt positive strategies to confront the Japanese industrial challenge.

The Japanese government reacted more stiffly than in the past to these proposals and issued a statement denying that Japanese exports were causing high unemployment and inflation in Europe and calling on European businessmen to work harder to export to Japan. The statement pledged that the government would continue to advise Japanese private enterprises not to export goods such as televisions and cars in 'a torrential manner'.

By the end of 1980, a consensus was apparently emerging among Japanese industry exporting to the European market that prudence was of the essence. But no new agreement on export limitation was reached either between the European and Japanese industries or at the official level. In February 1981, the EC Commission issued a warning by setting up import surveillance measures on Japanese cars, TVs and machine tools. These measures were statistical rather than protective because they only required that Japanese imports be counted after arrival. But the implication was that the next step could be to set up import licensing measures. The Commission also announced that it would seek to have the 'Japan problem' placed on the agenda of the Ottawa Summit of the industrial countries that July.

The industry giving the most trouble was the car industry, both in the EC and in the US where declining markets had not prevented the Japanese from increasing their shares. Both the American and the European manufacturers began demanding a cutback of Japanese imports. The Japanese were unwilling to come to any agreement with the Europeans until they had reached a settlement with the Americans because America is a much larger market for their exports. All the Europeans could do was insist that any agreement reached with the Americans should not lead to a diversion of Japanese car exports on to the European market and that the EC should secure a similar self-restraint agreement.

In America the International Trade Commission had ruled in November 1980 that Japanese car imports were not causing damage to the US industry, which only had itself to blame for declining market shares because Detroit had failed to switch its production in time to small cars. So the Japanese were reluctant to hold back their exports. When they finally agreed to do so in May 1981 it was only after very strong US political pressure and an American undertaking that the US auto industry would use the breathing space to restructure.

Immediately the EC demanded a similar agreement. This the Japanese authorities refused to grant, arguing that the EC was not in the same position as the US because Italy, France and Britain already had limitations on imports of Japanese cars, which was indeed the case. At which the EC Commission accused the Japanese of flooding the European market while keeping the Japanese market closed with complex regulations. The Japanese remained unmoved, pointing out that the Japanese market had been fully opened in recent years and also implying that because the Commission had no effective control over the member states' policies towards Japan, it felt itself obliged to huff and puff in an attempt to cover its weakness. Meanwhile Japanese negotiators came to an export limitation agreement with the Belgian and Dutch governments. Most important of all, an 'understanding' was reached between Bonn and Tokyo that Japanese car exports to Germany in 1981 would not be more than 10 per cent higher than in 1980.

As these 'understandings' were being reached, the Japanese Prime Minister, Mr Suzuki, paid official visits to the main EC countries, stressing his country's desire to strengthen its political ties with Europe. In other words he had come to talk politics, not trade. In most capitals he found that his interlocutors had the opposite concern; trade questions were uppermost in their minds. The irony of this situation was not lost on the small number of observers who remembered the previous visit of a Japanese Prime Minister to Europe (that of Mr Ikeda in 1962). He had then been scornfully dismissed as an 'electronics salesman' by General de Gaulle because of his willingness to discuss such pedestrian matters as trade quotas in contrast to the General's lofty concern with geopolitics.

The danger of the Europeans and Japanese once again talking at cross-purposes during Mr Suzuki's visit was avoided by masterly timing: the announcements of Japanese limitations of automobile exports preceded or coincided with the Prime Minister's arrival in each country. A statesmanlike tone prevailed and there was general acknowledgement of the need to place Europe–Japan relations on a sound political basis. The Prime Minister sought to mollify the EC Commission, which had been side-tracked by the member states over the automobile agreements, by expressing the willingness of his government to come to an agreement with the Community as a whole over Japanese car exports in 1982 –

provided the Community could reach a common policy on this issue and speak with a common voice.

The defusing of the bilateral trade frictions was also helped by the antipathy felt by both the Europeans and the Japanese towards US deflationary economic policies and high interest rates which were acting as a break on economic recovery in Europe and Japan. Indeed these were the concerns mainly voiced at the Ottawa Summit of industrial countries in July 1981, not so much the problems posed by Japanese exports.

But the relief was only temporary. By the autumn of 1981 it was once again clear that both the EC and the US were going to have historically high trade deficits with Japan. In October, a high-powered Japanese business mission led by the chairman of Keidanren, Mr Inayama, visited the EC. It was met with a similar reception as Mr Doko's mission had met five years before. Blunt accusations that Japan's market was closed, and in some capitals of the EC lengthy lists of demands, including that the Japanese government set up import targets and institute a special tax rebate for Japanese importers of European machinery.

If the object of Mr Inayama's mission was to assess the political and economic climate in the EC with a view to further encourage Japanese direct investments in Europe, his high-handed reception can hardly have persuaded him that the time was ripe.

Meanwhile, the pressure from the US was far stronger. In the Congress, with elections in autumn 1982, there was much talk of passing reciprocity trade legislation whereby Japan would be required to import as many cars, for example, as the US imported from Japan. The effects of such narrow mercantilist legislation would have been the formal burial of the post-war multilateral free-trading system. Both Japan and the EC urged the US administration to head off such protectionist pressures in Congress. In addition, the Japanese government moved swiftly to answer US (and European) complaints that the Japanese market was still partially, and unfairly, closed to imports from its main trading partners.

A special Committee for International Economic Measures was set up in the ruling Liberal Democratic Party under the vigorous leadership of Mr Esaki Masumi. The new Committee was able to cut across ministerial rivalries and quickly announced two sets of measures to further ease access to the Japanese market, such as advance tariff cuts, the removal of sixty-seven out of a combined EC and US list of ninety-nine non-tariff barriers, and the estab-lishment of a new Office of Trade Ombudsman to handle specific complaints of foreign businessmen.

The continuation of Japan's export restraint for another year in key sectors such as cars was also reluctantly agreed. Moves were even started to begin to relax the barriers in the only clearly protected sector of the Japanese market, agriculture, despite the fact that the LDP majority was based on the agricultural vote and despite the fact that Japan was already the largest market in the world for US agricultural products, $6 billion worth of which had been imported in 1981.

As these measures were being taken in the early spring of 1982, Mr Esaki visited Washington and the main European capitals to explain them. Not for the first time, Japanese moves to conciliate Western opinion were taken as an admission that the Western case had been justified and that the Japanese mar-ket had indeed been partially and unfairly closed to Western exports.

Nevertheless, the market-opening measures taken by the Japanese government in the first half of 1982 did serve to tempor-arily defuse criticism of Japan. The US Congress dropped the draft bills calling for strict reciprocity and at the Versailles Summit in June 1982, just as at the Ottawa Summit the previous year, problems of trading with Japan were not on the agenda.

Actual trade results of the market-opening measures were not immediately apparent. Indeed there was even a decline of European and American exports to Japan in 1982. If the EC's deficit with Japan was down slightly for the first time in fifteen years it was because of the significant decline of Japanese exports to the EC, blocked by various restraints in most major sectors.

The trade frictions of 1980–82, while arising out of fundamental-ly similar circumstances to those of 1976, were marked by the ever greater competitiveness of Japan in particular sectors, notably cars. On the European side there was more willingness than in the past, at least amongst informed opinion, to acknowledge that the problem was not one of unfair Japanese trade practices, but rather of the wide gap in productivity between certain European and Japanese manufacturing industries.

Having followed the course of Europe–Japan trade frictions in the 1970s and early 1980s, the reader may at this point be asking himself why such alarums and excursions were necessary in the first place. I also found myself asking this question from time to time. Eventually I came to the conclusion that although the immediate effect of the trade frictions was to stir up negative emotions, they did have one positive result in that they forced both Europeans and Japanese to become more aware of each other and of the nature of the problems with which both were faced. But before examining the matter in further detail, it is now time to glance briefly at the arguments and counter-arguments, the accusations and counter-accusations, made by both sides.

We have already seen that in the decade 1960 to 1970, Europe–Japan trade was more or less balanced, and the European position was a defensive one, limited to preventing 'sudden influxes' of Japanese goods. In the decade 1970–80, as the European deficit with Japan began to rise rapidly, the question began to be asked whether the European market was more open to Japanese imports than the Japanese market was open to European imports. In other words, was Japan operating with an unfair advantage?

The arguments on the European side that Japan was still partially closed to European exports were often ill-informed and out of date, but some were legitimate and based on actual and recent experience of the Japanese market.

First, two key background points: it was correctly argued that trade liberalization and the easing of foreign investment controls came much later in Japan than similar moves in Europe. Thus, it was argued that Japanese traders had had the advantage of earlier access to the European market than European exporters to the Japanese market. For example, if there were many more dealers handling Japanese automobiles in Europe than there were dealers handling European cars in Japan, this was partly because the Japanese auto-makers had been able to spend many years investing in and building up dealer networks in Europe. But while they were doing so, foreign investments in Japan were still restricted, and the Japanese auto industry, during the period of its growth, was protected from outside competition. By the time the imports of cars were liberalized, the domestic industry was sufficiently strong to maintain its control of the market against any new-comers. The policy of building up import substitution industries was standard practice of the Japanese authorities in the 1950s and 1960s. The fruits of these policies were harvested in the 1970s and 1980s.

Secondly, the very slowness with which Japan had begun to liberalize her market in the late 1960s, and the fact that she had only continued to do so in 1971–2 and again in 1981–2 under strong US and European pressure, suggested to many Europeans, who still remembered the heavily protected Japanese market of the 1950s and early 1960s, that the Japanese were reluctant to really open their market, that it was, in short, still partially closed. This mistrust is a good example of the poor communications between the two sides. It would be foolish and unfair to blame the Japanese for European ignorance and the tendency to cling to old images. Nevertheless Japanese readers will perhaps acknowledge that the pattern of waiting until strong external pressure has built up, and an internal consensus has formed, before taking action, does often suggest extreme reluctance to take the action in the first place.

The view that the Japanese market was not fully opened to foreign imports naturally also received apparent confirmation from the fact that Japan was beginning to score huge trade surpluses with Europe.

All sorts of arguments were adduced to support the view that despite *de jure* liberalization, the Japanese market was *de facto* still partially closed.

The complaints about high tariffs protecting Japanese domestic industries became less common after the successful completion of the Kennedy round of tariff cuts and even more so as the Tokyo round drew to a conclusion, although particular exporters, for example, of biscuits, questioned why it was necessary to maintain a 38 per cent tariff.

The argument shifted to so-called non-tariff barriers (NTBs) or government regulations covering imports which inhibited, or were claimed to inhibit, free movement of goods and services. A typical example has already been mentioned, the testing and type approval of automobiles.

Real and imaginary trade barriers exist in every market, and there is no doubt of the problems they can cause on the Japanese market. They probably act more as a discouragement to enter the market, however, than as a real cost factor. The trouble was there were many who appeared to use trade barriers as an excuse for European failure to penetrate the Japanese market. Indeed those who complained of such barriers most loudly often seemed to be businessmen who had either never been to Japan, or if they had, only some years previously, when the market really was protected. It was also noticeable that those who had had least success on the Japanese market were the most ready to grasp at the accusation of trade barriers.

Other accusations from the European side included the contention, which had been last heard at the time of the Great Depression, that the yen exchange rate was being unfairly manipulated in such a way as to keep its value artificially low. German banks and businessmen tended to be outspoken on this point, feeling that the Deutschmark before its decline in 1981 was too high in relation to the yen, making German exports to Japan too expensive, and thus contributing to the German deficit with Japan which since the early 1970s has been by far the largest bilateral deficit of all the European countries. Accusations of a 'dirty float' were never substantiated, but the fact that steps toward reforming and liberalizing Japanese capital markets and foreign exchange transactions were extremely slow in coming, only encouraged such suspicions in the 1970s. Moreover the track record of European banks in Japan bore witness to the tight control exercised by the authorities. In other capital markets around the globe European banks had proved themselves fully competitive. In Japan, however, their share of banking activity is still rather small (although their number has grown considerably in recent years).

It was also said on the European side that the large Japanese trading companies maintained a near oligopoly of imports and favoured the domestic groups of industry (*keiretsu kigyō*) to which they belonged. Thus the French Prime Minister, in a discussion in December 1980 with leading Japanese businessmen, while acknowledging the 'insufficiencies' of French industry, was reported to have recalled that the Japanese market was difficult to approach because of non-tariff barriers and a 'screen' of trading companies which prevented the establishment of after-sales networks.[26] It was also frequently held that Japanese companies (especially public corporations) follow a patriotic instinct to buy Japanese even if it meant paying higher prices. The Japanese distribution system was said to be a barrier to imports, although the domestic producer had to use the same system. We saw in Part I that it was commonly said the Japanese government and business acted in 'collusion' (the Japan Inc. image) to keep imports out when necessary, or to subsidize export industries. It was frequently claimed by European exporters that, whatever the goodwill expressed at the upper levels of Japanese officialdom, at the operational levels, in the customs or in the regulatory agencies, for example, there was a dilatoriness and lack of enthusiasm towards imports reflecting an older more protective phase of Japanese industrial and commercial policy.

To substantiate all these various claims, it was pointed out that Japan alone of the advanced industrial democracies had an import share for manufactured goods of 30 per cent, or considerably less, of total imports. Given this relatively small ratio of manufactured goods imports to total imports, it was hardly surprising that practically every other advanced industrial country by the 1970s had a deficit in its manufactured goods trade with Japan. Nor was it felt to be a matter of pure coincidence that foreign shares of the Japanese market in major industries such as ships, steel, automobiles, tobacco or banking were in the region of only 1 or 2 per cent.

Starting in 1977, the US and European negotiators began pressing Japan to play a more active role in the world economy by stimulating domestic demand and by reducing her enormous balance of payments surpluses. This led to Prime Minister Fukuda's undertaking at the London Summit in 1977 that Japan would achieve 6.7 per cent GNP growth that fiscal year and reduce the surplus. When she did not achieve these goals on time, this too touched off, however unfairly, the old talk of Japan being unreliable.

Similarly, in 1978, Japan undertook 'to take all appropriate steps to increase imports of manufactures . . . and that the share of these imports in Japan's total imports would increase steadily and return within a reasonable period of years to a more normal level under current international economic circumstances' (EC–Japan Joint Communiqué, 24 March 1978). The trouble was economic circumstances soon changed – oil prices shot up in 1979–80 and as a result the relative share of manufactured imports in Japan's total imports, far from increasing, actually declined.

Other points were made to show that Japan was operating with an unfair advantage and enjoying a 'free ride' in the international arena.

For example she had few defence responsibilities and was not particularly generous in her aid programme to the developing countries.

In 1981, the US spent 5.8 per cent of its GNP on defence. The USSR spent about 14 per cent; Britain 5.0 per cent; Germany 4.3 per cent; France 4.2 per cent and even neutral Sweden and Switzerland 3.2 per cent and 1.8 per cent respectively. Japan spent 0.9 per cent.

Despite growing awareness in Japan that a larger defence budget was called for (from 0.9 per cent to 1.0 per cent?), decisive steps to translate this awareness into action were slow in coming. Meanwhile the allies were informed that Japan could not do as much as she had hoped because of budgetary difficulties. Hardly a very convincing argument when Europeans and Americans were daily reminded that Japan's economy was outperforming theirs by far.

Another field where Japan's contribution was held to be incongruously small in comparison with the size of her economy was the extent of her official development assistance (ODA). Here again, many of the other advanced industrial democracies, relatively speaking, have tended to be more generous, despite the fact that their economies have not been doing so well as Japan's.

Between fiscal 1978 and 1980, under very considerable external pressure, Japan doubled her official development assistance to reach 0.33 per cent of GNP (compared with 0.47 per cent average in the EC). In addition aid was extended to countries of strategic importance to the Western alliance such as Pakistan, Thailand, Egypt and Turkey. In 1981, a new five-year programme to double Japan's ODA and also to increase the grant element of the aid was adopted. Even so, by 1985, Japan's ODA will be average, it will not be outstandingly generous.

In the 1930s the Europeans accused the Japanese of 'social dumping', because Japanese wages were much lower than in Europe. Today this is no longer the case, but the Japanese are still commonly regarded in Europe as exceptional in that their values towards life and work and leisure are felt to be different from those in Europe and in the United States. The Japanese work harder, take fewer holidays and spend far less time complaining about their lot. Or so it seems from the outside. They also put up with cramped housing, crowded roads, and few public amenities such as urban parks or sports facilities. Investments are concentrated instead in industry and all energies appear to go into competing with rival Japanese companies to capture ever larger shares of world markets in a growing number of key industries. Japan, it is often claimed, has therefore an 'unfair' competitive advantage with her more luxurious trading partners, who spend more on improving living standards than on improving the competitiveness of their industries.

Japan is, in other words, in fundamental ways different from Europe and America. A leading French executive was only reflecting this widely held view when he said, 'It is another world, we are not fighting with the same weapons.' Or, as the Director General of the Confederation of British Industries put it in the summer of 1981, 'We cannot turn our people into Japanese. The difference in productivity between Europe and Japan is so large that we cannot bridge it in the short term.' To the Chairman of Germany's most powerful trade union I.G. Metall, on the other hand, it was not a question of the impossibility of catching up with the Japanese but of the danger of being dragged down to their level: 'To work like the Japanese,' he said, 'with their labour conditions and social practices, would be to revert to the stone age.'

I have summarized very briefly the main European (and US) criticisms of Japan during the years after 1976. They began with the contention that Japanese exports were over-concentrated and were built up too rapidly; next came the view that the trend for Japan's surplus to increase every year was intolerable and that it was the result of the Japanese market either being opened too late or not being fully opened to European exports. It was also held that the huge Japanese balance of payments surpluses were acting as a deflationary pressure on the international economy and they should be reduced by stimulating Japanese domestic demand and thus increasing her imports. This last complaint was of course abandoned when Japan's current account moved into the red.

Finally it was often said that Japan had an unfair advantage in that her defence and aid contributions were small and also in that her domestic investments were concentrated in industry rather than in social overheads.

There is no doubt some validity in most of these contentions, which only took on their full force when buttressed with detailed and specific examples, and when considered in the light of the particular phases of the world economy at that time. In Part IV, I list a number of actions which could be taken to improve Europe–Japan relations and hence suggest by implication which complaints were valid and which were spurious.

Often in the popular presentations of the EC's and the US case, the main contentions were fuzzy and they were linked together in a false causality. Thus it was sometimes said that if Europe managed to open the Japanese market fully, Europe's deficit with Japan would be reduced and the Japan trade problem would be solved. This is of course not necessarily a logical outcome at all. We have seen that the opening of the Japanese market did not lead to a boom in European exports, which were often insufficiently competitive and inadequately launched and followed up, to secure many breakthroughs similar to those made by the Japanese on European markets. Moreover, even if European exports to Japan increased, fears in Europe of market disruption in sensitive sectors would remain. The problems caused by Japanese exports to Europe, in other words, would still continue.

Furthermore, amid all the oft-repeated talk about the Japanese market not being fully opened to foreign imports, nobody asked why if this was really so, the Japanese in most years actually imported more per capita from the EC and the USA than did the Europeans and Americans from Japan! The figures in Table 10 speak for themselves.

Notable about the EC–Japan trade is that by 1980, per capita, the EC had caught up and was importing as much from Japan as Japan imported from the EC.

The larger amount imported by Japan from the USA than from the EC is explained by the huge imports of agricultural goods from the USA. If these are subtracted and only manufactured goods are considered, then Japan imported only $155 per capita from the USA in 1980, only slightly more than the USA imported from Japan.

The problem, as Table 11 illustrates, did not lie so much with the level of Japan's imports, as with the high level of her exports per capita (together with the speed of their build-up and their concentration in three or four key sectors).

The notion too that increased GNP growth rates in Japan would lead to an increase of domestic demand and therefore to a reduction of trade surpluses is also simplistic. High growth rates

Table 10. Imports per Capita in the Bilateral Trade between Japan, the EC, and the USA 1970, 1975 and 1980

	Japan's imports per capita from the EC	The EC's imports per capita from Japan	Japan's imports per capita from the USA	USA imports per capita from Japan
1970	US $15	7	54	29
1975	30	23	104	53
1980	67	67	209	140

Source: Japan's imports, Ministry of Finance, Tokyo (CIF); EC imports, Eurostat (CIF); USA imports, Department of Commerce, Washington (free alongside price).

also require more exports. Moreover the supposition that increased Japanese domestic demand would lead to more imports from Europe is another example of a false linkage. What happened was that imports of raw materials or manufactured goods from Japan's neighbours increased – not imports from Europe.

Finally a false causal connection was often made between Japanese exports in a given sector and high unemployment in that sector in Europe, leading to the accusation that Japan was 'exporting unemployment'. As the Minister of Industry in France put it in 1981, 'Every Japanese car imported equals five French workers out of a job.' The Minister did not explain why imports of cars from other countries did not have a similar effect. Perhaps he believed that imports of goods from a given country should be exactly balanced by exports of the same type of goods to that country (the so-called 'reciprocity' argument). Or perhaps he was trying to justify the French government's limitation of imports of Japanese cars to 3 per cent of the market share.

The danger of such false linkages is clear: not only do they obscure the root causes of the problem but they also invite popular frustration and resentment when the achievement of one step fails to lead to the next. They therefore contribute to the fear and distrust of Japan which break out from time to time in Europe and can be seen in headlines in the European press such as 'Commercial War – the Japs attack!', 'A Yen for Victory!', 'The Japanese are preparing to devour us', 'Will Japan lead us to World

Table 11. Exports per Capita in the Bilateral Trade between Japan, the EC, and the USA 1970, 1975 and 1980

	Japan's exports per capita to the EC	The EC's exports per capita to Japan	Japan's exports per capita to the USA	USA exports per capita to Japan
1970	US $ 8	6	53	23
1975	51	11	100	45
1980	142	24	268	109

Source: Same as Table 10, based on FOB (free alongside price for the USA).

War III?'. In part these reflect the editor's search for an eye-catching headline to a story which is usually as unsensational for the general reader as only international trade can be. Such headlines also certainly reflect the unfavourable images inherited from previous generations of Japan as a belligerent enemy and an unfair trading partner.[27]

Policies intended to resolve trade frictions, if clumsily presented, can end by stimulating them.

The possibility that Europe's deficit with Japan is at least in part the result of a lack of competitiveness in certain of its industries is understandably perhaps not always given prominence in the presentation of its case. But this point is of course recognized in Europe, and by an increasing number of people, who fully realize that European industries can never become competitive on the Japanese market unless they are competitive on their own markets. Some of those who had early held this view were already quoted in Part I. In making this point in late 1977 in an article in a *Le Monde* Special Supplement on Japan, I concluded that 'today the EC has a choice: either make a better job of restructuring its industries or resign itself to losing markets to more competitive trading partners. To continue to complain of the bilateral trade deficit with Japan as the result of Japanese protectionism only serves to obscure the problem, not to resolve it.'[28]

The article was based on a detailed study of Japan's changing export structure and her rapid switch from labour-intensive industries, such as textiles, to capital- and knowledge-intensive industries, such as automobiles and electronics. This study, which circulated amongst government departments in Europe and was eventually published in Paris, reached three important conclusions.

First, the EC's failure on the Japanese market in industries such as cars, ships and electronics was paralleled by its declining share in these industries on the US market. The failure then was presumably the result of a decline in the Community's competitiveness in these industries rather than the result of special unfavourable conditions keeping its exports out of the Japanese market.

Secondly, although it was probably possible for the EC to reduce the sharpest tensions in its trade relations with Japan in the short term by various measures such as negotiating Japanese export restraints, in the long run, the Community would not be able to compete with Japan, on its own markets, on the Japanese market, or on third markets, unless it regained its competitiveness by effectively restructuring its industries.

Thirdly, if the Community wished to avoid being caught between the greater competitiveness of the newly industrializing countries (in labour-intensive industries) and the US and Japan (in knowledge-intensive industries) then again it would have to restructure its industries, especially knowledge-intensive industries, before it was too late.[29]

The same basic point concerning competitiveness was made a year later in a report of the EC Commission analysing the causes of the EC–Japan trade frictions. Despite the fact that it was a confidential internal document, it leaked to the press in the spring of 1979. The report became notorious in Japan because two phrases, about Japanese living conditions ('What Westerners would regard as little more than rabbit hutches') and working habits ('workaholics'), were quoted out of context and became the focus of an initially somewhat emotional reaction. What the report actually said was, 'the basic consideration is the relative economic strength and *competitiveness* of Japan'. It then paid tribute to the 'hard work, discipline, corporate loyalties, and management skills of a crowded, highly competitive island people'. It went on to say that in Europe 'the Protestant work ethic has been substantially eroded by egalitarianism, social compassion, environmentalism, state intervention and a widespread belief that working hard and making money are antisocial'.

The preamble of the report put its finger on the reasons for the Japanese surplus with Europe – not unfair Japanese trading practices or non-tariff barriers keeping European exports out of Japan, but, it implied, the lack of competitiveness of certain European industries as compared with their Japanese counterparts. Such plain speaking in an official document, even an internal paper such as this one, is rare in bureaucracies, which normally find it more expedient to address the margin of a problem, rather than its essential core, which is either too embarrassing or too unpleasant to reveal. On this occasion the message in the preamble was a novel and a bitter one for Europeans to swallow. In order to make sure the paper was read in Europe, blunt language was used.

The body of the document surveyed the different policies followed by the Community in its relations with Japan and assessed their effectiveness. In the concluding paragraphs various future actions which the Community might take were spelt out, including the possibility, if all else failed, of considering measures which would reduce Community imports from Japan.

The week in which the report leaked to the press I found myself in Tokyo in the unusual position of receiving complaints from both Japanese and European friends. The Europeans were annoyed that the Commission spoke so frankly about Europe, and the Japanese appeared totally to miss the point of the paper, and feeling that they had been insulted, concentrated solely on the term 'rabbit hutch'. It was a busy week.

Many complained that such crude language should not have found its way into a policy paper. To these the best I could reply was that the paper was an internal document not intended for public consumption. Secondly I reminded them of the practices of the estimable Walter Bullinger, the Foreign Minister in Harold Nicolson's *Public Faces*, who 'tried to give his minutes that personal note which differentiated the pronouncements of Cabinet Ministers from the suggestions of civil servants. A homely turn of phrase here and there: the avoidance generally of technical or professional expressions; the introduction even of a few topical catchwords, of a few examples even of current slang.'

The phrase 'rabbit hutch' as a description of Japanese housing immediately became a catchword in Japan in a manner very similar to the sudden spread of the expression 'economic animals' in the early 1970s. Only weeks after it had appeared in the press, it was used as a slogan in the spring labour offensive to argue for better living conditions. Later in 1979, a leading newspaper listed the phrase as amongst the 'Best Ten Catchwords' of the 1970s and the top catchword of 1979.[30]

To some the phrase was taken as an indication of European racial prejudice by its implication that the Japanese were sub-human.[31]

But the majority did not draw such an extreme conclusion as a nationwide poll by the *Asahi Shimbun* indicated. The poll investigated attitudes towards the Tokyo Economic Summit and included the following questions and responses:

In some circles in Europe, there is the view that 'the Japanese people are workaholics, living in rabbit hutches'. Do you feel displeased to be viewed in such a way, or do you not feel so?

Displeased .... 43 per cent
Do not feel so .... 49 per cent
Other answers; no answer .... 8 per cent

Do you think that the expression that 'the Japanese people are workaholics, living in rabbit hutches' describes the present situation in Japan, or do you not think so?

Describes it .... 58 per cent
Do not think so .... 32 per cent
Other answers; no answer .... 10 per cent

While nearly two thirds of those polled felt there was some truth in the phrases, it is equally significant that nearly half did not like having this pointed out by a foreigner.[32]

Partly as the result of the publicity gained by this EC working paper in Europe as well as in Japan, the need has increasingly been felt to broaden the scope of the EC–Japan dialogue to include the exploration of the possibility of industrial co-operation, joint research into new energy resources and other areas of mutual benefit.

The Japanese response to European complaints has usually been co-operative when it is a problem which can be solved by Japanese voluntary export control ('orderly marketing'). Some efforts have also been made to ease regulations governing imports into Japan and to remove NTBs, and some recognition is given to the difficulties facing the foreign exporter to the Japanese market. Much more could no doubt be done. Some of the lines for further action are discussed in Part IV.

But on the whole the Japanese response to complaints from Europe of an increasing bilateral trade deficit with Japan has been that European businessmen should make greater *efforts* on the Japanese market.

This is very much in line with the reflex which credits the other side with the opposite qualities of one's own. The Japanese self-image is of a frugal, hardworking and disciplined people. If the Europeans or others have difficulties on the Japanese market, then it must be because they lack those very qualities which enable Japan to build up her industries and her exports. In other words Europeans must be extravagant, lazy and undisciplined. This basic Japanese view is wittily expressed in the popular cartoon Fuji Santarō.

Japanese visitors to Europe in the Meiji period a hundred years ago noted that the Europeans were so lazy that their post offices were closed on Sundays. Later, during the Great Depression, it was pointed out in Japan that Japanese labour was frugal and worked hard, while in the West, 'labour aims at working the shortest possible hours, doing the minimum amount of work and getting the highest possible wage'.[33]

Forty-five years later in 1977, a senior official in MITI was putting forward exactly the same argument as the main reason for Europe's deficit with Japan:

A comparison between the labour force of Europe and that of Japan shows clearly that European workers lack discipline . . . The decline of Britain, in my opinion, is basically attributable to the fact that discipline has waned . . . Workers (in Europe) are like undisciplined troops. They stop marching and go to bed . . . Europeans today lack spirit . . . Europe is seriously lacking the will to develop the Japanese market.[34]

There is no doubt some truth in such statements which are borne out by labour attendance statistics, strike statistics and general observations. They do not explain everything though – why, for example, Germany, with its more disciplined workforce than Britain, usually has a much larger deficit with Japan than Britain does.

Nor is the weakness of certain European industries, such as textiles or steel, necessarily caused by the laziness of workers in those industries. Japan too has depressed industries, such as textiles or aluminium smelting, and I never heard it argued in Japan that the workers in those industries were especially lazy. Obviously, the reasons for the weakness of a particular industry may lie in structural conditions which go beyond the working habits of a particular country. For example, lower wages in developing countries, or high costs of imported raw materials. To ascribe Europe's structurally weak industries to the laziness of European workers is to draw a simplistic veil over a complex problem shared by all developed countries, including Japan.

In other industries, the problem is not only the laziness or lack of discipline of European workers as compared with their Japanese counterparts, although these may often contribute to the core of the problem, but also the relatively low productivity in many European industries caused by insufficient investment in new plant and equipment and new technologies, and in some cases by the failure to build up large production runs in order to reduce unit costs.

Turning now to the different question of 'efforts', or their lack, in exporting to a foreign market. How can such efforts be judged? Two reasonable indications are, how many businessmen take the trouble to go to the market they wish to sell in, and how much head-offices are prepared to invest in overseas marketing or manufacturing.

Take the first indicator. Thousands of Japanese businessmen and bankers are stationed in the EC in more than a thousand offices. Six thousand alone come from the major trading companies. Many tens of thousands more go to Europe on business trips. In Germany, which has the largest concentration of Japanese companies in Europe, there were no less than 430 Japanese business offices in 1980 and 13,500 resident Japanese. Düsseldorf, familiarly known as 'Japandorf', is now Japan's major financial centre in Europe. About 5,000 Japanese live there and its hotels registered 64,000 Japanese visitors in 1981. Naturally the European market is much larger than the Japanese market and it has immediate spinoffs into neighbouring countries, as well as being a leading centre of world market information, from insurance to shipping, from cocoa to copper. So you would expect at least three or four times more Japanese businessmen to be stationed in Europe than Europeans in Japan.

But what is the actual situation? How many European business-men and bankers are stationed in Japan? The answer is straight out of the sixteenth century. There are about as many Christian missionaries from the EC in Japan as there are businessmen. Until the mid 1970s more long-term visas were issued to missionaries than to businessmen from Europe. Even today, there are only ten thousand resident in Japan from all the ten EC countries put together. Of these only a couple of thousands are doing business – about the same number as are active as missionaries and teachers. The Japanese visa authorities are strict. It can therefore be safely assumed that the missionaries are indeed engaged in propagating Christianity and not in business activities. In 1964, 1,162 long-term missionary visas were issued to nationals from EC countries, compared with 892 long-term commercial visas. By 1974, the businessmen, although catching up slightly, were still behind. In that year 1,103 missionary visas were issued compared with 1,033 commercial visas. The United States, both in 1964 and 1974, had about the same numbers of long-term commercial visas as the EC but twice as many missionary visas.

Despite the number of missionaries they have been no more successful than the businessmen: less than 1 per cent of the Japanese population has been converted to Christianity.[35]

In 1981, the total number of businessmen to go to Japan from the EC on short visits came to 62,000 – less than the number of Japanese businessmen who booked into hotels in Düsseldorf that year.

Another rather convincing statistic is the number of European business offices in Japan; they actually decreased between 1961 and 1975 – from 67 to 45 (over the same period the number of Japanese trading offices in Europe increased from 88 to 458). The decrease in the numbers of European business offices in Japan over these years was nothing unique; the same was happening all over Asia.[36]

Compare too the efforts put into export promotion. The semi-official Japan External Trade Organization (JETRO) maintains twelve offices in the EC manned by officials who speak the languages of the countries in which they are stationed. In addition among the 250 or so Japanese diplomats who were stationed in the EC in 1981, there were commercial, financial, and agricultural attachés, part of whose job was to promote Japanese business interests. In comparison, the EC countries maintain a handful of individual export promotion officials in Japan, most of whom do not speak the language. A considerable number of the just over a hundred diplomats from EC countries stationed in Japan in 1981 were active in export promotion; but of this number only a few were from the EC Commission working exclusively on EC economic and trade interests as a whole.

Turning now to the second indicator of 'efforts' on a given foreign market, the amount of investments put into that market.

By March 1980 the accumulated direct investments of all nine EC countries in Japan amounted to 340 million dollars. Of this 134 million dollars, or 39 per cent, was from the United Kingdom. Next came Germany with 110 million (32 per cent) and then France with 40 million (12 per cent) and finally Italy with only 2 million dollars. The United States had 1.5 billion dollars invested in Japan by 1980.

Large sums of money. But not so very large when compared with Japanese investments in the EC, which by the same year came to 3.7 billion dollars or nearly ten times more than the EC invested in Japan. Per capita the ratio is 19 to 1 in Japan's favour. And Japan's investments in the EC have been increasing much faster than the EC's investments in Japan. The same applies to Japanese investments in the US. Per capita the ratio is eleven to one in Japan's favour.

The different level of investments in each other's market has certainly been affected by the later liberalization of the Japanese market than that of the EC. Customs relating to company takeover in Japan make it more difficult for a foreigner to break in than in Europe. Also the Japanese market has been traditionally much more self-sufficient than that of Europe, and its industries today are extremely competitive. It is not an easy market therefore in which to find an entry.

But there is no doubt that the relatively small number of European businessmen in Japan and the relatively low level of European investments there are yet further indications of the overall decline of European involvement in Asia. Europe's weakness in selling to the Japanese market is but one example of this general trend which in certain cases is also exacerbated by declining competitiveness of European exports. It is not then *in the first instance* something exceptional arising from the special conditions of the Japanese market.

Japanese strength in selling to the European market, on the other hand, is one result of what we found in Parts I and II. In a word, the Japanese have taken enormously more interest in Europe than the Europeans have done in Japan.

In view of the evident imbalance in efforts to exploit each other's markets, it should come as no surprise to find that there was a widespread feeling in Japan, at least after 1976, that because of prejudice, she was made a scapegoat for the failures of the EC's economy in recent years, and the wave of anti-Japanese sentiment in Europe was felt to be inspired by jealousy of Japan's economic successes.

These arguments and counter-arguments began to be heard in the nineteenth century. They have increased in intensity as Japan has built up her modern industry and they were heard most clamorously when Europe was in recession, as in the years 1929–32 or again in the 1970s and early 1980s.

Behind the arguments there stands a simple truth – Japan is the first Asian country to have gradually reversed its trading relationship with Europe by developing a fully competitive industry, not only light industry, but also heavy knowledge-intensive industry as well. The industrial structures of Japan and Europe are therefore no longer complementary – they are competitive.

Increasingly too Japan has been drawing ahead of Europe in the levels of efficiency of key industries. A trend which shows every sign of continuing as the investment/innovation gap between the two widens. How to maintain free trade and to avoid frictions under these conditions will be one of the main problems facing both Japan and Europe in the 1980s and 1990s. Some suggestions for coping with the problem are put forward in Part IV where the view that the issues involved are more numerous than the evident lack of European efforts on the Japanese market is further elaborated.

17

Positive Results of
Trade Frictions?

Until the 'Doko Shock' in 1976, the EC's 'dialogue' with Japan, as
I mentioned earlier, was conducted in a highly formalistic manner, with the EC officials making warnings, and the Japanese
officials scoring defensive points. Not much was effected and the
EC's bilateral deficit continued to increase every year.

The reason for the EC's failure to get its message across was
that the Europeans did not make sufficient efforts to have it heard
in the right quarters in Japan. Few European politicians or
industrial leaders visited Japan, partly because they did not take
Japan very seriously, but mainly because everybody was much too
concerned with finding ways to combat the post-oil-shock stagflation at home. For the same reason Japanese politicians and
business leaders during these years were not very disposed to
react to general warnings from the EC, even if they heard them.
Instead, from time to time, they acted on specific problems caused
by their exports in a given industry or a given country. For the
rest, the overriding priority was to survive against fierce competition at home and abroad and one way of doing this was to
export.

There were other reasons too why the EC's warnings were
ignored. Japanese officials drew the conclusion that the EC was
no longer as strong as its early promise had suggested it might
become. US–Soviet détente had removed one of the main objec-
tives of building a strong Europe. And following the oil shock of
1973, which was the first serious and dramatic external threat to
Europe since détente, the EC did not react as a whole, but each of
its member states pursued their own individual advantage. As an

American commentator put it, 'Europe of the 1970s presents a melancholy picture of fragmentation, internal squabbles and aimlessness.'[37]

The Japanese are a practical people. Their main experience of dealing with Europeans since the sixteenth century has been of dealing with individual nation states. These they played off against each other very successfully. Then in the late nineteenth century the Japanese themselves adopted the institutions and trappings of the European nation state. In the twentieth century their one attempt to set up regional co-operation around Japan had disastrous results still felt to this day. In other words, history has not disposed the Japanese to take the political aims of a unified Europe or regional blocs with anything more than a grain of salt and a pretty troublesome grain at that.

In addition, there is the very real difficulty for all the European Community's interlocutors, including Japan, of accurately assessing the balance between the powers of the EC as such and the sovereignty of each member state. A balance which is continually shifting and which inevitably affects the EC's efforts to co-ordinate at the supranational level the particular sectoral interests of each member country. In certain sectors, for example, cars or TVs, the EC is not a single unified market because of special restrictions or import regimes in individual member states. This problem of assessment, and real or apparent disunity in the EC, has from time to time encouraged those who prefer to see Europe as nothing more than a number of individual countries. A typical statement of this view was made by a member of Prime Minister Ohira's Cabinet in a 1979 interview in answer to the question 'Do you consider Japan's trade dispute with the European Common Market more serious than your trade conflict with the US?' The reply was: 'For Japan, the relationship with the United States is much more important. The European Community is one large organization with which we have a relationship. But basically that amounts to a series of bilateral relationships between Japan and West Germany, Britain, France, etc. Therefore we feel we should address problems in a bilateral manner.'[38] This perception of Europe is perhaps a shade superficial and out of date, being based on past perceptions, nevertheless it has on occasion proved a useful guide to securing Japan's narrow commercial advantage.

The Japanese are acutely conscious of hierarchy, in international relations, just as much as in social or in business life. The EC in the post-oil-shock years appeared to be sliding down in the international power stakes. Its institutions tended accordingly to be somewhat downgraded in the Japanese official mind and EC Commission requests to Japan were brushed aside as being insufficiently specific, no more than a hodge-podge of the individual positions of the member states. Moreover, so long as the Commission was able to exert little or no control over the commercial or self-restraint agreements reached by the member states with Japan, so long that is as there was no united EC policy towards Japan, and so long 'as the Community lacked an effective industrial policy, it was too weak to do little more than cry 'wolf' to Japanese exports. In doing so, it seemed to many Japanese, the Commission did more to stimulate fears of protectionism than it did to calm them. In a similar manner the Commission's efforts to put together a common Community policy towards Japan appeared to contribute more to politicize even local trade problems, which it sought to elevate to the European level, than it did to resolve them. In other words, the Japanese could see neither the necessity nor the advantage of dealing with the EC as a whole. Instead they continued to settle each problem bilaterally with the individual member states. An approach frequently encouraged by the member states themselves which, despite rhetorical support for a united Community policy towards Japan, often preferred to come to a deal directly with Tokyo when the crunch came.

Although the EC–Japan regular bilateral consultations were inaugurated in 1973 by the EC's external relations commissioner and by the Japanese foreign minister, and although the joint communiqué at that time stipulated that the consultations should be held at both the ministerial level and the level of experts, after the oil shock they were downgraded to sub-Cabinet level where they remained for the next four years. No Japanese ministers went to Brussels between late 1973 and 1977.

Finally, because of the weakness of the Europe–Japan link, buttressed neither by security nor direct political interests, as is the US–Japan link, there was far less willingness in Japan to make concessions to Europe than there was to make concessions to the US. The continued existence in Europe of a small number of discriminatory quantitative restrictions against Japanese imports has been cited by Japan's chief trade negotiator during these years as a further reason for Japanese reluctance to make concessions to the Europeans. Nor is it forgotten in Japan that in the difficult early post-war years when the Europeans were setting up protective and discriminatory barriers against Japanese exports, the Americans were granting the Japanese privileged access to their market and advising them how to sell on it.[39] It should also be noted that there is no sizeable Japanese lobby in Europe as there is in the US: a lobby which can call on a very considerable body of academic and expert opinion on Japan, which is lacking in Europe.

It is significant that when the logjam of the muted EC–Japan dialogue was broken, it was done by a Japanese business leader. This supports the view that the EC had delivered its essentially political and business message for the previous three years to the wrong 'windows' and perhaps, too, in an over-formalistic manner. Amongst some officials in Tokyo, Mr Doko was not very popular. It was considered that he had interfered in government affairs, and as a 'rank amateur' in international relations had been responsible for upsetting the comfortable rhythm which the essentially fruitless EC–Japan talks had followed since 1974.

But the logjam was broken and suddenly, in large measure because of the trade frictions, both sides began to take each other much more seriously. Contacts increased enormously and it became the accepted wisdom in ever widening circles to stress the need to strengthen the Europe–Japan side of the US–Japan–Europe triangle.[40] From 1977, in increasing tempo, the Heads of State and Prime Ministers of nearly all the Community countries paid official visits to Japan which were reciprocated. An increasing number of ministerial contacts also took place in these years. In 1979 the Summit Conference of world economic powers was held in Tokyo. Commissioners, European ministers and Japanese cabinet members began shuttling backwards and forwards between Europe and Japan. In 1979, the head of Japan's Defence Agency visited NATO headquarters and the following year the

West German Defence Minister paid an official visit to Tokyo. In 1981 the Japanese Prime Minister visited the main European countries (the first such visit since 1962) and in 1982 Mr Mitterrand became the first French President ever to visit Japan. The first regular contacts between the Japanese Diet and the European Parliament took place in 1977, and they were held annually from 1978 onwards. The regular twice-yearly high-level consultations between the EC Commission and the Japanese authorities were now once again upgraded from time to time to ministerial level. In 1974, the Commission had opened a permanent diplomatic delegation in Japan, while in 1979, the Japanese Foreign Ministry was finally allocated the budget, for which it had been asking for years, to open a second mission in Brussels especially to the Community.

The immediate effect of the EC–Japan trade frictions, which broke out in the autumn of 1976 and again in 1980, was to trigger emotional reactions which reinforced popular hostile images on both sides, thereby making the repetition of such emotional outbursts that much more likely.

The positive outcome of the trade frictions was that they stimulated both sides to make an effort to understand the other in the light of the actual situation confronting each in the post-oil-shock world.

A final point remains to be made about the outbreak of EC–Japan trade frictions in 1976 and in 1980 (and the same point could be made about the previous round in 1971–2). It is that the frictions appeared to follow the well-known pattern of *Europe only waking up to Japan when Japan had become impossible to ignore, and Japan only waking up to an external situation when it had reached the boiling-point*. Then both sides reacted to the 'shock' over-emotionally and in a state of panic.

Possibly the strength of inherited and outmoded images which each holds of the other, plus the lack of regular and effective communications, make this shock-therapy approach to heightening mutual awareness inevitable, at least until both sides get used to the idea of listening to each other as normal day-to-day interlocutors.

PART IV

What is to be Done?

18

How to Improve Economic and Trade Relations between Europe and Japan

In Parts I and II the range of inherited metaphor available to Europeans and Japanese today to think about each other and to describe each other was examined in detail. It emerged that both sides tended to see the other in terms of past images, rather than in terms of present-day realities. For the Europeans, Japan was lost in a romantic Oriental haze from which she would burst forth now and again, usually as a threat. For the Japanese, Europe was wrapped in a cultural cloud, which would regularly evaporate into an unpleasant vapour. It also emerged that the psychological distance from Europe to Japan appeared to be much greater than from Japan to Europe.

The extent to which prejudice and outmoded images could influence reality was shown in Part III in the analysis of Europe–Japan trade frictions.

It is now time to take a look at the reasons for the poor communications between Europe and Japan and to suggest how they can be improved.

People communicate as much by their actions as by their words. We judge somebody's attitude towards us not only by what he says, but more importantly, by how he acts towards us. Actions 'speak' louder than words. In the final resort, to reach a rounded judgement of somebody else, we take account both of his words and of his deeds and of the fit between the two. Likewise in assessing communications between cultures we have to examine two different modes of communication.

First, unconscious or unintended communication, the non-verbal signals conveyed by actions and interpreted by the other side in the light of its current preoccupations. In the case of Europe and Japan, this 'dialogue through action' has been mainly concerned with bilateral trade. No amount of verbal communication can alter the sometimes contradictory and unexpected signals conveyed by decisions in the trade field.

The second way in which cultures communicate is by conscious verbal messages usually conveyed by specialist intermediaries; through academics who explain one culture to another; through journalists and other opinion leaders who convey information on a day-to-day basis; through government spokesmen and the diplomatic channel and through all the multifarious contacts of politicians, businessmen, students, athletes, housewives and others who just happen to meet each other.

To resolve the 'trade frictions' between Europe and Japan therefore it is not enough simply to take actions in the trade field. It may well be that the 'communications gap' is so great that such actions will be misinterpreted. It is even less effective to try and resolve the problem simply by increasing public relations activities and other forms of conscious communications.

In the same way, to resolve the 'communications gap' between Europe and Japan it is necessary not only to increase contacts and build up more effective communications, but also to ensure that decisions taken in the trade field are such as to enforce the desired message.

If the 'dialogue through action' between Europe and Japan has been most intense in the trade field in recent years, it has proved an inefficient form of communication because it periodically broke down into trade frictions. These frictions triggered negative images on both sides which increased the communications gap, thereby making future outbreaks of frictions more likely. While Europe had similar trade problems from time to time with America, it also had a much wider 'dialogue through action' with the Americans (political and security fields) as well as a tradition of contacts and verbal communications at every level (shared cultural heritage). This has meant that Europe's trade problems with America have easily been fitted into a wider context and been kept in proportion as only one strand in the bilateral relations. Europe's trade problems with Japan, on the other hand, are more liable to get out of control, to be given exaggerated attention and to provoke exaggerated reactions, because there is no wider set of communications links into which trade frictions can be reduced to their relative importance. All the more reason then that suggestions for improvement of trade relations include measures to broaden the dialogue between Europe and Japan.

The diagnosis of Europe–Japan trade frictions over the last hundred years was given in Part III. The brief prognosis which follows is divided into three parts: what the Europeans and Japanese could do together, and what each could do separately to help avoid trade frictions in the future. Then the related question of improving channels of communication is taken up.

Joint Actions

To the extent that Europe and Japan share many of the same political values and face many of the same economic problems, they are objective allies. It is in their common interest to ensure that the values which they hold important continue to be guarded and to be taken fully into account in all international decisions. Great care should be taken therefore to include Japan into allied consultations as much as possible. At the very least the aim should be to avoid giving the Japanese the impression that they are being deliberately excluded from allied summitry as was so clumsily done at the Guadeloupe Summit of December 1978, and again during the discussion amongst the allies following the Soviet invasion of Afghanistan in the winter of 1979. On every issue of international politics the aim should be to encourage Japan to take a more active role in the Western alliance. Nor should bilateral economic disputes ever be allowed to obscure our fundamental identity of purpose with Japan.

Although direct security co-operation between Europe and

Japan is far less important to both than the security ties linking each with the United States, there are surely areas where Europe and Japan could both benefit by increasing such co-operation, which is at present almost nil. The incentives are not hard to find: the Soviet Union is considered the main threat to both, so it matters greatly to Japan what happens in the European theatre, the focus of Soviet military power. Likewise Europeans recognize that instability in the Asia-Pacific region could readily affect the distribution of Soviet forces. Responses to Soviet military interventions in other parts of the world also require co-ordination as also do economic relations with the Soviet bloc and strategic aid to friendly countries such as Thailand, Egypt or Turkey.

European sales of military equipment and technology to China could eventually have more immediate repercussions in Japan than in Europe (if only by stimulating a greater Soviet presence in East Asia), so the speed and extent of the build-up of China's military power is another important question of mutual concern. Because Europe and Japan depend so heavily on regular supplies of oil from the Middle East, both have an enormous stake in contributing to stability in that region. Finally, both Europe and Japan have a major stake in the outcome of arms control and arms reduction talks.

Given these mutual interests and recognizing the necessity of a comprehensive global approach to national and regional security, Europe and Japan have little to lose and much to gain by instituting, as a first step, regular exchanges of information on security matters in a trilateral framework with their main ally, the United States.

In the economic sphere, it is vital for both Europe and Japan to ensure stable relations with the developing countries, solutions to the oil problem and continuing access to raw materials. None of these questions can be settled by Europe or Japan alone, but they stand a far better chance of reaching an effective solution if Europe and Japan can act together. The same naturally applies to the maintenance of a free and open world trading system and the necessary conditions for its continued functioning – a stable international monetary system and adequate safeguards, rules of conduct, and standards to guarantee fair play on all sides.

In the bilateral trading relations the first step to be taken is to agree on the terms of the dispute. What is being argued about, what is being requested and what is being denied. Until there is an agreed analysis of the problems dividing Europe and Japan, there can be no agreement on solutions and on who is responsible for implementing what. This may seem an excessively simple or naive observation, but as we saw in Part III too often these basic questions were not resolved, leaving both sides talking at cross-purposes with each other.

Take the problem, for example, of the over-concentration and too-rapid build-up of Japanese exports to Europe. A real problem which was temporarily solved by a variety of measures depending on the particular circumstances. So far so good. Then there was the separate question of European access to the Japanese market. It usually involved different export sectors and its solution required different measures. Yet the two problems were linked together although the solution of the one could not lead directly to the solution of the other. Even if the trend for Europe's deficit with Japan to grow every year was halted by a rapid increase of European exports to Japan, the difficulties caused by Japanese exports in sensitive sectors of the European market would remain. Many other examples of such false linkages were given in Part III. Their danger lies in the frustration they invite when one step fails to lead to the next.

Another cause of confusion was the failure to distinguish different kinds of problem. For example, there were clearly long-term questions, such as changing Japan's import structure or restructuring European industry, upon whose successful resolution various elements of the dispute depended. Then there were other difficulties which were short-term, such as the balance of payments position or the economic conditions of a country in a given year. Again, these different types of question and the widely different time periods required for their resolution tended to be lumped together. The Europeans would put forward requests and the Japanese would respond by accepting some and rebutting others on an ad hoc basis as each one came up. Neither side to the dispute seemed particularly willing to sort out the different strands.

No doubt the lumping together of separate issues and the assumption of all sorts of linkages which are more apparent than real is not so much a European or a Japanese characteristic, but something shared by both, a disease of the bureaucratic mind caused by bureaucratic procedure. If there is a problem with another country a file is opened. If there is a further problem with that country then it is added to the file. When there are enough problems on the file a negotiation is started. In the terms of the negotiator's logic all the different problems are linked because each can be used as a bargaining point to influence the outcome of the others. Even minor issues can play a major role in a negotiation and it is often part of the negotiator's skill to be able to present a minor shift in his position as a major concession, and to leave major issues, or issues over which he has no competence or influence, safely unidentified.

Typical of the inability to agree on the terms of the dispute was the failure to agree on what constitutes an 'open market'. If the degree of a market's openness is measured by the formal structure of tariffs and quotas, then by the conclusion of the Tokyo round of multilateral trade negotiations, Japan's market was as 'open' as that of the EC or of the US. If non-tariff barriers such as the administration of industrial standards, or customs procedures and so forth, are taken into account, then again it would be difficult to decide whether the Japanese market was less open than the European countries or the US. Indeed the argument about Japan's market in the last resort often came down to the accusation that it was closed by 'non-specific' barriers such as national cultural attitudes towards foreign trade. In this view the distribution system in Japan functioned to keep foreign goods out and even the Japanese language was held by some to constitute a so-called 'non-specific' barrier.

Again and again Western businessmen and officials who put forward such arguments seemed to be saying that it was self-evident that our markets were fully open and the Japanese was not, because our imports from Japan were so much larger than our exports to Japan. The false nature of this line of reasoning was already mentioned in Part III. Japan is a much smaller market than either the EC or the US, whether measured in terms of population, GNP or volume of foreign trade. So there is no reason to suppose that Japan's imports from these markets should be of the same order in absolute terms as Japan's exports to them. Indeed when measured in per capita terms we saw that Japan was importing as much from the EC as was the EC from Japan, and more from the US than the US was from Japan (see Table 10).

Another glaring example of the inability to define the terms of the dispute was the failure to agree on a common set of statistics or even on how to measure trade flows. The Europeans measured their debt with Japan using European statistics. The Japanese used their own. In some years there was upwards of a 50 per cent difference between the two sets of statistics. It is true that over a two- or three-year period the trend lines were the same, but the timing of changes in the trends could differ considerably. One result of using different statistics was that in most years Europe's debt with Japan looked much higher to the Europeans than to the Japanese. This is because import figures include costs of transport and insurance whereas export figures do not. So Europe's imports from Japan, which were already much larger than her exports to Japan, appeared that much larger. In order to avoid such differences visible trade should be measured according to a formula such as used by the IMF which subtracts transport and insurance from imports. In this way both imports and exports would be measured in terms of their freight on board (FOB) price. Which currency to use to measure trade flows is another question upon which agreement should be reached before mutual accusations are exchanged.

The situation was even worse when it came to estimating invisible trade trends between Europe and Japan (payments, transfers, transport and tourism). According to the Japanese negotiators, arguing on the basis of Japanese statistics which recorded gross debits, Japan in 1980 had a 3.4 billion dollar deficit with the EC. The Europeans using their figures, which recorded net receipts, put this at closer to one billion dollars. Not surprisingly there was absolutely no agreement possible on the trends in the bilateral current acount balance.

The first and most obvious joint step to be taken to avoid

fruitless arguments is therefore to agree on the terms of the dispute including what constitutes an open market and to agree on a common measure of trade flows.[1]

Trade frictions between Europe and Japan have been taking place on and off for several generations. Their timing and causes have usually followed the same pattern. A domestic business downturn in Japan, or an external factor such as huge increases in the price of oil, leads to more than usual pressures to export. Reflecting Japan's previous negative balance of payments, the yen at such times tends to be cheap thus giving Japan's exports an added advantage. The trouble is that these conditions have co-incided with recession in Europe and America and that Japanese exports have been concentrated in labour-intensive sectors often already in decline or suffering from unemployment. The result has been trade frictions with all sorts of accusations that Japan operates with unfair advantages or uses unfair trading practices, keeps her market closed and exports unemployment.

What has happened, in other words, is that Japan has managed to react more rapidly to global recessions than either Europe or America, so that it has seemed to some that Japan's export-led recovery was at the expense of European and American economic recovery.

If the causes of the frictions are clear, it should be possible for the EC and Japan to warn each other in time to be able to take remedial actions before the outbreak of actual frictions. The institutional framework for bilateral consultations already exists. It remains to be seen whether bureaucratic systems are capable of taking action before a crisis forces them to do so.

Another fruitful field for joint action is industrial and technological co-operation. There is much the Europeans could learn from the Japanese in industries such as robotics or microchips. Conversely the Japanese could probably gain through technological co-operation in industries such as aeronautics and development of aerospace technologies or pharmaceuticals. Already such co-operation exists. It not only leads to useful cross-fertilization, but it also brings European and Japanese industrialists and executives into more meaningful contacts than as distant observers to their respective government authorities arguing about the biscuit tariff in Geneva.

Technological co-operation including joint research and development projects could also prove extremely useful to both sides in areas such as information technology, exploitation of marine resources, biotechnology and new forms of energy. The basis for such co-operation already exists in various bilateral treaties and agreements. It only needs to be extended.

Joint ventures between Japanese and European companies in third countries is a form of co-operation which has not always been a happy one so far, but given time and patience on both sides, it could bring obvious benefits, particularly in heavy and capital industries including oil and mineral exploration.

Finally, both sides should continue to bring industrial and safety standards, including testing and approval procedures in Japan and in Europe, into line with the best international practice. Such standards should be introduced with adequate prior notification and mutual consultation and with regard for possible effects on international trade, including imports. Tests already conducted to international norms and certified by officially accepted agencies should be recognized without requiring that they be repeated in the importing country.

Joint actions between Europeans and Japanese, at the level of government, industry or trading firm, already exist in many spheres. They should however be intensified. Not only are such actions beneficial in themselves, but they also serve to broaden and diversify the dialogue between Europe and Japan.

Because of the high degree of interdependence between the economies of Europe, Japan and the US, it would make sense on all major issues, not only to hold prior consultations on a bilateral basis, but also to give advance warning to the third partner or to hold trilateral consultations.

European Actions

We turn now to the actions which each side could take unilaterally to prevent the outbreak of trade frictions, and start with the Europeans.

A clearer understanding of the causes of Europe's trade problems with Japan is required. On the import side I am reminded of a story told by F-X Ortoli, the former President of the EC Commission. During the French–Italian 'wine war' of the early 1970s, in which French producers complained of a flood of Italian imports, Ortoli received a French delegation, whose leader with admirable clarity remarked: 'We are faced with two difficulties with Italian wine, namely its quality and its price. It is too good and it is too cheap.' The same could be said of most of Japan's exports to Europe. If they sell well it is for the simple reason that they are popular amongst consumers, who appreciate not only their high quality and their price, but also the excellent delivery schedules and after-sales service.

While I was stationed in Tokyo a colleague once made much the same point when she wryly remarked how amusing it was to observe trade negotiators coming all the way to Tokyo to complain bitterly of deficits with Japan. And then to see the same negotiators rushing to the shops to buy Japanese cameras, calculators and anything else they could carry, before returning home.

The first thing to acknowledge then is that Japan's trade surpluses with the EC have been made possible by the high quality and strong competitiveness of her exports.

To complain that the cause of the EC's deficits with Japan was that the Japanese market has been closed to European and other foreign exports by tariff or non-tariff barriers is to ignore common sense and everything we know about the changing patterns of European trade. In short, the EC's exports to Japan increased during the 1970s at about the same rate as its exports to the rest of the world. So did Japan's exports to Europe. The difference was that Japan's world exports were increasing at twice the speed of the EC's world exports. During these years the EC was scoring declining shares on most Asian markets including Japan. The same was also true of the EC's share on developed markets such as the United States. And the reasons were the same: increased competition from Japan and the newly industrializing countries on the one hand, and on the other, declining competitiveness of European exports. This decline was brought about by low productivity in many key export industries such as textiles, steel, ships, cars and electronics, which in turn was the result of relatively low levels of investment over the preceding decade in new technology and equipment, ever higher costs of labour, as well as labour unrest. In short, the results of a decade of stagflation and economic malfunctioning in many of the European economies, whose extreme form, the English disease, at times showed signs of infecting the whole continent.

Europe's share of world exports has also declined because a larger percentage of its trade is now concentrated in markets closer to home, in particular as the result of European integration within the EC. Even here, many of its key industries have only been able to survive because they have been protected from outside competition by one means or another, whether overt or concealed, whether direct or indirect.

No amount of blaming Japanese trade surpluses or of protecting Europe's ailing industries is going to cure the disease. Indeed to do so can only prolong it by directing attention from its root causes.

In the nineteenth century, Japan reacted to the Western industrial challenge first by shutting her doors and hoping the Westerners would go away. When it was only too clear that they would not, the Japanese embarked on an all-out and carefully planned programme to learn what it was that made the West so powerful and successful. They recognized their weakness and decided to catch up.

Today the tables are turned and Europe is faced with an industrial challenge from Japan. When this finally became clear in the 1960s, the initial reaction was negative. Now there are signs of a more positive approach, but it still remains to be seen whether this will lead to a carefully planned effort to learn what it is that has given key Japanese industries such a competitive edge over Europe.

Competitiveness on a given market today is the result of investment decisions and marketing strategies taken yesterday. The relatively poor performance of European exports to Japan, compared with Japan's exports to Europe in the 1970s, was the result of decisions taken or not taken in the 1960s. But the same pattern need not be repeated in the 1980s and 1990s if the right decisions are taken now.

The Japanese have made perfectly clear what kind of exports their industrial restructuring programme will lead to tomorrow. They intend to continue to move out of energy- and labour-intensive industries into technology- and knowledge-intensive industries – biotechnology, communications, microchip electronics, optics, computers, both hardware and software, numerically controlled machine tools, industrial robots, aircraft, satellites, medical equipment, pharmaceuticals and consumer durables such as videotape recorders. The only way to export successfully to a strongly competitive market is to get into the market early on. The Japanese market is not competitive in every sector. Far from it. But already the Japanese authorities are preparing the ground by encouraging research and by strengthening their industries of tomorrow. Unless the Europeans can start to meet this challenge by (i) restructuring their own industries in growth sectors of tomorrow and (ii) investing in the Japanese market to lay down the infrastructure for exports in these sectors, they will find that the Japanese will take the lead in a select handful of the new industries in their own market, and then in the world market, just as they did in steel, ships, cars, bearings and home electronics in the 1970s.

The main impetus to act will have to come from the private sector in Europe because, as Japan shifts the cutting edge of her exports away from labour-intensive industries to knowledge-intensive industries, the political impact of her exports will be diminished, at least in the early stages of the process.

A number of additional steps could be taken to prevent a repetition of the failures of the 1970s.

- Encouragement of much greater practical knowledge of Japan in Europe, including Japanese industrial and investment plans for the 1980s and 1990s.
- Encouragement of European investment in Japan, including joint ventures and company takeovers, particularly for distribution, after-sales service and other infrastructures for the sale of European goods. Where volume was sufficiently high

to justify it, investment in manufacturing industries in Japan. Also, consideration of manufacturing investments in relatively low-labour-cost countries (South Korea, Malaysia, Singapore) with the intention of exporting to the Japanese market.

- Much greater export promotion activities, especially of high volume sales items to the Japanese market (it is after all not an isolated market in Asia but one of the world's largest markets).

- In a number of EC countries, chiefly Italy and France, there are about fifty quantitative restrictions against Japanese imports. In most cases these are relics of the 1950s and 1960s. Although discriminatory these are neither exclusively against Japanese imports nor do they cover items of any especial importance today. But in less than a dozen cases there are quantitative restrictions which are exclusively directed against Japanese imports and some of these actually cover major items (such as imports of Japanese cars into Italy which are limited to 2,200 per year). To the extent that these restrictions have often been cited by Japanese negotiators as a major impediment to improving relations with the EC, and especially where they no longer represent anything more than a relic of the past, they should be removed as quickly as possible.

Naturally none of these steps would make any sense, except in the context of a more outward looking Europe which was willing to take a leaf out of the book of more successful trading partners, such as Japan, and which was determined to halt the drift towards protectionist policies at home and concentration of external trade on preferential markets.

Yet even if this change of direction was to come about, and even if all these steps were to be taken, they could not succeed without a number of moves being made on the Japanese side. It is to these that we now turn.

Japanese Actions

The following Japanese actions could help prevent future outbreaks of trade frictions with the EC.

The majority of Japan's trading partners, including the EC,
have a deficit in their manufactured goods trade with her. Most
countries have no more than a 1 or 2 per cent share of the
Japanese market in such huge sectors as cars, steel, ships, home
electronics or tobacco.

Is everybody else out of step, or is it just possible that there is
something on the Japanese side which has prevented greater
foreign penetration of her markets? If the EC was the only foreign
trading partner of Japan having a deficit with her, I would have
long since concluded that this was *solely* the result of the EC's lack
of competitiveness and general decline of interest in distant and
difficult markets. Indeed this is precisely what Japanese spokesmen have often argued.

The argument would be far more convincing, however, if it was
not for the fact that nearly all other countries appear to experience
similar problems on the Japanese market, and not only in the
industries in which Japan proved herself so competitive in the
1970s.

The heart of the problem lies in the Japanese import structure
as it has developed during the post-war years. By the 1970s, alone
of the advanced industrial countries, Japan was importing a
relatively small share of industrial or manufactured goods, never
more than 30 per cent of total imports, and falling as low as 20 per
cent in 1975 and 22 per cent in 1980 because of the higher bill for
oil imports in those years. Most European countries and the
United States on the other hand imported both absolutely and
relatively a far greater amount of manufactured goods. Thus in
1981, Japan imported only $288 per capita of manufactured
goods, compared with twice as much in the USA and almost twice
as much in the EC. The reasons for this disparity are clear, as a
glance at Table 12 will show. While Japan imports roughly the
same relative amounts of foodstuffs as the EC and the USA
(about 10 per cent of total imports), she imports far more energy
and raw materials which together accounted for 65 per cent of her

Table 12. Population, GNP, Import Structure and Exports of the EC, the USA and Japan 1981

		EC	USA	Japan
Population	(million)	271	230	118
GNP (GDP for EC and Japan)	(billion $)	2,418	2,925	1,127
Total imports	(billion $)	338	261	143
Imports per capita	($)	1,247	1,134	1,211
Imports as percentage of GNP		14	9	13
Imports of foodstuffs	(billion $)	34	18	16
Foodstuffs imports as percentage of total imports		10	7	11
Foodstuffs imports per capita	($)	125	78	136
Raw materials imports	(billion $)	35	12	20
Raw materials as percentage of total imports		10	6	14
Raw materials imports per capita		129	52	169
Energy imports	(billion $)	116	81	73
Energy imports as percentage of total imports		34	31	51
Energy imports per capita	($)	428	352	619
Manufactured goods imports (SITC 5–8)	(billion $)	140	141	34
Mftd goods imports as percentage of total imports		41	54	24
Mftd goods imports per capita	($)	517	613	288

		EC	USA	Japan
Total exports	(billion $)	302	234	152
Exports per capita	($)	1,114	1,017	1,288
Exports as percentage of GNP		12	8	13

Note: Figures have been rounded to nearest decimal point so that totals may not always add up exactly.

Imports of the EC represent imports of the ten member countries from outside the EC. Likewise exports are exports from the EC of the ten to rest of the world.

Sources: EC, Eurostat, USA, Department of Commerce; Japan, Ministry of Finance. All imports CIF except for the USA which are FOB. Exports FOB.

total imports in 1981 compared to 39 per cent for the EC and 36 per cent for the USA. So the share of manufactured imports in Japan's total imports is correspondingly low (24 per cent in 1981 compared to 41 per cent for the EC and 54 per cent for the USA).

Since the EC primarily exports manufactured goods and since 85 per cent of its exports to Japan are of such goods, export opportunities on the Japanese market are very much smaller than on its own markets or the US market.

There is, of course, nothing immutable about an import structure. It results from a number of factors, chief among which are a country's endowment of energy and raw materials, its geographical setting and historical pattern of external trade and, finally, the industrial and economic policies followed by its government.

The biggest difference in resource endowment between Japan on the one hand and the EC and the USA on the other lies in Japan's poor endowment of primary energy. Taking into account all energy sources including coal, crude oil, natural gas, hydro-electric and nuclear electric power, the EC, with Britain's North Sea oil, Holland's natural gas and Germany's coal, produced per capita four times more energy than Japan. The USA produced per capita fifteen times more than Japan. Japan and the EC consume per capita roughly equivalent amounts of energy, but Japan in 1981 only produced 11 per cent of total energy consumption while the EC was able to meet 45 per cent of its energy requirements and the USA 73 per cent. In other words Japan's dependence on imported energy is far higher than either the EC or the USA (89 per cent compared to 55 per cent and 27 per cent respectively). For this reason no less than a half of Japan's imports are made up of oil and other energy products compared to only a third in the EC and the USA.

Unlike most European countries, Japan has not in the past been surrounded by equally advanced neighbours, allowing close horizontal integration and the growth of an extensive two-way trade in manufactured goods. All these factors encouraged a more autarkic development of Japan's economy than of most European countries or the United States. In addition, one of the aims of government economic planners in Japan in the post-war period has been to reduce imports of manufactured goods and to build up a competitive manufacturing industry in Japan. Another aim was to maintain rapid economic growth. Both policies were enormously successful; among their results was an industrial structure heavily weighted toward manufacturing industries, including a number of world export leaders, and an ever increasing demand for raw materials imports. The other side of the coin was a level of manufactured imports far below that of her main competitors in both relative and absolute terms. Opportunities on European and American markets were therefore much greater for Japanese exporters than for European and American exporters to the Japanese market. The Japanese were not slow to make the most of the opportunities which offered. The result has been huge surpluses in her manufactured goods trade with both the EC and the US and most of her other trading partners as well. Another result has been the very small shares achieved on the Japanese market by foreign exporters – either the advanced industrial countries or the newly industrializing countries.

Because of the relatively small amounts of manufactured goods imported by Japan, there is therefore little or no chance that the EC will be able to increase rapidly and substantially its exports to

Japan. Unless, that is, either the objective situation in which Japan finds herself changes, or there is a shift in Japanese economic and industrial policies.

Already there is recognition inside Japan of the need to adjust the industrial structure to integrate the external trade of the country more into the international division of labour, allowing a higher ratio of manufactured goods imports where comparative advantage lies outside Japan. This move will be encouraged by the shift of emphasis in the economy from concentration on manufacturing industry to long overdue efforts to improve the quality of life – housing, drainage, roads, hospitals, parks and the like. The political support for this shift in emphasis will no doubt come from post-war generations more inured to the comforts of life than their elders. There will also be added emphasis on social welfare as the structure of the population tilts further towards older age groups. De-emphasis of heavy industry, especially energy-intensive industries, coupled with slower rates of growth, will lead to a falling share of raw materials imports.

Externally the emergence of newly industrializing countries (NICs) in Asia (such as South Korea, Taiwan, Singapore or Hong Kong) at a time when labour costs are high in Japan and there is a need to switch away from energy-intensive, high-pollution industries, means that for the first time Japan has acquired neighbours from whom it makes good sense to import goods rather than manufacture them domestically.

Because they can score where Japan is weakest, they will score first. Indeed this is precisely what has been happening in recent years. In 1970, the Asian NICs had only about a 10 per cent share of Japan's imports of manufactured goods. By 1980, this had risen to 25 per cent (correspondingly the EC share over the same period fell from 25 per cent to 20 per cent and the US share fell from 40 per cent to 30 per cent).

Increased imports from the NICs would be a welcome contribution by Japan, which currently imports far less both relatively and absolutely from them than does the US or the EC, although 70 per cent of developing-country manufacturing industry is situated in East Asia – closer to Japan than to Europe or America.

Apart from these major changes in the Japanese economy and industrial structure, changes which have already begun but which will take years to achieve, a number of practical steps have now begun to be taken which should greatly assist European and other foreign exporters to the Japanese market.

The steps include:
- A policy review of such obviously protected sectors as agriculture, including manufactured tobacco
- Purchasing decisions of public corporations to be made open to foreign bidders
- Foreign companies to be allowed reciprocal opportunities for takeovers as Japanese companies enjoy in Europe
- Foreign banks to be allowed the same operating conditions as Japanese banks enjoy in Europe; greater liberalization and internationalization of capital markets; full liberalization of insurance sector
- Continued efforts to bring testing and approval procedures in line with the best international practice (already mentioned where it more properly belongs under 'Joint Actions')
- Strict enforcement of regulations governing the prohibition of import cartels.

On the export side, Japanese companies should avoid 'torrential downpours' of exports in particular sectors or particular markets. This is all the more likely to happen because at the moment the modern sector of Japanese industry which acts as world export leader concentrates its efforts in only a handful of export items – cameras, cars, electronics, ships and steel. The government could try and encourage a greater diversification of exports in order to spread their impact. It should also keep a sharp eye open and, if necessary, be prepared to encourage the continuation of the various kinds of export restraint which have been practised up until now in potentially dangerous situations.

Pricing policies of exporting companies can also do much to help reduce trade frictions. Prices should be adjusted taking into account price levels in export markets and not, for example, adjusted as an immediate reflex to foreign exchange fluctuations.

In the 1960s, the Americans jumped the hurdle of nascent

European protectionism by switching from exports to direct investment in manufacturing industry in Europe. By the end of the decade they were deriving far more revenue from their investments there than from their exports. These investments also provided a bridgehead for popularizing American management methods and the American way of life in general.

More Japanese direct investment in manufacturing in Europe could play an important role in preventing trade frictions especially where such investment provided employment on a scale sufficient to take the sting out of the main accusation against Japanese imports, namely that they increase unemployment. Those Japanese factories which have already been set up, for example, the thirty or so in Great Britain, have created an excellent impression of Japanese management methods, and they have on the whole received a very positive press. The conditions for such investments usually include requirements to buy a certain percentage of local components, or to sell a minimum amount of the product on external markets. Such conditions may not be totally welcome, but the advantages in gaining local support may well prove to be the determining factor.

Now to turn to the question of Japan's contribution to the alliance linking her to the US and through the US to the other advanced industrial democracies. Without calling into question her peace constitution, there is clearly room for Japan to contribute a little more than she does at present. That she can afford to, there can be no reasonable doubt. In 1981, Japan's GNP amounted to 20 per cent of the total GNP of the six most important members of the Western alliance, but her defence expenditures only came to 4 per cent of their total defence expenditures.

Per capita, in 1981, the United States spent $760 on defence; Britain $512; France $483; Germany $405; Italy $155, and neutral Sweden and Switzerland $455 and $154 respectively. Japan spent $98.[2]

But before embarking on increased military expenditures, both Japan and her allies should be clear as to the nature and extent of her defence role. For a start, what are the defence requirements facing Japan? How can Japan's defence capability be improved?

Should Japan continue a 'miniskirt' strategy under the US nuclear umbrella of leaving her extremities exposed and protecting only her vital parts? Should she adopt a 'midi' approach and seek for example to cover her economic lifelines, the oil routes in Southeast Asia, by increasing naval and air strength? Or should she take a 'maxi' policy and build her own nuclear shield? For the moment no clear consensus has emerged, although the second alternative would appear to be ruled out for the time being in Japan, and the third to be completely unacceptable.

If Japan does increase her defence capability her arms manufacturers will probably succeed in having the current rules forbidding arms exports relaxed. Weapons manufacturers in Europe and America may well then find themselves with rapidly declining overseas markets.

The second edition of the *Encyclopaedia Britannica* (1780) noted amongst the various positive and negative traits of the Japanese people that they were 'uncharitable'. Two centuries later, the relatively low level of Japan's aid to developing countries, as well as her record of caring for the Indo-Chinese refugees, while not exactly a scandal, were nevertheless not up to the standard which could reasonably be expected of such a rich country.

This is probably one of the rare examples when a centuries-old image has remained unchanged for the simple reason that the reality itself until very recently had not fundamentally altered.[3]

The joint actions to improve relations between the EC and Japan outlined above have no hope of succeeding, unless both sides are prepared to take the half dozen individual, but complementary, actions listed for each. Nothing can be achieved if both sides continue to put the onus to act on the other as they have done in the past. The Europeans, for example, blamed the Japanese for exporting with an unfair advantage and keeping their domestic markets closed. They rarely addressed themselves to the root causes of the problem in Europe, namely lack of competitiveness and failure to take the Japanese market seriously. The Japanese, on the other hand, frequently blamed the Europeans for lacking the will to export to Japan and for protecting industries which were declining because of European laziness. They rarely acknowledged that the structure of the post-war Japanese economy was geared to a vertical division of labour (imports of raw materials/exports of manufactures) rather than to a horizontal division of labour with advanced industrial countries such as those in Europe. Nor did they recognize that Europe's greater integration into the horizontal division of labour with newly industrializing countries has meant that its labour-intensive industries have been placed under severer strains than faced by Japan, which until recently has been more isolated.

Both sides need to acknowledge their own responsibility for improving trade relations and to be able to take the necessary actions, confident that the other is doing the same. In doing so, full recognition should be paid to the efforts of the other. To achieve these aims a broader dialogue is required between Europe and Japan and more efficient channels of communication than exist at present.

19

How to Improve Communications between Europe and Japan

So far, various courses of action have been suggested which could lead to improved relations and understanding between Europe and Japan. Here it is now time to examine how best to improve channels of communication between the two. As before the onus is on both sides to act. In this case, to put it in a word, for the Europeans to develop a talent for listening and learning and for the Japanese to convey clear messages.

As with individuals, so with countries – if you wish to be understood, it is essential to be clear in your own mind what role you are playing, what image you wish to project and what message you wish to convey. In Part I we saw that Japan's image has been often distorted and inaccurate in Europe. This is certainly the result of European ignorance. But it also derives from the Japanese inability to pay sufficient attention to projecting a clear and unambiguous message abroad, whether through actions or deliberate efforts to convey a particular message. This inability is exacerbated today by the uncertainty as to what role the country should be playing on the world stage.

The fact that Japan's image in Europe today is fragmented and arbitrary complicates the bilateral relations. It is a cause of concern, because Japan's actions will be interpreted in Europe in the light of these fragmented images.

If you wish to influence what other people think about you, it is essential to find out what is already in their minds, what images they hold, what expectations they cherish. How does the other see the world and how does his perceptions of your actions differ from your own? In answering such questions, the net should be cast wide, because images nestle in every nook and cranny of the collective mind. Some of the main lines of inquiry were suggested in Parts I and II.

The next step is to examine the flow of conscious, verbal or intended communications between Japan and Europe. Is a clear message being sent out? Is the message being distorted by incompetent intermediaries? What role can public-relations activities play in improving communications?

To start with the first question.

Sending a Clear Message

It is generally agreed that Europeans, having formulated their thoughts, are better at conveying them to others, as well as better at presenting their culture to outsiders, than are the Japanese. Europeans have had a lot of practice at this, whose negative aspect has been mentioned repeatedly in previous chapters, namely, that too often they see themselves as teachers and slip into an arrogant didacticism which prevents them from hearing what others are saying. At meetings between a European and a Japanese, or at international fora in which they both take part, the European will often do 90 per cent of the talking and afterwards will say, 'Well, I think he understood what I was trying to tell him.' At which, if you ask him what he thought the Japanese was trying to say, you will be met by incomprehension and the defensive retort, 'He did not seem to have very much to say at all.'

At any level Europeans make much greater efforts to spread their culture abroad than do the Japanese. Government budgets for assisting the arts and promoting cultural activities, for example, are enormously greater than in Japan. One wonders why. Often the European governments can far less afford such expenditures than the Japanese government. The reasons are, of course, more fundamental than merely fiscal. Nor does the explanation lie in the greater degree of state intervention in Europe than in Japan.

The Japanese, it is probably true, feel more strongly than most other peoples, and certainly more than Europeans and Americans, that the most important things, such as 'innermost sincerity' (*magokoro*), should not, indeed can not, be expressed verbally. Non-verbal, intuitive communication is taken as a sign of solidarity, of real understanding. The importance attached to 'visceral understanding' (*haragei*) in Japan hardly makes for easy communication with foreigners. Indeed there is no doubt that it has been one of the principal sources of misunderstanding between Japanese and foreigners.

The virtue of reticence in the individual in Japan has its equivalent at the national level; blowing one's trumpet is frowned upon – it is more effective to 'kill one's enemy with silence' (*mokusatsu*), that is to shame him by refusing to acknowledge his existence, than it is to drown him with a flood of words. Rhetoric is not a form of art which flourishes in the schools and public halls of Japan. Verbosity is not unknown there, but on the whole, that most tedious instrument for inflicting boredom on one's fellow men is more commonly found in Europe.

No doubt Japan's public reticence is in part derived from habits of mind inculcated through those long centuries when it was death to attempt to explain anything about the country to outsiders. The strong sense that Japan is isolated and unique is matched by the feeling that her culture is not universal and that even if the Japanese should try and explain it, foreigners would not possibly be able to understand. In the same way it is a strongly held view in Japan that the Japanese language is uniquely difficult for foreigners to learn. Objectively this is an unwarranted assertion, but nevertheless one which appears to be validated by the extremely small numbers who make the effort to master Japanese. Conversely it is said over and over again that the Japanese are bad at learning foreign languages. The reason usually given is that Japan was so long isolated from the rest of the world. Equally important reasons are the bias against verbal communication and an education system which stresses learning the grammar of foreign languages over acquiring the ability to speak them.

No doubt language difficulties are one of the major sources of misunderstandings between the Japanese and other peoples. At the same time the reserve of many Japanese abroad is the result of inability to handle the necessary foreign language with sufficient skill to risk breaking out of a safe silence.

That said, however, it is also true that the memories of the jingoistic bombast of the militarists during the Pacific War, followed by crushing defeat, have also reinforced a whole generation in their preference for silence and a low profile in international affairs. A preference which, after all, appears to have been validated by the spectacular success story of Japan's economic growth over the last thirty years. Why then, it is often argued, discard a winning formula? To many too, although Japan may have become a relatively rich country, it is also felt to be powerless because the indispensable sources of her wealth, oil and raw materials, have to be almost entirely imported from an unstable world. The feeling that Japan is isolated and fragile contributes to a certain hesitancy on the world stage.

Whatever the reasons, the Japanese, especially of the older generations, still tend to see themselves not only as militarily and economically weak, but also as culturally backward, as learners, rather than teachers. Thousands more Japanese students go abroad than foreign students go to Japan. Thousands more foreign books are translated into Japanese than Japanese books are translated into foreign languages.

The zest for foreign knowledge and culture has been one of the strengths of modern Japan. But surely the time has now come, as was suggested at the end of Part II, to reassess this old priority and for the Japanese to ask themselves whether they have something more to contribute to the world than consumer durables. In the words of Saji Keizo, introducing a symposium appropriately entitled *Japan Speaks*, 'Although Japan has become a major economic power in the world today, she has yet to express her unique cultural heritage in universal terms . . . If Japan is to find a viable role in the world community and contribute to the true progress of that community, she must discover anew, from an international perspective, the essence of her own culture and national character. Japan must also develop the means and ability to express this essence.'[4] At the very least the costs of being misinterpreted or misunderstood by other countries have now become so high that a major effort to project a clearer message would appear to be only prudent.

*

The world has changed radically since the nineteenth century, but the Europeans find it just as hard as the Japanese to break out of past patterns of thought. Europocentricism, that Copernican prison of the mind, is still strong in Europe today even though the conditions which may have made it justifiable in the past have long since ended. Europe no longer stands at the pinnacle; it is no longer the world centre of power, of knowledge and of innovation to which all other countries could be expected to turn for their enlightenment. The decline of Christianity has led to the weakening of the view that non-Christians are inferior and have therefore to be taught the truth. The colonial era is long since ended and with it the sense of superiority towards non-white peoples which was an effective barrier to learning from them. Today countries like Japan are open to the world, and speedy travel and communications make contacts much easier than ever in the past. Also today both Europe and Japan participate as neophytes in the homogenized American world culture.

In former times, it could be argued, there were insufficient incentives for Europeans to regard Japan as anything more than a marginal offshoot of China, not worth taking very seriously. Today, the fact that the Japanese can maintain higher rates of growth, that they have far fewer people unemployed and that they appear to be able to adjust their industries rapidly to be able to continue to produce competitive exports in the post-oil-shock world, all present adequate incentives for the Europeans to find out how the Japanese manage it. There is also the stimulus of the Japanese industrial and trade challenge – unless the Europeans can learn their lessons quickly, they will continue to lose markets to the Japanese both at home and throughout the world.

If the Japanese should switch from learning to teaching, then it is time the Europeans switched from teaching to learning.

There are already promising signs that these changes have begun. With 600,000 researchers and annual expenditures in 1980 of $24 billion, Japan is the world's third largest centre of technological development (after the USA and the USSR). Much of this activity has beneficial effects well beyond Japan's own borders. Already in 1977 and in 1978, there was an unprecedented shift to a positive balance in her technology trade, meaning that Japan is beginning to export more technological ideas, methods and processes than she imports. There are also signs that many Japanese are more open to the idea of Japan playing a more active role in international affairs. Individual companies and industrial foundations are making growing contributions to promoting the knowledge of Japan in foreign countries. The Japan Foundation sponsors exhibitions abroad on modern Tokyo and modern Japanese design as well as on Edo culture.

On the other hand, there are also promising signs that more and more Europeans are realizing that they have all sorts of things to learn from Japan. Several examples were quoted in Part I. Another is the scheme launched in 1979 by the EC Commission to send twenty-five young European executives per year to Japan for eighteen months to study Japanese language, culture and business practices. In itself the scheme is no doubt a mere drop in the bucket compared to all the many thousands of Japanese students and young officials and businessmen who have studied in Europe since the Meiji Restoration, nevertheless it is a possibly significant pointer of the way attitudes are gradually, all too gradually, changing in Europe.

So far, however, these are only indications of the beginnings of a shift in emphasis, the shift itself has yet to take place. That will only be achieved when the Europeans are sufficiently shaken to feel an imperative need to stop teaching and to start learning again, and when the Japanese are sufficiently self-confident to feel that they have something worth contributing to the world.

For the moment, the Europeans are just beginning to realize that Japanese industrial and technological structures may be worth studying. But, like the Japanese in the nineteenth century, they are still convinced that their own spirit (culture, values) is much superior to anything which Japan has to offer.

Public Relations

All governments and most government agencies conduct public relations both at home and abroad, just as do private corporations. In a sense the Japanese government had already begun in the early Meiji period with the establishment of the Rokumeikan which was intended to present a modern image of Japan to foreigners. Then, in 1898, the Foreign Ministry began collecting in a systematic way comments about Japan in foreign newspapers and journals. During the Russo-Japanese War this activity continued, and it formed the basis of an all-out effort to correct the yellow peril image of Japan in the West. Newspapers were bribed, editors were offered decorations, journalists were taken on junkets and friends of Japan were encouraged to express their views; a special press agency to disseminate news about Japan was set up in Germany and roving officials were seconded from their regular duties to go to Europe and America to argue, refute and propagandize.

In the years which followed, on and off such public relations activities continued. In the 1930s, for example, a deliberate effort was made to justify Japanese actions in China through radio broadcasts, pamphlets, especially commissioned books, goodwill missions overseas and conducted tours of Japan for foreign visitors. Particular efforts were made to bring school teachers to Japan because it was assumed that a favourable impression created on them would have ripple effects on the generation of their students. In 1936 Domei news agency began full-time dissemination of Japanese propaganda. In terms of the Japanese-American relationship, 'more time, attention and funds were probably devoted to cultural exchanges in the years preceding Pearl Harbor than in any previous period'.[5]

Possibly the single most effective piece of public relations after the war (apart from the Tokyo Olympics) was the decision in the 1960s to present an image of Japan as a northern country both technologically advanced and of great scenic beauty. The resultant photograph of the 'bullet' train flashing sleekly past a snow-capped Mt Fuji became extremely well known abroad and no doubt helped convey the additional message which its sponsors intended, namely that Japan was not to be confused with a tropical Asian country!

Judging from the data collected in Part I on European images of Japan, these PR activities were not too successful. Westerners were not at all impressed by the Rokumeikan – what won their attention were the government's activities in building a modern state and army. Again, during the Russo-Japanese War, Japan's propagandists probably did no more than provide arguments for those already disposed to take her side. In the 1930s, Japanese efforts to persuade the West that her activities in China were benevolent fell on deaf ears. If cultural exchanges before Pearl Harbor served to reassure Americans of the truth of the aesthetic image of Japan and to close their eyes to preparations for war, then it was a brilliant propaganda success. It is more likely however that such people-to-people cultural exchanges had little or no influence on government decision makers. Even the enormous circulation of the photo of the bullet train streaking past Mount Fuji was apparently insufficiently effective to mitigate the polluted monster image of Japan.

It would seem that official public relations can at best provide effective arguments to those already disposed to listen and to take a sympathetic view. It can sugar the pill for those who have decided to take the pill, but it cannot persuade them to take the medicine in the first place.

The most effective official PR is that which limits itself to explaining and providing further information about government aims and activities in as objective a way as possible. It should provide a steady flow of information – on failures as well as on successes.

In most periods positive images of Japan have usually been present in Europe, even when negative images have been predominant. Naturally official PR should seek to confirm the positive images and to correct the negative ones.

So far so good. But PR can only succeed if there is a story to be told. The trouble is today that Japan is a country in search of a role; she will only be able to find her voice when she has decided her role. In the meantime Japanese PR has to find ways to explain to increasingly sceptical audiences a number of awkward questions. For example, is Japan pulling her weight in the military alliances linking the parliamentary democracies? Is Japan operating under unfair advantages in her trade relations with the US and the EC in that the structure of her economy is not geared to importing manufactured goods? Is it fair that Japan should import far fewer manufactured goods from the newly industrializing countries (relative to total imports) than do the EC and the US? Why does Japan do less for developing countries than so many others? There are many people who would answer these questions by the simple answer – because the Japanese are selfish.

Rather than just shrugging off such negative reactions as arising from ignorance, misunderstanding or prejudice, it might be worth while to consider whether Japan could play a more positive role in her relations with foreign countries, and, having decided what that role is, to explain it with greater clarity than has been the custom up until now. For example, in replying to those foreigners who urge Japan to rearm, it often seems as if Japanese spokesmen prefer to deflect such advice by ambivalently replying, 'Yes, yes, we agree we ought to consider doing more and please rest assured we *intend* to do so, but at the moment it just happens that we have certain budgetary and political difficulties.' Would it not be preferable to say simply, 'Yes, of course, we are considering our own self-interests. But rearmament is not in Japan's interest at the moment and so we do not intend to embark upon it.'

The advantages gained by Japan in adopting a low profile in the post-war years were no doubt great. But we have now entered a new period of history in which the dangers of fuzziness may be equally great.

Because I believe the Europeans need no encouragement to talk about themselves and explain their positions to others, I have limited my comments on European PR to the particular question of the EC's presentation of its case to others. Firstly, as an ex-EC Commissioner, Mr Simonet, has remarked, 'European policies lack clarity.' The reasons are not hard to find; EC decisions are usually tortuous compromises between an exceptionally high number of interested parties – between the bureaucracies, politicians and parliaments of ten countries; between the half-dozen institutions of the Community itself; between the courts, the industries, the unions and the media – all of ten countries. Even insiders find it hard to know what is going on and why. And the general public in Europe is confused or just not interested.

The situation is not improved by the language in which Community policies are expressed. This is either the legalistic technical jargon of administrative regulations suitable to the subject matter, or it is the officialese of spokesmen or drafters of communiqués, experts in using words to hide more than they reveal. After one meeting of an EC Council of Ministers in 1979, an exasperated correspondent of *Le Monde* compiled a short guide to such EC officialese:

Action, agreed to take appropriate:	did nothing
Co-ordinate, will closely:	have agreed to differ
Decisions, concrete:	aspirations
European union:	complacent retrospect
In principle:	not
Note of, takes:	dismisses
Reaffirms:	is bored by
Satisfaction, expresses:	is alarmed
With a view to:	in the hope of thwarting

Decision-making in all our countries today is multipolar and complex and the language of government bureaucrats is not that of poets and philosophers. That said, the uncertain nature of the EC – something more than a customs union but less than the United States of Europe – and the uncertainty as to what role it should be playing make its policies and their expression exceptionally opaque.

To make matters worse, because of its special nature, the Community often speaks with a confusion of tongues. This has frequently happened in its relations with Japan. In November 1976, just after the European Council solemnly called on Japan to reduce her shipbuilding capacity, a Danish shipping company ordered six bulk carriers from Japanese shipyards. In December 1980, to take another example, a month after a Council of Foreign Ministers of the EC had called once again for a united strategy towards Japan, the co-ordinator of French policy on Japan who had been especially appointed by the French President stated to the press that, 'the French government has chosen to negotiate bilaterally with Japan . . . because the different European countries have chosen such different positions'. And in case anybody had failed to get the message, he added, 'The Commission in Brussels wants to negotiate on appearances, but I wish to negotiate on the basis of realities.'[6] Again, in May 1981, the EC Council of Ministers called for a united strategy towards Japan and empowered the Commission to seek a self-restraint agreement on exports of Japanese cars to the EC analagous to the agreement reached by the US with Japan. Within weeks of the decision, however, Germany and the Benelux had come to bilateral agreements with Tokyo on this issue thus effectively undermining the Community approach. Not for the first time the Commission was left uninformed, frustrated by the member states and humiliated before Japan.

Given this sort of confusion and fumbling, can anyone blame third countries such as Japan for finding it hard to distinguish who speaks for the EC?

Lastly, the PR of the EC is faced with the difficult task of explaining policies which to the outsider appear too often as negative or ludicrously ineffective in their results. It is no easy matter, for example, to try and explain why it is that the EC's efforts to keep foreign imports out of Europe appear to receive so much more attention than efforts to promote its own exports to foreign countries. Nor can 'butter mountains' and 'wine lakes' be easily presented in a positive light to consumers faced with rising food prices.

The day that the EC comes to play a more positive role, its public image will no doubt improve, and the work of its PR specialists will be made somewhat more easy.

There is no hope of a policy being understood, or of improving relations with a foreign country, unless a clear message is sent. As a minimum, therefore, the EC should ensure that three things are done, once an external policy decision has been taken:

1. Explain clearly to the affected country what the policy is and the reasons why it was adopted;
2. Put the explanation in plain language, not in jargon; and
3. Speak with one voice.

The Scholars

Turning now to the actual transmission of messages between Japan and Europe and the interpretation of each to the other by professional mediators such as academic specialists, journalists or diplomats: are they doing their job well?

The initial response, based on the copious evidence of bungled communications cited in previous chapters, must be clearly not.

Take the academic specialists. Particularly amongst European Japanologists, with whose work I am more familiar than that of Japanese 'Europeanologists', there seems to be an inability to focus their studies on matters of contemporary interest and, having done so, to convey their findings in such a way as to have any hope of changing the world or influencing the way people perceive it.

There is over-specialization in the hands of language experts who tend to justify their own role as intermediaries by emphasizing the differences between Europe and Japan. There is also an over-emphasis on past culture at the expense of the present, perhaps because it is felt to be more esoteric and hence better suited to academic investigation. This is related to the bias of many of the early enthusiasts of things Japanese whose romantic search for the exotic led them to highlight what were often untypical and marginal aspects of Japan. Another academic bias is over-reliance on the written word. It seems almost as if the acquiring of a difficult foreign language ensures that the expert will forever afterwards lay most value on the past written record.

Academic experts on Japan have been slow to acquire new disciplines such as sociology, economics or comparative literature. When they have managed to do so they pursue their special field with hardly a glance at related disciplines. This 'tunnel approach' is also found in both Europe and Japan in the fierce loyalty to one country or culture. European Japanologists are usually totally ignorant of other countries around Japan, and Japanese experts on Germany, for example, will ignore France, and a specialist on Italian culture will rarely know Germany. This single-country focus is particularly regrettable today when regional co-operation and integration in both Europe and in East Asia make it virtually impossible to follow events in one country without understanding how they fit in with what is going on around it. Another disadvantage of the single-country approach is that it often leads to the uncritical acceptance of that country's own self-image.

Many of these criticisms apply as well to journalists and diplomats, all of whom to the extent that they share the same guild mentality of professional cultural intermediaries, tend to overemphasize the differences between cultures, and focus their attention on the supposedly unique and unusual features of the culture they are writing about. They also tend, like all specialist groups, to fall too easily into the habit of talking exclusively to members of their own group, neglecting to address themselves to the public at large.

Given this formidable catalogue of weaknesses of European academic experts on Japan, I am always astonished that the Japanese government and big industry from time to time make gifts of large sums of money to traditional academic centres of Japanology in Europe. Surely they cannot believe that Europeans need yet another translation of the *Tale of Genji*?

When it comes to the students, the contrast is striking: Western students in Japan seem mainly to study the arts, whereas Japanese students in the West study for the most part science and technology. Each, in other words, is pursuing the old image of the other.

The following four proposals are put forward to improve the educational contribution to mutual understanding between Europe and Japan:

1. A much more effective way to encourage greater knowledge of modern Japan in European universities would be not to give grants to the traditional centres of Japanology (except in the limited sense of language schools) but rather to encourage knowledge of Japan in general undergraduate courses. The aim would be to make knowledge of Japan part of the normal education of young people, not an exotic option. A first step, in other words, towards closing the enormous gap in Europe between the knowledge of Japan held by specialists and the ignorance of Japan among the general public. At

the graduate or faculty level, funds should be made available to economists, doctors, lawyers, chemists and engineers and any others who expressed a serious interest in finding out about the Japanese experience in their special fields. Their influence spreads far wider in the university than the Japanologist's has ever done.

2. As part of the attempt to get more Europeans to go to Japan, more travel scholarships and grants could be made available to students. Government and business should be encouraged to contribute funds as much as the universities. The establishment of a Japanese equivalent of the Fulbright awards would have great impact.

3. In Japan it is regrettable that there are not more centres of European studies. Such centres could allow the staff as well as the students to escape the narrow confines of single-country specialization and achieve a more balanced and useful knowledge of modern Europe. There could also be a much greater opening of the Japanese university system, including the elite state universities, whose doors still remain closed to foreign staff.

4. In most countries it is recognized that fluency in foreign languages, especially English, is vital for communicating with the rest of the world. So provision is usually made in the education system for early exposure to speaking a foreign language or two. In Japan, on the other hand, fluency in speaking English is positively discouraged by the numerous examinations on written English and its grammar which students are forced to take in order to get in to the right schools and universities. The result is that most students can get no serious exposure to foreign languages until after they graduate from university. And by then it is usually too late to acquire fluency. Those who for one reason or another do go abroad and become fluent in foreign languages often find themselves penalized in the job market when they return to Japan. If Japan wishes to play a full role and to develop an effective voice in today's world culture, she must reform her educational system in such a way as to encourage fluency in foreign languages at an early age and to give much greater

recognition to young people who manage to achieve such a vital skill.

The Journalists

Turning now to the journalists, those popular cultural mediators par excellence, the situation has its encouraging as well as its disappointing aspects. In general, information about Europe is fed back to Japan accurately and in considerable detail. On the other hand, information about Japan in Europe is often inaccurate, appears only sporadically and is found usually tucked away in the business section of newspapers.

While I was in Japan I kept a careful watch on Japanese newspaper coverage of Europe, especially the EC. It was usually accurate but lacking a sense of flair. There were only very few occasions when the Japanese foreign correspondent appeared to have been able to tear himself away from official briefings and actually go out and investigate a story. As a consequence the coverage was a bit wooden and although detailed would sometimes miss the point. In contrast the same reporters were often much better informed when it came to writing about the visit of a Japanese politician to Europe.

Reporting on Japan is in the hands of some 250 accredited foreign correspondents from all over the world. At any given moment there are also some several hundred journalists visiting Japan on special assignments. Of the accredited Tokyo foreign correspondents in 1981 about sixty were working for news media in the EC countries (compared with about eighty Japanese correspondents stationed in the EC). The majority were from England (twenty-two) and Germany (eighteen) with ten from France and three from Italy. Only thirteen of the sixty were working for radio or TV stations.[7]

With a handful of notable exceptions, the foreign correspondents are usually unable to speak or read Japanese, so it is perhaps hardly surprising that the reporting out of Tokyo rarely gives the impression of being well informed. Even the best of the correspondents, however, face a discouraging lack of interest in stories filed from Tokyo. Much of what they send home either never appears or is relegated to a corner of their newspaper.

The following steps could be taken to improve the level of reporting on Japan:

1. Undertake systematic study of the coverage of Japan in the European media, including that originating from the Tokyo correspondents, in order to pinpoint the main strengths and weaknesses in the European reporting of events in Japan. Next it would pay to try and make up the weakness by doing what every other major country does, namely distribute scholarships to journalists to enable them to train in Japan.

2. The practice of discriminating against foreign correspondents in Tokyo by excluding them from the Japanese journalists' 'clubs' attached to ministries, politicians and political parties should be brought to an end. (A step in this direction was taken in 1979 when the Foreign Ministry Club was opened to foreign correspondents.) Nor is there any obvious reason why the Japanese government spokesman, the Chief Cabinet Secretary, should exclude foreign correspondents from his numerous press briefings.

3. There is probably a good case to be made for Japan to set up a more extensive news service, not only to bring foreign news into the country as is the case now, but also to disseminate Japanese news abroad.

The Diplomats

Both academic specialists and journalists can be judged by their output. The same cannot be said of diplomats whose reporting and activities are shrouded in a veil of secrecy. This was not always the case. In the old days, many of the best European experts on Japan were diplomats.

They would be trained to fluency in the language and then posted and reposted in the country for long periods. As the last and greatest of the scholar diplomats, Sir George Sansom, put it, they were not 'faced with quintuple bits of nonsense, piles of misleading statistics and even the awful likelihood that somebody may distort the studies by giving a call on the trans-oceanic telephone'.[8]

Today the scholar-diplomat has long since ceased to exist; diplomats are kept too busy, not only by the flood of communications but also by the endless stream of visitors who jet into town.

It is not only the European embassies in Tokyo which are kept busy by a stream of visitors – jet travel is world wide and Japanese embassies in Europe are faced with exactly the same calls on their time. Indeed Japanese diplomats frequently point out that they are kept busier in this respect than their European colleagues because so many more Japanese visit Europe than vice versa.

After the invention of the cable and the telephone, it is often said, embassies became little more than post offices. This is to do them a grave injustice – they have also come to perform the functions of travel agents.

In the old days, the embassy was often the only source of information and knowledge about a country which the home government could rely on. The ambassador for months or years on end was the senior and only representative of his country. The embassy was a vital and often independent link between nations. Today all that has changed with the proliferation of many different channels of communication and opportunities for direct meetings.

As many of the traditional functions of the embassy have declined, whittled away by more rapid or effective channels of communication, the discreet veil of secrecy surrounding the diplomat's activities has become ever more impenetrable. It is therefore almost impossible to judge how effective diplomats are at keeping the information flow between governments accurate. But one thing is certain: diplomats and foreign ministries will always be vulnerable to criticism, because like other cultural intermediaries, they are marginal in the strict sense of the word – they stand on the fringes between countries. The more diplomats retreat into a privileged sanctuary, the more they lay themselves open to such criticisms. There is a good case then for:

1. Opening wider the privileged ranks of the diplomats to ordinary mortals.
2. Requiring diplomats to be judged by the same standards as

anybody else, that is to say by their output. Without damage to confidentiality this could be made much more freely available, both in the country in which the diplomat is stationed and back at home.

3. Making greater efforts on the European side to ensure that at any given time several members of the embassy staff are fluent in Japanese.

Scholars, journalists and diplomats are only three of the different types of mediators between our countries. They are full-time professionals though. I have suggested some ways in which they could do a better job. But there are many other mediators – politicians, businessmen, labour leaders, students, athletes, to name some of the more important part-time ones. Recent years have seen an increase in their interaction and exchanges, but much more could be done to bring them together and to assist their efforts at mutual comprehension. For a start the traffic is still too much a one-way affair of Japanese going to Europe. More must be done to encourage Europeans to go to Japan.

The aim should be to increase the opportunities for meaningful contacts, and to increase the channels of communication. Only then can there be a shift from chance symbols to regular signals; from a limited number of outdated stereotypes to a full range of apposite images; from the capricious and emotional to the fixed and considered.

Nothing can be achieved until the Japanese define more clearly the role they wish to play on the world stage, and having decided it, make massive efforts to be better understood.

Nothing can be achieved unless the Europeans, in reacting to external pressures, respond positively with a newly awakened desire to learn.

Notes

Part 1   The Upside-Down Land:
Japan as Seen by the Europeans

1   Ministry of Foreign Affairs, Tokyo, 'Survey of public opinion towards Japan in five EC countries' (*EC gokakoku tai Nichi seiron chōsa*), Tokyo, 1978.

2   On the European image of the Orient see Steadman, J. M., *The Myth of Asia*, New York, 1969; Said, E. W., *Orientalism*, London, 1979 and Martino, P., *L'Orient dans la Littérature Française au XVIIe et au XVIIIe siècle*, Paris, 1906.

3   Cooper, M., *They Came to Japan; an Anthology of European Reports on Japan, 1543–1640*, Berkeley, 1965.

4   Lach, D., *Asia in the Making of Europe*, vol. I: *The Age of Discovery*, Chicago, 1965, pp.687–8.

5   Alcock, R., *The Capital of the Tycoon, A Narrative of Three Years Residence in Japan*, 2 vols., New York, 1863, vol. I, pp.357–8.

6   Lowell, P., *The Soul of the Far East*, Boston, 1888, pp.1–2.

7   Lewis, J. in the *Far Eastern Economic Review*, 20 April 1979, p.70.

8   Chamberlain, B. H., *Things Japanese*, London and Tokyo, 1890, pp.480–82.

9   Hearn, L., *Japan, an Attempt at Interpretation*, Boston, 1904, pp.7–8.

10   *The Economist*, London, 31 December 1977, p.34 and Clark, G. writing in the *Japan Economic Journal*, 5 June 1979.

11   Quoted in Cooper (see n.3), p.4. On this period in general see Boxer, C. R., *The Christian Century in Japan, 1549–1650*, Berkeley, 1951.

12   When the first members of the Japanese mission to Europe (1584–6) were received by Philip II of Spain they presented him with a gold screen on which was a map, not of Japan, but of China. See Lach (n.4), p.693.

13   Ministry of Foreign Affairs, Tokyo (see n.1).

14 Quoted in Boxer, C. R., *Jan Campagnie in Japan, 1600–1850*, The Hague, 1950, p.170.

15 Kaempfer, E., *History of Japan*, London, 1726–8, reprinted 3 vols., Glasgow, 1906, vol. III, p.301.

16 *Encyclopaedia Britannica*, 1st edition (1771), vol. II, p.210; 2nd edition (1780), vol. V, pp.3816–20; 6th edition (1823), vol. V, pp.33–40. The 7th edition (1842), vol. XIII, pp.510–22 quotes the 'Raffles Report' as being written by his physician, Dr Ainslie. The report if it was ever published has not survived.

17 Review of MacFarlane's *Japan* in the *Christian Remembrance*, vol. XXIV (1852), p.448.

18 See Miner, E. R., *The Japanese Tradition in British and American Literature*, Princeton, 1958 and Schwartz, W. L., *The Imaginative Interpretation of the Far East in Modern French Literature*, Paris, 1927. Among the many excellent books on Japanese influences on European painting, see Yamada, C. F., *Dialogue in Art, Japan and the West*, Tokyo, 1976 and Wichmann, S., *Japonisme*, London, 1981.

19 Dumas, Alexandre, *Francillon*, Paris, 1887, Act IV, Scene 2.

20 *The Mikado*, London, 1885.

21 De Beauvoir, *Pékin, Yeddo, San Francisco, Voyage autour du Monde*, Paris, 1872, p.160. Quoted by Lehmann, J. P., *The Image of Japan, From Feudal Isolation to World Power, 1850–1905*, London, 1978.

22 Arnold, E., *Seas and Lands*, London, 1898, pp.240–43.

23 Quoted in Cooper (see n.3), pp.64–5.

24 On Loti, see Nishimoto, K., *Loti en Face du Japon*, Quebec, 1962 and Ono, S., *A Western Image of Japan: What Did the West See through the Eyes of Loti and Hearn?* Geneva, 1972.

25 Loti, P., *Madame Chrysanthème*, Paris, 1887, p.239.

26 Norman. H., *The Real Japan*, London, 1892, p.239. Thirty pages of quotations from Western authors eulogizing Japanese women are contained in Ashmead, J., *The Idea of Japan: 1853–1895, Japan as Described by American and Other Travellers from the West* (unpublished Ph.D. thesis, Harvard University, Cambridge, Mass., 1951), pp.400–32.

27 James, H., 'Pierre Loti', in *Essays in London and Elsewhere*, New York, 1893, pp.151–87.

28 Puccini had a number of predecessors, the first of whom was Saint-Saens, whose *La Princesse Jaune* (1872) tells how a young Dutch scientist – perhaps modelled after the German Japanologist Von Siebold – becomes infatuated with a Japanese statuette and under the influence of drugs fancies himself in Japan. Other light operas on

butterfly themes include Sidney James, *The Geisha* (1896) and Pietro Mascani, *Iris* (1898).

29 Chéradame, A., *Le Monde et la Guerre Russo-Japonaise*, Paris, 1906, pp.3–5. See also Pozdneyev, D. M., *Japan, Present and Future, in the Eyes of Western Writers*, St Petersburg, 1895.

30 Holland, C. (pseud. of C. J. Hankinson), *My Japanese Wife*, London, 1895; 21st edition, 1916, and also by the same author, *Mousmé*, London, 1902.

31 *Poupée Japonaise* by Champsour, Paris, 1903; *Petite Mousmé* by Hautemer, Paris, 1907; *Poupée Parfumée* by Bouquet, Paris, 1925; *Thisen, La Petite Amie Exotique* by D'Estray, Paris, 1905; *Burmese Days* by Orwell, London, 1934; 'Masterson', in Maugham, *Complete Short Stories*, vol. IV, pp.266–75, London, 1951.

32 Fleming, I., *You Only Live Twice*, London, 1964, pp.1, 190.

33 Valéry in Preface to Bezombes, R., *L'Exotisme dans l'Art et la Pensée*, Paris, 1953, p.vii.

34 Hearn (see n.9), p.361.

35 Bacon, A. M., *Japanese Girls and Women*, Boston, 1902, p.262.

36 Kipling, R., *From Sea to Sea*, vol. XIII of *Writings in Prose and Verse of Rudyard Kipling*, New York, 1920, pp.408, 442.

37 Bird, I. L., *Unbeaten Tracks in Japan*, New York, vol. I, p.236.

38 Morri, Yasotarō, *Sunrise Synthesis, Aspects of Changing Japan*, Tokyo, 1935, p.14.

39 Curtis, W. E., *The Yankees of the East*, New York, 1896, vol. I, p.253.

40 Loti, P., 'Un Bal à Yeddo', in *Japoneries d'Automne*, Paris, 1889, pp.77–106. The German observer was Netto, C., *Papierschmetterlinge aus Japan*, Hamburg, 1898.

41 Hearn, L., *Glimpses of Unfamiliar Japan*, Boston, 1894, vol. I, p.665.

42 Hearn, L., *Japanese Letters*, 1922, quoted in Ono (see n.24), p.170.

43 Kipling (see n.36), p.402.

44 Kipling (see n.36), pp.418–19.

45 Villenoisy, F. de, *La Guerre Sino-Japonaise, ses Conséquences pour l'Europe*, Paris and Limoges, 1895.

46 Norman, H., *The People and Politics of the Far East*, London, 1895, p.2.

47 Pinon, R., 'La Guerre Russo-Japonaise et l'Opinion Européenne', *Revue des Deux Mondes*, vol. XXI, May 1904, pp.191–2.

48 *The Times*, 11 February 1904, quoted in Lehmann (see n.21), upon whose excellent study I have drawn heavily for this period.

49 Falkenegg, Von, *Japan, die Neue Weltmacht*, Berlin, 1905, quoted in Lehmann (see n.21).

50 Pinon (see n.47), pp.218–19, quoted in Lehmann (see n.21).

51 'Parabellum' took up the theme of a war between Japan and the United States in the bestselling German novel *Bansai!* published in Leipzig in 1905. There were many other popular novels on the same theme at this time.

52 Théry, E., in *Journal*, 11 February 1904.

53 Preface by the diplomat-politician and Nobel Prize winner Estournelles de Constant in Théry, E., *Le Péril Jaune: La Transformation du Japon*, Paris, 1901.

54 Pinon (see n.47), pp.194–5.

55 Ministry of Foreign Affairs, Tokyo (see n.1).

56 Spencer's letter is quoted in Hearn (see n.9), pp.481–4. On Swedish reactions to the Japanese victory see Burgman, T., *Svensk Opinion Och Diplomat Undur Rysk – Japanska Kriget 1904–1905*, Stockholm, 1965.

57 France, A., *Sur la Pierre Blanche*, Paris, 1904, quoted in Lehmann (see n.21), pp.154–6.

58 Plomer, W., *Autobiography*, New York, 1976, pp.181–2.

59 Pinon (see n.47), p.217.

60 Barrett, J., 'New Japan, Schoolmaster of Asia', *Review of Reviews*, December 1902.

61 Morri (see n.38), p.18.

62 Kipling (see n.36), p.370.

63 *Evening Standard*, London, 24 September 1937, quoted in *Japanese Aggression and World Opinion*, compiled by Press Bureau, Chinese Delegation, Geneva, 1937.

64 Woodcock, G., *The British in the Far East*, London, 1969, p.212; Manchester, W., *American Caesar, Douglas MacArthur, 1880–1964*, New York, 1979, pp.187–8.

65 Hitler, A., *Mein Kampf*, English translation, Boston, 1943, pp.290 –91; *Hitler's Secret Conversations, 1941–1944*, New York, 1972, *passim*; Presseisen, E. L., 'Le racisme et les Japonais: un dilemme Nazi', *Revue d'Histoire de la Deuxième Guerre Mondiale*, vol. XIII, 4 July 1963. Martin, B., *Deutschland und Japan im Zweiten Weltkreig*, Göttingen, 1969.

66 Petit, L., *Pays de Mousmé! Pays de Guerre!*, Paris, 1905; Apellius, M., *Cannoni e ciliegi in fiore*, Rome, 1941; Benedict, R., *The Chrysanthemum and the Sword*, Boston, 1946.

67 *Vision*, Paris, 15 March 1971, pp.15–16. There is a useful collection of excerpts and analyses of European and American criticisms of Japan in recent years in *OuBei no tai Nichi hihan no bunrui, bunseki* (report by Nomura Research Institute, published by Keizai Koho Centre,

Tokyo, 1980). Ogura, K., 'Japan–US Economic Frictions' (*Nichibei keizai masatsu*), Tokyo, 1982 is an excellent study.

68 *Time*, 2 March 1970, pp.25–6.
69 *EC Bulletin*, 3–1971, pp.26–7.
70 *Time*, 2 March 1970, p.29.
71 *Newsweek*, 7 May 1979, p.4 and *Japan Times* questionnaire, 26 June 1979.
72 Nakamura, M., unpublished paper, Tokyo, 1979.
73 *Overland Monthly*, July 1896, quoted in Iriye, A., *Mutual Images: Essays on American-Japanese Relations*, Cambridge, 1975, p.75.
74 Guillain, R., *The Japanese Challenge*, Paris, 1969; Scharnagl, M., *Japan: The Planned Aggression*, Munich, 1969; Hedberg, S., *The Japanese Threat*, Paris, 1970; Jecquier, C., *The Japanese Industrial Challenge*, Lausanne, 1970; Delassus, L., *Japan: Monster or Model*, Lausanne, 1970; Price, V., *The Japanese Miracle and Peril*, New York, 1971; Efimov, J., *Stop the Japanese Now*, Paris, 1971.
75 *Japan Times* questionnaire of 26 June 1979; Koestler, A., *The Lotus and the Robot*, London, 1960.
76 *The Economist* correspondents, *Consider Japan*, London, 1963. The articles upon which the book is based first appeared in *The Economist* in September 1962.
77 Federation of British Industries, *Report of Mission to the Far East, August to November 1934*, London, 1934.
78 'Pacific Century, 1975–2075', *The Economist*, 4 January 1975, pp.15–35.
79 'Proceedings of Parliamentary Committee on Science and Technology (Japan Sub-Committee)', *Hansard*, 14 July 1977, pp.71–88.
80 'Report on Trade with Japan of the Subcommittee on Trade of the Committee on Ways and Means', US House of Representatives, Washington, 5 September 1980, Preface.
81 Ministry of Foreign Affairs, Tokyo (see n.1). The Japanese Foreign Ministry conducted the second poll in January 1982. An opinion poll conducted in France by NHK in 1981 revealed that more than 50 per cent of those polled did not know where Japan is and one third could not name the capital.
82 Centre for Youth Policy, Prime Minister's Office (eds.), 'Japanese youth as compared with world youth' (*Sekai no seinen tono hikaku kara mita Nihon no seinen*), Tokyo, 1978, pp.112–13.
83 Benedict (see n.66), p.2.
84 Scidmore, E. R., *Jinrikisha Days in Japan*, New York, pp.369–70.
85 Chamberlain (see n.8), p.303.

86 Kimpei, Shiba, *Oh, Japan! Yesterday, Today and Probably Tomorrow*, Tenterden, 1979, p.201.
87 *Newsweek*, 21 January 1974, p.56.
88 Koestler (see n.75), p.175.
89 Ballon, R., 'A European Views the Japanese', *The Wheel Extended*, Special Supplement, No. 2, 1978, pp.1–5.

Part II The Cultural Museum:
Europe as Seen by the Japanese

1 Natsume, Sōseki, 'The Enlightenment of Modern Japan' (Gendai Nihon no Kaika), a talk given in 1911, quoted in Yamanouchi, Hisaki, *The Search for Authenticity in Modern Japanese Literature*, Cambridge, 1978, p.77.
2 Doi, Takeo, *The Anatomy of Dependence*, Tokyo, 1973.
3 Dore, R. P., 'Japan and the Third World', unpublished paper, July, 1979.
4 Katō, Shūichi, 'Japanese Writers and Modernization', in Jansen, M. (ed.), *Changing Japanese Attitudes towards Modernization*, Princeton, 1965, pp.425–46.
5 Tani, Shinichi and Sugase, Tadashi, *Nanban Art*, New York, 1973.
6 Tani and Sugase (see n.5).
7 Shiga, Shigetaka, *History of Nations*, Tokyo, 1888, p.139.
8 On *Rangaku* see Keene, D., *The Japanese Discovery of Europe, 1720–1830*, Stanford, 1969.
9 Sugita, Genpaku, *Dawn of Western Science in Japan*, 1815; English translation, Tokyo, 1969, pp.38, 43. See also Keene (n.8), pp.20–24.
10 Sugita (see n.9), pp.16–17.
11 Keene (see n.8).
12 French, G. L., *Shiba Kokan*, New York, 1974.
13 Quoted in Keene, D., *World within Walls, Japanese Literature of the Premodern Era, 1660–1867*, Tokyo, 1976, p.46.
14 Aizawa, Seishisai, 'New Proposals' (*Shinron*), 1825, translated in De Bary, W. T., Tsunoda, R., and Keene, D., *Sources of Japanese Tradition*, New York, 1958, vol. I, pp.95–6.
15 Shionoya wrote these words in 1859. They are translated in Van Gulik, R., 'Kakkaron: A Japanese Echo of the Opium War', *Monumenta Serica*, 1939, vol. IV, pp. 478–545.
16 Fujita, Tōko (1806–54), a leading spokesman of the Mito school whose slogan was 'Reverence the Emperor, expel the barbarians', quoted in Chang, R. C., *From Prejudice to Tolerance: A Study of the Japanese Image of the West, 1862–1864*, Tokyo, 1970, p.61.

17 Chang (see n.16).

18 Fukuzawa, Yukichi, *The Autobiography of Fukuzawa Yukichi*, New York, 1966 (first published 1899), p.21.

19 Chang (see n.16), p.184, quoting the *Diary of a Delegation to Washington*, 1861.

20 Fukuzawa (see n.18), p.216.

21 Fukuzawa (see n.18), pp.43, 21.

22 Fukuzawa (see n.18), p.91.

23 Satow, E., 'Diary of a Member of the Japanese Embassy to Europe, 1862–1863', *The Chinese and Japanese Repository*, XXIV, 1865, p.368.

24 Fukuzawa, Yukichi, *An Outline Theory of Civilization*, Tokyo, 1973, Foreword (first published 1875). On the role of foreign experts in Japan, see Jones, H. L., *Live Machines: Hired Foreigners and Meiji Japan*, Seattle, 1980 and on the role played by overseas students, see Watanabe, M., 'Japanese Students Abroad and the Acquisition of Scientific and Technical Knowledge', *Journal of World History*, vol. IX, no. 1, 1966, pp.254–93.

25 Nakamura, Hajime, *Parallel Developments*, Tokyo, 1975, pp.507–8.

26 Deguchi, Kazuo, *Shuppan o Manabu Hito no Tame ni*, Tokyo, 1979, gives the list of bestsellers. On the adaptation of Samuel Smiles to Japan, see Kinmonth, E. J., *The Self-Made Man in Meiji Japan: From Samurai to Salaryman*, Berkeley, 1981. The popularity of Samuel Smiles's teachings for individual advancement were matched by the influence in Japan of such social Darwinists as Bluntschli of Herbert Spencer who argued that the survival of the fittest applied as well to nations as to individuals (see below, Part III, n.7).

27 Hattori, Busshō, *Tokyo Shin Hanjo Ki*, 1874, translated and quoted in Keene, D., *Modern Japanese Fiction*, New York, 1956, pp.34–6.

28 Baelz, E., *Awakening Japan: The Diary of a German Doctor*, Bloomington, 1974, p.239.

29 Fukuzawa (see n.24), p.175.

30 Fukuzawa (see n.18), p.120.

31 Akutagawa, Ryūnosuke, 'The Ball', in *Short Stories by R. Akutagawa*, translated by Shaw, G. W., Tokyo, 1930, pp.99–122.

32 Natsume, Sōseki, *Bungakuron*, quoted in Yamanouchi (see n.1), p.48.

33 Nakae, Chōmin, *Kindai Nihon Shisō Taikei*, quoted in Lifton, R. J., Kato, S., and Reich, M. R., *Six Lives, Six Deaths*, New Haven, p.133.

34 Pyle, K. B., *The New Generation in Meiji Japan, Problems of Cultural Identity*, Stanford, 1969, p.74.

35 Tokutomi, Sohō, *Jiden*, quoted in Pyle (see n.34), p.85.

36 Chamberlain, B. H., *Things Japanese*, Tokyo, p.263.

37 Morri, Yasotarō, *Sunrise Synthesis, Aspects of Changing Japan*, Tokyo, 1935, p.145.

38 Fukuzawa (see n.18), p.335.

39 Okakura, Tenshin, *The Book of Tea*, Boston, 1906, p.9.

40 Kawakami, Hajime, *Binbō Monogatari*, Tokyo, 1917.

41 Mushanokōji, Saneatsu, *Love and Death*, translated by Marquandt, W. F., New York, 1958.

42 Tokutomi, Sohō, 'Commentary on the Imperial Rescript Declaring War on the United States and the British Empire', translated in De Bary (see n.14), p.293.

43 Shillony, Ben-Ami, *Politics and Culture in Wartime Japan*, Oxford, 1981, pp.134–77.

44 Chūō Chōsasha, *Suki na Kuni, Kirai na Kuni* (Countries liked and disliked), Tokyo. This opinion poll has been conducted every three months since 1964.

45 Nihonjin Kenkyūkai (eds), *Nihonjin no tai Gaikoku Taido* (Japanese attitudes towards foreign countries), Tokyo, 1977. On early Japanese images of Germany, see Opitz, F., 'Die Entwicklung des japanischen Deutschlandbildes', and on recent images see Zahl, K. F., 'Die Deutschen – in den Augen der Japaner', *Zeitschrift für Kulturaustausch*, 1980, no. 2, as well as other articles in the same issue. A fascinating catalogue of a recent exhibition of pictures of each other's countries painted by Japanese and German schoolchildren shows the extraordinary degree to which the most obvious stereotypes are still passed from one generation to the next: *Hakenkreuz und Butterfly, Japanische Schüler sehen uns, Deutscher Schüler sehen Japan*, Stuttgart, 1981.

46 Nippon Research Centre, 'A Research Report on the Study of Japanese Attitudes towards the European Communities', Tokyo, 1979.

47 Poll on attitudes towards foreigners released by the Prime Minister's Office, Tokyo, October, 1980. The second poll is quoted in Nihonjin Kenkyūkai (see n.45), pp.45–78, which was based on a survey conducted in the late 1960s.

48 Nihonjin Kenkyūkai (see n.45), pp.91–2, quoting a 1967 survey.

49 Kanagaki, Robun, *Aguranabe* ('The Beefeater'), Tokyo, 1871, translated in Keene (see n.27), p.32.

50 Morri (see n.37), p.120.

51 Kokuminsei Chōsa, Tokyo, 1958, 1963, 1968, 1973 and 1978.

52 Nakagawa, Yatsuhirō, 'Japan, the Welfare Superpower', *Journal of*

Japanese Studies, vol. V, no. 1, 1979, pp.5–56 (originally appeared in *Bungei Shunjū*). The bestselling author he quotes is Fukada, Yusuke (also writing in *Bungei Shunjū*, March 1977).

53 Amaya, Naohiro, 'Ushiwakamaru Strategy for Trade Frictions', *Kanchō Nyūsu Jihyō*, January 1977.

54 Tourism White Paper *Kankō Hakusho*, Tokyo, 1979.

55 Nihon Kōtsū Kōsha, *Nyūsu to Shiryō*, Tokyo, 1981.

56 Fukada, Yusuke, *Shin Seiyō Jijō*, Tokyo, 1976.

57 Kokuminsei Chosa, 1978 and *Asahi Jyānaru*, vol. XXI, no. 32 (17 August 1979).

58 Ishida, Takeshi, 'Weight of the Past in the Japanese Vision of Europe', unpublished paper, Tokyo, 1979.

Part III   Open Markets and Double-Bolted Doors

1 Ono, Yeijirō, *The Industrial Transition in Japan*, Boston, 1890, p.104.

2 Smith, Adam, *The Wealth of Nations*.

3 Keene, D., *The Japanese Discovery of Europe, 1720–1830*, Stanford, 1969, p.109.

4 Itō, Hirobumi recording Ōkubo's words, translated in De Bary, W. T., Tsunoda, R. and Keene, D., *Sources of Japanese Tradition*, New York, 1958, vol. II, pp.158–9.

5 There was an emotional hostility towards foreign goods in the 1860s as recorded by Fukuzawa Yukichi: 'Stores dealing in foreign goods were attacked for no other reason than that they sold foreign commodities which "caused loss" to the country,' Fukuzawa, Yukichi, *The Autobiography of Fukuzawa Yukichi*, New York, 1966 (first published 1899), p.223.

6 Sugi, Kōji and Nishimura, Shigeki in *Meiroku Zasshi* no. 24 (December 1874) and no. 29 (February 1875), quoted in Braisted, W. R., *Meiroku Zasshi*, Tokyo, 1976, pp.302–4, 356–8.

7 Herbert Spencer, the social Darwinist, had an enormous reputation in both China and Japan in the late nineteenth, early twentieth centuries, presumably because the implication of his philosophy is that there is no immutable law making one nation more powerful than another – it only requires efforts and effective political and economic policies to boost a nation up the path to progress. Spencer wrote to Baron Kentarō in 1892 answering his requests for advice on Japanese policy towards the foreign powers. He gave his permission for the advice to be passed to Prime Minister Itō, on the condition that it not

be made public in his lifetime to avoid arousing the animosity of his fellow Englishmen. Spencer's letter of 26 August 1892, which I have quoted from, was published in *The Times* of London on 18 January 1904, just after his death. Its publication did not give rise to a storm of animosity, possibly because the conditions to which Spencer addressed himself had been bypassed by events with Japan's successful renegotiation of the unequal treaties. It is also possible that readers of Spencer's letter could see some sense to his arguments. The letter is reprinted in Hearn, L., *Japan, An Attempt at Interpretation*, Boston, 1904, pp. 481–4.

8   Chamberlain, B. H., *Things Japanese*, London, 1890, 5th edition, 1905, p.261.

9   Norman, H., *The Real Japan*, London, 1892, pp.356–7.

10 Norman, H., *The People and Politics of the Far East*, London, 1895, pp.380–83.

11 Norman (see n.10), p.383.

12 Murray, David, *Japan*, 1906, pp.381–2, quoted in Lehmann (see Part I, n.21), p.131.

13 Brooks Adams quoted in Iriye, Akira, *Across the Pacific*, New York, 1967, p.66.

14 Groupe d'Études du Pacifique, *Les Conséquences du Développement Économique du Japon pour l'Empire Français*, Paris, 1930. On 21 September 1931, Britain came off the gold standard. The pound fell and the yen rose in relation to it by 30 per cent. On 13 December 1931 Japan also went off the gold standard and the yen began to fall. The immediate effects of the British decision to come off the gold standard can be compared with the Nixon shock of August 1971, at least insofar as regards effects on Europe–Japan trade relations.

15 Federation of British Industries, *Report of Mission to the Far East, August to November 1934*, London, 1934, pp.20–21.

16 Storry, R., 'The English-language presentation of Japan's case during the China Emergency of the late nineteen-thirties', in Nish, I. and Dunn, C. (eds), *European Studies of Japan*, Tenterden, 1979, pp.140–48.

17 'The Essence of National Defence and Proposals for Strengthening It' (*Kokubō no Hongi to Sono Kyōka no Teishō*), Ministry of War, Tokyo, October 1934.

18 Asahi, Isoshi, *The Secret of Japan's Trade Expansion*, Tokyo, 1934.

19 Ushiba, Nobuhiko and Hara, Yasushi, *Nihon Keizai Gaikō no Keifu*, Tokyo, 1979, pp.242, 371. See also Hanabusa, Masamichi, *Trade Problems between Japan and Western Europe*, Royal Institute of International Affairs, London, 1979.

20 'Le Japon et la Communauté', *EC Bulletin* 12–1969, pp.17–21; pp.244–65.

21 As established by the European Community decision of 9 October 1961 (see *EC Bulletin* 3–1969, p.69).

22 *EC Bulletin* 3–1971, pp.26–7.

23 The division of Japan's industries into categories such as labour-intensive or knowledge-intensive accords with the cluster pattern of capital, knowledge (two years college and above) and labour inputs when these are plotted on a simple graph. See Wilkinson, Endymion, 'Changement de Structure des Exportations du Japon, 1955–1976 et ses Implications pour la Communauté Européenne', *Chroniques d'Actualité de la S.E.D.E.I.S.*, Paris, vol. XVIII, no. 8, April 1978, pp.244–65.

24 *Japan Economic Journal*, 18 November 1975.

25 *Newsweek*, 11 October 1976.

26 The French Prime Minister, M. Barre, is quoted in *Le Monde*, 11 December 1980, p.39. On non-tariff barriers see Little, A. D., Inc., *The Japanese Non-tariff Barrier Issue: American Views and the Implications for Japan–US Trade Relations*, Tokyo, 1979.

27 The headlines appeared in the following papers: *Pourquoi Pas*, Brussels, 17 February 1977; *The Economist*, 10 June 1978; *Paris Match*, 15 September 1980; *New Statesman*, London, 8 September 1978.

28 Staunton, George, 'Tokyo: aller au fond des choses', *Le Monde*, 12 December 1977.

29 Wilkinson (see n.23), and for a more recent report which reaches similarly gloomy conclusions see the EEC Commission document, 'The Competitiveness of European Industry', Brussels, March 1982.

30 *Asahi Shimbun*, 10 December 1979.

31 *Japan Economic Journal*, 7 July 1979, p.6.

32 *Asahi Shimbun*, 26 June 1979, pp.1, 12, 13.

33 Asahi, Isoshi, *The Secret of Japan's Trade Expansion*, Tokyo, 1934.

34 Amaya, Naohiro, 'Ushiwakamaru Strategy for Trade Frictions', *Kanchō Nyūsu Jihyō*, January 1977 (in Japanese).

35 The numbers of missionaries and businessmen from the EC in Japan were computed from the statistics of visas issued by the Visa Department, Ministry of Justice, Tokyo; the number of Christians in Japan is taken from *Asahi Nenkan*, Tokyo, 1978, p.444.

36 Statistics from *Tōgin Shuhō* (The Bank of Tokyo Weekly), vol. XXI, no. 23, 9 June 1977, pp.1–7. The same article shows that the number of American business offices in Japan was increasing between 1963 and 1975.

37 Laqueur, A., *A Continent Astray: Europe 1970–1978*, Oxford, 1979.
38 Mr Tokusaburō Kōsaka (at the time Director-General of the Economic Planning Agency) in an interview with Alan Field, *Newsweek*, 16 April 1979.
39 Ushiba and Hara (see n.19), pp.170, 317.
40 The trilateral idea appears to have been first launched by the Japanese. During Prime Minister Ikeda's trip to Western Europe in 1962, he advocated to Western leaders that 'the free world should be supported by three pillars, that is, North America, Western Europe, and Japan and Asia'. Masaya Itō, *Ikeda Hayato*, Tokyo, 1967, p.153, quoted in Hanabusa (see n.19), p.4.

Part IV What is to be Done?

1 Some of the problems of defining what constitutes an open market are summed up in 'Report of Japan–US Economic Relations Group', *Japan Economic Journal*, 9 June 1981, pp.30–32. See also Schmiegelow, H., *Japans Aussenwirtschaftspolitik: Merkantilistisch, liberal oder funktionell?*, Hamburg, 1981, and Little, A. D. Inc., *The Japanese Non-tariff Barrier Issue: American Views and the Implications for Japan–US Trade Relations*, Tokyo, 1979.
2 See *The Military Balance, 1981–1982*, London, 1981. Japan emerged from US occupation in 1952 with a constitution containing an article (IX) that states in part: 'land, sea and air forces, as well as other war potential, will never be maintained. The right of belligerency of the state will not be recognized.' Under pressure from the United States during the Korean War, the Japanese established a 75,000-man national police reserve, which developed into a 250,000-man Self-Defence Force, but they have consistently interpreted Article IX as prohibiting the dispatch of troops overseas. In 1976, the Japanese government decided that for the present, defence expenditures in each fiscal year should not exceed 1 per cent of GNP. Japan's defence budget has thus been lowest in proportion to GNP of any major power in the world, In addition, successive Prime Ministers of Japan have adhered to three non-nuclear principles – Japan will not manufacture nuclear weapons, will not maintain such weapons on its territory, and will not permit them to be introduced into its territory. For a recent discussion see Johnson, U. A. and Packard, G. R., *The Common Security Interests of Japan, the United States, and NATO*, Cambridge, Mass., 1981 and also Satoh Yukio, *The Evolution of Japanese Security Policy*, Adelphi Papers, 1982.
3 The recent steps to improve Japan's aid programme are summarized

on pp.202–3. Japan has only recently ratified the 1951 International Convention on the Status of Refugees or its 1976 Protocol. The Convention allows refugees, once they have been accepted for residence, the same benefits as citizens. Currently 750,000 Koreans are denied such benefits although many of them are second-generation immigrants entirely brought up in Japan and only speaking the Japanese language. The relatively small numbers of refugees from Indo-China who have been allowed into Japan are in a similar underprivileged position.

4   Introduction to the International Symposium *Japan Speaks* by Saji Keizo, President of the Suntory Foundation, Osaka, 1980.

5   Schwantes, R. S., 'Japan's Cultural Policies', in Morley, J. W. (ed.), *Japan's Foreign Policy, 1868–1941: A Research Guide*, New York, 1974, pp.178–9. On the earlier period see Valliant, R. B., 'The Selling of Japan: Japanese Manipulation of Western Opinion, 1900–1905', *Monumenta Nipponica*, XXIX, 4, 1972, pp.415–38.

6   *Le Monde*, 6 January 1981.

7   *The Japanese Press*, Nihon Shimbun Kyōkai, Tokyo, 1982.

8   *Report of the Governing Body*, School of Oriental and African Studies, University of London, 1955–6, pp.79–84.

Index